Praise for
ASH PRINCESS

AN INSTANT *NEW YORK TIMES* BESTSELLER!

"A DARKLY ENCHANTING PAGE-TURNER you won't be able to put down." —*Bustle*

"TENSE AND IMAGINATIVE, this story of a diminished yet vengeful princess inciting a rebellion to recapture her rightful place of power strikes a timely chord. *ASH PRINCESS* IS A SMART, FEMINIST TWIST ON A TRADITIONAL TALE OF A FALLEN HEROINE, with plenty of court intrigue, love, and lies to sweeten the deal. Good luck putting this one down." —Virginia Boecker, author of the Witch Hunter series

"The story leaps and twists like a swordswoman, and its blade carves the characters anew and divides them against themselves. THIS SEARING PAGE-TURNER IS A COMPELLING EXAMINATION OF THE COMPLEXITIES OF BOTH EVIL AND RESISTANCE." —Sarah Porter, author of *Vassa in the Night*

"Sebastian has created A DARK AND SPELLBINDING EPIC in *Ash Princess*. Brace yourself, because Theodosia Houzzara—wounded, driven, and deadly—is going to carve out a place for herself in your heart." —Sara Holland, *New York Times* bestselling author of *Everless*

"An EMOTIONALLY COMPLEX, BREATHTAKINGLY SUSPENSEFUL series starter." —*Booklist*

"Sebastian has built a BEAUTIFUL AND COMPLEX world." —*VOYA*

"Delivering a narrative that crackles with POLITICAL INTRIGUE, POWERFUL and DEBILITATING MAGIC, and THE VIOLENT MECHANISMS OF COLONIZATION . . . [*Ash Princess* will] submerge readers in a turbulent and ENTHRALLING PLOT." —*Kirkus Reviews*

"[Theodosia's] trip from downtrodden princess to queen is an ENGAGING one that FANTASY FANS WILL ENJOY . . . [as will] FANS OF THE SELECTION SERIES BY KIERA CASS and THE HUNGER GAMES TRILOGY." —*SLJ*

"[*Ash Princess*] provides a window into THE COMPLEXITIES OF HUMAN INTERACTION and EMOTION, FAMILIAL TENSIONS, and THE FALSE PUBLIC FACE THAT IS SOMETIMES REQUIRED IN POLITICS AND AT COURT . . . culminating in a CLIMACTIC ENDING ripe for a sequel." —*Publishers Weekly*

"Sebastian brings interest to Theodosia's character through her internal battle . . . and the threats she must navigate provide NAIL-BITING TENSION. . . . Readers will want to follow her into the coming revolution in a promised sequel." —*The Bulletin*

D0059279

WITHDRAWN

Books by Laura Sebastian

ASH PRINCESS

LADY SMOKE

Sebastian, Laura,
Ash Princess /
[2018]
33305244896423
mh   05/02/19

ASH PRINCESS

LAURA SEBASTIAN

EMBER

This is a work of fiction. Names, characters, places, and incidents either
are the product of the author's imagination or are used fictitiously. Any resemblance
to actual persons, living or dead, events, or locales is entirely coincidental.

Text copyright © 2018 by Laura Sebastian
Cover art copyright © 2018 by Billelis
Map illustrations copyright © 2018 by Isaac Stewart

All rights reserved. Published in the United States by Ember,
an imprint of Random House Children's Books, a division of Penguin Random
House LLC, New York. Originally published in hardcover in the United States
by Delacorte Press, an imprint of Random House Children's Books,
a division of Penguin Random House LLC, New York, in 2018.

Ember and the E colophon are registered trademarks of Penguin Random House LLC.

Visit us on the Web! GetUnderlined.com

Educators and librarians, for a variety of teaching tools,
visit us at RHTeachersLibrarians.com

The Library of Congress has cataloged the hardcover edition of this work as follows:
Names: Sebastian, Laura, author.
Title: Ash princess / Laura Sebastian.
Description: First edition. | New York : Delacorte Press, [2018] |
Summary: Held captive by the brutal Kaiser since age six when
she witnessed her mother's murder, Theodosia, called Ash Princess,
is now sixteen and prepared to reclaim the throne by any means necessary.
Identifiers: LCCN 2017024454 | ISBN 978-1-5247-6706-8 (hc) |
ISBN 978-1-5247-6707-5 (glb) | ISBN 978-1-5247-6708-2 (ebook)
Subjects: | CYAC: Princesses—Fiction. | Courts and courtiers—Fiction. |
Kings, queens, rulers, etc.—Fiction. | Prisoners—Fiction. | Fantasy.
Classification: LCC PZ7.1.S33693 Ash 2018 | DDC [Fic]—dc23

ISBN 978-1-5247-6709-9 (pbk.)

Printed in the United States of America
10 9 8 7 6 5 4 3 2 1
First Ember Edition 2019

Random House Children's Books supports the First Amendment
and celebrates the right to read.

FOR JESSE AND EDEN.

May you always do the right thing,
even when it's hard.

———•—•———

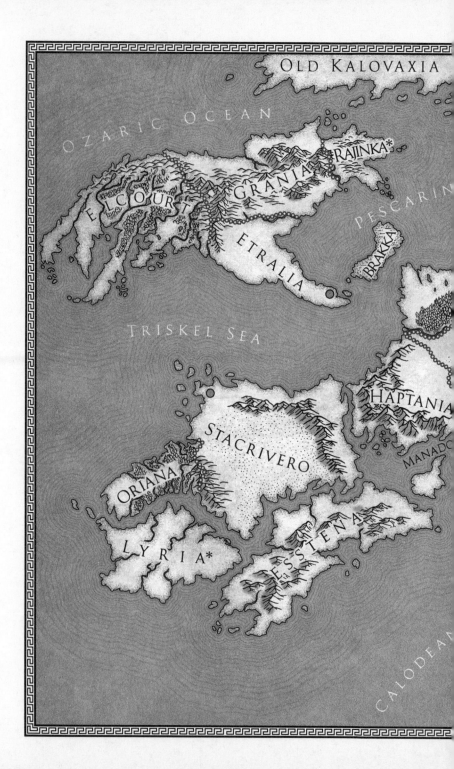

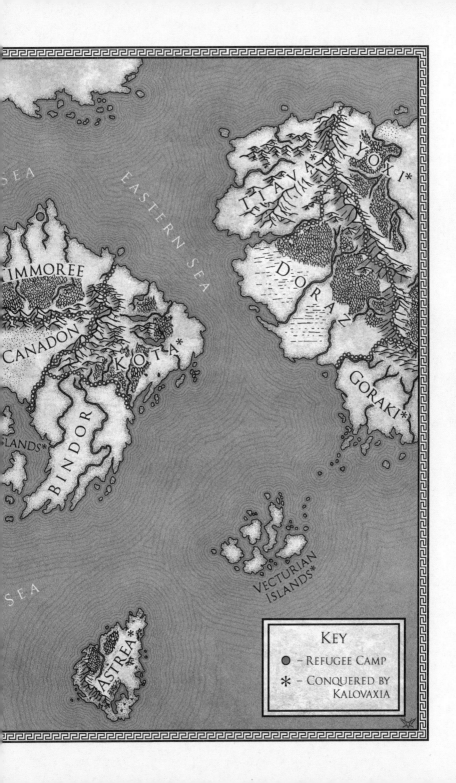

SEA

EASTERN SEA

EASTERN SEA

T'IAVAT

YOXI*

IMMOREE

DORAN

CANADON

KOTA*

GORAKI*

SLANDS*

BINDOR

SEA

VECTURIAN
ISLANDS*

ASTREA*

KEY

● – REFUGEE CAMP

✳ – CONQUERED BY
KALOVAXIA

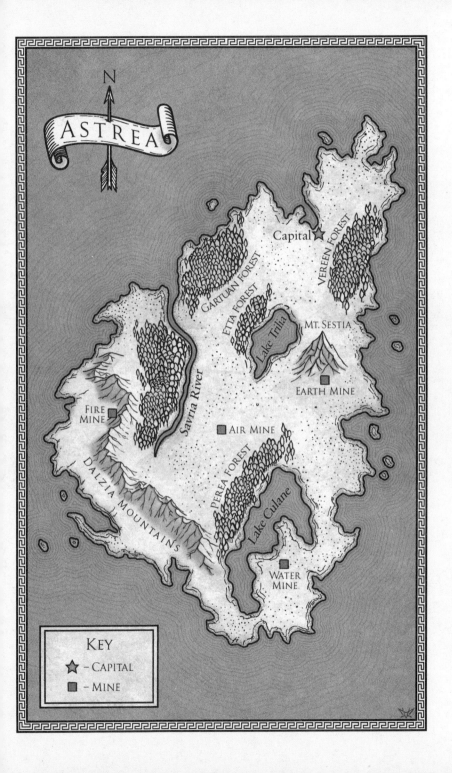

PROLOGUE

T HE LAST PERSON WHO CALLED me by my true name was my mother, with her dying breath. When I was six years old, my hand was still small enough that hers covered it completely. She squeezed it so painfully tight that I hardly noticed anything else. So tight that I hardly noticed the silver of the knife pressing against her throat or the fear in her eyes.

"You know who you are," she said to me. Her voice didn't waver, even as drops of blood bloomed where the blade cut her skin. "You are our people's only hope, Theodosia."

And then they cut her throat and they took my name.

THORA

---·---

"THORA!"

I turn to see Crescentia barreling toward me down the gilded palace hallway, pink silk skirts lifted as she runs and a broad grin spread across her lovely face.

Her two maids struggle to keep up with her, their emaciated frames drowning in homespun dresses.

Don't look at their faces, don't look, I tell myself. Nothing good ever comes of looking, of seeing their dull eyes and hungry mouths. Nothing good ever comes of seeing how much they look like me, with their tawny skin and dark hair. It only makes the voice in my head grow louder. And when the voice grows loud enough to push past my lips, the Kaiser grows angry.

I will not anger the Kaiser and he will keep me alive. This is the rule I've learned to follow.

I focus on my friend. Cress makes everything easier. She wears her happiness like the sun's rays, radiating it to warm those around her. She knows I need it more than most, so she doesn't hesitate to fall into step next to me and link our arms tightly.

She is free with her affection in a way only a few blessed people can be; she has never loved someone and lost them. Her effortless, childlike beauty will stay with her until she is an old woman, all dainty features and wide crystalline eyes that have seen no horrors. Pale blond hair hangs in a long braid pulled over her shoulder, studded with dozens of Spiritgems that wink in the sunlight pouring through the stained-glass windows.

I can't look at the gems either, but I feel them all the same: a gentle pull beneath my skin, drawing me toward them, offering me their power if I'll only take it. But I won't. *I can't.*

Spiritgems used to be sacred things, before Astrea was conquered by the Kalovaxians.

The gems came from the caves that ran beneath the four major temples—one for each of the four major gods and goddesses of fire, air, water, and earth. The caves were the center of their powers, so drenched in magic that the gems inside them took on magic of their own. Before the siege, the devout would spend years in the cave of the god or goddess they swore allegiance to. There, they would worship their deity, and if they were worthy, they would be blessed, imbued with their god's or goddess's power. They then used their gifts to serve Astrea and its people as Guardians.

Back then there weren't many who weren't chosen by the gods—a handful a year, maybe. Those few went mad and died shortly after. It was a risk only the truly devout took. Being a Guardian was a calling—an honor—yet everyone understood what was at stake.

That was a lifetime ago. *Before.*

After the siege, the Kaiser had the temples destroyed and

sent tens of thousands of enslaved Astreans to the caves to mine the gems. Living so close to the power of the gods is no longer a choice people make, but one that is made for them. There is no calling or allegiance sworn, and because of that, most people who are sent to the mines quickly lose their minds and, shortly after, their lives.

And all that so the wealthy can pay a fortune to cover themselves in gems without even uttering the names of the gods. It's sacrilege to us, but not to the Kalovaxians. They don't believe. And without the blessing of the gods—without the time spent deep in the earth—they can possess only a shadow of a true Guardian's power, no matter how many gems they wear, which is plenty for most of them. The Water Gems in Cress's braid could give a trained Guardian the power to craft an illusion strong enough to create a new face entirely, but for Cress they only lend her skin a glow, her lips and cheeks a pretty flush, her golden hair a shine.

Beauty Gems, the Kalovaxians call them now.

"My father sent me a book of poems from Lyre," she tells me. Her voice grows tense, as it always does when she speaks of her father, the Theyn, with me. "We should take it up to the pavilion and translate it. Enjoy the sun while we still have it."

"But you don't speak Lyrian," I say, frowning. Cress has a knack for languages and literature, two things her father has never had the patience for. As the Kaiser's best warrior and the head of his army, the Theyn understands battle and weaponry, strategy and bloodshed, not books and poetry, but he tries for her sake. Cress's mother died when Cress was only a baby, so the Theyn is all she has left by way of family.

"I've picked up a few phrases here and there," she says,

waving a hand dismissively. "But my father had the poet translate some so I can puzzle out the rest. You know how my father enjoys his puzzles."

She glances sideways at me to see my reaction, but I'm careful not to give one.

I'm careful not to imagine Cress's father pressing his dagger to a poor scrawny poet's neck as he hunches over his work, or the way he held it to my mother's so long ago. I don't think of the fear in her eyes. Her hand in mine. Her voice, strong and clear even then.

No, I don't think of that. I'll go mad if I do.

"Well, we'll solve them quickly, between the two of us," I tell her with a smile, hoping she believes it.

Not for the first time, I wonder what would happen if I didn't suppress a shudder when she mentioned her father. If I didn't smile and pretend he wasn't the same man who killed my mother. I like to believe Cress and I have been friends long enough that she would understand, but that kind of trust is a luxury I don't have.

"Maybe Dagmær will be there," Crescentia says, dropping her voice to a conspiratorial whisper. "You missed her . . . bold fashion choice at the countess's luncheon yesterday." Her eyes glint with a smile.

I don't care. The thought comes sudden and sharp as a bee-sting. *I don't care if Dagmær attended the luncheon in the nude. I don't care about any of it.* I push the thought down deep and bury it, as I always do. Thoughts like that don't belong to Thora; they belong to the voice. Usually it's only a whisper, easy enough to ignore, but sometimes it grows louder and spills into my own voice. That is when I get into trouble.

I anchor myself to Cress, her easy mind, her simple pleasures.

"I doubt anything can top the ostrich feathers she was covered in last month," I whisper back, making her giggle.

"Oh, it was far worse this time. Her gown was black lace. You could practically make out her intimate attire—or lack thereof!"

"No!" I shriek, pretending to be scandalized.

"Yes! They say she's hoping to entice Duke Clarence," Cress says. "Though why, I can't imagine. He's old enough to be her father and he smells like rotten meat." She wrinkles her nose.

"I suppose when you consider her actual father's debts . . ." I trail off, arching an eyebrow.

Crescentia's eyes widen. "Really? Where did you hear that?" she gasps. When I only smile in response, she sighs and elbows me lightly in the side. "You always know the best gossip, Thora."

"That's because I listen," I say with a wink.

I don't tell her what I'm really listening for, that I sift through each vapid rumor for whispers of Astrean resistance, for any hope that someone is still out there, that someday they might rescue me.

In the years after the siege, there were always stories about rebel Astreans striking out against the Kaiser. Once a week, I would be dragged out to the capital square to be whipped by one of the Kaiser's men and made an example of while the heads of fallen rebels stood rotting on pikes behind me. I knew those faces most of the time: Guardians who had served my mother, men and women who had given me candy and told me stories when I was young. I hated those days, and most of the time I hated the rebels because it felt like *they* were the ones hurting me by incurring the Kaiser's wrath.

Now, though, most of the rebels are dead and there are only whispers of rebellion, fleeting afterthoughts of gossip when the courtiers run out of other things to talk about. It's been years since the last rebel was caught. I don't miss those punishments, always more brutal and public than any others, but I do miss the hope that clung to me, the feeling that I was not alone in the world, that one day—maybe—my people would succeed and end my misery.

Footsteps grow louder behind us, too heavy to belong to Cress's slaves.

"Lady Crescentia, Lady Thora," a male voice calls. Cress's hold on my arm tightens and her breath catches.

"Your Highness," Cress says, turning and dropping into a curtsy, pulling me with her. The title sends my heart racing, even though I know it's not the Kaiser. I would know his voice anywhere. Still, I don't fully relax until I rise from my curtsy and confirm that I'm right.

The stranger shares the same long wheat-blond hair and cold blue eyes, the same square jawline, as the Kaiser, but the man in front of me is much younger, maybe a year older than I am.

Prinz Søren, I realize, surprised. No one has spoken of his return to court, which is surprising because the Kalovaxians are infatuated with their Prinz far more than they are with the Kaiser.

The last time I saw him was almost five years ago, when he was a scrawny twelve-year-old with round cheeks and a wooden sword always in hand. The man in front of me is no longer scrawny, and his cheeks have lost that childish roundness. A sword still hangs in the scabbard on his hip, but it isn't wooden anymore. It's a pockmarked wrought-iron blade, its hilt glittering with Spiritgems, for strength this time.

As a child, I saw Earth Guardians strong enough to haul boulders three times their weight as if they were nothing but air, but I doubt the Prinz's Spiritgems do much more than add an extra few pounds of force to his blows. Not that it really matters. Over the five years of Søren's training with the Theyn, that sword has drawn more than its fair share of blood. The court is always abuzz with whispers of the Prinz's prowess in battle. They say he's a prodigy, even by Kalovaxian standards. The Kaiser likes to treat the Prinz as an extension of himself, but Prinz Søren's achievements only serve to highlight the Kaiser's own shortcomings. Since taking the throne, the Kaiser has grown lazy and content, more interested in feasting and drinking than taking part in battles.

I wonder what the Prinz is doing back after so many years, though I suppose his apprenticeship with the Theyn is over. He's officially an adult now, and I can only assume he'll be leading his own armies soon.

He gives a shallow bow and clasps his hands behind his back. His placid expression doesn't change; it might as well be carved from marble. "It's good to see you both again. I trust you've been well."

It's not a question, really, but Cress still answers with a flustered *yes,* tucking a strand of hair behind her ear and smoothing the folds of her skirt, barely able to meet his eyes. She's been swooning over him since we were children, along with every other girl our age who grew up imagining herself a prinzessin. But for Cress, it's never been a hollow fantasy. Astrea is only one of the territories her father has won for the Kaiser. They say her father has taken more kingdoms than any other warlord, and no one can argue that the elevation of his daughter to prinzessin would be a just reward for such loyalty. Since Cress came of age six months ago, the whispers about such a match have grown deafening at court.

Another reason for his return, maybe?

If those whispers reached Søren, wherever he's been, he doesn't show it. His eyes glide over Cress as though she were nothing but air and light, landing instead on me. His brow furrows, the same way his father's does when he looks at me, though at least it isn't followed with a smirk or a leer.

"I'm glad to hear it," he says to Cress, cool and clipped, though his eyes stay on mine. "My father is requesting your presence, Lady Thora."

Fear wraps around my stomach like a hungry python, tightening, tightening, until I can't breathe. The urge to run rears up in me and I struggle to keep my legs still.

I haven't done anything. I've been so careful. But then, I don't have to do anything to earn the Kaiser's wrath. Anytime there's a hint of rebellion in the slave quarter or an Astrean pirate sinks a Kalovaxian ship, I pay the price. The last time he summoned me, barely a week ago, was to have me whipped in response to a riot in one of the mines.

"Well." My voice quavers despite my best efforts to keep it level. "We shouldn't keep him waiting."

For a brief moment, Prinz Søren looks like he might say something, but instead, his mouth tightens and he offers me his arm.

TRAITOR

—◆ · ◆—

THE OBSIDIAN THRONE STANDS ON a dais at the center of the round, dome-roofed throne room. The great, hulking thing is carved from solid black stone in the shape of flames that appear to kiss whoever sits upon it. It's plain, almost ugly, amid all the gold and grandeur that surround it, but it is certainly commanding, and that is what matters.

The Kalovaxians believe that the throne was drawn forth from the volcanoes of Old Kalovaxia and left here in Astrea for them by their gods, ensuring that they would one day come and save the country from its weak and willful queens.

I remember a different story, about the Astrean fire god, Houzzah, who loved a mortal woman so much he gave her a country and an heir with his blood in her veins. That story whispers through my mind now in a familiar lilting voice, but, like a distant star you try to look at directly, it's quick to fade if I focus on it. It's better left forgotten, anyway. It's safer to live only in the present, to be a girl with no past to yearn for and no future to have ripped away.

The thick crowd of courtiers, dressed in their finery, parts easily for Prinz Søren and me as we make our way toward the Kaiser. Like Cress, the courtiers all wear blue Water Gems for beauty and clear Air Gems for grace—so many that to look at them is almost blinding. There are others as well—red Fire Gems for warmth, golden yellow Earth Gems for strength.

I scan the room. Amid a sea of pale, blond Kalovaxians, Ion stands out in his place off to the side of the throne. He's the only other Astrean not in chains, but he's hardly a welcome sight. After the siege, he turned himself over to the Kaiser and begged for his life, offering his services as an Air Guardian. Now the Kaiser keeps him around to use as a spy in the capital and as a healer for the royal family. And for me. After all, I'm not as much fun to beat if I black out from the pain. Ion, who once swore himself to our gods and my mother, uses his gift to heal me only so the Kaiser's men can break me again and again and again.

His presence is an unspoken threat. He's rarely allowed at court functions; he usually only appears during one of my punishments.

If the Kaiser intended to have me beaten, he would want to do so somewhere more public. He hasn't ruled it out, though, which is why Ion is here.

The Kaiser aims a pointed look at Søren, who drops my arm and melts into the crowd, leaving me alone under the weight of his father's stare. I'm tempted to cling to him, to anyone, so I won't have to be alone.

But I'm always alone. I should be used to it by now, though I don't think it's the kind of thing a person ever grows used to.

The Kaiser leans forward in his seat, cold eyes glinting

in the sunlight that pours through the stained-glass roof. He looks at me the way he might a squashed bug that dirtied the bottom of his shoe.

I stare at the dais instead, at the flames carved there. Not angering the Kaiser is what keeps me alive. He could have killed me a thousand times in the last decade and he hasn't. Isn't that a kindness?

"There you are, *Ash Princess*." To anyone else, the greeting might sound pleasant, but I flinch. There is always a trick with the Kaiser, a game to play, a thin line to balance on. I know from experience that if he is playing at kindness now, cruelty can't be far behind.

Standing at his right side with her hands clasped in front of her and her head bowed, his wife, Kaiserin Anke, lets her milky eyes dart up through sparse blond lashes to find mine. A warning that makes the python coil tighter around my stomach.

"You requested my presence, Your Highness?" I ask, dropping into a curtsy so deep I am almost flat against the ground. Even after a decade, my bones still protest the posture. My body remembers—even when the rest of me forgets—that I am not made for curtsying.

Before the Kaiser can answer, a guttural cry shatters the still air. When I rise, I notice a man standing to the left of the throne, held in place between two guards. Rusted chains are wrapped around his gaunt legs, arms, and neck so tightly they cut through his skin. His clothes are tattered and blood-drenched and his face is a mottled mess of broken bones and torn skin. Beneath the blood, he's clearly Astrean, with tawny skin, black hair, and deep-set eyes. He looks much older than me, though it's impossible to say exactly how old he is with all the damage that's been done to him.

He is a stranger. But his dark eyes search mine as if he knows me, imploring, begging, and I rake through my memories—who could this be and what does he want from me? I have nothing for him. Nothing left for anyone. Then the world shifts beneath my feet.

I remember those eyes from another lifetime, set in a gentle face a decade younger and unbloodied. Memories surge forward, even as I try to press them down.

I remember him standing at my mother's side, whispering something in her ear to make her laugh. I remember his arms coming around me as he lifted me up in the air so I could pick an orange from a tree; I remember how he smiled at me like we shared a secret.

I push back those thoughts and focus instead on the broken man standing before me.

There is one man always mentioned in connection with the rebellions. One man who has a hand in every move made against the Kaiser. One man whose name alone is enough to send the Kaiser into a wild-eyed rage that leaves me whipped so hard I have to stay in bed for days. One man whose acts of defiance have caused me so much pain, but who has been my one spark of hope when I dare let myself imagine there is an *after* to these infernal years.

No wonder the Kaiser is so happy. He's finally caught the last of Astrea's Guardians, and my mother's closest guard. Ampelio.

"My Queen," he says. His voice carries so that everyone gathered in the silent throne room hears his treason.

I shrink back from his words. *No, no, no,* I want to tell him. *I am no one's queen. I am Lady Thora, Princess of Ashes. I am no one.*

It takes me a moment to realize he's speaking Astrean, speaking forbidden words once used to address my mother. *My mother.* In another life, I was another girl. Another kind of princess. That girl was told that one day she would be queen, but she never wanted that to be true. After all, being queen meant living in a world where her mother no longer existed, and that had been unfathomable.

But that girl died a decade ago; there is no help for her now.

The man lurches, weighed down by his chains. He's too weak to make it to the door, but he doesn't even try for it. Instead, he topples to the ground at my feet, fingers grasping the hem of my dress and staining the pale yellow silk red.

No. Please. Part of me wants to drag him up and tell him he's mistaken. Another part wants to shrink away from him because this is such a lovely dress and he's getting blood on it. And yet another wants to scream at him that his words are going to ruin us both, but at least *he* will have the mercy of death.

"He refused to speak to anyone but you," Kaiser Corbinian says in an acid voice.

"Me?" My heart is beating so hard in my chest that I'm surprised the whole court can't hear it. Every eye in the room is on me; everyone is waiting for me to slip, desperate for the slightest hint of rebellion so that they can watch the Kaiser beat it out of me again. I will not give it to them.

I will not anger the Kaiser and he will keep me alive. I repeat the mantra to myself again and again, but the words have grown limp.

The Kaiser leans forward on his throne, eyes bright. I've seen that look too often before; it haunts my nightmares. He is a shark that has caught the scent of blood in the water. "Don't you know him?"

This is the Kaiser's favorite kind of question to ask. The kind without a right answer.

I look back at the man, as if struggling to place him, even as his name screams through my mind. More memories come and I force them back. The Kaiser is watching me carefully, waiting for any sign that I am not under his thumb. But I can't look away from this man's eyes.

In that other life, I loved him.

He was my mother's most trusted Guardian and, according to just about everyone, my blood father—though even my mother couldn't say that for certain.

I remember searching his face for similarities to my own after I heard the rumor for the first time, but I found nothing conclusive. His nose had the same slope, and his hair curled around his ears in the same way mine did, but I looked far too much like my mother to be sure of anything. That was before, though, when my eyes were childishly wide and shapeless, impossible to place on my mother's face or anyone else's. Now the resemblance is so clear it hits me like a knife to my gut.

As a Guardian, he would travel often to keep the country safe with his fire magic, but he always returned with sweets and toys and new stories for me. I often fell asleep on his lap, my hand clutching the Fire Gem that always hung around his neck. Its magic would buzz through me like a lullaby, singing me to sleep.

When my mother died and the world I knew turned to dust, I waited for him to save me. That hope waned with every Guardian's head the Kaiser had piked in the square, but it never disappeared. I still heard whispers about Ampelio's rebellions, and those kept my hope alive, even after all the other Guardians fell. Few and far between as they were, I clung to them. As long as he was out there, as long as he was fighting, I knew he would save me. I never let myself imagine, even in my worst nightmares, that I would see him like this.

I try to empty my mind, but it's futile. Even now, a dim hope flickers in my heart that this day will have a happy ending, that we will see another sunrise together, free.

It's a stupid, dangerous hope, but it burns all the same.

Tears sting at my eyes, but I cannot let them fall.

He doesn't wear his gem now. Taking it was the first thing the Kaiser's men would have done when they captured him. For an untrained courtier, a single gem can barely provide enough warmth to keep them comfortable on a winter's night, but Ampelio was blessed. One gem was all he would need to burn this palace to the ground.

"This is the famed Guardian Ampelio," the Kaiser says, drawing out each word mockingly. "You must remember him. He's been sowing treason throughout the mines, trying to rally them against me. He even instigated the riot in the Air Mine last week. The Theyn found him nearby and brought him in."

"Wasn't it an earthquake that incited the riot?" The words slip out before I can stop them. They don't feel like my words really. Or rather, they don't feel like Thora's.

Kaiser Corbinian's jaw clenches and I recoil, readying for a strike that doesn't come. Yet.

"Caused by him, we suspect, in order to rally more people to your cause," he says.

I have a retort for that, too, but I bite it back and let confusion cloud my features. "*My* cause, Your Highness?" I ask. "I wasn't aware that I had a cause."

His smile sharpens. "The one seeking to, as they say, 're-store you to your rightful place as Queen of Astrea.'"

I swallow. This conversation is taking an entirely new direction, and I'm not sure what to make of it. I think I'd almost prefer the whip to whatever new game this is.

My eyes drop to the ground. "I'm not anyone's queen, and there is no Astrea anymore. I am a lady now, by Your Highness's mercy, and a princess only of ashes. This is my rightful place, and the only one I desire."

I can't look at Ampelio as I recite the line that has been burned into my heart over the years. I've said it so often the words have stopped meaning anything, but saying it now in front of him causes shame to run through my veins.

The Kaiser nods. "I said as much, but Astreans are stubborn old mules."

The throne room erupts into laughter. I laugh, too, but it is a sound wrenched from my gut.

The Kaiser turns to Ampelio, his expression a mockery of sympathy. "Come and bow before me, *mule*. Tell me where I can find your rebels and you can spend the rest of your days in one of the mines." He grins at the broken man still lying at my feet.

Agree! I want to yell. *Pledge your loyalty to him. Survive. Do not anger the Kaiser and he will keep you alive. These are the rules.*

"I bow before no one but my queen," Ampelio whispers, tripping over the hard edges of the Kalovaxian language. Despite his low voice, his words carry throughout the room, followed by gasps and murmurs from the court.

He raises his voice. "Long live Queen Theodosia Eirene Houzzara."

Something shatters within me, and everything I've held back, every memory I've repressed, every moment I've tried to forget—it all comes rushing forward and I can't stop it this time.

Theodosia. It's a name I haven't heard in ten years.

Theodosia. I hear my mother saying it to me, stroking my hair, kissing my forehead.

You are our people's only hope, Theodosia.

Ampelio always called me Theo, no matter how my nanny, Birdie, chided him for it. I was his princess, she said, and Theo was the name of a dirt-streaked ragamuffin. He never listened, though. I might have been his princess, but I was something more as well.

He was supposed to save me, but he never did. I've been waiting for ten years for someone to come for me, and Ampelio was the last scrap of hope I had.

"Maybe he'll answer to you, Ash Princess," the Kaiser says.

My shock is dim, drowned out by the sound of my name

echoing again and again in my mind. "I . . . I couldn't presume to have that power, Your Highness," I manage.

His mouth purses in an expression I know all too well. The Kaiser is not a man to be refused.

"This is why I keep you alive, isn't it? To assist as a liaison to bullheaded Astrean scum?"

The Kaiser is kind to spare me, I think, but then I realize once again that he doesn't spare me out of kindness. He keeps me alive to use me as leverage against my people.

My thoughts are growing bolder now, and though I know they are dangerous, I can no longer quiet them. And for the first time, I don't want to.

I've been waiting for ten years to be saved, and all I have to show for it is a scarred back and countless dead rebels. With Ampelio caught, there is nothing more the Kaiser can take from me. We both know he is not merciful enough to kill me.

"May I speak Astrean?" I ask the Kaiser. "He might feel more at ease. . . ."

The Kaiser waves a hand and slumps back into his chair. "So long as it gets me answers."

I hesitate before dropping to my knees in front of Ampelio, taking his shredded hands in mine. Even though the Astrean language is forbidden, some of the courtiers here must understand it. I doubt the Kaiser would let me speak it otherwise.

"Are there others?" I ask him. The words sound unnatural in my mouth, though Astrean was the only language I spoke until the Kalovaxians came. They pried it away from me, made it illegal to speak. I can't remember the last time an Astrean word passed my lips, but I still *know* the language somewhere deeper than thought, as if it's embedded in my

very bones. Still, I have to struggle to keep the sounds soft-edged and long, unlike the halting and throaty speech of the Kalovaxians.

He hesitates before nodding. *"Are you safe?"*

I have to pause a moment before speaking. *"Safe as a ship in a cyclone."* The Astrean word for cyclone—*signok*—is so close to the word for harbor—*signak*—that only a practiced ear would understand. But one might. The thought is paralyzing, but I push past it. *"Where are the others?"* I ask him.

He shakes his head and drops his gaze from mine. *"No-where,"* he chokes out, though he draws out the second syllable to sound more like *"everywhere"* to lazy ears.

That doesn't make any sense. There are fewer Astreans than Kalovaxians—only a hundred thousand before the siege. Most are slaves now, though there were rumors they were working with some allies in other countries. It's been too long since I've spoken Astrean; I must have mistranslated.

"Who?" I press.

Ampelio sticks his gaze to the hem of my skirt and shakes his head. *"Today is done, the time has come for little birds to fly. Tomorrow is near, the time is here for old crows to die."*

My heart recognizes the words before my mind does. They're part of an old Astrean lullaby. My mother sang it to me, and so did my nanny. Did he ever sing it to me himself?

"Give him something and he'll let you live," I say.

Ampelio laughs, but it quickly turns into a wheeze. He coughs and wipes his mouth with the back of his hand. It comes away bloody.

"What life would it be at the mercy of a tyrant?"

It would have been easy enough to slur together a pair of

consonants and make the Astrean word for *tyrant* sound like the one for *dragon,* the symbol of the Kalovaxian royal family, but Ampelio spits out the word with enough emphasis, directing it at the Kaiser, so that even those who don't speak a word of Astrean can understand his meaning.

The Kaiser leans forward in his chair, fingers gripping the arms of the throne so tightly they turn white. He gestures to one of the guards.

The guard draws his sword and steps toward Ampelio's prone form. He presses the blade to the back of Ampelio's neck, drawing blood, before lifting the sword again to ready the killing strike. I've seen this done too many times to other rebels or slaves who disrespected their masters. The head never comes off on the first swing. I ball my fists in the material of my dress to keep from reaching out to shield him. There is no saving him now. I *know* that, but I can't fathom it. Images swim before my eyes, and I see the knife drawing across my mother's throat. I see slaves whipped until the life leaves their bodies. I see Guardians' heads on pikes in the capital square until the crows take them apart. I've seen people hanged for going against the Kaiser, for having the courage to do what I haven't.

Run, I want to tell him. *Fight. Beg. Bargain. Survive.*

But Ampelio doesn't flinch from the blade. The only move he makes is to reach out and tether himself to my ankle. The skin of his palm is rough and scarred and sticky with blood.

The time is here for old crows to die. But I can't let the Kaiser take another person from me. I can't watch Ampelio die. I can't.

"No!"

The voice forces its way through the fractured bits of me.

"No?" The Kaiser's softly spoken word echoes in the silence and raises goose bumps down my spine.

My mouth is dry, and when I speak, my voice rasps. "You offered him mercy if he spoke, Your Highness. He did speak."

The Kaiser leans forward. "Did he? I may not speak Astrean, but he didn't seem particularly forthcoming."

The words flow before I can stop them. "He had only half a dozen comrades left, after all your great efforts to destroy them. He believes the remaining men and women were killed in the earthquake in the Air Mine, but if any survived, they are supposed to meet him just south of the Englmar ruins. There is a cluster of cypress trees there."

There is at least a fraction of truth in that. I used to play in those trees every summer when my mother took her annual tour of the town that had been leveled by an earthquake the year before I was born. Five hundred people had died that day. Until the siege, it was the greatest tragedy Astrea had ever faced.

The Kaiser tilts his head and watches me too closely, as if he can read my thoughts like words on a page. I want to cower, but I force myself to hold his gaze, to believe my lie.

After what feels like hours, he motions to the guard next to him. "Take your best men. There's no telling what magic the heathens have."

The guard nods and hurries from the room. I'm careful to keep my face impassive, even while I want to weep with relief. But when the Kaiser turns his cold eyes back to me, that relief turns hard and sinks to the pit of my stomach.

"Mercy," he says quietly, "is an Astrean virtue. It is what

makes you weak, but I'd hoped we saved you from that. Perhaps blood always wins out in the end."

He snaps his fingers and the guard forces the hilt of his iron sword into my hands. It's so heavy that I struggle to lift it. The Earth Gems glint in the light, and their power makes my hands itch. It's the first time since the siege that I've been allowed to handle any kind of gem, or any kind of weapon, for that matter. Once, I would have welcomed it—anything to make me feel like I had a little bit of power—but instead, my stomach lurches as I look at Ampelio lying at my feet and realize what the Kaiser expects me to do.

I shouldn't have spoken up; I shouldn't have tried to save him. Because there is something worse than watching the light leave the eyes of the only person I have left in the world—it's driving the sword into him myself.

My stomach twists at the thought and bile rises into my throat. I grip the sword, struggling to box myself up again and bury Theodosia even deeper before I end up with a sword at my throat as well. But it can't be done this time. Everything feels too much, hurts too badly, hates too fiercely to be contained now.

"Perhaps sparing your life was a mistake." His voice is casual, but it makes the threat all the clearer. "Traitors receive no pardons, from me or the gods. You know what to do."

I barely hear him. I barely hear anything. Blood pounds in my ears, blurring my vision and my thoughts until all I can see is Ampelio lying at my feet.

"Father, is this really necessary?" Prinz Søren steps forward. The alarm in his voice surprises me, but so does the strength behind it. No one has ever contradicted the Kaiser.

The court is as surprised as I am, and they break their silence with whispers that are only interrupted when the Kaiser slams his hands against the arms of the throne.

"Yes," he hisses, leaning forward. His cheeks are a vicious red, though whether it's anger at his son or embarrassment at being questioned it's difficult to say. "It is *necessary*. And let it be a lesson to you as well, Søren. Mercy is what lost the Astreans their country, but we are not so *weak*."

The word *weak* falls like a curse—to the Kalovaxians there is no worse insult. Prinz Søren flinches from it, his own cheeks coloring as he takes a step back, eyes downcast.

At my feet, Ampelio shudders, his grip on my ankle twitching.

"Please, My Queen," he says in Astrean.

I am not your queen! I want to scream. *I am your princess, and you* were *supposed to save* me.

"Please," he says again, but there is nothing I can do for him. I have seen dozens of men before him executed for far less than this. It was foolish to think that he would be spared, even if the information I gave had been true. I could beg the Kaiser until my throat was raw and it wouldn't do any good. It would only end with a blade at my back as well.

"Please," he says again before launching into rapid Astrean that I struggle to keep up with. *"Or he will kill you, too. It is time for the After to welcome me. Time to see your mother again. But it is not your time yet. You will do this. You will live. You will fight."* And I understand. I almost wish I didn't. His blessing is its own kind of curse.

No. I can't do it. I can't kill a man. I can't kill *him*. I'm not the Kaiser, I'm not the Theyn, I'm not Prinz Søren. I'm . . .

Something shifts deep inside me. *Theodosia,* Ampelio called me. It's a strong name—the one my mother gave me. It's the name of a queen. It doesn't feel like a name I deserve, but here I stand, alone. If I am to survive, I *must* be strong enough to live up to it.

I must be Theodosia now.

My hands begin to shake as I lift the sword. Ampelio is right; someone will do it, whether it's me or one of the Kaiser's guards, but I will make it quicker, easier. Is it better to have your life ended by someone who hates you or someone who loves you?

Through the thin, torn shirt he wears—more red than white now—I feel the vertebrae of his spine. The blade fits below his shoulders, between two protruding ribs. It will be like cutting steak at dinner, I tell myself, but I already know it won't be like that at all.

He turns his head so that his eyes meet mine. There is something familiar in his gaze that wrings my heart in my chest and makes it impossible to breathe. There is no doubt left in me. This man is my father.

"You are your mother's child," he whispers.

I tear my eyes away from him and focus on the Kaiser instead, holding his gaze. "Bend not, break not," I say clearly, quoting the Kalovaxian motto before I plunge the sword into Ampelio's back, cutting through skin and muscle and bone to strike his heart. His body is so weak, so mangled already, that it's almost easy. Blood gushes up, covering my dress.

Ampelio gives a twitch and a shallow cry before going limp. His hand slips away from my ankle, though I feel the bloody handprint left behind. I withdraw the sword and pass it back to the guard. Numb. Two other guards step forward to drag the body away, leaving a trail of slick red in its wake.

"Take the body to the square and hang it for everyone to see. Anyone who tries to move it will join him," the Kaiser says before turning back to me. His smile pools in the pit of my stomach like oil. "Good girl."

Blood soaks my dress, stains my skin. Ampelio's blood. My father's blood. I curtsy before the Kaiser, my body moving without my mind's consent.

"Clean yourself up, Lady Thora. There will be a banquet tonight to celebrate the fall of Astrea's greatest rebel, and you, my dear, will be the guest of honor."

I drop into another shallow curtsy and bow my head. "Of course, Your Highness. I look forward to it."

The words don't feel like my own. My mind is churning so deeply I'm surprised I can find words at all. I want to scream. I want to cry. I want to take that bloody sword back and stab it into the Kaiser's chest, even if I die in the process.

"It is not your time yet," Ampelio's voice whispers through my mind. *"You will live. You will fight."*

The words don't bring me any comfort. Ampelio is dead, and with him my last hope of being rescued.

THEODOSIA

I'M NOT TEN STEPS DOWN the hall when a hand grips my shoulder, restraining me. I want to run, run, run until I'm alone and I can scream and cry until nothing is left in me but emptiness again. *You will live. You will fight.* Ampelio's words whisper through my mind, but I'm not a fighter. I am a frightened shadow of a girl. I am a fractured mind and a trembling body. I am a prisoner.

I turn to find Prinz Søren, a sliver of concern cracking through his stoic expression. The hand that stopped me is now light on my shoulder, the palm and fingertips surprisingly rough.

"Your Highness." I'm careful to keep my voice level, hiding the tempest tearing through me. "Does the Kaiser need something else from me?"

The thought should terrify me, but instead, I feel nothing. I suppose I have nothing left for him to take now.

Prinz Søren shakes his head. He lets his hand drop from my shoulder and clears his throat.

"Are . . . are you all right?" he asks. His voice sounds strained, and I wonder when he last talked to a girl. When he last talked to anyone but other soldiers.

"Of course," I say, though they don't feel like my words. Because I am not all right. I am a hurricane barely contained in skin.

My hands begin to shake, and I tuck them into the folds of my skirt so the Prinz won't notice.

"Was that the first time you've killed?" he asks. He must see the panic flash in my eyes, because he hastens to continue. "You did well. It was a clean death."

How can it possibly be clean when there was so, so much blood? I could take a thousand baths and still feel it on me.

Ampelio's voice echoes through my mind: *You are your mother's child. The time has come for little birds to fly. You will fight. My Queen.*

A memory surfaces and I don't try to smother it this time. His hand around mine as he walked me down to the stables. Him lifting me up to sit on his horse so I towered above him, on top of the world. The horse's name was Thalia and she liked honey drops. The feel of his hand at my back, keeping me safe; the feel of the sword, slicing through his skin.

Bile rises in my throat but I force it down.

"I'm glad you thought so," I manage.

For an instant, he looks ready to ask another question, but he only offers me his arm. "May I escort you back to your room?"

I can't refuse the Prinz, though I want to. I am in tatters and I don't know how to smile and pretend I'm not. Thora is so much simpler. She is a hollow thing with no past and no future. No desires. No anger. Only fear. Only obedience.

"When I turned ten," Prinz Søren says, "my father brought

me to the dungeon and gave me a new sword. He brought out ten criminals—Astrean rabble—and showed me how to slit their throats. He did the first, to demonstrate. I did the other nine."

Astrean rabble.

The words rankle me, though I've heard them called worse. *I've* called them worse under the Kaiser's always-watching gaze, pretending I'm not one of them. I've mocked them and laughed at the Kaiser's cruel jokes. I've tried to distance myself from them, pretended they were not my people, even if we share the same tawny skin and dark hair. I've been too afraid to even *look* at them. All the while, they've been enslaved and beaten and executed like animals to teach a spoiled prinz a lesson.

Now that Ampelio is dead, no one is left to rescue them either.

Bile rises up again, but this time I can't hold it back. I stop and retch, the contents of my stomach spilling all over the Prinz's suit. He jerks back and for a painfully long moment we can only stare at one another. I should apologize; I should beg for forgiveness before he tells his father how weak and repulsive I am. But all I can do is clamp my hand over my mouth and hope that nothing more comes up.

The shock in his eyes fades, replaced with something that might be pity.

He doesn't try to stop me when I turn and dash away down the hall.

*   *   *

Even when I'm back in my room, stretched out on my bed, alone, I can't fall apart. I can hear my personal guards settling into the small rooms on the other side of the walls that the Kaiser had installed after the siege. Their boots click against stone floors and their sheathed swords clatter down. They are always here, always watching through three thumb-sized holes. Even when I sleep, even when I bathe, even when I wake up screaming from nightmares I only half remember. They follow me everywhere, but I never see their faces or even hear their voices. The Kaiser refers to them as my Shadows, a nickname that has spread so far and wide that I think of them that way myself.

They must be laughing now. The little Ash Princess lost her stomach over a bit of blood, and all over the Prinz, too! Which of them will get the honor of telling the Kaiser that story? None of them, more than likely. The Prinz will tell it himself and the Kaiser will know of my weakness in minutes. He will only try harder to beat that weakness out of me. This time, he might succeed, and then what will be left of me?

My door opens and I sit up. It's Hoa, my maid. She doesn't look at me, instead focusing on undoing the buttons that run down the back of my bloodstained dress. I hear her sigh with relief when she realizes that the blood isn't mine this time. Cool air hits my flesh as the fabric falls away, and I stiffen for the sting as she peels off the bandages on my back. Her fingers are gentle as she checks on my welts, making sure they're healing properly. When she's satisfied, she dabs on ointment from a jar Ion gave her and replaces the bandages with fresh ones.

Because I cannot be trusted with an Astrean slave, the Kaiser gave me Hoa instead. With her light gold skin and straight black hair that falls to her waist, I assume she must be from one of the eastern lands the Kalovaxians invaded before Astrea, but she's never told me which one. She couldn't if she wanted to, because the Kaiser's sewn her mouth shut. Thick black thread crosses over her lips in four X's from corner to corner, taken out every few days to allow for a meal before being sewn again. Immediately after the siege, I had an Astrean maid named Felicie, who was fifteen. I thought of her as a sister, and when she told me she had a plan for our escape, I followed her without question, so sure that all my dreams of rescue were coming true. I even believed my mother was still alive somewhere, waiting for me.

I was a fool.

Instead of giving me freedom, Felicie delivered me straight to the Kaiser, just as he'd instructed her.

He personally gave me ten lashes, and then he slit Felicie's throat, telling me he had no more use for her. He said it was to teach me a lesson that would last longer than my welts, and I suppose it did. I learned to trust no one. Not even Cress, really.

Hoa gathers my bloody dress in her arms and nods toward the washbasin, a silent instruction to get cleaned up, before she leaves again to launder the dress.

When she's gone, I sit down at my vanity and rinse my mouth with water from the basin, getting rid of the taste of sickness. I dip my hands in next to clean the specks of blood from them. My father's blood; my blood.

Again I feel like I'm going to be sick, but I force myself to take deep breaths until it passes. The eyes of my Shadows weigh heavy on me, waiting for me to fall apart so they can report it to the Kaiser.

In the vanity mirror, I look the same as I did this morning. Every hair curled and pinned in the Kalovaxian style, face powdered, eyes rimmed with kohl and lips stained red. Everything is the same, even though I am not.

I take the small white towel hanging over the edge of the bowl and dip it into the water before rubbing it over my face. I scrub until all the powders and paints come away, coloring the towel as they do. It took Hoa the better part of an hour to apply them this morning, but it takes me less than a minute to wash them all off.

My mother's face looks back at me from the mirror. Her freckles dance over my nose and cheeks like unmapped constellations. Her olive skin glows like topaz in the candlelight. Her hair shines, the color of deep mahogany, though hers was always down and wild, never held back so severely from her face like mine. The eyes are not her eyes, though. Instead, Ampelio's dark hazel eyes stare back at me, deep-set, with heavy lashes.

Though these are flaws that Kalovaxian beauty standards demand I hide, I remember how people spoke about my mother's beauty, how they wrote poems and sang songs in her honor.

I blink and I see the Theyn's knife pressing into my throat—into my mother's throat. I feel the bite of the steel, see beads of blood well up. I blink again and it's only me. Only a broken girl.

Theodosia Eirene Houzzara. The name whispers through me again, followed by my mother's dying words.

Would she forgive me for killing Ampelio? Would she understand why I did it? Or does she turn her back on me from her place in the After?

He's with her now, I have to believe that. He's with her because he gave his life to spare me, though that isn't fair. He risked everything for Astrea, while I have done nothing but try to appease the monster who destroyed us.

I can't play the Kaiser's game anymore. I can't follow his rules and keep him amused while my people wear chains. I can't laugh and talk about poetry with Crescentia. I can't speak in their hard, ugly language. I can't respond to a name that isn't the one my mother gave me.

Ampelio was the last person I thought could rescue me, my last hope that this nightmare could end one day. I thought I'd killed that hope when I killed him, but I realize now that I didn't. The hope inside me is not smothered yet. It is dying, yes, with only a few embers left. But I've seen fires rekindled with less.

Hoa still hasn't returned, so I paint my face again, covering up every last trace of my mother. My true name feels heavy on my tongue after hearing Ampelio speak it earlier, and I want to hear it again. I want to *say* it, to banish Thora from my mind for good, but I don't dare.

Theodosia, Theodosia, Theodosia.

Something in me is waking up. This is not my home. I am not their prize. I am not content with the life they have so kindly spared.

Ampelio can't save me anymore, but I won't let his sacrifice be in vain. I have to figure out how to save myself.

CROWN

THE DRESS THE KAISER SENDS for me to wear is bright vermilion with no sleeves and very little back. It's similar to the loose, simple chiton styles my people wore before the Conquering. Strangely, in recent years, Astrean styles have become popular among the younger courtiers, as opposed to the structured heavy velvets the Kalovaxians wore when they first arrived. But I don't think the Kaiser picked it with style in mind. With my shoulders and back bare, my scars are exposed and his message can be read all the clearer.

Astrea is defeated. Astrea is broken. Astrea is no more.

I've always been ashamed of the red, gnarled skin of my back. The record of Astrea's rebellions can be traced there. Each time Astrean pirates sank one of the Kaiser's ships, each time one of the mines tried to revolt, each time a slave spit at their master, it was carved into my skin. The scars are ugly and monstrous and a constant reminder of what I am.

But now, sitting in front of the vanity mirror while Hoa braids my hair, it's not shame I feel. Now, fresh hate trickles through my veins like water from thawing ice. I've been pushing it down for so long that it feels good to finally let it overtake me. It's an aimless aura of hate, though. It needs a focus. It needs a channel. It needs a plan.

But I am isolated here—there is no one to turn to for help. All I know of what goes on outside the palace comes from overhearing Kalovaxian courtiers, and it's usually been filtered through so many people by then that I'm not sure how much truth is in it. There are Astreans in the capital, but all of them are slaves and most of them are younger than I am and kept malnourished and weak. And though I hate myself for thinking it, I'm not sure I can trust them.

The Theyn. Even though the very thought of him makes me want to vomit again, I can't deny that if there's anyone who is likely to have accurate information about Astrean rebellions, it's him. There's the possibility Cress has overheard him saying something relevant, but the world outside the palace holds little interest for her, so it doesn't seem likely she'd remember anything important. No, I'll have to speak with the Theyn himself tonight, though being around him always makes me feel like I'm six years old again, watching him slit my mother's throat.

I am sure he doesn't like me any more than I like him, but if I corner him with Cress at my side, if I widen my eyes and let my voice tremble as I act like I'm frightened that Ampelio was working with someone, that whoever it is will try to come and take me away, he'll have to tell me something. Admittedly, he'll tell me there's no one left no matter what the truth is, but for all his skills in battle, the Theyn is a horrible liar.

Cress herself pointed out the tells to me once, how his skin turns a flustered red under the long yellow beard that takes up most of his face. How he makes too much eye contact, how his nostrils flare.

Either way, I'll have a better idea of what's going on with the rebellion.

Hoa fastens another braid back with a plain pin. Her eyes meet mine in the mirror, and for an instant I could swear she reads my thoughts as clearly as words on a page. Her eyes narrow, but after a moment she looks away, braiding the last section of my hair and securing it in place.

There's a knock at the door, and without waiting, a servant enters with a gold box. The final part of my ensemble.

Inside is a crown modeled after the one my mother wore: a circlet of flames that cuts across the forehead and reaches up a few inches, licking at the air.

Hoa places it on my head with a featherlight touch. It's a routine we've been through too many times to count, so often that it's become banal, but this time is different. This time, I let myself remember how my mother would sometimes let me wear her crown, how it was so big it would fall down around my neck. But while my mother's crown was wrought from black gold and set with rubies, the one the Kaiser sends me is molded from ashes, and as soon as it is in place, it begins to crumble, streaking my hair, skin, and dress.

My mother was known as the Fire Queen, regal and strong. But I am the Ash Princess, a living joke.

The stares lie heavy on my skin as soon as I step into the banquet hall, followed by whispers and titters that warm my cheeks. Flakes of ash come down with each step I take, each infinitesimal move of my head, fluttering against my cheeks and shoulders and chest. I pretend not to notice, keeping my head high and letting my eyes glide over the courtiers until they catch on one stare in particular. The Prinz's eyes are so much like his father's that my chest constricts until I can hardly breathe. I look away, wanting to sink through the floor and disappear entirely as I remember how I vomited on him earlier. His stare has a purpose to it, though, which is not to gawk or gloat, but to draw my eyes back to his. I won't give in.

I have my own purpose. While he watches me, I watch the shadows, where the slaves wait with their sunken eyes until they're needed. They are mostly children and adolescents, though there are a few older women as well. No one who could prove a threat, physically. They are all frail bones jutting out beneath sallow skin, with missing teeth and thinning clumps of hair.

Don't look, the old voice urges, but I ignore it now. I need to look. I need to see. "There you are," Crescentia says, tearing my attention away from the shadows. She appears at my side and loops her arm through mine, even as ashes flake down to cover her as well. Her cheerfulness cuts through the tension in the room, and everyone else's attention dissipates. They remember, as I do, what happened the first time the Kaiser sent me the ash crown, how Crescentia—then only seven—brushed her thumbs along my cheekbones and smeared the ashes into thick lines.

There, she'd said so softly that no one else heard her. *Now you're truly ready for battle.* The small act of defiance earned me ten lashes, and I'm sure the Theyn punished

Cress as well. Now, she ignores the crumbling crown as stubbornly as I do.

"I heard all about the trial," she says softly, her forehead puckering. "Are you all right?"

Trial seems like an odd word for it. There were no arguments made, no jury, no judge. It was a murder, and I executed it myself.

Logically, I know I didn't have a choice. But that doesn't ease my guilt.

"It's done," I tell her, waving a hand dismissively. As if it's so easy to rid myself of the memory of the blade biting into Ampelio's skin. "I do hope Hoa will be able to get the blood out, though. It was such a pretty dress, didn't you think?"

"Oh yes. I'm so terribly jealous, Thora. Yellow looks awful on me, but you pull it off so beautifully," she says, squeezing my arm as she leads me toward the far end of the banquet table, away from the royal family and Prinz Søren's probing gaze.

The Theyn, I notice with a sinking stomach, isn't here. He must have already left again. Off to another battle, another invasion, another slaughter.

"Ash Princess." The Kaiser's voice sends ice down my spine, but I suppress a shudder as I turn toward it, pleasant smile at the ready. His pale blue eyes are hard over his goblet of wine, raised in a mock toast to me. His bloated face is already a drunken red. "You're the guest of honor. Your place is here." He gestures to an empty seat next to Prinz Søren.

The squeeze Crescentia gives my hand is comforting as I leave her side to approach the Kaiser.

I curtsy at his feet, and when he extends a hand toward

me, I kiss the ring on his smallest finger—the ring my mother used to wear, and her mother before her.

I start to rise, but his hand brushes my cheek, holding me in place. I struggle not to recoil. Some battles aren't worth fighting. Some battles I can only ever lose. So I lean into his touch like the loyal subject I have been groomed to be, and I let him mark me with an ash handprint.

His hand falls away and he smirks, satisfied, before gesturing for me to sit. As I rise, I notice the Fire Gem pendant hanging from the gold chain around his neck. I would know that gem anywhere. It was Ampelio's. The one he would let me play with, even though my mother scolded him for it whenever she saw him.

"Spiritgems aren't playthings," she would say.

But that might have been her only order he ever disobeyed. I loved holding it in my tiny hands, but it frightened me too— the warmth and power flooded through me like my blood was turning to fire in my veins. It sang to me like we belonged to one another.

Seeing it now, around Corbinian's thick neck, fills me with a different kind of fire, and it's all I can do to stop myself from lunging toward him and using that chain to choke the life from him. But I know Ampelio didn't die for me so I could do something so foolish.

I force my eyes away from it and take my seat next to the Prinz.

Where before his eyes were stuck on me like mud, now he acts like I'm not here at all. He never lets his eyes leave the plate of food in front of him. He can't have told his father about the incident earlier, or I would have already paid for it. But why not? The Kaiser trades favor for information, and even though Prinz Søren is his only son and heir, he must be struggling for favor more than anyone. The Kalovaxian monarchy is rooted more in strength than blood, and half the time when an old monarch dies, he refuses to name his son as successor and the other families at court take the opportunity to make a grab for power. The history books say that it's always bloody and that the process can drag on for years.

But the Prinz isn't weak. Even before he returned, the court was abuzz with his heroics in battle, how strong and valiant he was, what a great kaiser he would make one day. The Kaiser hasn't fought in battle in decades now—unusual for kaisers, who often remain warriors until their deaths. Prinz Søren's strength is only highlighting the Kaiser's weakness, and that is something I'm sure the Kaiser will make him pay for now that he's back at court.

I don't know why the Prinz wouldn't take what favor he could.

A slave boy appears next to me, piling my plate with fish grilled with spices in the Astrean tradition. Most Kalovaxians have a difficult time stomaching Astrean food, but on nights like this they insist on trying. It's more of a symbol than anything else, after all. The food, the music, the clothes are all Astrean, but Astreans themselves—*ourselves*—are no longer allowed to exist.

This music picks up and my mind goes back to my mother. It's the kind of music she used to dance to, her skirts flaring out around her legs as she twirled, spinning me with her until we were both dizzy and giddy. It's the kind of music she and

Ampelio used to sway to, their arms wrapped tightly around each other. These people don't deserve to hear it; they don't deserve any of this. I keep my hands in my lap to hide my clenching fists.

The slave boy bumps against my shoulder as he places another fillet on my plate, and I think nothing of it. I don't let myself look at him this close to the Kaiser, who has had Astreans beheaded in front of me for an innocent glance. I have enough blood on my hands for one day.

I stare at my plate instead, watching as ashes flake down, counting them. It's the only way I'll make it through dinner without screaming.

The slave bumps my shoulder again, this time for no reason at all. The Kaiser, mercifully, is deep in conversation with some visiting lord whose name I don't know, but the Kaiserin's milky, distant eyes flicker to me and narrow briefly before darting away.

Everyone says she's going mad, but I've seen a clarity in her eyes at times that is paralyzing, as if she's waking up in a world she suddenly doesn't understand. Tonight that clarity is not there. The main course hasn't even been served yet and she's already deep in her cups.

No one else notices the Kaiserin. As usual, their eyes glaze over her like she's a ghost, pale and silent and eerie. I'm not entirely sure she isn't.

My plate is piled with more fish than I can possibly eat, but the boy doesn't move away. He must have a death wish.

"Is there anything else you need, my lady?" he asks in my ear. "Wine, perhaps?"

Something in his voice prickles a memory, though I can't place it. I steal a glance, hoping not to be noticed, and when my eyes meet the slave's, I freeze.

His face is gaunt, and he has black hair cropped close to his scalp. His chin is covered in stubble and there's a hardness in his jaw, like he's either angry or hungry. A puckered white scar slices across deep olive skin. But I see the shadow of an apple-cheeked boy sitting next to me in the palace playroom before the siege, always competing for our teacher's favor as she taught us how to write. I remember Astrean words that flowed like water from our quills, his name and my name side by side. I see races I always lost because my legs weren't as long as his. I see solemn green eyes inspecting my scraped knee and I hear his gentle voice telling me it'll be fine, to stop crying.

"Blaise."

I don't realize I've said it out loud until Prinz Søren turns to me.

"Pardon?" he says.

"I . . . I said please. Wine would be lovely. *Please*."

Prinz Søren turns to face front again but I'm frozen in place, looking at Blaise over my shoulder. I can't stare at him this long; it'll raise suspicion. I know that, but I can't make myself turn away, because he's *here*, like some spirit I summoned. How can he be here?

Blaise holds my gaze for a second that is heavy with words we can't speak, questions we can't ask. He gives a curt nod before turning away, but his eyes are loaded with a promise. I face forward in my seat again, but questions thunder through my mind. What is he doing here? If he had been working in the castle, I would have noticed it before now, wouldn't I? Appearing today of all days can't be a coincidence.

"Lady Thora." Prinz Søren's low voice draws me out of my thoughts, and I angle toward him and pretend everything is normal. His bright eyes land on mine, shift to the handprint his father left on my cheek, and dart away. He looks to the Kaiser, who is paying too much attention to the slave girl pouring him more wine to notice anything else. She's younger than I am—fourteen, maybe. It makes my skin crawl, but it's nothing I haven't seen before.

Still, Prinz Søren's voice is quiet, barely audible over the music and conversation. "About what happened—"

"I'm so sorry, Your Highness," I interrupt, turning my attention back to Søren, suddenly embarrassed. "You must understand that I was in shock. As you were astute enough to realize, it was the first time I had . . ." I trail off. I can't say the words. Saying them out loud will make them irreparably true. "Thank you for not telling anyone."

"Of course," he says, looking surprised. He clears his throat. "As bumbled as my attempt might have been, I was only seeking to . . ." It's his turn to break off. "I wanted to ease your mind."

The kindness in his words takes me aback, especially when he's looking at me with the Kaiser's cold blue eyes. It's difficult to meet them, but I try. "My mind is easy, Your Highness," I assure him, forcing a smile to my face.

"Søren," he says. "Call me Søren."

"Søren," I repeat. Even when gossiping about him with

Crescentia, I don't know that I've ever said his name out loud. He's always been "the Prinz." I'm struck by how Kalovaxian a name it really is, with its hard edges and long "o." It sounds like a sword slicing through the air and finding its target. It's strange, the power names have over us. How can there be such a difference between Thora and Theodosia when both are me? How can just saying Søren's name aloud make it so much harder to lump him in with the Kaiser and the Theyn and all the other Kalovaxian warriors?

"Then you must call me Thora," I say, because it's the only response I can give, even if the name tastes bitter in my mouth.

"Thora," he repeats, lowering his voice. "What I meant earlier was that I remember my first kill, and I think it will always haunt me."

"Even if they were only Astrean rabble?" I ask, struggling to keep the bite out of my voice.

I must not have succeeded, because he goes quiet for a moment. "Uri, Gavriel, Kyri, Nik, Marios, Dominic, Hathos, Silas, and Vaso," he says, counting them off on his fingers. It takes me a moment to realize he's listing the names of the men he killed seven years ago. "The one my father killed was called Ilias. It's not something I'm proud of; I'm sorry if I led you to believe otherwise."

The words are stiff and clipped at the edges, but there's no mistaking the feeling beneath them, straining to break free. There is something laid bare in his eyes that I've never seen before. Not from any other Kalovaxian, not even Cress.

Before I can puzzle out how to respond, Blaise appears at my shoulder again, pouring blood-red wine into my goblet. It takes all my self-control not to look at him.

On the other side of the table, a slave girl drops a tray, sending fish skidding across the stone floor. Everyone turns to stare as she hastens to clean up, even the Prinz. Søren.

"Midnight tonight," Blaise whispers in my ear. "Kitchen cellar."

I turn, but he's already disappeared into the crowd.

The slave girl who dropped the tray is grabbed by two guards and dragged from the room. She will be whipped for her clumsiness at best, killed at worst.

Before she's gone, her eyes lock onto mine and a small, tight smile flickers across her mouth. She isn't clumsy at all. It was a distraction, and one that might cost her her life. I can't imagine how I'll be able to meet Blaise tonight, but I will have to try.

ALLY

———— • ————

MY MOTHER ALWAYS TOLD ME that if we prayed to the gods, they would protect us from harm. Houzzah, god of fire, would keep us warm. Suta, goddess of water, would surround our island and protect us. Ozam, god of air, would keep us healthy. Glaidi, goddess of earth, would keep us fed. There were a dozen other minor gods and goddesses of everything from beauty to animals, though I've forgotten most of their names by now.

But I also remember how when the Kalovaxians came, we both prayed and prayed and prayed and it didn't matter. I didn't believe they would kill her, because the gods would never allow it. She would be queen until old age took her—it was her due. Even when the blood spilled from her neck and her hand grew slack around mine, I still didn't believe it. I thought my mother was immortal even after the light left her eyes.

Afterward, I wept. Then I raged, not just against the Kalovaxians but against my gods as well, because they had let my mother die when they should have protected her. The Kalovaxians forced me to replace them with their gods—

similar in domains, but more vengeful, less forgiving—but it didn't matter one way or another. That part of me, the part that believed, had broken.

I try praying now as I lie in bed and wait for midnight. I pray desperately and hopelessly, to all the gods I remember from either religion. Mine feel more like ghosts now, echoes of ancestors I met once but remember more from stories than memories.

I never let a word pass my lips. In the silence, my Shadows' presence is even heavier. Heresy is a death offense, and I'm sure they would fight one another for the chance to tell the Kaiser, if only so that they could finally be rid of what must be a truly terrible job. They aren't even supposed to talk to one another, though they break that rule often. I usually fall asleep to them whispering.

Now the room is silent for the first time in my memory. They're supposed to sleep in shifts, and that is one rule I know they always follow, because all three of them snore horribly and I only ever hear one at a time.

One snore erupts from the northern wall, so deep it almost feels like the floor shakes.

If it's North's turn to sleep, East and South usually snicker at his snore, but they don't now. I close my eyes and listen, trying to strip away North's snore to hear anything underneath.

And there it is—a whimper of a snore from East, like a mewling puppy.

The Kaiser will be furious if he finds out both of them are sleeping. He doesn't like to take chances, and my Shadows, like most Kalovaxians, are too terrified of him to risk his wrath.

If only South is watching me tonight, there must be something I can do. One Shadow is easier to mislead than two, though not by much. It's still one dedicated and deadly man whose entire job revolves around watching every move I make.

But then I hear it: a third snore, this one raspy and light, easy to mistake for a particularly riotous wind pouring through the cracked window.

The realization floods me with joy that's all too quickly replaced by dread. What are the chances that on the same night Blaise appears and arranges a meeting, my Shadows are all asleep for the first time in ten years? Much lower than the chances that I'm walking into a trap. Felicie comes to mind again and I can see the Kaiser's angry, red face and the whip in his hand.

This time, the punishment will be worse.

But if it isn't a trap, if Blaise is really waiting in the kitchen cellar and he was in league with Ampelio, how can I *not* go?

When the moon is high in the sky and I'm sure most everyone is asleep, I throw my quilt off and slip from the safety of my bed. There is still no sound from beyond the walls, so I inch closer to one of the holes, my heart pounding in my chest.

The snores are unmistakable now from each of the holes. The Shadows are all well and truly asleep. It's possible, of course, that they all ate and drank too much at the banquet and fell into a deep sleep, but I don't believe in coincidences. The thought that I'm walking into another one of the Kaiser's traps paralyzes me for a moment, but I push on. I cannot be a coward anymore.

The icy stone floor feels like needles on the soles of my feet as I tiptoe across it, but my steps are quieter without shoes. Barefoot, I make my way to the door and pause with my hand on the doorknob. It would be so easy, I think, to crawl back into my bed, to banish thoughts of Blaise and Ampelio and my mother to the back of my mind for good. I could bury it all deep inside. I could refrain from angering the Kaiser and he would continue to keep me alive.

But I think of the blood staining my dress, my hands. Of Ampelio.

I suck in a deep breath and force myself to turn the doorknob and push the door open just wide enough to slip through out into the hall. The doors to the Shadows' rooms are all closed, but there are wine goblets left on the floor outside them. Some kind soul must have brought them drinks from the banquet. Or maybe not so kind, depending on what else was in the wine.

Clever, Blaise. I stifle a smile before realizing that for the first time in ages, no one is watching me. I let myself really smile. For a moment, I think of them asleep in their tiny rooms, and the temptation to spy on *them* for once passes over me, but I can't risk waking them.

The smile stays fixed on my face as I continue down the hall. The cellar is in the west wing of the palace, beneath the main kitchens, so I need to turn left. Or is it to the right? In the dim light from torches lining the walls, I can't be sure of anything. All it will take is one wrong turn, one wrong corridor, one person where they aren't supposed to be. The thought almost sends me running back for my bed, but I know it's only a slower death that awaits me there.

I have to make a choice. I have to trust myself. I go left.

The sounds of late-night revelers travel up the grand staircase and down the halls to me—music and drunken laughter, shouts of glee at Astrea's expense. A toast is raised to the Ash Princess, and they make lewd jokes I've heard so often they roll off my back like water. The easiest path to the kitchens leads right past them, down the stairs and just around a corner—a terrifying prospect, considering their current state—but there is a reason Blaise designated the kitchen cellar, and it isn't only because it's dark and deserted at this time of night. It's because of the tunnels.

When we were children, before the siege, Blaise was determined to explore all the passages hidden within the castle, drawing up dozens of scrawled maps that only he could read. And since his mother and mine were close friends and always together, he was often forced to let me tag along. I discovered them as well. We didn't come close to finding all of them, but in the year or so we spent looking, we found dozens. Including one that leads from the east wing of the palace to the kitchen cellar.

It's the kind of memory I thought long lost, like most of my memories before the siege, but seeing Ampelio today and then Blaise has them all coming back to me.

Still, it would be only too easy to miss the entrance after so many years. The darkness doesn't help and I didn't dare bring a candle. The voices of the revelers are moving now, getting closer, but they head down another passageway, away from me, and I let out a sigh of relief.

When I come to what I am almost positive is the right hallway, I reach out and trail my fingers along the wall. Ten years ago, the stone was at eye level, so now it should be about waist height. How can it be possible that I've grown so much, when it feels like yesterday that I watched my mother die?

But then, it was also another lifetime.

I've nearly given up finding it when I run my hand over a stone that juts out slightly from the rest.

Like Guardian Alexis's nose, Blaise had said with a snicker when we'd first found it. Guardian Alexis was an Air Guardian who had a nose that arched like a bow ready to snap and who liked to tell jokes I didn't understand. He must be dead now.

I twist the stone once clockwise, twice counterclockwise, before giving the wall a firm shove with my shoulder. It takes a few more shoves before a hidden door hinges open, but that's a good thing. It means no one has used this tunnel in quite some time. With one last look back to make sure I'm not being followed, I step inside and push the door closed behind me.

The tunnel is narrow and dark but I press forward, feeling along the dust-draped walls to find my way. I should have brought a candle. And shoes. No one has been in this tunnel for a decade, and the stones that make up the walls and ground are coated in dirt and dust that cling to my hands and the soles of my feet.

I walk and walk and the path twists on longer than I remember, curling in ways that make me certain I'm going in circles. Every so often, muffled voices leak through the stones, and though I know their owners can't know I'm here, I hold my breath as I pass. One way or another, I'm sure now that this will end in my death, but it doesn't matter. Even if all this is for nothing and I am killed for it, even if it is a trap, I'm doing the only thing I can.

Finally my foot touches wood and I stop. I drop to a crouch and sweep away the dust and dirt on the door I know is beneath me as best I can, feeling around for the cold metal handle. It appears under my hand and I turn it only to find it rusted shut. I have to throw all my body weight against it to turn it a quarter of the way. I turn it again and again, until my arms burn, and the door inches open wide enough for me to slip through.

"Hello?" I whisper into the darkness below.

If I remember correctly, it's a ten-foot drop to the stone floor of the cellar, and with my bare feet I can't possibly make it without help.

The sound of shuffling footsteps moving closer.

"Are you alone?" he whispers up to me in Astrean. It takes a few seconds for the words to register.

I have to translate my response in my mind before I say it, hating myself as I do. Even my *thoughts* are Kalovaxian now.

"Are *you*?" I ask.

"No, I thought I'd bring a few guards and the Kaiser along."

I freeze, though I'm fairly sure he's joking. He must hear my hesitance, because he sighs impatiently.

"I'm alone. Jump and I'll catch you."

"I'm not six years old anymore, Blaise. I'm a good deal heavier," I warn.

"And I'm a good deal stronger," he answers. "Five years in the Earth Mine will do that."

I can't manage a reply. Five years enslaved in a mine, five years that close to the raw power of the earth goddess, Glaidi. No wonder he looked so haunted. My decade in the palace has been a nightmare, but it doesn't compare to even half that time in a place like that. Once, those mines were holy places, but I can't help but feel the gods abandoned us during the siege.

"You were in the mines?" I whisper, though I don't know why I'm surprised. Most Astreans were sent to the mines. But if Blaise was there for five years and didn't go mad, he's stronger than the boy I remember him being. I doubt he can say the same of me.

"Yes," he says. "Now hurry up and jump, Theo. We don't have much time."

Theo.

Theodosia.

I ignore the nagging urge to turn back, and I slide through the hole legs first. For less than a second, I fall freely before Blaise's arms come under me, one beneath my knees and the other at my back. He sets me down immediately.

It takes my eyes a moment to adjust to the dark, but as they do, his face comes into focus. Unlike in the banquet hall, I can truly look at him now without any consequences. His face is long, the way his father's was, but with dark green eyes he inherited from his mother. There is nothing on his bones but hard muscle and ashen olive skin. A long, pale scar cuts from his left temple to the corner of his mouth, and I shudder to imagine what could have caused it. He always dwarfed me by a few inches, but now I have to look up to catch his eyes—there's nearly a foot of difference between us, never mind the broadness of his shoulders.

"Ampelio is dead," I tell him when I finally form words.

The muscle in his jaw jumps and his eyes dart away from me. "I know," he says. "I heard you killed him."

The bite in his voice makes my breath hitch.

"He asked me to," I say quietly. "He knew if I didn't, the Kaiser would have had someone else do it and then my own life would have been forfeit as well. Now the Kaiser believes I am loyal to him above my own people."

"Are you?" he asks. His eyes are locked on mine, searching them for the truth.

"Of course not," I say, but my voice wavers. It's the truth, I know it is, but just saying it is enough for me to remember the Theyn's whip biting into my skin, the Kaiser's cruel eyes on me, reveling in my pain every time he so much as suspected my loyalty to him wasn't bound in iron.

Blaise stares at me for a long moment, sizing me up. Even before he speaks, I know I've been found wanting.

"Who are you?" he asks me.

The question is a wasp sting.

"You're the one who wanted to meet me here, who risked both of our lives in the process. Who are *you*?" I reply.

He doesn't flinch, instead keeping his gaze trained on me in a way that feels like he's reading me down to my bones.

"I'm the one who's going to get you out of here."

He says it so gravely, but it sends a wave of relief through me. I've been waiting for a decade to hear those words, for a glimpse of freedom. I never thought it would come like this. But shiny as this new hope is, I can't bring myself to trust it.

"Why now?" I ask him.

His eyes finally drop from mine. "I promised Ampelio that if anything happened to him, I would do whatever it took to save you."

My chest feels hollow. "You were working with him," I say.

I had already figured as much, but hearing him say his name still hurts.

Blaise nods. "Ever since he rescued me from the Earth Mine three years ago," he says.

That hurts worse. I know that Blaise's life in the mine was much more painful than my life here is. Still, while I was waiting for Ampelio to save me, he saved Blaise instead, and I can't deny the way that digs under my skin.

"What happened to the serving girl at the banquet?" I ask, ignoring the feeling and focusing on something else. "Is she . . ."

I can't say the words, but I don't need to. He shakes his head, though his eyes are still far away. "Marina is . . . a favorite of the guards. They won't kill her. It's why she volunteered. She'll meet us on the ship."

"The ship?" I ask.

"Dragonsbane's ship," he says, naming the best known of the Astrean pirates. His actions are responsible for more than a few of the scars on my back. Blaise must see my confusion, because he sighs. "It's hidden about a mile up the coast from here, in a cove just past the forest of cypress trees."

I have a vague idea of the area he's talking about, though I haven't left the capital since the siege. I can see the tops of the tall cypresses from Cress's window. Still, I don't want to let myself believe what he's saying until he says the words.

"We're getting you out. Tonight," he says, and everything in me uncoils.

Out. Tonight. I didn't allow myself to think about that possibility when I came down here; didn't allow myself even a glimmer of hope that tonight would end with me being free from the Kaiser's hold. But now I do. Freedom is close enough to touch, but the thought terrifies me as much as it excites me. I've been close to freedom before, after all, and it hurts so much when it's yanked away again.

"Then what?" I ask him, unable to keep giddiness from leaking into my voice. I can't help it. The idea of freedom is working its way through me, and even though I feel like it can be yanked away as quickly as it was offered, it's *hope,* and it's more real than anything I've felt in a decade.

"There are countries that have taken in Astrean refugees," he tells me, counting them off on his fingers. "Etralia, Sta'crivero, Timmoree. We'll go to one of those, make a new life there. The Kaiser will never find you."

The hope flooding my veins sputters. It doesn't die, but it twists into something new and unexpected. In all my fantasies of being rescued, I never saw it going like this. I thought of Ampelio coming to me with anger and armies and a plan to retake Astrea. I hate living under the Kaiser's thumb, but this palace is my home. I was born here, and I always imagined fighting to retake my mother's throne and sending the Kalovaxians back to the desolate wasteland of their home country.

I took my first steps here. The thought of leaving my home behind is what I've wanted for ten years, but the idea of never coming back? That feels like a punch to the gut.

"You want to run?" I ask quietly.

Blaise flinches at the last word. He was raised in this palace, too, after all. Leaving it behind can't be easy for him either, but he doesn't back down. "This has never been a fight we could win, Theo. With Ampelio, there was a chance, but now . . . All the Guardians are dead. The forces Ampelio managed to gather scattered after he was captured, and they weren't many to begin with. Maybe a thousand."

"*A thousand?*" I repeat, my stomach sinking. I am shocked. "There are a hundred thousand Astreans."

His eyes fall away from mine, looking instead at the stone floors. "There *were* a hundred thousand," he corrects, grimacing. "The last numbers I heard put us closer to twenty."

Twenty thousand. How is that possible? The siege took many lives, but could it have been so many? We are a mere fraction of what we were.

"Of those twenty thousand," Blaise continues, ignoring my shock, "half are in the mines and unable to escape."

That I know. The mines were heavily guarded before the Air Mine riot last week; I'm sure the Kaiser doubled the number of guards there since.

"But if you escaped, there must be a way," I point out.

"I had Ampelio. We don't," he says, but doesn't elaborate. "Of the other ten thousand, Dragonsbane smuggled about four thousand to other countries, which leaves six thousand in Astrea—maybe three thousand here in the capital. None of them have ever fought a day in their lives. Many are children who have never lived in a world not run by the Kaiser. They've never raised a weapon. One thousand were willing to try."

I barely hear him. While I played the Kaiser's games, eighty thousand of my people died. Every time the whip bit into my skin and I cursed my country and the people trying to save it, my people were slaughtered. While I've danced and gossiped with Cress, they went mad in the mines. While I've feasted at the table of my enemy, they starved.

The blood of eighty thousand people is on my hands. The thought turns me numb. Soon I will mourn them, and once I start I don't know if I'll ever be able to stop, but I can't do it now. I force myself to think instead about the twenty thousand people who are still alive, people who have been waiting for ten years for someone to save them, just like me.

The time has come for little birds to fly, Ampelio said before he told me to kill him, to end his life to save my own. He can't save us anymore, but someone has to.

"There are ten thousand in the mines," I say when I can speak again. The words come out hoarse and desperate. "Ten thousand strong, furious Astreans who would be happy to fight, after everything they've endured."

"And the Kaiser knows that, which is why the mines are even better guarded than the capital," Blaise says, shaking his head. "It's impossible."

Impossible. The word ruffles me and I ignore it.

"But the thousand you mentioned," I say. "We can get them back, can't we? If we work together."

He hesitates before shaking his head. "By the end of the week, every Astrean in the country will know that you were the one who killed Ampelio. They'll have a hard time trusting you after that."

The idea sickens me, but I'm sure the Kaiser anticipated that very response when he ordered me to kill Ampelio. Another way to cut me off from my people, by making them hate me as much as they hate him.

"We'll explain it to them. They know the Kaiser by now,

they know his games. We can change their minds," I say, hoping it's true.

"Even if we can, it won't be enough. It's still one thousand civilians against one hundred times as many trained Kalovaxian soldiers."

I bite my bottom lip. "And Dragonsbane?" I press. "If he's on our side, we can fight. He must have made allies in his travels, he must know people who can help." Dragonsbane has been a burr in the Kaiser's boot since the siege, attacking his ships, sinking several fortunes in Spiritgems he meant to sell, smuggling weapons to Astrean rebels.

But Blaise looks unconvinced. "Dragonsbane's loyalty is to Dragonsbane." He says it like he's quoting words he's heard too many times. "We're on the same side now, but it's best not to place too much faith there. I know it isn't what you want to hear—it isn't what I want to *say* either—but any hope of revolution died with Ampelio, and there wasn't much hope to begin with. All we can do now is leave, Theo. I'm sorry."

I've been dreaming of freedom every day since the siege, waiting and waiting and waiting for just this moment, when someone would take me as far away from this place as possible. I can have a new life on some faraway shore under an open sky, no Shadows watching, no having to worry about every word I say, every flicker of my expression. I would never have to see the Kaiser again, never feel the whip bite into my back, never have to bow at his feet. I would never again have to wonder if this would be the day he would finally break me beyond repair.

Freedom is close enough to touch. I can walk away and never look back.

But as soon as I think it, I know it isn't true.

Ampelio spent the last decade trying to save Astrea because it was our home. Because there were people—like Blaise—who needed him. Because he swore oaths to the gods to protect Astrea and its magic at any cost. His blood is on my hands now, and though I know it was unavoidable, I still took a hero from a world with precious few of them.

Eighty thousand people. It's an unfathomable number. Eighty thousand mothers, fathers, children. Eighty thousand warriors and artists and farmers and merchants and teachers. Eighty thousand unmarked graves. Eighty thousand of my people who died waiting for someone to save them.

"I think I'd like to stay," I tell him quietly.

Blaise turns to me, dumbfounded. "What?"

"I appreciate all the trouble you've gone to, really I do—"

"I don't know what that monster did to you, Theo, what lies he's spun, but you aren't safe here. I was there tonight when he had you on display like a trophy. It's only going to get worse."

How it could be worse I can't begin to fathom. I won't think about it. It'll only weaken my already tentative resolve.

"We don't have their numbers, Blaise. You're right: if we come at him on an even field, we lose and the rebellion Ampelio gave his life for will have been for nothing. But if I stay, I can get information. I can find weaknesses, figure out their plans. I can give us a chance to take our country back."

For a moment, he almost looks like the boy I knew. The boy I chased and clung to, no matter how he tried to get rid of me.

"You can't tell me I'm wrong," I say. "I'm your best shot."

He shakes his head. "It's too dangerous. You think we haven't had spies before? We've had dozens, and he always finds them. And don't take this the wrong way, but they were a lot more stable than you are."

"I'm *fine*," I protest, though we both know it's a lie.

He watches me for a moment, searching my face for any sign of hesitation he can use against me. I don't give it to him.

"Who are you?" he asks.

It's such a simple question, but I falter. We both know it's a test, and one I cannot fail. I swallow, forcing myself to meet his eyes.

"My name is Theo—"

The name catches in my throat and I am a child again, cowering on the cold stone floor while the Kaiser and the Theyn stand over me.

"Who are you?" the Kaiser asks calmly.

But every time I tell him, the whip cracks against my skin and I scream. It goes on for hours. I don't know what they want from me, I keep telling them the truth. I keep telling them my name is Theodosia Eirene Houzzara. My name is Theodosia. My name is Theo.

Until I don't. I tell them I am no one.

That is when they stop. That is when the Kaiser crouches next to me with a kind smile and places a finger under my chin, forcing me to look at him. That is when he tells me I am a good girl and gives me a new name like it's a present. And I am grateful to him for it.

Warm hands grip my shoulders, jerking me back and

forth. When I open my eyes, Blaise's face is inches from mine, eyes dark and harder than I remember them.

"Your name is Theodosia," he tells me. "Say it."

I lift my hand to touch his cheek, tracing his scar. He flinches.

"You used to have such a lovely smile," I tell him. My voice breaks. "Your mother said it would get you into trouble one day."

He drops his hands as if my skin burned him, but he still watches me like I'm a savage animal. Like I could attack him at any moment. I wrap my arms around my stomach and lean back against the wall.

"What happened to her?" I ask, quietly.

I don't think he hears me at first. He turns his face away, swallows hard.

"Killed in the siege," he says after a moment. "She tried to stand between the Kalovaxians and your mother."

Of course she did. Our mothers were friends from the cradle, "closer than blood," they used to say. I called her Auntie. Gruesome as it is, it would have been quick at least. For that, I'm thankful.

My legs give out and I sink to the dirty ground.

"And your father?" I ask him.

He shakes his head. "The Kalovaxians have experience conquering countries. They knew to kill the Guardians and warriors first," he tells me. "Ampelio was the last one."

"I tried to make it painless," I murmur. "It was the least I could do. He was already in so much pain, though. . . . I don't know if it helped."

Blaise nods, but doesn't say any more. Instead, he sinks to the ground next to me, crosses his legs, and suddenly it almost feels like we're children again at our lessons, waiting for our teachers to make sense of the world around us. But none of our world makes sense.

"Theodosia," he says again. "You need to say it."

I swallow as the shadows close in again. But I can't let them overtake me. Not now.

"I am Th . . . Theodosia Eirene Houzzara," I tell him. "And I am my people's only hope."

For a moment, he stares at me. He's going to say no and I'm not even sure he's wrong to.

Instead, he lets out a long, pained exhale and tears his gaze away. He suddenly looks much older than seventeen. He looks like a man who has seen too much of the world. "What kind of information?" he asks finally.

My smile feels brittle. "They aren't infallible, no matter what the Kaiser likes to believe. The riot last month, in the Air Mine?"

He looks away from me. "The one that killed a hundred Astreans and injured more than twice that?" he asks.

"Instigated by an earthquake, of all things. The Astreans saw their opportunity to revolt and they took it. The Kaiser said Ampelio caused it, but he was a Fire Guardian, not Earth. Of course, the Kaiser doesn't rely on logic or facts. He said Ampelio caused it, and that's good enough for the Kalovaxians," I say. "Besides, it killed nearly as many Kalovaxians," I add.

His thick eyebrows dart up. "I didn't hear that."

"The Kaiser must have kept it quiet. He wouldn't want anyone to know how much damage a group of Astrean rebels could do. You know the Theyn?"

Blaise's face darkens and he gives a grunt of acknowledgment.

"His daughter thinks of me as a friend, and she has loose lips," I say, though guilt ties my stomach into knots as I say it. Cress *is* my friend, but she's also the Theyn's daughter. It's easiest to think of them as two separate people.

"I'm surprised they allow her around you, then," he remarks.

I shake my head. "I'm just a broken girl to them, a bleeding trophy from another land they've conquered," I say. "They don't see me as a threat."

He frowns. "And the Kaiser? Do you have anything on him?"

"It's difficult," I admit. "He's careful to appear more god than human. Even the Kalovaxians are too frightened of his wrath to risk gossiping, at least not where they can be overheard."

"And the Prinz?" he presses.

The Prinz. Søren, he asked me to call him. I hear him tell me the names of the Astreans he killed on his tenth birthday again, though I'm sure there have been many more killings since then. He can hardly remember all their names, can he?

I push the thought aside and shrug. "I don't know him well; he's been training at sea for the last five years. He's a warrior, and a good one from what I've heard," I say, thinking more about our conversation at the banquet, how he followed me after Ampelio's execution to make sure I was all right when no one else thought twice about me. "But he has a weakness for heroism. I suppose it traces back to wanting to protect his mother. The Kaiser doesn't seem particularly attached to him, even as an heir. I think he's intimidated by him. As I said, the Kalovaxians don't love the Kaiser, they *fear* him. I'm sure many of them are waiting for the day the Prinz replaces him."

Blaise's expression is guarded, but I can see his mind working. "Have you heard anything about berserkers?"

The word is strange, though it's certainly Kalovaxian. "Berserkers?" I repeat. "I don't think so, no."

"It's a kind of weapon," he explains. "There have been . . . whispers about them, but no one's been able to discover what they do firsthand. Or at least survive to report on it."

"The Theyn's daughter might know something," I say, desperation leaking into my voice. I need to stay here, I need to be useful, I need to do *something*. "I can try to find out more."

He gives a loud exhale, leaning his head back against the wall. He's pretending to consider it, but I know I have him. I'm not offering much, but he has no other options.

"I'll have to find a way to stay in contact," he says finally.

Relief floods through me, and I can't help but laugh. "You certainly can't drug my Shadows again."

He looks surprised that I figured it out, but shrugs. "They'll think they got carried away at the banquet, and they definitely won't want the Kaiser to find out about it."

"The Kaiser finds out about everything," I tell him. "This time, the Shadows might take the fall, but if there's a pattern—even a hint of a pattern—he'll find a way to blame me for it."

He thinks for a moment, chewing on the inside of his cheek.

"I might have an idea, but I'll need some help first," he says. "It might be a few days. I'll find you—don't risk coming looking for me. In the meantime, see what you can do about the Prinz."

"What do you mean?" I ask.

He looks me over, sizing me up again, but this time in a different way, one I can't quite put my finger on. "You said he likes the idea of being a hero," he says, a grim smile pulling at his mouth. "Aren't you a maiden in need of rescuing?"

I can't help but laugh. "I'm hardly of any interest to him. The Kaiser would never allow it."

"And spoiled prinzes always want things they can't have," he says. "You notice a lot, but did you notice the way he looked at you?"

I think of the way he watched me at the banquet, how he asked if I was all right, but the idea still seems ridiculous.

"The same way he looked at anyone, I'd imagine. With an expression carved from stone and frost behind his eyes."

"That wasn't how it appeared tonight," he says. "The Prinz could be a priceless source of information."

The idea of Prinz Søren having feelings for anyone is laughable. I doubt there's a heart in his chest at all. Still, I can't help but think of how he asked me to call him by his name.

"I'll see what I can do," I say.

Blaise rests a hand on my shoulder. His skin is warm, despite the chilly cellar. This close, I can see his father in him, in the fullness of his mouth and the square shape of his jaw. But there is so much anger in him, more anger than our parents ever had to know. It should frighten me, but it doesn't. I understand it.

"One month," he tells me after a moment. "In one month, we leave, no matter what."

One month more under the Kaiser's thumb seems like an eternity. But I also know that it isn't nearly enough time to turn the tide; it isn't enough time to do much of anything. But it'll have to be.

"One month," I agree.

Blaise hesitates for a moment, looking like he wants to say more. "These people destroyed our lives, Theo," he says finally, his voice breaking over my name.

I step toward him. "That is a debt we will repay," I promise.

The words themselves don't shock me as much as the vehemence behind them. I don't sound like myself, even to my own ears. Or at least, I don't sound like Thora. But when Blaise's eyes soften and he pulls me into an embrace, I wonder if I'm starting to sound like Theodosia.

It's been so long since anyone besides Cress has touched me like this, with genuine love and comfort. I almost want to pull away, but he smells like Astrea. He feels like home.

PLOT

———— ◆•◆ ————

Every muscle in my body screams when Hoa enters my room and draws the curtains to let the sun in. I want to roll over and beg to go back to sleep, but I can't risk anything that could seem suspicious after Blaise's stunt with the guards. I was up until nearly dawn scrubbing the grime from my skin and stuffing the unsalvageable nightgown into a hole in the underside of my mattress, terrified that at any moment those three sets of snores would stop and I would be caught, but mercifully they were still sleeping when I finally drifted off.

Hoa will notice the nightgown missing soon, but there are much simpler explanations for that than treason.

Yesterday feels like a dream—or more like a nightmare—but it wasn't. It might be the only real day I've lived in the last decade. The thought gives me energy enough to sit up and blink away my bleariness. I drag through the motions of getting ready, and if Hoa notices my daze or the difference between the nightgown I wear and the one she dressed me in last night, she gives no sign.

As she wraps vivid orange silk around me and pins it at my shoulder with a lapis lazuli pin, my mind is far from idle.

If Blaise is right and the Prinz is interested in me, I'm not sure where to start. I've seen Kalovaxian courtship rituals play out many times, ending in marriage or death and nothing in between, but whatever the Prinz wants from me, it won't be marriage. His father would never allow it. The Kaiser may have given me a title and other luxuries, but he will never grant me any more rights than any other Astrean slave.

"Lower," I tell Hoa.

Her forehead creases in confusion, so I move the pin down myself. It's only a couple of inches, but it causes the neckline to dip low and expose more of my chest. I've seen courtesans show far more skin—even Dagmær routinely wears much more scandalous things. Still, Hoa's eyes are disapproving. If she knew what I was doing, she would applaud me, wouldn't she? Or maybe she would tattle to the Kaiser before I could so much as draw a breath.

As soon as Hoa finishes arranging my hair and painting my face, there's a knock at the door, and without waiting for an answer, Crescentia glides in wearing a dress of sky-blue silk. A small leather-bound book is clasped in her hand. Like my dress, hers is draped in the Astrean style. Though I'd missed the loose flowing chitons for years while I was forced to sweat in fitted Kalovaxian velvets, it always turns my stomach to see anyone, even Cress, wear Astrean dresses. It feels like another thing that's been taken from me. I wonder if she knows that it's loose to facilitate movement, that it's made for dancing and riding and running. Now it's merely ornamental, just as we're supposed to be.

"Hello, darling," she chirps, eyes darting briefly to my lowered neckline. I wait for a pointed comment, a barb like she throws when Dagmær wears something outrageous, but she only smiles. "I thought we could take a walk outside today, maybe down to the beach? I know how you love the sea, and I could use some help with these poems. Lyrian is more challenging than I anticipated."

I was six when I first met Crescentia, and lonely. No one spoke to me, and I wasn't allowed to speak to anyone. I was, however, required to attend meals in the banquet hall and lessons with the noble children.

Not that the lessons actually mattered, since my Kalovaxian was rough at best and the teacher spoke too quickly for me to keep up with her. I all but disappeared into my own mind; fantasies of being rescued and finding my mother alive played over and over in my head. Anyone who wanted to pull me out of my fantasies had a hard time of it, though the Kaiser had given permission for any person of Kalovaxian blood to strike me.

The other children were the most vicious. They pinched and slapped and kicked me until I was black and blue and bloody, and no one stopped them. Even the teacher only watched with a wary eye, ready to step in if it looked like any irreparable damage was being done. That was where the Kaiser drew the line. I wasn't of any use to him if I was dead.

The worst was Nilsen, who was two years older and looked like a block of pale wood, yellow and hard-edged and just as wide as tall. Even his face reminded me of the swirls and rings in the wood grain. He had a fascination with water that wasn't unusual for Kalovaxians, but it took on a sadistic twist that I'm not sure even the Theyn was capable of.

The first time, he shoved my head in a water basin and held me there, thick fingers digging into the back of my neck as I thrashed against him. I had the good sense—or maybe it was foolishness—to kick him between the legs and break away when he doubled over, both of us gasping for breath.

Luckily, I caught mine first and ran.

Unluckily, he learned from his mistake.

The next day, his two friends held me in place, and no matter how much I struggled and tried to kick, I couldn't get free. My lungs burned and the edges of my mind began to blur. I was almost looking forward to passing out—maybe even seeing my mother again in the After—when suddenly the hands were gone and I was pulled out by a much gentler grip.

My dazed mind thought that she was a goddess at first. The Astrean fire god, Houzzah, had a daughter named Evavia, who was the goddess of safety. She sometimes took the guise of a child to do her work, and I certainly could have used her help. I only caught a glimpse of Nilsen and his friends as they fled the room as fast as their stubby legs could carry them.

"Are you all right?" She spoke Kalovaxian slowly so I could understand her.

I couldn't form words, only cough, but she rubbed circles on my back reassuringly—a maternal gesture I recognized later as strange, considering that her mother had died when she was an infant.

"They won't come after you," she continued. "I told them my father would burn the skin from their bones if they ever laid a finger on you again." She had to mime for me as she spoke, but I understood well enough.

Houzzah was more than capable of such a feat, but as the spots cleared from my vision and my mind came back to earth, I realized this girl was no goddess. Evavia might take the guise of a child, but none of my gods would ever look like a Kalovaxian, and this girl was the epitome of them, from her pale skin and flaxen hair to her small, delicate features.

As I caught my breath, she told me her name and proclaimed that we were friends, as if it were as simple as that. To Crescentia, it was. She makes friends as easily as she breathes, and for reasons I still don't understand, I became her favorite. There are moments when I wonder if it's something her father pushed her into in order to better keep an eye on me, but I also know that she cares for me in a way I'll never be able to match. I love her, but today I can't look at her without seeing her father dragging his dagger across my mother's throat.

In a strange way, I think part of what drew us together was our shared loss—we're both girls with dead mothers.

I glance at her dress, which has been sewn with small pieces of aquamarine around the hem and neckline that match her eyes perfectly.

"Oh no, Cress," I say with a sly smile. "You're far too pretty to only go down to the beach today." I pause as if the idea is just coming to me, though I've been putting together a plan since last night. "Do you know what the Prinz is doing? We could just happen to wander by. . . ." I lift my eyebrows meaningfully.

Cress's cheeks turn pink and she bites her bottom lip. "Oh, I wouldn't dare."

"Plenty of other girls would dare," I tell her. "He's grown up handsome, don't you think? Even Dagmær might decide he's a better prize than that ancient duke she's been angling for."

She chews harder on her lip and smiles. "He is awfully handsome, isn't he? Taller than I thought he would be. Last time I saw him, I had a few inches on him, but now he towers over me. My father says he's an excellent warrior as well, the best he's seen in years."

"How long will he be here, do you know?" I ask.

"My father says he's back for good," she says, cheeks dimpling as her smile widens. "He'll still go off when he's needed in battle, but this will be his home now. The Kaiser is insisting he join the court. A marriage likely won't be far off, now that he's seventeen."

"And I'm sure every other girl in court has gotten that same idea in her head, Cress. You'd be wise to get ahead of them quickly. So where is the Prinz today?" I ask again.

She hesitates a breath more, but I know I have her. "Inspecting new battleships," she admits. "In the South Harbor."

"Perfect," I say brightly, taking her hand in mine and leading her from the room. "We'll get to see the water as well, then, just like you wanted to."

Battleships. Why on earth would the Kalovaxians need more battleships? Houzzah knows they have plenty already.

I tear my thoughts away from that idea as we leave Hoa behind. She isn't allowed in public spaces, so it's only Crescentia's two maids who accompany us. And my Shadows, of course, though they'll keep a careful distance.

This time, I force myself to look at the slaves. I won't keep ignoring them; they deserve more from me than that. Who were they before the siege? I don't even know their names.

Crescentia never addresses them, only snapping her fingers when she needs assistance.

The younger of the two looks up and meets my gaze briefly, and something sparks in her eyes before she averts them. I'm not sure whether it is deference or hatred.

DRAKKAR

———— ◆ · ◆ ————

I REMEMBER WALKING TO THE SOUTH Harbor with my mother when I was a child. It only takes fifteen minutes or so on foot, but Crescentia prefers carriages. Her slaves ride outside, next to the coachman, to leave more room inside for us. I don't know what we need so much room for. The carriage is spacious enough that both of us could lie down on the benches and still leave enough room for both girls to sit as well.

"Does my hair look all right, Thora?" Crescentia asks me, patting at it idly as she looks out the window.

"It's lovely," I assure her. And it is—everything about Crescentia is lovely. But after meeting with Blaise, every word I say to her has the shadow of a lie.

"You look very pretty, too," she says, glancing at my neckline again before her eyes dart back up to my face. She's quiet for a moment, but her eyes are probing, as if she can see all my secrets laid bare. For a second, I could swear she knows about my meeting with Blaise, but that's impossible.

"You're acting strange today," she says after a moment. "Are you all right?"

The truth bubbles up inside me. Of course I'm not all right, I want to tell her. I killed my father, eighty thousand of my people are dead, and I'm risking my life plotting treason. How can I possibly be all right?

I've never had to keep secrets from Cress before; she's the first person I want to tell anything. But I'm not a fool. Cress might love me, but she loves her country more. She loves her father more. In a strange way, I can't even begrudge her that. After all, can't the same be said about me?

"I'm fine," I say instead, forcing a smile she sees through immediately.

"It isn't anything to do with that awful trial, is it?" she asks.

Again, her use of the term *trial* scratches at my skin like jagged fingernails. I ignore it and give her a brief nod. The *trial* isn't the best explanation to give Cress for the difference in my behavior, but it's at least a partial truth. "It was quite alarming."

It's such an understatement that it's almost laughable, but there isn't anything funny about it. I hope she'll take the hint and change the subject, but instead, she leans toward me.

"He was a traitor, Thora." Her voice is gentle, but there's a warning there as well. "The treason law is clear and decreed by the gods themselves. The Kaiser had no choice, and neither did you."

Not my law, I think. *Not my gods.*

And besides, what of the Kaiser's treason? He had my mother removed from her gods-given throne. Crescentia's father cut her gods-blessed throat. If treason should be left up to the gods, why are men like her father and the Kaiser still alive while my mother and Ampelio are dead?

"You're right," I lie with a smile. "I feel no guilt over the man's death, truly. No more than I would feel for stepping on a roach."

The words taste foul, but the lines of her expression smooth as she takes my hands in hers. "My father told me that the Kaiser was impressed with your loyalty," she says. "The Kaiser thinks the time is right to find you a husband."

"Does he?" I ask, raising my eyebrows and trying to hide my surprise and horror at the idea.

Cress and I often talked about marrying any number of the boys our age. It was a game to us, our favorites changing as often as our gowns, but the constant was that we would do it together. We would marry brothers or friends and raise our children to be as close as we are. It was a lovely fantasy, but that's all it ever was. A marriage will never happen, I realize— I'll be long gone by then. Soon the time will come when I will never see Cress again, and I can't help but mourn this. She'll always think of me as a traitor. Any children we might one day have will grow up on opposite sides of a war.

"What else did they say?" I ask, though I don't think I actually want to know.

Something dark flickers across her expression and she leans back again, releasing my hands. "Oh, I can hardly remember. More of the same, really, about how you're proving to have the heart of a true Kalovaxian."

I wonder what else was said that she refuses to repeat. Did they gloat about my mother's death? Or did they make comments about my marriage bed? Maybe they called me a savage or demon-blooded. It wouldn't be the first time I've heard any of those things, but Crescentia's been sheltered enough to miss them. Everything in her world is so pretty and shiny and full of good intentions. I don't have the heart to crush that.

"That's very kind of them," I tell her with what I hope passes as a demure smile. "Did they have anyone particular in mind?" I ask, already dreading the answer. After all, whoever the Kaiser has picked out for me won't be one of the boys Cress and I gossiped about.

She hesitates for a moment, eyes darting away from mine, confirming my fear. She busies herself by smoothing out the folds of her already pristine skirt. "Lord Dalgaard has expressed a great deal of interest in you, apparently." She struggles to sound conversational, but doesn't quite manage. I don't blame her. Whatever horrible name I was expecting, Lord Dalgaard is infinitely worse.

In his seventy years, Lord Dalgaard has had six wives, each younger than the last and each dying suspiciously within a year of her marriage. His first wife lived long enough to give him an heir before her body washed up on the shore of what-ever country the Kalovaxians had invaded at the time. She was too mangled to tell what exactly had happened to her. Other wives were claimed by fires, by mad dogs, by falls from cliff tops. Even before they died, they wore bruises the way other women wore jewels, curling around their necks and arms and littering any other scrap of exposed skin. His wealth and closeness with the Kaiser made him untouchable, but his rep-utation was making finding a seventh wife tricky.

Of course, his marrying me would suit everyone just fine. He would have a wife no one would care what he did to, the Kaiser would collect a hefty price, and I would be even more a prisoner than ever.

I turn my focus out the window to hide my face, but immediately wish I hadn't. Outside, the capital whirrs by, and though the city has been this way for most of my life, it makes my stomach turn.

Once, beautiful villas of polished sunstone stood proudly along the shore, glittering in the sunlight like the ocean itself. The streets were broad and lively, watched over by sandstone sculptures of the gods that towered tall enough to be seen from the palace windows. Once, the capital was a pretty scene where even the poorest corners were at least whole and clean and cherished.

Now the villas are in disrepair from the siege. Even after ten years, chunks are missing from walls and roofs, patched up poorly with straw and plaster. The limestone doesn't shine the way it used to, now caked with dull white sea salt. Once-busy streets are all but abandoned, though every so often I see an emaciated, specter-like frame peer at us through a broken window or disappear into an alley.

These are my people, and I have failed them with my fear, with my inaction. While I've cowered, they've starved, and my mother has watched me from the After with shame.

When the carriage finally turns in to the harbor and pulls to a stop, I let out a breath I didn't realize I've been holding.

Here, there is life again. Ships crowd the harbor, with more lurking offshore, waiting. Dozens of patchy cats stalk the docks like they're in charge, even while they beg sailors for scraps of fish. The Kalovaxian crews work hard, yellow heads glowing in the sun, but they are all well fed at least. Their pleasantly drunk, raucous voices chant sea songs while they build and scrub and scrape barnacles from the ships' undersides. It's strange that there aren't any Astrean slaves to do the hard work, though I must admit it's a wise choice. The cannons that line the ships on both sides can easily wipe out an enemy ship—or a Kalovaxian one, depending on who is manning it.

Seeing this lifts my spirits. If the Kaiser doesn't trust my people with weapons, he must still fear us.

I make a mental tally of the ships so that I can report back to Blaise about them. There are three drakkars in port, mounted with wooden dragon heads at the bows and large enough to carry a hundred warriors each. Farther offshore, there is a ship so large I doubt it could fit in the harbor at all. It's double the size of the drakkars, and I shudder to think of how many warriors it holds. There are also a dozen small ships bobbing in the waves around it, but as unassuming as they seem next to the large ship, they aren't to be under-estimated. They aren't designed to be big, they're designed to be fast. Each one can hold fifty people, maybe less, depending on what else it's carrying.

Blaise mentioned a new weapon, something called a ber-serker, but maybe it's a kind of ship. The Kalovaxians have so many names for their ships, I can't keep them all straight.

I add up the ships and the men it would take to sail them—nearly two thousand warriors at full capacity, much more than what's needed for one of their usual raids. And these are only the new ships. There are others in the East Harbor, older but still effective, that could triple that number. What is the Kaiser planning that requires so many? Even as I wonder, I know exactly how I'm going to find out.

At first glance, Prinz Søren blends in with the rest of the crew. He's helping to rig a gold sail emblazoned with the Kalovaxian sigil of a crimson dragon. His simple white cotton shirt is rolled up to the elbows, exposing strong, pale forearms. Corn-silk hair is tied back from his face, emphasizing his angular jaw and cheekbones.

Crescentia must have spotted him as well, because she lets out a light sigh next to me.

"We shouldn't be here," she says to me, her hands clasped tightly in front of her.

"Well, it's too late now, I suppose," I say with a mischievous grin. I loop my arm through hers and give it a reassuring squeeze. "Come on, think of it as bolstering the spirits of our brave warriors before they embark for . . . where? Do you know?"

She laughs, shaking her head. "The North, more than likely. To deliver gems."

But these aren't cargo ships. If they were loaded with Spiritgems in addition to those cannons and the ammo to go with them, they would sink before they left the port. Crescentia doesn't know the difference and I can't even fault her for that. If the siege hadn't happened and I'd grown up a naive and spoiled princess, I doubt I'd have any interest in boats either. But most Kalovaxians love their boats more than some of their children, and I had thought maybe it would be something Ampelio and the other rebels could use against them when they rescued me.

We draw the eyes of the crew as we approach, eliciting shouted greetings and a few vulgar comments that we pretend not to hear.

"Is the Prinz looking?" Crescentia whispers. Her cheeks flush and she smiles sweetly at the ships we pass.

I paste a smile on my face as well, though some of these men must have fought in the siege and those who are too young must have fathers who did. *Twenty thousand left*. Blaise's words echo in my head and my stomach twists. These people murdered tens of thousands of my people, and I have to smile flirtatiously and wave like I don't hate them with every part of me. But I do it, as nauseated as it makes me.

Prinz Søren is so focused on rigging the sail that he doesn't look up with the rest of his crew. His expression is drawn taut in concentration as he ties intricate knots, brow furrowed and mouth pursed. When he pulls the knot tight and finally looks up, his eyes find mine first and linger for a beat too long before shifting to Crescentia. Blaise might be right, ridiculous as it is. I may be a damsel in distress, but the Prinz can't very well save me from his own people, can he? From his father, from himself? A monster can't also play the part of the hero.

He passes the rigging to a member of his crew and comes to the edge of the boat, hopping down easily onto the dock and landing a few feet in front of us. Before he can even straighten up, Crescentia and I are both in deep curtsies.

"Thora, Lady Crescentia," he says when we rise again. "What brings you to the docks today?"

"I was craving some sea air, Your—" I break off when he gives me a look, reminding me of our agreement last night. "Søren." But at the sound of his given name, Crescentia gives me a sharp, suspicious look. It seems I can't win, so I hastily shift focus. "We didn't realize it would be such an event. What are all the boats for?"

His expression wavers slightly. "Nothing of importance. Dragonsbane is just causing a little trouble along the trade route. Sank a few of our trade ships last week. We're going to bring him and his allies in," he says.

I can't bring myself to believe him. Not completely, at least. Not with this much artillery. The Theyn keeps hand-drawn maps hanging on the walls of his sitting room, and though they were never of much practical interest to Cress and me, we used to marvel at the beauty of them and note the differences between the artists' depictions, how a narrow stream in one was painted as a wide river in another. But I do remember that in no version was the trade route wide enough to hold a boat the size of the one off the coast. In each map, the route was like a piece of string winding through the Haptain Mountains.

"I'm sorry we interrupted your plans," Søren continues. "I can't imagine much fresh sea air makes it past this lot unsoured."

"Don't be silly. It's an honor to see so many Kalovaxian men working so hard for the country," I tell him.

I may be laying it on a tad thick. Even Crescentia shoots me a bemused look.

"And you'll be leading them?" she asks, turning her attention back to Søren.

He nods. "My first time leading a crew of my own," he admits, his voice thick with pride. "We leave in a week's time. These are just the finishing touches. The crew goes through them personally, as a way of aligning ourselves with the ship. It's an old Kalovaxian custom," he explains to me.

"Well, the *old* Kalovaxian custom is for the crew to build the boat itself," Crescentia adds with a dimpled smile. "But it was amended when the boats kept falling to pieces. Warriors don't make the best shipsmiths."

Søren's eyes spark with a laugh that doesn't quite make it out of him, but she looks pleased with herself. Her dimples deepen.

"That they don't," he agrees. "But we can be trusted with the rigging and finishing. Barely. Would you like a tour?" he asks.

Crescentia opens her mouth to politely decline, but I get there first.

"Yes, please," I say. "That sounds fascinating."

She pinches the inside of my arm but tries to hide her irritation from the Prinz. Inspecting boats is not how she wanted this day to go, and even I have to admit that *boats* and *fascinating* do not belong in the same sentence. But this is a chance to get information.

Søren leads us to the rickety ladder fitted against the hull and helps hand Crescentia up first. Over her shoulder, she shoots me an annoyed look that I try to match with an encouraging one. She has a tendency toward seasickness, and among Kalovaxians, this is seen as a matter of great shame. I'll have to give her an explanation later to quell her irritation. If she wants a crown so badly, I'll say, she'll need to put up with some discomfort.

When Søren hands me up next, I let my fingers linger on the bare skin of his arm a few seconds longer than necessary, the way I've seen Dagmær do at parties. It's a brief touch, barely noteworthy, but the grip of his other hand at my waist tightens. I feel his eyes on me, but I can't look at him. My cheeks warm as I pull myself onto the ship and then straighten my dress. Cress fidgets next to me, smoothing her hair and adjusting the neckline of her dress, her cheeks bright pink.

Seconds later, Søren is with us, gesturing around at the ship.

"Drakkars can hold a hundred people a ship," he explains, confirming my estimation. "Every drakkar is fitted with twenty oars and twelve cannons," he adds as he offers each of us an arm.

We start toward the prow, the ship rocking gently beneath us. I've been on Kalovaxian ships only a handful of times over the years, and I can't help but admire how they're built— sleek, simple vessels designed for speed, powered by a complicated set of sails and riggings and oars. They're very different from the Astrean sailboats I remember from my childhood trips around the country with my mother. Those were toys. These are weapons.

His sailors stop their work as we approach, and bow deeply.

"Men, we have the honor of a visit from Lady Thora and Lady Crescentia, the Theyn's daughter," he tells them.

There's a murmuring of polite words, though they all seem to be directed at Crescentia, which isn't surprising. These men revere her father as a living god.

"And this, ladies, is the finest crew in the world," Søren says with a grin.

One of the crew, a young man a little older than Søren

with surprisingly dark hair and gold skin, rolls his eyes. "He always says that."

"As I should, Erik," Søren answers, grinning back. "I assembled all of you myself, didn't I? Why would I want anyone but the best for my crew?"

"There's no accounting for poor judgment, Søren," Erik volleys back, "even if you are a prinz."

"Especially since you're a prinz," an older man with a ruddy, sunburnt face and a large gut adds with a laugh.

The difference between Søren and his father is jarring. I've seen his father have men executed for less insubordination, but Søren's laugh joins his men's instead, and it feels even more disorienting. Søren looks so much like the Kaiser that it's easy to think of them as somewhat interchangeable—just like these warriors are the same, more or less, as the ones who stormed the palace all those years ago.

"Are you feeling all right, Lady Crescentia?" Søren asks, concerned.

I look at my friend, who has, I realize, turned quite green in the few minutes we've been on board, despite the fact that the ship is well tethered and barely rocking.

"Oh dear," I cut in, because I suspect that if she opens her mouth to speak, something else entirely might come out, and the Prinz has been vomited on enough for one week. "I didn't want to say anything earlier, but Crescentia hasn't been feeling well today. We thought a spot of sea air would do her good, but that doesn't seem to be the case. We might be better off going back to the castle." I put a comforting arm around her shoulders and she sags against me.

"It could be a good idea to let her settle before a rough carriage ride back," Søren reasons. "If I may, there's a cool place to sit beneath the trees, there. Would you mind?" he asks her.

Despite her queasiness, Crescentia can't agree fast enough. I move to go with them, but Søren stops me. "Stay for a few more minutes," he says. "Erik will continue the tour. You seemed so interested before."

"I was. I *am*," I agree, a little too quickly. "Are you all right, Cress?"

Crescentia nods as she straightens up so she isn't leaning on me anymore. Her eyes are nearly twice their usual size as they flit between Søren and me. She looks even greener, but somehow I think that's more to do with nerves about being alone with the Prinz than the sea itself. I give her a reassuring smile as Søren helps her off the ship.

I'm supposed to be seducing the Prinz, not passing him off to Crescentia, but that can wait for another day. These ships were built for something, and I have a strong suspicion that it wasn't to defend a trade route from a pirate who was—as of my meeting with Blaise last night—hiding behind a forest of cypress trees a mile outside the capital.

"Which parts of the ship were you interested in seeing, Lady Thora?" Erik asks me.

As we begin to walk, the other crew members go back to their duties, not sparing me another glance. If Cress were still here, they would be hanging on each word and gesture, but fine clothes or not, I am still Astrean and therefore not worthy of their attention. Which will only make it easier to gain information.

I don my most innocent smile and link my arm through Erik's.

"I've heard stories about the berserkers. Are they as fearsome as they sound? I would love to see one."

His forehead creases, and he's quiet for a few seconds before answering. "I'm sorry, Lady Thora. We don't have any on board at the moment and . . . well, I'm not sure the Kaiser would approve of showing you any, if you don't mind me saying so."

"Oh, of course," I say, biting my lip and fidgeting with the end of my braid. "I'm flattered, really, to be thought of as so dangerous."

He laughs, the tension smoothing from his forehead. "Anything else you would like to see?"

I think for a moment, tilting my head to one side and trying to look slow-witted, even while my mind is churning. "I'm not entirely sure. It's been such a long time since I was on a boat, sir," I say finally.

I can tell by looking at Erik that he has no title. He's too dark in hair and skin, and the palms of his hands are rough with hard calluses. His clothes have been torn and mended a dozen times over. If I had to guess, I would imagine he's not full Kalovaxian, but rather the product of the siege of Goraki—the last country the Kalovaxians conquered before Astrea—taken pity on by whichever highborn man fathered him.

His neck flushes red at my address and he hastily waves it away. "There are no *sirs,* or *lords,* or even *prinzes* on a ship, Lady Thora," he says.

"Then perhaps there should be no *ladies* either," I reply, earning a laugh.

"Fair enough," he says. "Why don't we start with the bow and work our way back?" he suggests.

"Oh yes, please," I say, following him toward the front of the ship. I keep my eyes wide and eager, ready to hang onto his every word. If he's feeling confident and important, he's more likely to let something slip he shouldn't. "I would love to get a better look at the dragon figurehead. Is it true they're as popular in the North as birds are here?"

"I wouldn't know, La—*Thora*. I've never been farther north than Goraki," he says, solidifying my suspicion.

"Well, they must be magnificent at any rate, though I don't know if seeing them is worth braving the cold weather," I say.

An idea suddenly occurs to me, though I know it's a dangerous one that could turn bad very quickly, especially after my berserker question might have already raised his suspicions. But the threat of a partnering with Lord Dalgaard is nipping at my heels.

"I hope it won't get too chilly in . . . oh, where was it Søren said you were going? I've never been very good at geography," I say with my best attempt at looking sheepish.

He gives me a sideways glance, but if he finds anything strange about the question, he doesn't say. He clears his throat.

"The names do tend to run together," he agrees. "But not to worry—the Vecturia Islands are only a bit north of here."

That was easier than I expected. *Too* easy, I can't help but think—though why should Erik think my question was anything other than an idle query from an idle mind? It's practically small talk.

The Vecturia Islands. I repeat the name over and over in my mind, determined to remember it. Something about it pricks my memory, but I can't place it. Hopefully, Blaise will be able to the next time I see him.

Crates of ammunition are stacked next to cannons. I run the numbers in my head quickly. From what I can tell, it looks like each box can hold roughly ten cannonballs, and there are five boxes sitting at each cannon. Søren said there were twelve cannons. . . . That's six hundred shots altogether. And there are a fleet of these warships, with the largest operating as the command ship, where Søren will give orders from.

"There are an awful lot of cannons," I say as we walk past another cluster of them.

"The Vecturians are barbarians," Erik says with a dismissive shrug, though that word chafes. It's the same word the Kalovaxians use to describe Astreans, though the Kalovaxians are the ones who thrive on war and bloodshed. "We aren't anticipating too much trouble, but we need to be prepared," he continues.

I decide to press my luck.

"That sounds dangerous," I say, biting my lip. "I can't imagine what would make that journey necessary."

He opens his mouth to answer, but after a second of hesitation, he closes it again. "Kaiser's orders," he says with a tight smile. "I'm sure he has his reasons."

"He always does," I reply, hoping my smile looks more natural than it feels.

ELPIS

THE YOUNGER OF CRESCENTIA'S SLAVES is waiting for me on the dock when we disembark. I tell Erik that I'll pray for his safety before leaving him.

As I approach the girl, her eyes dart around in an effort to avoid mine. "The Prinz escorted Lady Crescentia back to the palace," she says, "but they promised to send the carriage for us soon." She's skinny to the point of malnutrition, yet her cheeks still have a childish roundness. Her large, dark eyes are sunken deep in her face, making her look far older than I'm sure she is.

She doesn't curtsy, but then, Astrean slaves never curtsy to me anymore. It can too easily be construed as paying deference to a sovereign, and more than a handful have lost their lives for it. The Kaiser has done everything in his great power to isolate me from my people. Even when there are Astrean slaves around, we can never speak, and most of them won't even look at me. I never used to understand it. I thought he was simply cruel in putting up so many walls around me. But if I hadn't been so lonely, if I hadn't felt so separate, maybe I wouldn't have been so desperate to break myself into what he wanted me to be.

No one can say that the Kaiser isn't smart. But now I'm determined to be smarter.

The Kaiser would never have approved leaving me alone with an Astrean, even with my Shadows nearby. But maybe this is one of the inches of freedom that executing Ampelio has bought me. I won't waste it.

"I would prefer to walk, if you don't mind," I tell her. "What do they call you?"

She hesitates, doe eyes darting around briefly. She knows my Shadows are here, too. "Elpis," she says, so quietly that I barely hear her.

"Do you mind walking, Elpis?" I ask her.

She chews her bottom lip for a few seconds until I'm worried she'll draw blood. "We'll have to walk through the slave quarter, my lady," she warns. "It will be empty this time of day, mostly, but . . ."

"I don't mind if you don't."

"I . . . I don't mind," she says, her voice strengthening. "We don't have a guard, though."

"We have my Shadows," I say, though they're more to keep me leashed than to keep me safe, and I doubt they'd step in unless it looked like I might be killed or disfigured. They certainly wouldn't lift a finger to help Elpis. She must know this, too, because she looks at me warily.

"Of . . . of course, my lady."

I can't blame her for her discomfort. She was younger than I was when the siege happened. Astrea is little more than a ghost story to her. I'm not sure if that makes her a more or less dangerous person to trust. There is so much more than a whipped back at stake this time. I need to be sure of Elpis.

I'm tempted to look around for my Shadows as we walk, but I know by now that I won't see them and it'll only make me appear suspicious. Maybe I'll catch sight of a scrap of black fabric darting through a nearby alley, or hear a handful of soft footsteps, but nothing more. They're trained to be neither seen nor heard, and I'm sure they have Spiritgems aplenty to aid them in that. I've heard that cloaks lined with Air Gems can make the wearer invisible for a time, and nearly soundless.

They'll tell the Kaiser about this, though I doubt they'll dare get close enough to hear what we talk about. He won't be pleased to hear that I exchanged words—no matter how innocent—with an Astrean slave. Thora's voice sounds again in my mind, urging me to stay safe, but Blaise's is louder. *Twenty thousand.*

"Do you live in this area with your parents?" I ask her as we walk.

"Yes, my lady," Elpis says carefully. "Well, with my mother, at least, and my younger brother. My father died in the Conquering."

The Conquering is what the Kalovaxians call the siege. It makes it sound more honorable, I suppose, to conquer something wild rather than to lay siege to something defenseless.

"I'm very sorry to hear that," I tell her. "What does your mother do?"

"She was a botanist before, but now she's a seamstress for the Theyn and Lady Crescentia."

"How old is your brother?" I ask.

She hesitates. "He'll be ten soon," she says, a hard edge coming to her voice. "He's my half brother."

"Oh," I say, glancing at her uncertainly. Even at court, there are women who have children out of wedlock, and it's far less shameful for a widow than a maiden. If my math is correct, the siege would have just ended when her mother became pregnant. The pieces fit together and I realize what Elpis isn't saying.

Conqueror's Rights allowed warriors to terrorize and rob and enslave my people without fear of retribution, but I'd never thought of all that would entail. *Rape.* I won't let myself think around the word or use one of the many euphemisms to try to dull it. Another injustice my people have faced. Another thing I swear will be paid for.

Elpis isn't as practiced at hiding her anger as I am. It plays over her face like words on a page, evident in the tension in her jaw and the intense focus of her eyes. She could turn a person to stone with a gaze like that. It's an anger I know too well.

Elpis isn't loyal to the Kaiser, I'm sure of it. But that doesn't mean she'll be loyal to me. I'm not her queen, after all; I'm a spoiled, sheltered girl who is friends with the one who keeps her chained.

I have to take a moment to translate my words to Astrean in my mind before I say them. "Does he look like them?" I ask her quietly, dropping my voice to a whisper. I keep a tight hold on my smile so that it will fool my Shadows into thinking I'm babbling about something silly and inconsequential. Hopefully, after years of watching me do nothing of interest, they won't expect anything more now.

I am poking at a bruise. Elpis flinches at my words, but I don't back down. I need her anger; I need her to know it isn't hers alone to bear, that I am on her side.

Her eyes narrow and she opens her mouth to answer before clamping it shut again. "Yes," she says shortly in Kalovaxian before switching to Astrean and lowering her voice so that even I can barely hear her. "What is it you want from me, my lady?" she asks me, her voice tight.

The streets are deserted, though there are sunken eyes watching from broken windows. Children too young to work, the ill, the elderly. Hoa must live somewhere around here when she's not with me. The thought strikes me as strange—it isn't something I'd ever wondered about.

"What do *you* want?" I ask Elpis.

Her eyes dart around, searching for the Shadows, too, the ears that are always listening, the eyes that are always watching. They're not here, though, I assure myself. Not close enough, anyway. But I don't fully believe it. I've been wrong too many times before.

"Is this a trick, my lady?" she asks, switching back to Kalovaxian.

She doesn't trust me. And why should she? She's watched me for years with Cress. She would be a fool to trust me, and she's lived too rough a life to be a fool.

If anything, the fact that she doesn't trust me makes me trust her.

"No, it's not a trick." I look around again and see it—a telltale glimmer in the air, but a good twenty feet away, lurking in the shadow of a crumbling building. They won't hear me, but I force a high, false laugh, keeping my smile frozen and speaking in Astrean for extra measure.

Elpis is bewildered. "Smile," I tell her, and she instantly obeys, though there's a touch of fear in her eyes. "They tried to break me, Elpis, and they nearly succeeded. I let my fear cow me, I let *them* cow me. But I'm done. I'm going to make them pay. For everything they've done to us, to our country. To our fathers and our mothers. Will you help me?"

I hold my breath. Elpis has grown up in this world, she has never known anything else. She could turn against me for her freedom and enough food to keep her family satiated, and I couldn't even blame her for it. It's a difficult world for Astreans to survive in, and I haven't seen the worst of it. I am no more her ruler than the Kaiser is, and what does she care, really, so long as she's safe and warm and fed?

But when her eyes meet mine, they are burning with venom. Her gaze is lethal, but not to me. Her anger only feeds mine, until we are matched, hate for hate.

"Yes, Your Majesty," she whispers, stumbling over the Astrean words. I'm surprised she even knows them.

Your Majesty. The Kalovaxians don't use that term, so the only person I've heard referred to that way was my mother. I know Elpis means well, but hearing it now makes my heart ache.

I'm not anyone's majesty, I want to tell her.

"Are there people you trust implicitly?" I ask.

"Yes," she says, without hesitation.

"That's the wrong answer. You trust no one until they have earned it. I've made that mistake before and suffered for it. But the Kaiser won't find punishing you worth his time. He'll kill you, do you understand?"

She bites her lip before remembering that we're being watched. "Yes, I get the joke," she says with a laugh that sounds surprisingly natural. She doesn't bother to lower her voice or speak in Astrean. Good girl, giving them something, even if it's nothing.

"The only person I want you to trust is a boy. He was serving the banquet yesterday. A little older than me, with black hair cut close? Taller than most men, with bright green eyes. And a scar here," I add, tracing a finger from my temple to the corner of my mouth, but making it look like I'm scratching an itch.

Elpis nods slowly. "I believe I know him," she says.

"You think, or you know?" I press.

"I . . . I know," she says, sounding more certain. "There aren't many young men working in the palace, but one started two days ago. He had paperwork releasing him from the mines?"

Forged, I'm sure, and not likely to last long before that's discovered.

"That's the one," I say in Kalovaxian.

She gives me a small smile. "You could have just said the handsome one. He's had all the girls swooning over him."

I stifle a laugh. "Can you get a message to him?"

"Yes, it shouldn't be difficult. Lady Crescentia doesn't notice much, particularly when she has a new book to occupy her mind. Her father keeps closer tabs on us, but he left to survey the mines yesterday afternoon."

More useful information, though hardly the good kind. I can only imagine what the Theyn's visit to the mines will entail, but I'm sure it will come with a body count.

"Good," I say. "Introduce yourself to him. Tell him I sent you." I know he won't believe her—it's exactly what the Kaiser's spy would say to catch us. "We were children together in the palace, before the siege. Our nanny's name was Sofia, but we called her Birdie because she had the prettiest voice. If he questions your story, tell him I said that."

"And what would you like me to tell him?" she asks me.

"Tell him . . . tell him I have some news and I need a way to meet with him in person."

GARDEN

———◆•◆———

Days PASS FILLED WITH FEAR that any moment now my Shadows will tell the Kaiser I spoke with Elpis. It won't matter that they didn't hear what was said, I'll pay for it all the same. It was worth it—I know it was worth it—but that doesn't make it any easier to wait for the ax to fall. I sleep little, and when I do manage to dream, all I see is Ampelio dying over and over again. Sometimes Blaise takes his place. Sometimes Elpis. Sometimes it's Crescentia lying at my feet, begging for her life while I hold a blade to her throat.

No matter who it is, the dream always ends the same and I always wake screaming. My Shadows don't react. They're used to it by now.

It's been four days since seeing the ships. Five days since I met with Blaise. All I have been able to do is wait for him to make contact like he said he would. It's almost easy to slip into life as Thora again, attending luncheons and dances and spending afternoons with Cress in her father's library. But I force myself to remember who I am.

I keep my mind busy and think about the Vecturia Islands. What could be happening there that requires a fleet of warships and the Prinz himself as a commandant? It *could* be that the Prinz was telling the truth and Erik was only confused—that Dragonsbane is troubling the trade route. But the more I think about it, the less sense that makes. They wouldn't need that many ships with that much ammunition if they were squaring off against just Dragonsbane's small fleet. Dragonsbane might be a thorn in the Kaiser's side, but removing it would require a knife, not a cannonball.

Yet Vecturia isn't Astrea, I remind myself. Their problems aren't mine, and I have my own people to think about.

And it might turn out to be nothing. Prinz Søren and Erik were secretive, yes, but it's possible it's to hide something else. I've heard tales of Prinz Søren's skills in battle, but they've always been secondhand and they could be greatly exaggerated in order to make the Prinz appear godlike.

If I could just speak to Blaise again, I could tell him what I know and see what he thought about it. He might even have another piece of the puzzle to help make sense of it. But there has been no word from him since our meeting in the cellar. He said he had an idea about how we could speak more, but I'm starting to lose hope. There have even been some darker moments when I wonder if I made him up.

There's a knock at the door—stiff and formal, not Cress's light, melodic tap. Hoa is heating up a pair of hair tongs in the fireplace, so I go to answer it. My feet are made of stone. The only people who knock like that are guards, and I don't have to guess at what they want. My welts from the mine riot haven't fully healed yet. The idea of a whip reopening them sends shudders through me that won't be quelled.

I shouldn't have spoken to Elpis. I shouldn't have met with Blaise.

I take one last shaky breath before opening the door. A stern guard stands on the other side dressed in a crimson jacket, and my heart all but ceases to beat. He isn't one of the Kaiser's men, though. Great as their numbers are, I would know their faces anywhere by now. They're burned into my memory so deeply they even haunt my nightmares. This man isn't one of them but I don't know if that's better or worse.

He produces a square envelope from the pocket of his jacket and passes it to me, his expression frozen in a thin, straight line.

"From His Royal Highness, Prinz Søren," he says, as if the royal crest emblazoned on the front weren't enough of a clue. "He asked that I wait here for a reply."

Numb with relief and shock, I tear the envelope open with the corner of my pinky nail and skim the Prinz's hastily scrawled words.

Thora—

I'm sorry for abandoning you the other day, but I hope you enjoyed the tour. Allow me to make it up to you with lunch before I leave?

—Søren

I read the words twice, looking for hidden meanings, but only see exactly what is written. It's the sort of letter Cress receives from boys who are trying to court her. Could it be that Blaise was right about the way the Prinz looked at me? The letter lacks the usual poetry and flattery of a love missive, but that's not surprising, considering Søren's demeanor. I doubt he would know a poem if one was written on the sails of his precious ships. But I cannot ignore the last line—the invitation to spend time alone together.

I know this opportunity to gather more information is one I can't pass up, yet I still feel guilty. I imagine Cress pacing her own rooms over the last few days, anxiously awaiting a letter like this from the Prinz. The few times I've seen her since the harbor, she's been giddy and bright-eyed, going over every moment of their time together in such fine detail I could swear I was there myself. But what I didn't tell her is that while Søren was courteous with her and did all the chivalrous things—held doors open, handed her into the carriage, escorted her back to her rooms and said goodbye politely at the door—it sounded like he was doing his duty and no more.

Not like this. Having lunch with me is certainly not a duty, and his father will be furious when he finds out. Søren must have known that when he wrote the letter, but he did so anyway.

For a long moment, I can only stare at the paper in my hands, thinking over what I should say back, what I should wear, what I should talk to him about, all the while aware of the guard's eyes on me. It's only after a moment that I realize the best path to take, the one that will most assuredly keep the reins in my hand. Blaise did say that Søren would want me all the more because he can't have me.

I look up at the guard and give him my sweetest smile,

though it doesn't seem to do much good. His face remains frozen.

"I have no reply," I tell him. "Good day."

With a bob of a curtsy, I close the door firmly before he can protest.

The autumn air is thick and heavy on my skin as I walk through what was once my mother's garden. My memory of her is still hazy, but I feel her presence stronger here than anywhere else. I remember color and a smell so heady it would wrap around me like a blanket—the scent of flowers and grass and dirt. It clung to my mother even when she spent all day in the throne room or walking through the city.

She was never happier than she was here, with dirt staining her skirts and life in her hands.

"The smallest seeds can grow the greatest trees, with enough care and time," she would tell me, placing her hands over mine to guide them as we planted seeds and patted damp earth over them.

Ampelio used to say that if she weren't a queen, she would have made a formidable Earth Guardian, but Astrean laws said she couldn't be both. Of course, favor from the gods wasn't hereditary. Though she gave me a small patch of the garden to work alongside her, I couldn't even get weeds to grow there.

Nothing grows anywhere in the garden anymore. Without my mother's diligent care, it grew wild, and if there is one thing the Kaiser cannot stand, it is wildness. He set fire to it all when I was seven. I saw the flames and smelled the smoke from my bedroom window, and I couldn't stop crying, no matter how Hoa tried to quiet me. It felt like I was losing my mother all over again.

Nine years later, and the air here still tastes of ashes to me, though the charred remains have long been cleared, the dirt paved over with square gray stones. My mother wouldn't recognize it now, with its hard floor and the few trees that break through the cracks to provide skeletal fingers of shade. There isn't any color—even the trees have better sense than to sprout leaves.

The garden was always a busy place, before. I remember playing with Blaise and the other palace children when the weather was nice. There would be dozens of courtiers milling through the trees and bushes in chitons dyed a myriad of vivid colors. Artists with their paints or instruments or notebooks sitting alone as they worked. Couples sneaking off together for not-so-secret rendezvous.

Now it's deserted. The Kalovaxians prefer the sun pavilions set up on public balconies to better take advantage of the light and the sea breeze. I've been a few times with Crescentia, and though the Kalovaxians play and work and gossip and flirt there as well, it never feels the same. Burnt and broken as this place is, it is the only part of the palace that still feels like home.

Comfort isn't what drives me here today, though. I've been struggling to find places to meet with Blaise—once he gets in touch—but I can't get to the cellar again without raising the suspicions of my Shadows. There are precious few places in the palace where I actually feel alone. Even here—the garden is overlooked by thirty palace windows, and every now and then I catch a glimpse of my Shadows on their watch from inside, the black hoods of their cloaks up so I can't see their faces.

The garden is exposed, but that might not be a bad thing for a possible meeting place. There would be people who would *see* us together, but if he's working to prune the trees or scrub the stones it won't seem strange, and Kalovaxians have a bad habit of ignoring slaves. There is nowhere we could be overheard from, and that is what truly matters.

It's a flawed plan, of course. We wouldn't be able to say more than a few words to one another without raising suspicions. Flawed as it is, though, it's the best option I've found so far.

"Lady Thora."

The male voice makes me jump. Unlike Crescentia, I'm not accompanied by maids to keep my reputation pristine. My Shadows watch from a distance, of course, but their job is less to keep me safe than to keep me watched.

Still, I know that voice, and since his letter this morning, I've been waiting for him to find me.

Prinz Søren crosses the stone garden toward me, flanked by two guards whose orders are surely much different than my guards'. Though they are Søren's and not the Kaiser's—not the ones who have dragged me through the halls to answer for crimes I didn't commit, not the ones who have taken turns with the whip—their eyes are just as hard, and I have to suppress a shudder.

They are not here for me, not today.

I drop to a curtsy. "Your Highness," I say when I rise. "What brings you out here?"

He gives me a reproachful look. "*Your Highness.* I thought we talked about this."

"You did call me *Lady* first," I point out.

Søren grimaces, but his eyes are smiling. It seems to be as close as he gets to any actual signs of mirth. "Old habits, I suppose. Let's start again. Hello, Thora," he says, bowing his head slightly.

The name bristles against my skin, though it's more familiar to me than my real one.

"Hello, Søren. What brings you out here?" I repeat, tilting my head to one side.

He glances around the stone garden with disinterest. Through his eyes, I imagine, this place is nothing but a ruin.

"I was looking for you, actually," he says, holding an arm out to me. I have no choice but to take it.

"Me?" I say. Though I've been waiting for him to seek me out, I can't help but remember that the last time Søren came looking for me had been to bring me to Ampelio's execution. Could it be Blaise's now? Or Elpis's?

I must not hide my worry well, because he rests his free hand on my arm with a squeeze. I think he means to be reassuring, but it ends up feeling awkward and unsure. I suppose neither of us is used to compassion. Still, I appreciate the attempt.

"Nothing like that," he says, and my pounding heart immediately slows. "You look . . ." He clears his throat. "That dress is very pretty."

"Oh, thank you," I say, glancing away as if I'm flustered. As if I hadn't again intended it to show just an inch more skin than is common. This time, the top is conservative enough, with saffron yellow silk draping over both shoulders in wide swaths and a neckline high enough to cover my clavicle. I asked Hoa to pin the bodice tighter around my torso than I usually wear it so that it highlights the curve of my waist. She secured it with a ruby pin at my left hip as I instructed— higher than usual, so that the slit starts higher as well. Now each step I take reveals a glimpse of half of my leg. I practiced walking in it for almost an hour this morning in front of a mirror, trying to find the right balance between tantalizing and vulgar. If the way he's looking at me is any indication, I've succeeded.

"You're leaving soon, aren't you?" I ask, deciding to test him. "To secure the trade route from Dragonsbane?"

"In four days, yes," he says. And there it is—his eyes dart from me, giving away the lie.

So my gut was right—they aren't going to secure the trade route. I can't do anything with that information until I know for sure where they are going, but I still feel a rush of pride at being correct.

"I'm a bit nervous about it, to be honest," he admits.

"I don't see why you should be," I tell him. "From what I've heard, you're excellent in battle, and Dragonsbane only has a small fleet. I'm sure you'll do well."

He shrugs, but he averts his eyes again. "It's the first mission I've been put in charge of, without the Theyn's guidance. There are a lot of expectations resting on it, and I'm not . . ."

He trails off and clears his throat, looking flustered at his admission of weakness. Before I can think of a way to respond, he changes the subject.

"I'm sorry I couldn't continue your tour of the ship myself."

"Oh, don't be," I say lightly. "It was very kind of you to look after Crescentia, and Erik was a wonderful replacement. It's a beautiful ship. Does it have a name yet?"

"It does, actually. Or rather, *she* does. The crew . . ." His eyes dart away. "After you left, they—*we*—decided to name it for Lady Crescentia."

I couldn't care less about what he chooses to name his boat, but he's watching me for my reaction, and who am I to disappoint him? Let him believe I'm concerned with something so silly. I tighten my smile so that it looks vaguely forced. "That's a fine name. She was, after all, the first lady to step on board, wasn't she?"

"You both were," he says. "But . . ." He trails off again, unable to finish.

"But I'm not a lady," I fill in. "Not really. That's what they said, isn't it?"

He shakes his head but doesn't deny it. "They thought it would be bad luck. I disagreed, Thora, and so did Erik, for that matter. But . . ."

"I understand," I say, making it sound like I don't.

The trick with Søren, I've realized, is to let him believe he's seeing through me, past the act I put on for everyone else. But he can't, not really. There always has to be at least one more layer so that he'll keep looking.

I lower my voice for effect. "I heard what they said about

me," I continue, pretending to lay out my cards. "They think I'm your paramour. Only they used a fouler word that I won't repeat."

He believes the lie easily. His arm goes stiff beneath my fingers and his brow furrows. "Who said that?" he asks, angry and a touch afraid. I'd imagine the last thing he wants is that rumor getting back to his father.

"Does it matter?" I reply. "Of course they think that. Your guards likely think it, too." I glance their way, though they keep their eyes politely averted. "The one who delivered your letter certainly did," I add, knowing that the guard from earlier isn't present. "Even I would believe it if I didn't know better. Why else would you be seeking me out like this? Inviting me to lunch?"

I wait on edge for his response. He doesn't answer for a few seconds and I worry that I've pulled the rod before he could fully swallow the bait. He turns toward his guards and waves his hand. Without a word, they turn and go back inside, though I'm sure they're still watching.

"That isn't going to help things," I tell him, crossing my arms over my chest. "I don't have a chaperone, and—"

His ears redden and he turns back to me. "You did get my letter, then," he interrupts. "But you didn't reply."

I bite my lip. "I didn't think it would be appropriate to accept your invitation, but I wasn't sure I was allowed to refuse. No answer seemed the best answer."

"Of course you could refuse, if you wanted to," he says, looking surprised. "*Did* you want to?"

I let out a forlorn sigh and glance away. "It doesn't matter what I want," I tell him. Not answering will drive him all the more mad. "You should have asked Crescentia. She likes you, and she's a more appropriate companion."

I expect him to deny it, but he doesn't. "I enjoy spending time with you, Thora," he says instead. "And it was only a lunch."

It's easy to act like a damsel in need of rescuing. All it takes are wide eyes, tentative smiles, and a wolf at my heels. "I don't think your father would approve," I say.

He frowns and drops his gaze. "I wasn't planning on telling him," he admits.

I can't help but laugh. "Someone would have," I say. "You've been gone for a long time, Søren, but ask anyone— your father sees everything that happens in this palace. Especially where I'm concerned."

Søren's frown deepens. "You've been with us for ten years," he says. "You're more Kalovaxian than not at this point."

I think he means the words as a comfort, but they strike me like daggers.

"You might be right," I say instead of arguing. It's time to play the card Cress left me, the one that will make me more a damsel in distress to him than ever. "He's planning to marry me to a Kalovaxian man soon."

"Where did you hear that?" he asks, alarmed. I suppress a smile and try to look troubled, biting my lip and wringing my hands.

"Crescentia overheard her father and yours talking about it. I suppose it makes sense. I'm of age, and as you said, I've been a Kalovaxian now longer than I was an Astrean."

"Marry you to *who*?"

I shrug but let my expression cloud over. "She mentioned

that Lord Dalgaard offered the most to own the last Princess of Astrea," I say, letting just a touch of acid into my voice.

It's treason to even use that title to describe myself, but Søren seems to like flashes of honesty. It's a gamble, yes, but all of this is a gamble. One wrong move will leave me buried.

Søren swallows and drops his gaze. He's likely been in more battles than I can name, but the threat of Lord Dalgaard leaves him speechless. He glances past my shoulder to where his guards are waiting, just out of earshot.

I reach out to touch his arm lightly and lower my voice.

"I've done everything your father's asked of me, Søren, given him everything he's asked of me without complaint, trying to show that I can be a loyal citizen here. But please, *please,* don't let him do this," I plead. "You know about Lord Dalgaard and his poor wives. I have no dowry, no family, no standing. No one would care what happens to me. I'm sure that's part of the appeal for him."

His expression hardens into granite. "I can't go against my father, Thora."

I drop my hand and shake my head. I take a breath as if to steady myself and stand up a little straighter. When I look at Søren again, I let another layer of my mask fall into place, this one cold as ice.

"I'm sorry, Your Highness," I say stiffly. "I overstepped and I shouldn't have. I just thought you were . . . I wanted . . ." I shake my head and let my eyes linger on his, full of disappointment, before tearing them away and blinking hard, like I might cry at any second. "I should go."

I turn to leave, but just as I hope, he reaches out to take hold of my arm. From there, it's only a small twitch of a muscle, an infinitesimal drop of my shoulder that causes the already loose sleeve of my dress to fall, giving him a glimpse of the scars covering my back. He knew they were there; he was present when some of the older ones were given. Still, I hear his sharp intake of breath at the sight. I pull my arm from his grasp and hastily yank the sleeve back up to cover them, keeping my eyes lowered as if the scars shame me.

"I'm sorry," he says as I hurry away from him.

I'm not sure what exactly he's apologizing for, but it doesn't matter. I don't have to look at him to know that I have him where I need him: ready to leap to my rescue, even if it digs a chasm between him and his father in the process. All I have to do now is wait for the results and hope they don't cost me too dearly.

WALLS

H OA ISN'T IN MY ROOM when I return, but I'm hardly alone. The doors of my Shadows' rooms scrape open and closed, followed by sounds of them settling in: sheathed swords unclasping, helmets clattering to the floor. I ignore them, as I always do, and stand by the window, looking out at the empty garden so that they can't see my face.

How long will I have to wait for Søren's next move? If it comes at all.

I think of the look in his eyes when I turned away. This is only just starting. He'll go to his father with some pressing reason to end my engagement before it starts. He won't come out and say it's to protect me—Søren's too clever for that—but there are other ways, other reasons for a betrothal to fall through. Crescentia's had three marriage proposals too good to outright reject, but the betrothals never quite become official due to Cress's meddling.

I can only hope that the Kaiser doesn't suspect I had anything to do with Søren's sudden interest in my betrothal. At best, it'll mean another whipping. At worst, he'll marry me to Lord Dalgaard immediately. And then how long would it take before my mind truly broke? There would be no coming back from that. I would die Thora.

"When you turned down his lunch invitation, I thought you truly were mad," a voice says. Terror turns my blood to ice. I spin, but the room is empty.

"But he seems more interested than ever," the voice goes on. "Well done."

Blaise. His voice is muffled, but it's unmistakably him. *He's the mad one, coming here knowing full well that my Shadows watch my every move.*

"Here, Theo," he says. There's laughter there that reminds me of when we were children together, before laughter became such a rarity.

I follow the sound, walking to the eastern wall, to where one of my Shadows sits on the other side, watching. *A Shadow.*

"I seem to have underestimated you as well," I say. I peer through the hole in the wall to find Blaise's green eye staring back. "Though I'm sure you remember I have three Shadows?"

"Say hello to Artemisia and Heron," he says, sounding pleased with himself. "Art, Heron—Queen Theodosia Eirene Houzzara. It's a bit of a mouthful. Would you have them beheaded if we shortened it to Theo for the time being?"

Hearing that word again—*queen*—is still strange, especially hearing it in Astrean. It's my mother's title, or it was. Every time I hear it, I can't help wanting to look around for my mother, sure it's her they're referring to.

"So long as you don't call me Thora," I say, straightening up and glancing at the other walls, now occupied by other Astreans. "Artemisia, Heron, pleasure to meet you."

"The pleasure is ours," a low, soft voice says from behind the northern wall. Heron, I assume.

"You don't *look* batty," the third voice says from behind the southern wall, gritty and lilting. Artemisia.

"Art," Heron warns.

"I didn't say she was batty," Blaise interjects quickly. "I said . . . *sensitive*."

"You said *unbalanced*."

I open my mouth to snap out a retort but quickly shut it again. I'm not sure which of those terms bothers me more, but I can't deny the truth in any of them. Blaise saw me fall apart in the cellar. He must wonder how strong I really am.

"What happened to my real Shadows?" I ask instead of responding.

Blaise clears his throat, but it's Heron who answers.

"They've been . . . relieved of their duties," he says carefully.

Artemisia snickers. "Among other things."

I wait for their deaths to hit me, to feel *something*, whether it's relief or happiness or some unexplainable grief, but I feel nothing. I never saw their faces or spoke to them. I won't mourn them, but I don't hate them enough to celebrate their deaths either.

"And if they're found?" I ask.

"They won't be," Artemisia says. "We tied rocks to their corpses and dropped them in the ocean. They must be a hundred feet deep, at least. Give it a few days and there won't be anything left but bones."

She says it so distantly, as if she weren't speaking of people at all. Then again, I've heard Kalovaxians refer to Astreans as things instead of people; I can't exactly fault her for holding the same view of them.

"Any progress, Theo?" Blaise asks. "We saw that lovely meeting with the Prinz, but we couldn't hear a damn thing. What are you planning?"

"You did tell me that he's interested in me because he can't have me, didn't you?" I say. "So I'm becoming more interesting. And sowing tension between him and the Kaiser, which I imagine can only be good for us."

"Why?" Artemisia asks.

I shrug, but my smile is feral. "The Kalovaxians have every advantage. There are more of them; they're better armed and better trained; they have the advantage of already holding the land. Blaise was right when he told me we don't stand a chance against them on an even field. But if we could turn Søren against his father, the court will take sides, and they'll be distracted enough fighting each other that we might have a better chance. We'll still need to amass more numbers and more weapons, of course. It's not much of a plan," I admit. "But it seemed like a good place to start."

"If it works," Blaise says warily. His skepticism prickles at the back of my neck.

"It'll work," I say, though my own doubts pool in the pit of my stomach. "Søren is easy to twist; all I need to do is convince him that I'm in need of saving, and that his father and his people are the ones I need saving *from*. If I can turn Søren against them, at least half the court will eagerly follow in hopes of putting Søren on the throne without waiting for the Kaiser to die." No one has a reply to that, so I continue. "You saw his face in the garden. Do *you* think it worked?"

"Yes," Artemisia admits. "He had battle in his eyes, that one. The falling sleeve was a nice touch. I suppose that was intentional?"

I shrug. "He wants a damsel and I'm giving him one. How long have you been watching me, anyway?" I ask.

"Only today," Blaise says. "Your friend found us a couple of days ago. Elpis. We were already trying to find a way to replace your Shadows, but she'd seen their movements up close and knew how they operated, how often they reported to the Kaiser, when it would be easiest to overtake them. Their monthly report to the Kaiser is tomorrow night, so we knew we had to do it before then or they'd tell him about your conversation with her. They sleep in shifts; it was simple to replace them one by one."

Replace them. He says it as naturally as Artemisia did, as if killing came easily. Maybe for him it does, maybe it wasn't even his first kill. In fact, it likely wasn't if he escaped the mines and has been running with Ampelio as long as he has. The realization sits strangely. I can't help but think of him the way he was as a child, quiet and inquisitive. He wouldn't even kill bugs back then.

I push the thought aside and focus on the here and now. "Sooner or later, someone will miss them," I point out, irritated at their shortsightedness. "And what exactly are you planning to do when you meet with the Kaiser tomorrow? I've never seen their faces, but he certainly has."

"It's actually not as much of a risk as it seems," Heron says. His voice is quiet, but there's such a solid quality to it that I don't have to struggle to hear him. It's the kind of voice that reverberates through your whole body. "Your guards' only duty is watching you. The Kaiser is very particular about it, doesn't want any mistakes. They don't have families or attend any social events that you don't. No one will miss them."

"And this meeting with the Kaiser?" I press.

"Ah, that," Blaise says, but he doesn't sound wary. He sounds triumphant. "Artemisia and Heron were working in the mines as well before Ampelio snuck us out. Why do you think he would have freed us out of everyone there?"

"You're Guardians," I say as I realize it.

"Not technically," Artemisia says. "There was no formal training, though Ampelio tried to make up for that."

"Still, the gods saw fit to bless us with their gifts. Unlike most of the others forced to work down there," Heron says.

I don't have to see his face to know the words cost him. I've seen many awful things since the siege, but from what I hear, it's nothing compared to the nightmare of the mines. I've heard that a dozen people go mine-mad each week. They're immediately put to death in front of their friends and families, who must watch and not say a word or risk sharing their fate.

"Magic is well and good, but it doesn't make an even battlefield between the three of you and the Kaiser's guards when he learns who you are," I point out.

"That's just it, though. The Kaiser won't learn anything. Only one Shadow meets with him at a time, so the other two can stay with you. And Artemisia has the Water Gift," he says.

The pieces fall into place.

"Which includes crafting illusions," I finish.

"I got a good look at the guards when we overtook them,

good enough to impersonate them. It won't hold for long without a gem to channel through," she admits. "Fifteen minutes? Twenty, maybe. But from what we've heard about the Kaiser's briefings, it should be more than enough time."

Good enough. Should be. They aren't exactly heartening statements of confidence.

"You don't have a gem?" I ask. "Do any of you?"

The silence that follows is answer enough.

"Ampelio did," Blaise manages finally. "But he was taken with it. Not that it would have done any of us any good. As I said, Artemisia has the Water Gift, Heron has the Air—"

"And you have the Earth?" I finish for him.

"Yes," he says after a slight hesitation. "But the meetings with the Kaiser are short. Artemisia can hold an illusion that long without a gem, I've seen her do it."

For a moment, I don't know what to say. None of it is terribly inspiring, and so many things can go wrong with their plan. I don't have to ask to know that Ampelio would not have agreed to them replacing my Shadows or he would have done it himself years ago. If he were here now, he would want to wait, to make sure everything was perfect before he struck. But Ampelio waited for ten years and it was never the perfect moment. He waited and bided his time until they killed him.

I shake my head. "There must be a better way for us to keep in touch while I'm here."

"Like inviting a thirteen-year-old to be our messenger?" Blaise retorts.

He sounded like that when we were children, too. Like the year that separated us made him infinitely wiser than I could ever hope to be. *I'm* not even sure that bringing Elpis into this was the right thing to do, but I know it was the only thing I *could* do. "I trust Elpis," I say, lifting my chin a fraction of an inch and strengthening my voice. "I'll admit that I've made mistakes before. I've trusted the wrong people and I've paid dearly for that. The Kaiser enjoys setting traps for me to fall into. I barely trusted *you* when you appeared out of nowhere, but I did."

"It was a good choice," Artemisia puts in. "She's a smart girl, and observant. We couldn't have overtaken your Shadows without her."

"We could have," Blaise insists, sounding like an irritated older brother. "And we wouldn't have had to risk the life of a child."

"You weren't moving fast enough." The words spill out before I can think about them, but arguing with Blaise has always had this effect on me. He was always so calm and condescending and it never failed to reduce me to the petulant child he treated me as.

Which is why I decide I am not going to tell them about the threat of Lord Dalgaard hanging over my head now. Fear of becoming his next bride made me act rashly, and next to everything they have endured, I have no right to complain.

I clear my throat. "I gave her a choice. Elpis wanted to help."

"She's a *child*. She didn't know what she was agreeing to," Blaise insists, his voice becoming a growl.

"Come now, Blaise," Artemisia soothes. "Thirteen is hardly a child, not anymore."

Blaise's breathing stretches longer for a few beats. "She's

your responsibility, Theo. If something happens to her, that's on you," he says.

I nod, though my temper threatens to overwhelm me. Even if I'm paralyzed by doubt, I can't show it. I won't apologize.

He's quiet, but through the wall separating us, I can feel his anger simmering in the air.

"You can't talk to our queen like that, Blaise," Heron says. I can't know for sure without seeing his face, but he sounds a bit frightened.

Our queen. The title sounds strange, and I have to remind myself that he's talking about me, that I *am* their queen. I try not to think about Ampelio calling me the same thing before I plunged the sword into his back. I exhale, letting my anger go as well. "He can talk to me however he sees fit," I say quietly. "All of you can—and should."

Heron shifts behind his wall; then he gives a grunt of acknowledgment.

"The girl said you had news?" Blaise asks, no longer sounding upset.

"Oh," I say. In all the excitement, I forgot why I needed to talk to him in the first place. "Where exactly are the Vecturia Islands?" I ask.

"I've heard that name before . . . ," Blaise says.

"Vecturia is a cluster of islands northeast of here," Artemisia says, sounding bored. "Why?"

"I think the Prinz is taking at least two thousand troops to the islands in a few days, armed to the teeth with cannons," I say. "I don't imagine it's a social visit."

"You think or you know?" Artemisia asks.

I hesitate, weighing the evidence in my mind—the types

of ships, the heavy artillery, the fact that Dragonsbane can't have gotten all the way to the trade route if he was just outside the capital only last week. I think of Søren looking away in the garden when he told me again that he was going to the trade route, how obvious it felt that he was lying. It's all circumstantial, nothing I can prove outright, but I can feel it in my bones.

"I know," I say, hoping I sound more confident than I feel.

"Did they have berserkers?" Blaise asks.

I shake my head, then stop. "Well, I can't really say—I still don't have a clue as to what they are."

"Even with just their cannons and warriors, he'll destroy Vecturia," Artemisia says, more alert now. "There are five islands, but each can't have more than a few hundred people. A fraction of that will be trained soldiers, and they're all spread out. If they aren't ready for an attack, the Kalovaxians will pick them off one island at a time without a drop of sweat for their efforts."

"There must be something we can do to help them," I say.

Blaise shakes his head. "The Vecturians didn't lift a finger to help during the siege. If they had . . . well, we likely still would have lost, but we would have had a chance."

"Exactly," Heron says. "Is it heartless to say I care more about the dirt under my fingernails than them?" he asks. "This is no more than they deserve. If we'd stood together, we might not be in this mess. I certainly won't cry over them now."

As harsh as his words seem, I can't help but agree with them.

"Still," I reason, "we might need the Vecturians' help when we start gathering allies to take on the Kalovaxians. Let's not make the same mistake they did. Besides, when we *do* manage to take Astrea back, we won't keep it long if the Kalovaxians have taken over our neighboring country as well. They'll just regroup there and come back."

Blaise gives a labored sigh and I'm almost positive he's rolling his eyes. "Vecturia made it clear that they aren't our ally, and we need to save what little power we have for ourselves."

Part of me knows he's right. He gave me the numbers. One thousand of us against the tens of thousands of Kalovaxians in Astrea.

"If we help Vecturia, we could forge a new alliance. You said it yourself, our numbers don't stand a chance against theirs, but if we add another few hundred from Vecturia . . ."

"It still won't be near enough," Heron says. Even though I know he's trying to be kind, I can hear the impatience coming through in his voice. "And that's an *if*. It's far more likely we'd be sending warriors *we* need to die in a fight that isn't ours. Vecturia will still fall, and we won't be far behind."

What would my mother do? I wonder. But even as I ask myself the question, I know the answer. "It isn't fair. There are people on those islands and we're dooming them to carnage and slavery. If anyone should understand the stakes here, we should."

Artemisia scoffs. "Blaise was right. You've been locked in your cushioned cage too long, and it's turned your mind soft," she says. "We've seen more carnage than you ever will, felt more loss. We've starved and bled and lingered at the door of death so often we lost count. We know exactly what we're dooming Vecturia to, but they aren't Astrea, and therefore they aren't our concern."

"It's what my mother would have done," I say.

Again Artemisia scoffs, and if I could reach through the hole in the wall, I would slap her. But before she can say anything about my mother, Blaise cuts in.

"May the gods bless Queen Eirene forever in the After, but until the end, she was the queen of a peaceful country. Her reign was largely untested and easy; she never had to know war until the Kalovaxians came and slit her throat. She had the luxury of being a sympathetic queen. You don't."

There is no barb in his voice. It is a calmly stated fact, and as much as I would like to argue it, I can't right now. From her place in the After, I hope my mother understands. One day, I will be a magnanimous ruler. I will be everything the Kaiser isn't; I will be as gracious as my mother was. But first, I need to make sure my country survives.

"All right," I say after a moment. "We do nothing."

"Good choice," Artemisia says.

Though I don't know what she looks like, I'm sure she's quite smug behind that wall. I'm grateful to have them here, truly I am, but I can't help but feel I'm carrying far more weight than I was this morning, and that even more people are now waiting for me to fail. They're my allies—the only ones I have—but that doesn't mean we'll always be on the same side.

"You need to be prepared," I tell them. "Cushioned as my cage might seem, my life here isn't all flirtations and pretty dresses and parties. If something happens to me . . . you're going to let it happen. I don't care what it is or what sense of duty makes you want to try to defend me. Your attempt will fail, and then you'll be compromised as well—and that won't do anyone any good."

"Theo—" Blaise starts heavily.

"He won't kill me. I'm too valuable to him for that. Whatever he does to me, I will recover from it. The same can't be said for you. Swear it."

There's a stubborn silence for a long moment and I worry that they'll protest. I realize I'm asking them to go against Ampelio's dying wishes. He wanted me safe, but my country needs me to stand.

"I swear it," Artemisia says, echoed by Heron a breath later.

"Blaise?" I prompt.

He gives a grunt that I interpret as acceptance, but it isn't a promise.

Hoa returns a few minutes later with a basket of laundry in her arms, and my Shadows go silent. They aren't quite as practiced at it as my old Shadows were. I can hear them fidgeting more, breathing louder. If Hoa senses anything off, though, she gives no sign, and I wonder if I only notice because I know the truth. I didn't know anything was different about my Shadows this morning, after all.

Part of me wants to confess everything to Hoa, but as much as I want to believe I can trust her, I can't. And after everything Hoa has suffered at the hands of the Kaiser, asking her to stand up against him would be its own kind of cruelty.

I eat a quick dinner alone while Hoa folds the laundry, but the silence feels unbearably loud. I should be used to it. Most meals pass like this and I've more or less stopped noticing, but tonight is different. Everything is different. Blaise is so close, Artemisia and Heron too, and they're watching me as a queen. I'm painfully aware of how lacking I must seem.

After Hoa clears away my plate and turns to my armoire to pick out a nightgown, panic seizes me. She's going to change me into it. Which means my Shadows are going to see everything.

I've never had the luxury of being modest. For the last ten years, the old Shadows watched me change twice a day, and I never gave it a second thought. It was all I'd ever known. And my dress had been ripped to bare my back to hundreds— sometimes thousands—of people. It was a part of the punishment, a way of humiliating and dehumanizing me further. After all, how can anyone look at a bleeding girl in a ripped dress and see her as a leader? But Blaise and Heron and Art seeing me naked is different.

Hoa riffles through my armoire and I take the opportunity to shoot my most commanding look in each Shadow's direction and twirl a finger in the air, motioning for them to turn around. Not that I have any way of knowing they're obeying, but I trust them. I have no choice.

Still, I keep my back to them as best I can and face the curtained window instead as Hoa unclasps the shoulders of my chiton and lets it fall to the ground. Her warm fingers reach up to touch one of the healing wounds, causing me to flinch. She makes a muffled, disapproving noise in the back of her throat and leaves my side, returning seconds later with a pot of ointment that stinks of rot and dirt, given to her by Ion to help the healing along. After she applies it gingerly, she slips my nightgown over my head. The thin cotton sticks to the ointment, making it itch, but I know better by now than to scratch.

"Thank you," I say.

Her hand brushes my shoulder briefly before falling away. Without a sound, she slips from the room, leaving me alone.

But for the first time in a decade, I'm surrounded by allies. I'm not alone, I tell myself. And hopefully, I never will be again.

KAISERIN

— · —

IT'S BARELY NOON WHEN THE sharp, official knock sounds at the door and sends my heart pounding. My immediate thought is that the Kaiser is summoning me. If all went as I hoped, Søren found a way to question his father's decision without the Kaiser tracing it back to me—if he so much as suspects I had anything to do with it, he'll punish me for it and marry me off to Lord Dalgaard anyway.

My mouth is dry no matter how often I swallow, and I can't keep from shaking as Hoa goes to the door. I hide my hands in the folds of my dress and struggle to keep my scrambled, panicked thoughts from showing on my face.

I'm acutely aware of Blaise and the others behind the walls. I can't let them see me afraid. I need to show them that I can be strong and sure.

I cross to stand near Blaise's post, dropping my voice to a whisper while Hoa is distracted listening to the guard.

"Remember what we talked about. The humiliation at the banquet was a mild inconvenience compared to what will happen now. The Kaiser's punishments are brutal but not le-thal, so you will let it happen and stay silent. Do you understand?" I don't let myself mention Lord Dalgaard, as if not speaking about it will erase the threat.

He doesn't reply, but I can almost feel an argument brewing.

"I'm too valuable to kill," I assure him, softening my voice. "That's protection enough."

He grunts in response and I have no choice but to take that as assent.

Hoa flits back into the room, light on her feet, her expression inscrutable. She immediately starts tugging at my dress and smoothing out the wrinkles that have come from sitting around all morning.

"Is it the Kaiser?" I ask, letting real fear seep into my voice.

Her eyes dart to mine briefly before dropping. She shakes her head. Relief spreads through me, loosening the python around my stomach. I have to force myself not to burst into inexplicable laughter.

"The Prinz, then?" I guess as she combs my hair back and fastens it in place with a pearl-encrusted pin.

Another shake of her head.

I frown, wondering who else could throw her into such a frenzy. Briefly I consider the Theyn, which sends another shudder through me before I remember he's inspecting the mines. Still, it must be someone important, but no one apart from Crescentia—and now, apparently, Søren—pays me personal attention.

Hoa drags her eyes over me one last time, from the top of my head to my sandaled feet, before giving me a firm nod of approval and a none-too-gentle shove toward the door, where two guards wait.

I know better than to ask the guards where we're going. Most Kalovaxians—even those without titles—treat me as if I'm an animal instead of a girl. Though that isn't quite fair. I've seen plenty of Kalovaxians speak to their dogs and horses with some measure of kindness.

My Astrean gods are hazy in my mind, especially the dozens of minor gods and goddesses, but I'm fairly sure there is no god of spies among them. Delza, Suta's daughter and the goddess of deception, is likely the closest, though I'm not sure even she will be able to protect me from the whip.

The sound of my Shadows' footfalls are so common that I've almost stopped hearing them altogether, but now I'm all too aware of them. Despite his promise, I doubt that if it comes to a whipping or some other punishment, Blaise will be able to stay silent.

The guards lead me down the halls and I have to force my feet to keep moving forward. When I realize where we are going, my chest tightens until I can hardly breathe. I haven't been in the royal wing of the palace since before the siege, since it was my own home.

The guards' boots click against the granite floor and all I can think about is my mother chasing me down this hall, trying to wrangle me into a bath. The stained-glass windows are cracked and dirty now, but I remember how the afternoon light used to filter through them and make the gray stone walls look like the inside of a jewelry box. Paintings used to line the halls, landscapes and portraits of my ancestors done in rich oil paints with gilded frames, but now they're all gone.

I wonder what happened to them. Were they sold or simply destroyed? Imagining those paintings in a heap with a torch put to them breaks my heart.

This can't be the same hall I grew up in, where I lived with my mother. That hall lives in my memory, perfectly intact, but now that I see what's become of it I wonder if I will ever be able to remember it the same way again.

Still, as different as it is from the place I remember, it's haunted with the ghost of my mother, and her presence weighs down on my shoulders like the funeral shroud she was never given. I hear her laugh in the silence, the way it used to echo through the halls so it was the last thing I heard each night before I fell asleep.

We pass the door to the library, to the private royal dining room, to my former bedroom, and then the guards pull me to a halt in front of what was once the door to my mother's sitting room. I don't know what it is now, but I'm sure it can only be the Kaiser waiting for me on the other side with a whip in his hand.

The guards push me through the door into a dimly lit room, and I immediately drop to a curtsy without looking up, heart thundering against my rib cage. Any hint of disrespect will cost me. Footsteps approach—lighter and slower than I'd been expecting. Red silk skirts and golden slippers fill my vision while the cloying scent of roses tickles my nose, and I realize it isn't the Kaiser who's summoned me, it's the Kaiserin.

While she is a moderately more appealing option than the Kaiser, I'm not sure I'm grateful for it. At least with the Kaiser I know where I stand. I understand the rules of his games, even if he usually cheats. But I can't begin to guess what the

Kaiserin wants from me, and I fear that looking at her will feel like looking at my future if I fail to gain my freedom. How long will it be before my own eyes grow so empty and distant?

Hers have always been that way, I think, even when she first arrived in the palace after the siege, then in her mid-twenties with smooth skin, loose yellow hair, and a seven-year-old Søren clutching her hand. She flinched when the Kaiser kissed her cheek in greeting, eyes darting around the room in a way I'd already grown too familiar with. She was searching for help she would never find.

"Leave us," she says now. Her voice is no louder than a whisper, but the guards comply, shutting the door behind them with a *thunk* that echoes in the mostly empty sitting room. "I trust your back isn't broken enough to hinder your standing?" she asks.

I hasten to my feet, smoothing out my skirts as I do. The room is large but sparsely decorated. There are five enormous windows that line one of the walls, but they're each draped with thick red velvet curtains that keep out any trace of sunlight. Candles are lit instead: a taper stands four feet tall by the door and a dozen thumb-sized ones crowd the low table in the center. The heavy brass chandelier overhead is lit as well, but the room still feels dark and gloomy. There's a hodge-podge of seating thrown around the table, including red velvet tufted chairs, sofas, and a chaise, all with gilt frames. Despite being filled with so much fire, the room is chilly.

It's a different place entirely than it was when it was my mother's sitting room. I remember it bright and soft, with sunlight filtered through the stained-glass windows and a thick patterned rug that covered most of the floor. Cozy chairs and sofas surrounded a sunstone fire pit where she would sit at the end of the day with her closest friends and advisors. The memories are hazy, but I remember her laughing with Ampelio, a goblet of red wine in her hand, while I played with my toys on the rug. I remember him whispering something in her ear and her resting her head on his shoulder. I don't know if the memory is real, but I suppose it doesn't matter. I can hardly ask them about it.

I blink the thought away and force myself to focus on Kaiserin Anke. It's been years since I've been this close to her in anything but an official capacity, when her skin has been slathered with an apothecary's worth of creams and tints. Time hasn't been kind to her, leaving her face looking like a half-melted candle and her hair thin and patchy. The red silk dress is finely crafted, but it sags on her gaunt frame and makes her skin look even more sallow. She's still young—not more than thirty-five—but she looks much older, despite the Water Gems coiled around her neck.

"Your Highness summoned me?"

Her small, milky eyes rake over me from the top of my head to my toes, and her mouth purses. "I thought it best we speak privately before you go and do something foolish," she says. The roughness in her voice takes me by surprise. The rare times I've heard her speak in public, she's always sounded more like a child than a woman.

I glance around the room. There is no one waiting behind her, no one crouched behind the patch of armchairs or the sofa. There is no one behind me either; the guards and my Shadows remain on the other side of the thick door. At the volume she's speaking, no one else can hear her. Still, my stomach churns. "I don't know what you're talking about, Your Highness."

Her eyes linger on me a moment longer before her mouth curls into a tight smile and she clasps her hands in front of her. Each finger is ringed with a Spiritgem—every gem except for Earth. The Kaiser is sure to forbid his wife any strength, though she could certainly use it. "You're an accomplished liar, I'll admit that. But he's always better, isn't he?"

I fight the urge to swallow or look away. I hold her gaze. "Who is?" I ask.

Her smile is wan. "Very well, little lamb. We'll play your game."

The nickname prickles the back of my neck like an annoying insect I can't ignore. She used to call me by it when she first came to the palace after the siege. That was before I understood the magnitude of everything that had happened. That was before the Kaiser's punishments started. That was when I'd mistaken her cowardice for kindness.

"I don't know what you mean, Your Highness," I tell her, keeping my voice level.

She turns and walks away from me, gliding toward the chaise with the grace of a ghost before sinking down into it. "Has anyone ever told you how I became a kaiserin, little lamb?" she asks.

"No," I lie. I've heard a dozen versions of the story, each different. Even those who were there, who saw it happen with their own eyes, each has their own version of the tale, painting it as everything from a triumph to a tragedy.

She leans back in the chaise and lifts her chin a fraction of an inch. Her eyes are far away, even when she looks directly at me. "You might as well sit," she says.

Tentatively I cross the room and sit down in the chair closest to her. I try to mimic her prim body language, crossing my legs at the ankles and resting my hands in my lap. It's uncomfortable, but it's the way she always sits, even now, when there is no one to see her but me.

"I was born Printsessa of Rajinka, a small country on the Eastern Sea. A tenth child and a fourth daughter, of little importance outside the promise of a strong marriage. Luckily, one of our greatest allies had a son close to me in age. Our betrothal was sealed before my second birthday."

"The Kaiser?" I asked.

Her mouth twitches into something that might be a smile. "Not at the time, no. Prinz Corbinian was how I knew him. Everyone called him Corby, much to his great displeasure. I didn't meet him until I was twelve, but from that moment I was hopelessly smitten." She laughs softly and shakes her head. "It's difficult to picture now, I suppose, but he was a gangly boy with an easy smile. He made me laugh. We wrote one another such sentimental letters, you would hardly believe it."

I know that this story turns, eventually, to the Kaiser only speaking to her in cruelty and the Kaiserin going mad with fear and hate. Thinking of him as a boy penning soppy love letters is impossible, like trying to imagine a dog dancing a waltz.

"My wedding day was beautiful. There wasn't a cloud in the sky and I don't think I'd ever been happier—it was what I'd dreamt of for three years, it was everything I'd been raised for. You and I were raised in very different worlds, in that respect," she says, keeping her gaze on me until I glance away. She clears her throat and continues. "We were wed in the chapel at my family's palace, where I had first sworn myself to my god as a child. We only had one in Rajinka, you know. It was much less confusing."

She pauses to take a breath, or maybe to steady herself. I know, more or less, what comes next. In no version is it ever a pleasant story—not for the Kaiserin, at least.

"We said our vows under the watch of his gods and mine, and the whole time, he couldn't take his eyes off me. It felt like . . . it felt like we were the only two people in the chapel . . . like we were the only two people in the world. And when it was official, he raised his hand and gave a signal I didn't understand."

Though I know what happens, I still wait to hear her say it, barely breathing.

"His father's men turned their blades on their kaiser, their kaiserin, all of his siblings, to be safe. Even the little ones, barely out of their short clothes. A few of the noblemen as well—anyone whose loyalty Corbinian couldn't secure. And when that was done and the floors of the chapel were slick with Kalovaxian blood, they turned on my family and friends. Bringing weapons into a place of worship is a sin, so my people couldn't even defend themselves. It was a slaughter."

Her voice begins to shake, and I can't help wondering if this is the first time she's told this story. Who else would have listened? The Kaiserin keeps no confidantes, has no friends, no one at all who is wholly hers. And like me, there are parts of her she has to hide at all costs from the Kaiser.

"My parents, my sisters, my brothers, the girls I'd had lessons with, my aunts, my uncles, my cousins. All of them were dead before I even had time to scream. And when it was done, do you know what my love said to me?"

"No." My voice comes out hoarse.

"*'I've given you two countries to rule, my love. Now what will you give me?'*"

The words send a shiver down my spine. "Why are you telling me this?" I ask.

She closes her eyes and takes a moment to calm herself. Her shaking slows, and when she opens her eyes again, the cloudiness is gone, replaced by a fire I didn't think her capable of. "Because I know the spark of rebellion when I see it. There was a time when I knew that spark very well. But I need you to understand that you are playing a dangerous game with a dangerous man. And there are consequences when you lose— and you will lose. I know that as well."

I glance around the room, expecting to see holes in the walls, expecting to hear guards burst into the room ready to arrest us both for speaking against the Kaiser. She sees this and smiles.

"No, little lamb, I rid myself of my own Shadows years ago. All it took was a decade of docility and submission for Corbinian to call them off—or, I suppose, to give them to you. With enough time, you'll lose them as well. Once Corbinian stops seeing you as a threat, or you have someone he can use against you the way he uses Søren against me."

"I'm still not quite sure what you want from me," I tell her, but I know I don't sound convincing.

She lifts a shoulder in a shrug. "My son came to me last night. He had some . . . concerns about Corbinian's plans to marry you off and hoped that I could change his mind. He was smart, to come to me instead of going straight to his father. Of course, you were smarter still to seek out his help in the first place."

I force my expression into one of innocence, though I'm starting to think it's useless with her. "The Prinz and I have become friends, Your Highness. I was . . . troubled, understandably, when I heard the Kaiser intended to marry me off to Lord Dalgaard, and I turned to Søren. As a friend."

For a long moment, she's quiet. "I have taken the liberty of arranging an alternative marriage for Lord Dalgaard," she says finally. "One he found perfectly amenable."

"I am very grateful, Your Highness," I breathe. It might be the first true thing I've said to her.

Her thin eyebrows arch. "Aren't you curious to know whose well-being was traded for your own?"

I try to look chastened, but I can't quite manage it. The truth, damned as it might make me, is that I don't care at all which spoiled and vicious Kalovaxian girl the Kaiserin had to trade for me. I'd watch them all die without batting an eyelash.

Even Crescentia? a small voice asks in the back of my mind, but I ignore it. Cress is too valuable to marry off to someone like Lord Dalgaard. It would never happen.

"I would imagine, Your Highness, that the wisest choice would have been Lady Dagmær," I say. "Such a match would please everyone. Dagmær's father likely put up a fuss about Lord Dalgaard's history, but since it was you asking—and I assume adding a little extra to Lord Dalgaard's bid—he gave in easily enough."

She purses her lips. "You have a sharp mind, little lamb, and all the sharper still for keeping it hidden. But make no mistake: there will be another match made for you, likely a crueler one."

"I don't see who could be crueler than Lord Dalgaard." I say it, holding her gaze with mine.

"Don't you?" she asks, tilting her head to one side. "My husband would hardly be the first kaiser to rid himself of his wife to take a younger bride. I have nothing left to give him, after all," she says casually. "But you're young. You could give him more children and strengthen his hold on the country. And I've seen him look at you. I'd imagine the whole court has—my chivalrous fool of a son included. Corbinian isn't exactly subtle, is he?"

I try to speak but words fail me. The python is back, wrapping itself around my stomach and chest so tightly I'm sure it will kill me. I want to deny her words, but I can't.

She gets to her feet and I know that I should rise as well and curtsy, but I'm frozen in place. "Some advice, little lamb? Next time you close a window, make sure it doesn't open a trapdoor beneath your feet."

She's halfway to the door when I find my voice. "I don't know what I'm doing," I admit, barely louder than a whisper.

The Kaiserin hears me, though. She turns and regards me with that disconcerting, unfocused stare of hers. "You're a lamb in the lion's den, child. You're surviving. Isn't that enough?"

GEMS

I'M SHAKING AS I WALK down the hall, though I try to hide it. I smile pleasantly at the barrage of courtiers who just so happen to be taking leisurely strolls near the royal wing, but I don't really see them—just a blur of bland, pale Kalovaxian features bleeding together until they're one face. The Kaiserin's voice echoes in my head: "You are playing a dangerous game with a dangerous man." It's no more than I already knew, but hearing it from someone else—the Kaiserin, of all people—sets everything in a new light.

I'd thought that the worst things that could be done to me had already come to pass—the public whippings, executing Ampelio, watching my mother die. I'd never imagined something worse was possible. But being forced to marry the Kaiser would be just that. I would burrow so deep inside myself that I'm not sure I would ever break free.

I would die first.

It doesn't matter, I tell myself; it won't come to that. In a month I'll be gone from this place and I'll never have to look at the Kaiser again. Still, fear and disgust course through me at the prospect of the Kaiser sharing my bed.

My Shadows' footsteps fall into place a good distance behind me, and I resist the urge to look back at them. I feel their eyes on me, but I can't let them know how afraid I am. I can't let them know about this new threat either. Blaise would insist that we leave the city immediately. He would stow me somewhere safe while Astrea turned to dust.

When I slip back into my room, Hoa is smoothing the coverlet into place over my bed, but she stops and looks up at me in alarm. I try to shift my expression into something neutral, but can't manage. Not today.

"Leave," I tell her.

Her eyes dart to the walls—a silent reminder or an old habit, I'm not sure—and for a second she looks like she wants to do something, but she only nods and disappears out the door.

I go to stand at my window, less for the view of the gray garden and more because it's the only way to hide my face from my Shadows. Still, the weight of their stares is unbearable. I can practically hear Artemisia's throaty scoff again and Heron's beleaguered lecturing voice. I imagine Blaise rolling his eyes and deciding to take me out of here tonight because it turns out I can't do this after all and I don't know why I thought I could. I'm only the broken little Ash Princess who can't save herself, let alone her country.

I try to calm down, but the Kaiserin's words repeat over and over in my head. I remember the way the Kaiser has been looking at me in recent months. I never let myself think about it, as if that would make it untrue, but I know she's right. I know how this story will play out.

Tears sting my eyes, and I hastily wipe them away before the others can see.

Heron called me a queen yesterday, and queens don't falter; they don't get frightened; they don't cry.

The door opens quietly and I stiffen, hastily wiping my wet eyes on the back of my sleeve. When I glance over my shoulder, fake smile at the ready, Blaise is closing the door behind him, pulling his hood back.

"Blaise—"

He waves my words away dismissively. "There was no one in the hall, I made sure of it." His eyes skim over my face and I know I didn't hide my tears as well as I'd hoped. His hands fidget in front of him and he drops his gaze. When he looks at me again, there's a softness in his eyes that makes him look like a different person altogether. "What happened, Theo? You're paler than a Kalovaxian."

He's trying to make me laugh, but the sound that comes out of my mouth is halfway between a laugh and a sob. I glance down at my feet, focusing on stopping their shaking. It takes a few seconds and a couple of deep breaths before they still and I trust myself to speak.

"I need a weapon," I tell him, keeping my voice calm.

He looks taken aback. "Why?"

I can't tell him. As much as the words claw at my throat, I can't share this burden. I might not know Blaise as well as I used to, but I know exactly what he will do if I tell him about the Kaiserin's warning. And if we run, we won't have another chance to strike out at the Kaiser from this close.

"I just need one," I say.

Blaise shakes his head. "It's too risky," he says. "If anyone were to find it on you—"

"They won't," I say.

"Your maid sees you in nothing but your skin every morning and night," he points out. "Where exactly do you propose to keep it hidden?"

"I don't know," I admit in a whisper. Nausea rolls through me again and I sit down on the edge of my bed. The mattress gives as he sits down next to me, his leg not quite touching mine.

"What happened?" he asks again, his voice softer this time.

"I told you," I say, forcing a smile. "The Kaiserin is mad." I push thoughts of the Kaiserin and her warning out of my mind and focus on the positives. "My test worked, though. The Prinz cares for me enough to go against his father, even if he did it in a roundabout way. I can get closer and push him harder, I know I can. If we can get him to turn against his father publicly, it will cause a rift in the court."

As I say the words, a plan begins to form in my mind. Blaise must see where it's going, because a grim smile stretches across his face.

"A rift," he repeats slowly, and I can tell that his thoughts are mirroring my own. "A rift like that would become uncrossable if . . . say . . . the Prinz were to be killed under mysterious circumstances after confronting his father."

"Or not so mysterious," I add. "Certain clues might point to a member of the Kaiser's personal guard."

Already I'm thinking of just what those clues might be: a scrap of an undershirt sleeve with the Kaiser's sigil on it, ripped off in the scuffle, one of the leather ties the Kalovaxian men use to hold their hair back, a Spiritgem that fell out of a scabbard. Of course, to make it convincing, someone would need to pick one of the Kaiser's guards to frame. His undershirt would need to be ripped, his leather hair tie stolen, a gem pried from his scabbard. Heron could turn invisible and do it easily, so could Art if she were wearing a different face, but being able to control their gifts for ten to twenty minutes won't be enough this time. They would need gems.

"How would the court react to that?" Blaise asks, half to himself and half to me.

I purse my lips and turn the question over in my mind. "The Kalovaxians value strength, but the Kaiser has grown lazy since Astrea was conquered. He just stays in the palace letting others fight for him. Letting Søren fight for him. The Kalovaxian people love the Prinz—he's exactly what they think a ruler should be. If they thought the Kaiser killed him, at least half the court would revolt. It's happened before in Kalovaxian history—a weak ruler being overthrown, a new family fighting their way to the crown. It always starts with a civil war, those who are content with the current regime versus those who are not. We can flee the country after killing the Prinz, and while they pick each other off, we gather enough allies to come back and destroy them all."

The thought of it causes a smile to rise to my lips.

"Could you do it?" Heron asks from behind the wall.

"Do what?" I ask.

Heron clears his throat but doesn't answer.

"I think what Heron's asking is . . . ," Blaise starts, but he trails off. He opens his mouth and closes it again, dropping his gaze away from me.

"They want to know if you can actually kill someone," Artemisia says. "But I don't think they wanted to bring it up, since the only time you've taken a life, it was Ampelio's. I doubt the Prinz will lie at your feet and let you do it, and you can hardly overpower him, can you?"

She has a point, though I'm loath to admit it. "It's just the next step in a plan we already had in place," I say instead. "If I could overpower him, do you think the rest of the plan could work?"

The three of them are quiet for a moment. Next to me, Blaise's eyes are fixed on the wall in front of him, seeing nothing. I can practically see him thinking, running through the scenario in every direction.

"Yes," he says after a moment.

"It actually could work," Artemisia admits, sounding somewhat impressed.

"It *will* work," I say, my confidence growing. I feel buoyant suddenly, like my feet aren't quite touching the ground. We can do this—take our country back. Admittedly, there is only a slim chance of it working, but it's significantly more than it was before, now that we have a plan. It's a glimmer of hope in the pitch dark.

I don't let myself think too long about what, exactly, I just offered to do. Søren is my enemy, even if he's only ever showed me kindness. And now I know what it means to take a life, that it's something more than a blade and blood and a heart gone still. Now I know that it takes something from you in return.

There is something else nagging at me, too. I clear my throat. "On a separate note, I've been thinking about Vecturia a bit more—"

Blaise groans. "Theo, we agreed—"

"I never agreed," I interrupt, squaring my shoulders. "I'm

not content to brush the death and enslavement of thousands of people off my hands like they're nothing but flecks of dirt."

"They did that to us when the Kalovaxians came to our shores," Heron says.

"And I'm sure they'll regret that decision when Søren and his men attack. But the fact remains that the more the Kaiser digs his roots into the area, the more difficult it's going to be to remove him. When war does come, we'll already be fighting a difficult battle, but if they have a stronghold in Vecturia as well, they'll be able to attack from both sides and crush us easily. It won't be a fight; it'll be a massacre."

I wait for protests, but all three are silent. Blaise's eyes dart around the room, his mouth pursed. I don't sound like my mother this time, I realize. I sound more like the Kaiser or the Theyn dictating battle strategies, and I'm sure my Shadows notice that difference as well. Blaise is grasping for an argument, so I push forward before he can find one.

"And we are leaving here eventually. When we do, we're going to need to gather more forces, make stronger alliances. I know the Vecturians aren't enough, but they're a start. They're more than we have now, and they can do more than we can from here. I'm not suggesting that we send what few people we have into an impossible battle, but Artemisia said that Vecturia's weakness is in the distance between their islands, right? If we can get a warning there and give them the chance to unite, it would become a more difficult fight than Søren is anticipating."

Blaise nods slowly. "He might even turn back once he realizes he's lost the element of surprise."

"Is there a way to send warning?" I ask.

Blaise's brow furrows and he glances at Artemisia's wall. "Will your mother do it?" He sounds wary.

She hesitates. "It might take some convincing," she says. "And I'm still not sure it's the best idea."

"If you have any better ones, I'm open to considering them," I tell her.

Silence. Then, "I'll try."

"Thank you," I say, feeling a few inches taller. The threat of the Kaiser recedes a bit in my mind. I can do this. I can act like a queen.

It takes a few seconds for the implications of what they were talking about to hit me. "Wait. What does your mother have to do with anything?" I ask her.

Artemisia laughs. "She is the most feared pirate on the Calodean Sea. You might know her better as Dragonsbane."

For a moment, I can only stare at the wall she's hidden behind. The rebel Astrean pirate is notorious, but I've always heard Dragonsbane referred to as a *he*. It never crossed my mind that it could be a woman. A *mother*.

A surge of hope bubbles up in my chest and I can't help but laugh. If Dragonsbane is on our side, our chances just greatly improved. But when I turn back to Blaise, his jaw is set and he looks anything but relieved. I remember what he said about Dragonsbane in the cellar. She is not on our side, not really, even if our interests sometimes align.

But Astrea must be our common interest, right? This is her country, too, and she's done so much to help it. We have to be on the same side. After all, what other side is there for us?

Before I can ask Blaise more about it, he stands up and holds out a hand to me.

"We can't dawdle all day," he says, pulling me to my feet so that I'm facing him. This close, I can feel the warmth rolling from his skin. Even though he hasn't been outside in days, he smells like the earth after a rainstorm. He cups my cheeks gently, running his thumbs under my eyes to dry the leftover tears there. It's a surprisingly intimate gesture, from Blaise of all people, and I hear Heron cough awkwardly to remind us of his presence. Blaise clears his throat and steps back. "You have a prinz to charm," he reminds me before hesitating. "If you can hide a weapon where no one will find it, I can get you something. A dagger, maybe?"

Relief floods me even though I doubt I would know what to do with a knife if the moment came. Still, having it will make me feel better.

"A dagger would be perfect," I say as a gust of wind blows through the window and raises goose bumps on my skin, bringing an idea with it. "The season is turning. I'll need my cloak soon."

His brow furrows. "I suppose so," he says.

I smile. "How are your sewing skills, Blaise?"

"Abysmal," he says, though his eyes lighten. "But Heron's fingers are surprisingly nimble for such a big fellow. Part giant, isn't that right, Heron?"

"I'm big enough to crush you," Heron shoots back from behind his wall, but there's only good humor in his voice.

"Could you sew a dagger into the hem of my cloak?" I ask him.

"Easily," he says.

"Thank you," I say to both of them before smoothing my hands over my skirt. "How do I look?" I ask Blaise.

"Lower that neckline half an inch and he doesn't stand a chance," he tells me with a smirk.

I give him an annoyed shove toward the door, but when he's gone, I do it anyway.

Before seeking out Søren, I stop by Crescentia's rooms. I rarely visit her quarters for fear of having to see her father, but the Theyn is still *inspecting* the Water Mine, making sure everyone there remembers their place. He'll bring back a few new gems for Cress, as he usually does. It's no accident that her collection of Spiritgems rivals even that of the Kaiserin.

Which is why I'm hoping she won't miss a few now. If our plan has even a sliver of a chance of succeeding, my Shadows need gems.

Elpis answers the door and gives me a shy smile before leading me through the gilded maze of rooms that make up the Theyn's suite. These were Blaise's family's rooms once, but I doubt even he would recognize them now. The entire suite is a living crypt of all the countries the Theyn has brought to ruins.

Most of it comes from Astrea—the burnished brass chandelier hanging from the ceiling that once hung in my mother's study, the gold-framed mirror crowned with the face of Belsimia, the goddess of love and beauty, that watched over the city's bathhouse—but there are other pieces that Crescentia had to explain to me. Candlesticks from Yoxi, painted bowls from Kota, a crystal vase from Goraki. The Theyn isn't a sentimental sort by anyone's definition, but he does like his souvenirs.

I once asked Cress how long it's been since the court was in Kalovaxia, because no one ever talks about it, but she didn't know. She said it must have been a few centuries and that, effectively, there was no Kalovaxia anymore. The winters had grown colder and longer until there were no other seasons, until nothing could grow there, until the livestock perished, until the Kalovaxians loaded up their boats and left for a better country. It didn't matter that it belonged to someone else; they took it by force and they reaped everything it had to offer—slaves, food, resources—and when they'd driven the country into the ground and there was nothing left, they found somewhere new and started the whole process again. And again, and again, and again.

Astrea was the first country they found with magic. Maybe that's why they've been here the longest, though I'd imagine even this country is starting to run low, both on gems and the people to mine them.

Elpis leads me down the hall to Crescentia's room, neither of us daring to speak. In the small space of the hallway, I feel confident enough of our privacy to reach out and give her arm a reassuring squeeze.

"You did well," I whisper.

Even in the dim lighting, I can see her face flush with pleasure.

"Is there anything else I can do, my lady?" she replies.

Elpis is the perfect asset—a girl no one would look twice at stationed in the house of the Theyn. My mind spins with the sort of things she could overhear, the things she could do. But the Theyn did not get to be the Theyn by being a fool.

Blaise's voice echoes in my mind. *"She's your responsibility, Theo."*

"Nothing just now," I tell her.

Disappointment flickers in her eyes, but she nods her head and knocks timidly on the door.

"Lady Thora here to see you, my lady," she says, her voice barely loud enough to be heard on the other side of the thick wooden door.

"Thora?" I can hear the excitement in Crescentia's voice from here. "Come in!" she calls.

I give Elpis a smile of thanks before pushing the door open and slipping inside.

Crescentia's room is large enough to house an entire family, and the space is dominated by a canopy bed hung in diaphanous white silk. The coverlet, I know, is embroidered with golden thread, but just now it's littered with so many pastel dresses that it's impossible to tell. She's sitting at her vanity, pots of cosmetics open and brushes scattered haphazardly. Her painted jewelry box—another artifact from some fallen land, I'm sure—is open and its contents are in disarray.

Cress herself is wild-eyed and flushed, though as far as I can tell she hasn't left her room yet today. There's a tray of half-eaten breakfast abandoned on her bed, and she's still wearing her nightgown. Her blond hair is down in a mess of frizzy waves that haven't yet been tamed and braided by her maids.

"Busy morning?" I ask, moving a discarded dress from a chaise lounge by her window and sitting down.

A grin breaks over her face. "I finally heard from the Prinz!

He sent a letter this morning inviting me . . . well, inviting *us* to have lunch with him. He's smart to avoid the impropriety of us being seen alone together, I suppose. Isn't it exciting?"

"It is," I say, trying to match her enthusiasm. Søren, it seems, isn't to be dissuaded, and I have to admit, this is a smart move on his part. Having Crescentia there as a buffer might not stop other courtiers from gossiping, but most of them won't be gossiping about me at least. Still, it seems cruel to use Cress as a shield, especially when she's imagining herself half in love with Søren already. But with my new plan buzzing loudly through my mind, I can't spare Cress's feelings more than a cursory thought. After all, she's more enamored with the idea of him than anything else, and if the plan goes right, he'll be dead before she realizes that. Cress will get to feel like one of the tragic heroines she likes to read about, and I think she'll enjoy that almost as much as a crown.

"I suppose you're trying to decide what you should wear?" I ask.

"I have nothing," she tells me with a dramatic sigh, gesturing widely to the rest of her room, where dozens of dresses lie in an array of colors and styles. Some of them are loosely draped Astrean gowns with delicate embroidery and jewel-encrusted fibulae. Others are traditionally Kalovaxian, with tailored waists and bell-shaped skirts that require steel cages and layers of petticoats, done in a heavier fabric like velvet or wool. There are so many dresses that counting them feels like trying to count all the stars in the sky, though I'm sure I've only ever seen her wear a fraction of them.

I pick up the dress I pushed aside and hold it up. It's a lavender gown I've never seen her wear before, cut simply with a swath of sheer fabric that sweeps across the velvet bodice and drapes over one shoulder. The neckline and hem are covered with hundreds of tiny sapphires arranged to look like flowers.

"What about this?" I ask.

"Hideous," she proclaims without really looking at it.

"I think the color would look lovely on you," I insist. "At least try it."

"There's no point. It's all hideous," she says. "What does the Prinz like? Do you know? What's his favorite color?"

"I don't know anything more about him than you do," I tell her with a laugh, hoping the lie isn't obvious. I might not know Søren's favorite color or what kind of women's fashions he likes, but I know he's kind and that he must be closer to his mother than his father or he wouldn't have gone to the Kaiserin to break off my engagement. I know that even though he's a great warrior, he doesn't enjoy the act of killing, the way most Kalovaxians do. He remembered the Astreans' names, after all, nine years after his father forced him to kill them.

I push those thoughts aside. I told Art and the others that I would be able to kill him when the time came, and I can't do that if I see him as a nice person.

"You sat with him at the banquet, though," Cress points out, a delicately sharpened edge coming into her voice. "And you seemed close at the harbor—you even called him by his given name."

She's jealous, I realize, and the idea seems almost funny to me. It isn't funny, of course. I'm *supposed* to be making Søren fall for me, and it seems like he's certainly taking more of an interest in me than Cress, but the jealousy still feels strange coming from her. This is the girl who gave me her hand-me-down dresses, who snuck me pieces of bread when the Kaiser withheld my dinner, who leveraged her own status to make sure other court girls didn't insult me to my face. I've been sheltered in her pity for most of my life; the idea of her being jealous of me feels absurd.

But she *is,* and I've given her plenty of reason to be. Guilt lodges deep in my stomach. It's not enough for me to change my mind, but it's there all the same.

I open my mouth but quickly close it again, unsure of what to say, exactly, to convince her that I'm no threat. Cress is always so good at telling when I'm lying, though.

"After the rebel's execution," I say after a moment, choosing my words carefully, "I was disturbed. There was so much blood and I felt sick about it. Søren found me afterward in the hall and I suppose he took pity on me. That's when he told me to call him Søren. And then I thanked him by vomiting all over him." I cover my face with my hands in a show of mortification.

"Oh, Thora," Cress sighs, and her expression shifts. She looks relieved, though she tries to hide it. "That's awful! How embarrassing." She takes my hand and pats it soothingly, pitying me once more.

"It was," I say. "But he was so nice about it. That's what we talked about at the banquet. I apologized and he said it was nothing to worry about. He's very kind."

Cress bites her lip. "But you don't like him, do you?"

"Absolutely not." I laugh, trying my best to seem surprised.

"He's a friend, I suppose, but that's it. And he's certainly not interested in me. Do you think a boy has ever fancied a girl after she vomited on him?"

Cress smiles, relief flooding her face before she glances at the strewn dresses again and frowns. "No idea of his favorite color, though?" she asks.

"He probably likes black best. Or gray. Something gloomy and serious," I say, and do my best impression of stone-faced Søren, furrowing my brow and pursing my lips. It's enough to make Cress giggle, though she quickly covers her mouth with her hand.

"Thora!" she exclaims, trying to come off as chiding but failing miserably.

"Honestly, though," I say. "Have you ever seen him smile?"

"No," she admits. "But being a warrior is an awfully serious business. My father doesn't smile much either."

Small as it is, hearing Søren likened to the Theyn is enough to remind me who he is and what he's capable of. Maybe he is kind, but how much blood is there on his hands? How many mothers has *he* killed?

I force a smile. "I'm only saying that you deserve someone who will make you happy," I tell her gently.

She thinks about it for a moment, chewing on her bottom lip. "Being a prinzessin will make me happy," she says decisively. "And being a kaiserin one day will make me happier."

She sounds so sure of the future in front of her that I almost envy her, even though if I have my say she will never get it. Guilt hits again, but I try to ignore it. I can't feel bad about Cress not getting her storybook ending when my people are dying. Instead, I reach for another dress, this one a pale blue Kalovaxian gown embroidered with gold flowers. I shake it out and hold it up.

"This is lovely, Cress," I tell her. "The color will bring out your eyes."

She considers it for a moment, eyes darting between the dress and me. The wheels of her mind are turning. "It's *boring*," she says finally before looking down at my dress. "I adore yours, though."

"This?" I glance down at the blood-orange Astrean chiton I'm wearing. "You gave this to me months ago, don't you remember? You said the color didn't suit you."

It was something she did often, ordering the tailor to make dresses she knew wouldn't suit her so that she had an excuse to pass them on to me. Most of my gowns were once Cress's, and they're far more wearable than the ones the Kaiser sends me, which are usually designed to keep my back bare and my scars visible.

"Did I?" she asks, frowning. "I think I might be able to pull it off." Her mouth purses before curving into a grin. "I have a splendid idea, Thora. Why don't I try your dress on and you can try on one of mine? Just to see how it looks?"

I cannot for the life of me imagine what would be fun about that, but the only reply I can give is to wholeheartedly agree.

The orange color of my dress looks garish on her, clashing with her rosy skin and yellow hair—which was the reason she never wore it when it was hers—but she isn't dissuaded. She turns every which way in front of her mirror, looking at her reflection from all angles with a critical pleat to her forehead and a glow in her eyes that I'd find frightening if I didn't know her as well as I do. It's a look she's inherited from her father, but while the Theyn gets it in the heat of battle, Crescentia wears hers in a different kind of war.

It's only when she has me don a gray velvet Kalovaxian dress that covers me from chin to wrists to ankles in one shapeless heap that I realize it's me she's waging war against. I don't doubt that she believed me about the Prinz, but I suppose Cress isn't one to leave anything to chance.

"That color looks so darling on you, Thora," she says. Her smile is sweet but false. She tilts her head thoughtfully, letting her slate gaze travel over me. "Why, you look positively Kalovaxian, if you ask me."

Her words rankle, but I try not to show it, forcing a smile instead. "Not nearly as pretty as you, of course," I say, telling her what she wants to hear. "The Prinz won't be able to take his eyes off you."

Her smile grows somewhat warmer as she calls for Elpis to come dress her hair. Her already minuscule sense of subtlety disappears when she instructs the girl to make it look like mine. Elpis gives me a brief, furtive look before setting to work heating up a pair of curling tongs in the dying embers of Crescentia's fireplace.

"You'll need something pretty to pin it back with," I tell Crescentia, taking the opportunity to flip open the lid of her jewelry box and rummage through her wealth of baubles.

Like most court women, her collection is largely made up of Water and Air Gems for beauty and grace, with a few Fire Gems mixed in for warmth during the winter months. Unlike most women, Crescentia has one or two Earth Gems as well.

Usually they're built into sword hilts or embedded in armor to give warriors extra strength, and court women have no use for them, but it isn't surprising the Theyn wanted his only child to take extra strength where she could get it.

I find a gold hairpin studded with Water Gems so dark they're nearly black and hold it up. "This would complement the dress prettily, don't you think?"

She glances at the pin in my hair, set with simple pearls, lips pursing thoughtfully. "If you like it so much, you wear it. I'll wear yours."

Too easy, I think, struggling to look put out. I slide the pin from my hair and pass it to her, replacing it with the Water Gem one. I'm not supposed to have Spiritgems, the Kaiser made that plain decades ago, but either Crescentia has forgotten or she doesn't care at the moment. Either way, I'm not about to remind her.

The Water Gems send a thrum beneath my skin, working all the way down to my toes. The power dances under my fingertips, begging me to call on it. I have no cause to change my appearance, no thirst for water, but the need to use the gems pulls at me until it fills my mind with a pleasant buzz that is never quite enough.

This temptation was never there before the siege, when only Guardians carried a single gem each, but I remember holding Ampelio's Fire Gem and feeling its power course through me. I remember him cautioning me never to use it, his usually jovial expression suddenly somber and heavy.

I push aside the memory and focus on the task at hand and sift through the jewel box again, pretending to look for earrings for Cress. As ugly as the dress is, I'm grateful for the long sleeves. They make it easy to slip an earring and a brace-let against my wrist, hidden from sight. Pressed up against my pulse, the Spiritgems find a steady rhythm I can't ignore, echoing my heartbeat.

My fingers linger on a Fire Gem, though I know there's no need for it. If the other gems buzz through me pleasantly, the Fire Gem feels like stepping into a familiar dream. Every-thing around me turns soft and light and comforting. It wraps around me like my mother's arms, and for the first time in a decade, I feel safe. I feel in control. I need it more than I need to breathe. With just an ounce of power, just a touch of fire, I could maybe hold my own in this nightmare. And if I truly am descended from Houzzah, how can calling on his power be considered sacrilege? But I asked my mother the same question once, and I still remember her answer.

"A Guardian must dedicate themselves to their god above all else, but being queen means dedicating yourself to your country above else. You cannot do both. You can love the gods, you can love me, you can love whomever you wish to love in this world, but Astrea will always come first. Every-one and everything else gets only the leftover scraps. That was Houzzah's gift to our family, but also his curse."

I know that she was right, even as I wish she weren't. It would be so much easier if I could call fire to my fingertips the way Ampelio could, but how would I be any different from my enemies then? I'm as untrained as any Kalovaxian, and most days I don't give the gods a second thought. I only pray to them when I need something. If I were to set foot in the mines and try to seek their favor, try to train to wield a Spirit-gem, the gods would surely strike me down.

Seeing the Kalovaxians wield power that they didn't earn, that they didn't sacrifice for, has always made me sick to my stomach. I will not go against my gods and risk their wrath. Besides, I am too much like the Kalovaxians already. This is the line I will not cross.

LUNCHEON

Søren set up the royal family's private terrace for our lunch and spared no luxury in his effort. The table is carved from solid marble and so heavy that I'm sure it took a small army—and a fair share of Earth Gems—to drag it out here from the formal dining room where it normally resides. On the table is a painted vase filled with fresh-cut marigolds at peak bloom and four gold place settings. All of it belonged to my mother once, and if I try hard enough, I can see her sitting there, across from me, sipping spiced honey coffee and talking about silly things like the weather and my lessons, blissfully unaware of the battalions closing in around us.

The sun is high in the sky when Cress and I step out onto the pavilion, and it streams through the red silk awning, casting the space in a garish light, but the view from here is breathtaking—all rolling ocean and cloudless sky and a few ships so small they're the size of my pinky nail.

So much distance, I think. In ten years, I've never gone farther from the palace than the harbor. It's easy to forget how big the world really is, but from here I can see miles and miles of ocean in three directions.

One day soon, I'll be free again.

Prinz Søren and Erik stand up when Cress and I approach, both of them dressed in traditional Kalovaxian suits. I wasn't expecting Erik, but I'm glad to see him. He treated me like a person, which is more than I can say about most Kalovaxians. It's difficult to say whether Erik or Søren looks more uncomfortable in the layers of silk and velvet, though I suppose it must be Erik. At least Søren's suit was made to fit him. Erik's is clearly secondhand, too tight in some places, too loose in others.

"Ladies," Søren says, bowing as we curtsy. "I'm glad you could join us. You remember Erik. From the ship?"

"Of course," I say. I don't have to look at Cress to see the blank expression on her face. She only had eyes for the Prinz that day. I doubt she could have picked Erik out from a crowd if she'd been asked to.

"It's good to see you again, Erik," I add with a smile.

His quick blue eyes dart between Cress and me in amusement. "You as well, Lady Thora. You both look lovely, of course," he says, pulling my chair out for me. When he goes to push me in, he drops his voice low so that only I can hear it. "Did you lose a bet of some kind?"

I stifle a grimace. "Crescentia was kind enough to lend me her dress."

"Yes," he says, barely holding back laughter. "*Very* kind."

"And let me guess," I say wryly, glancing at Cress, who's already drawn Søren deep into a conversation about a letter she received from her father. "Our Prinz was kind enough to invite you to enjoy a good meal before you set off to Vecturia?"

He lifts a dark eyebrow and drops his voice as well. "I was mistaken, Thora. It's only trade-route issues. Far less interesting."

He's as bad a liar as Søren, unable to look at me when he does it.

I fake a laugh. "Trade routes, Vecturia. To me, one is as interesting as the other. I don't even know where Vecturia is," I lie.

He smiles, relieved. "I won't lie to you, Thora. I've got a month or so of hardtack and watered-down ale to look forward to. Søren offered me a good last meal as a distraction today, and I couldn't take him up on it quick enough."

He glances pointedly to the other end of the table, where Crescentia and Søren are in conversation about the Theyn, though Søren's eyes keep darting about like he's searching for an escape. They meet mine briefly before slipping away again.

I turn back to Erik, raising an eyebrow. "They make a sweet couple, don't they?"

"I don't think *sweet* is the word Søren would use," Erik says, lowering his voice to a whisper. "The Kaiser has been pushing the match since Søren got back."

Søren clears his throat loudly across the table, shooting Erik a pleading glance. "Erik actually got his start with me under your father's command as well," he tells Cress. "Isn't that right, Erik?"

"Duty calls," Erik murmurs to me before leaning toward Cress.

"That's true, Lady Crescentia. I was twelve at the time. It felt like I was meeting a god," he says. "In fact, would you do me the honor of taking a walk around the pavilion while we wait for food to arrive? I can tell you stories about him you'd find quite amusing."

Cress frowns, eyes narrow. She's about to refuse with some excuse or other, but Søren cuts her off.

"Erik is the most gifted storyteller, Lady Crescentia," he says. "I think you would enjoy walking with him for a moment."

Crescentia's nostrils narrow—the only outward sign of her displeasure, and one that likely went unnoticed by Søren and Erik. With a gracious smile, she rises and takes Erik's proffered arm, allowing him to escort her to the edge of the pavilion, casting a wary glance at me over her shoulder.

Søren reaches for the crystal wine decanter and moves his chair a few inches closer to mine as he pours me a glass, the liquid as red as fresh blood. He doesn't look at me, instead focusing on the task at hand and taking his time with it. A lock of golden hair falls into his eyes, but he makes no move to push it aside.

I'm painfully aware of Cress just a few feet away. Though she's out of earshot and politely listening to Erik's story about his first battle under the Theyn's command, her eyes dart to me every few seconds, wary and suspicious.

The whole court wants to see Søren and Cress married, it seems. Cress and her father certainly want it, and Erik said the Kaiser was pushing for it as well. The only one dragging his feet about it is Søren, and I don't understand why. Kalovaxian marriages are never about love—that's what affairs are for. Marriages are about power, and as such, marrying Cress should suit Søren just fine.

"Thank you," I say to him when my glass is full.

His bright blue eyes snap to mine and linger for a moment before he shakes his head and drops his gaze. He knows I'm not thanking him for the wine, but for talking to his mother for me, for saving me from becoming Lord Dalgaard's latest victim.

"Don't mention it," he says. I can't tell if it's modesty or a command.

We lapse into a tense silence again, full of things that can't be said, lies that I'm worried he'll see through. Just over an hour ago, I was casually planning to murder him, but sitting across from him now—a living, breathing person—it seems impossible. I fear my plots are written across my face. Finally the silence becomes unbearable and I settle instead for almost-truths.

"I don't think I've ever spoken to your mother privately before. It was . . . enlightening. I like her."

"She likes you, too," he says.

Across the pavilion, Cress's looks are getting more pointed, her eyes boring into me no matter how many reassuring smiles I give her. I angle away from Søren, deciding to stop looking at him as well. Which makes my job even more difficult; Søren will be leaving again soon, so my time is limited.

I can make it up to Cress later, ply her with excuses and flattery and delusions about Søren really being interested in her. For the first time in ten years, I let my own needs take precedence over Cress's.

Playing the damsel in distress always leaves me with a sour taste in my mouth, but I can't deny its effectiveness.

"I asked a lot of you when I asked you to stop my engagement," I whisper, making my voice small and fractured, like a dam about to break. "I'm so grateful that you did, truly, but I would hate to think doing so caused trouble for you. I just want to apologize—"

"You never have to apologize to me," he interrupts, startled. He lowers his voice. "After everything that's been done to you, the scars on your back, the things he's made you do. You should hate him. You should hate *me*."

"I don't hate you," I tell him, and I'm surprised to realize it's the truth. Whatever I feel for Søren, it isn't hate.

Pity, maybe.

Heron's voice echoes in my mind, asking me if I was capable of killing Søren. Yes, I'd told him then, and that's what the answer still has to be. Pity or no pity.

Søren's eyes search my face, but now I can't look at him. I keep my gaze trained on the gold silk tablecloth, remembering my mother's dark, freckled hands smoothing it down, tugging at its corners so that it lay flat. She always fidgeted when she was nervous, and I've inherited that habit. It takes all my self-control to keep my hands motionless in my lap, not to twist my napkin or twirl the stem of my wineglass. The Spiritgems are still caught firmly between the sleeve of my dress and my skin, but I'm worried that any movement will set them loose and I'll have no way to explain that.

Crescentia has stopped even pretending to pay attention to Erik, though he's gesturing wildly as he tells some exaggerated story. Her eyes are locked on mine, sharp, suspicious, and a touch resentful.

I sit up a little straighter and turn away from Søren's surprised face. "Cress," I say, infusing my voice with warmth and camaraderie, hoping it's enough to make her forgive me for monopolizing Søren's attention. "Come tell the Prinz about the book your father brought you from his voyage to Elcourt. The one about the one-handed knight?"

Crescentia leaves Erik behind without hesitation, hurrying back to the table and retaking her seat on Søren's other side, Erik retaking his own seat a moment later. Her face flushes with delight and she launches into a description of the folktale and the illustrations that accompanied it. Søren, for his part, listens raptly but I can barely pay attention to a word she's saying. The small distance between Søren and me no longer feels cramped with things unsaid. Now, it's full of unspoken promises.

I try not to look at him, not wanting to cause any more tension between Cress and me, but it's impossible not to. When our eyes catch halfway through lunch, it sends my heart racing.

Because I'm succeeding, I tell myself. I have him where I want him and soon—so soon—I'll be free. But that's not it, not entirely. There's more to Søren than I like to let myself think, and as much of a traitor as it makes me, I like him.

When the time comes, I'll still kill him. I just might feel a little bit guiltier about it than I thought I would.

PINCH

———— • ————

BACK IN MY ROOM, I slip the pin from my hair and examine
it. The Water Gems glint in the dim candlelight, a dark,
inky blue like the deepest part of the ocean. It's riskier to hold
on to it than the other jewelry I took, since Cress knows I have
it, but I wouldn't be surprised if that detail slipped through
the fairly spacious grates of Crescentia's mind.

As soon as I think it, guilt pools in my gut. Kalovaxian
as she might be, Cress is my only real friend among them.
Her behavior today might not have been gracious, but if our
friendship were a set of scales, today would be a raindrop
against an ocean, and I can't even blame her for it.

All Cress's life, her father has pushed her toward the Prinz,
filling her head with ideas of herself as a prinzessin and eventually a kaiserin. It's been a path carved for her since she was
still in the cradle, so of course she's going to fight for it. In
a strange way, I respect her for it. The Crescentia I thought I
knew wasn't much of a fighter at all.

I sit down on the edge of my bed and slip the other pieces
of jewelry I took from Cress's box from the sleeve of my
dress. Twenty Air Gems make up the chandelier earring, each

the size of a freckle, and the Earth Gems in the bracelet are even smaller, flecks of dust, practically, that blend into the gold chain of the bracelet almost seamlessly. Along with the pin, they're small enough to fit in one hand, but I can feel the slight buzz of power licking at the skin of my palm. For someone who's been gifted by the gods, they'll be much more powerful.

"I didn't realize you were such a fan of jewelry, Theo," Blaise's voice comes from the wall.

I look to the small hole and grin. "Actually, they're presents for you," I tell him, standing back up and walking toward his wall. I thread the bracelet through the hole.

"Not really my style," he says before giving a sharp inhale when the power hits him.

"Look closer."

"How did you . . ." He trails off.

"Crescentia has quite a collection. I'm hoping she won't notice a few things missing. Can you use it?" I ask.

He hesitates for a few heartbeats. "I think so," he says.

"What's going on?" Artemisia asks.

I cross to her wall. "Don't worry, I haven't forgotten about you two," I say, slipping the hairpin through her hole and then the earring through Heron's.

"A bit small, but it'll do," Artemisia says. "Strange setting, though, isn't it?"

"The Kalovaxian courtiers like to wear them as jewelry," I explain. "Water Gems for beauty, Air Gems for grace, Fire Gems for warmth, Earth Gems for strength."

"You're joking," Heron says, spitting the words out like they're poisonous. "They use them as *jewelry*?"

"Very *expensive* jewelry, as I understand it," I add. "They sell them for a fortune to countries in the North."

"Believe me, I hate the Kalovaxians as much as anyone, but I'm not sure I understand the difference," Artemisia says. "Ampelio wore his gem as a necklace, and so did all the other Guardians."

"A pendant," I correct, at the same time as Blaise and Heron.

"It was *earned,* not bought," Blaise says. "And it meant something, not just decoration. It was an honor, not a fashion trend."

"It was a symbol of the gods' favor," Heron adds, more force in his voice than I've heard from him. "If there was ever any doubt about the Kalovaxians being denied an Afterlife . . ." He trails off, the gems of the earring clinking lightly as he turns it over in his hands.

Artemisia snorts. "If the gods cared about any of this—or exist at all, for that matter—surely they would have stepped in by now."

The casual disdain in her words takes me by surprise, and from the stunned silence that follows her words, I know I'm not alone in that.

"You're a Guardian," I point out finally. "Surely you believe in the gods."

She's quiet for a long moment. "I believe in surviving," she says, but there is a sharpness in her voice that keeps me from asking more. "That's been hard enough."

"But you were blessed," Blaise says. "We all were. We were given power."

"I don't know if I've ever felt blessed," she admits. "I was given power, I can't deny that, but I have a hard time imagining it was given by gods. I figured it was something more chemical. Something in my blood—and yours—made us better receptors for the magic in the mines than other people."

"You believe it was just chance?" Heron asks, bewildered. "We were chosen more or less at random and others weren't?"

I hear her shift behind her wall. "It's better than the alternative, in my view," she says brusquely. "Why would the gods choose to bless me over everyone else in that mine? There were children there who went mine-mad. I can't believe there are gods who would spare me and kill them, and if they do exist, I want nothing to do with them." Her voice is all hard edges, but there's an undercurrent of pain there.

I might not know Artemisia well, but I know if I asked her about it, she'd stab me with that hairpin before I could finish the question.

Through the wall, I can almost feel Blaise's thoughts running the same path as mine. Throughout the past decade, the idea of the After has been all that's kept me going, and I don't have to ask Blaise to know that a part of him yearns for it as well. I've imagined my mother there, waiting for me. I've dreamt about her arms wrapping around me once again, the smell of flowers and earth still clinging to her, the way it did when she was alive.

It's one of the things I think of to stave off the temptation to use a Fire Gem. Tempting as that power may be, using a gem without the proper training—without being chosen by the gods—is sacrilege, and sacrilegious souls aren't allowed into the After. They're doomed to wander the earth as shades for the rest of eternity.

But I can't deny that Artemisia's words have lodged deep in my gut. There's a measure of truth in them that I can't deny—why *would* the gods allow us to suffer like we have for the last decade? Why wouldn't they have struck the Kalovaxians down as soon as they set foot on Astrean soil? Why didn't they protect us?

I don't like that I'm asking these questions. I don't like that I have no answers. Blaise and Heron must be similarly at a loss, because we lapse into silence.

When it gets to be too much, I clear my throat. "Well, I'm sure you're glad to know your labor in the mines was for such a pretty cause," I say, changing the subject. It must be close to teatime now, which means Hoa will be in soon with a tray of tea and snacks for me, since I don't have any other plans for the afternoon. "All of you turn away, I need to get out of this hideous thing."

I tug at the dress. It'll be difficult to get off without assistance, but the neck and sleeves are so tight it's difficult to breathe, and the heavy velvet itches. Hoa might only be a few more minutes, but I'm not sure I want to wait even that long.

"I wouldn't change into anything too comfortable," Blaise says, his voice muffled, hopefully because his face is turned away from me. "I have a feeling the Prinz will be paying you a visit later tonight."

My hands freeze at the buttons at the base of my neck. "What do you mean?"

"After lunch, he pulled me aside and asked me if there were any other entrances to your room," Blaise says.

"He pulled you aside?" I ask, alarmed.

"My hood was drawn—he didn't see my face," Blaise assures me.

I pause. "*Are* there other entrances to my room?" I ask, glancing around.

"One," Blaise says. "Ampelio told me about it. He was planning to use it to rescue you as soon as he could figure out a way to get past the harbor without notice."

"Oh." I feel a pang of longing. How different would my life have been if he'd found a way in? "Why would Søren want to sneak into my room?" I ask before I can dwell too long on that thought.

Heron laughs, a sound so deep it practically shakes the walls. "He's leaving tomorrow for who knows how long, and the two of you barely had a chance to speak at lunch. He had more to say to you, and I doubt he's the sort to wait weeks or even months to say it."

"Good," I say, managing to undo the buttons at my neck. With the collar loose, I should be able to breathe again, but the prospect of seeing Søren tonight makes it just as difficult as the dress had. Somehow I doubt he'll only want to talk, but the idea of doing anything more ties my stomach in knots. I clear my throat and try to hide my discomfort. "I have more to say to him as well if I'm going to turn him against his father."

I'm playing the game, I remind myself, and if a small part of me believes the lie, that only makes it more effective. So long as the larger part of me remembers what's real. I'll gather information. I'll turn him against his father. And when the time is right, I'll slit his throat and start a civil war. The idea makes me queasy, even if it was mine to begin with, but I hope the more I think it, the easier it will become.

"Hopefully, you'll be doing more than just talking, of course," Artemisia drawls, each word dripping in condescension. "You're meant to be making him fall in love with you, and that takes more than just words."

"I know that," I say, keeping my voice carefully detached. She's trying to rile me, and I'm not about to let her see how riled I am. I search through my wardrobe for something more appropriate. Something that looks casual enough, like I'm not expecting company, but still pretty. I settle for a simple chiton of turquoise blue tied at the waist with a wide gold sash. I undo the rest of the buttons on Cress's dress and let it fall to the floor before pulling the chiton over my head and tying it into place. "You can look now."

"I suppose Art's right," Blaise says, though he sounds uncomfortable. I hear him shifting behind the wall, the tap of his feet on the stone floor. "That *is* the goal, isn't it?"

It takes me a moment to realize he's asking a genuine question, but before I can respond, Heron jumps in.

"Kissing him shouldn't be too much of a challenge. He's handsome enough, for a Kalovaxian," he adds.

I shake my head. "It isn't that. I'll do what I have to. It's just . . ." I'm embarrassed to say it out loud. "I suppose I don't know *what* I'm doing."

"Whatever you're doing seems to be working just fine," Blaise answers.

"That's words, though. That's running and trusting that he's going to give chase. I've never really thought about what to do when he catches me," I admit.

Silence follows my confession, broken finally by Artemisia.

"Have you ever kissed a boy before?" she asks.

The question takes me off guard and makes my cheeks heat up.

"No," I admit. "There hasn't exactly been a wealth of opportunity. Apart from Crescentia—and now Søren—the Kalovaxians rarely show me any kindness. Certainly no romantic interest."

The Kaiser's leering grin surfaces in my mind and I can hear the Kaiserin's words echoing. *I've seen him look at you. . . . He isn't exactly subtle, is he?* But whatever *that* is, it isn't remotely romantic. It's something else that congeals in the pit of my stomach like rotten milk. I must look as queasy as I feel, because Heron laughs again.

"Come now, kissing the Prinz won't be *that* bad, surely," he says.

"I don't know," Artemisia adds tersely. "I wouldn't want the first person *I* kissed to be the son of the man who ruined my country. I'd want to vomit, too."

"He's not," Blaise says, his voice so quiet I don't understand him at first.

"You can't really be defending the Kaiser, Blaise," I say, sinking onto my bed and flopping back to look at the canopied ceiling. "Artemisia's summation is, if anything, frightfully kind."

Blaise clears his throat. "No. I'm saying that it won't be your first kiss."

It takes a moment for the words to make sense and another for me to understand exactly what he's talking about. It was so long ago all I really remember is the garden in full bloom, Blaise's rounder, unscarred face, and curiosity. I prop myself up on my elbows and look in the direction of Blaise's wall, wishing I could see his face now. It hardly seems fair that he can see mine. Is he blushing? His face used to get bright red when he was angry, but I don't know if I ever saw him embarrassed.

"That doesn't count," I tell him.

"What doesn't?" Artemisia asks.

Blaise doesn't answer her, so I do. "When we were younger—five or so—we saw other people kiss, you know, in the gardens and at banquets. Astrea wasn't nearly so prudish before the Kalovaxians invaded. And . . . well . . . I suppose we decided to try it out for ourselves—"

"No, doesn't count," Artemisia says before I can finish.

"A kiss is a kiss," Blaise mutters.

"Spoken like someone who's never had a real one either," she says with a snort.

"All right," Blaise says, and I can almost hear the scowl in his voice. "Enough idle talk. Artemisia, you have your meeting with the Kaiser tonight, and with Theo's present, it should be easy enough to get through."

"I could do it in my sleep," she says. "I'll just tell him that Theo—I mean *Thora*—is being a good little girl and not doing anything terribly interesting. Should be over quickly."

"After that, I need you to sneak down to the cypress grove and meet with your mother—see if she's made up her mind. You know how she can be. If she's going to beat the Prinz to Vecturia, she's going to need to leave tonight at the latest."

"My mother's ship is faster than any Kalovaxian vessel," she says with a sniff.

"And she'll have farther to go if she's going to warn all of the islands. I'd rather not take chances. Heron, can you use the Air Gems to make yourself invisible?" he asks.

"Easily," Heron says.

"Good. Why don't you explore the castle tonight? See what you can overhear."

"Finally," he says with a loud exhale. "No offense, Theo, but this room is too small for me."

"No offense taken," I assure him.

"While you're out, Artemisia, can you get Theo a dagger? Something thin and light that can be concealed easily?" Blaise continues.

"Of course I can," she says, sounding almost offended that he had to ask.

"If either of you isn't back by sunrise . . ." He trails off. I wait for him to finish. What is he going to do? Send people after them? Go looking himself? He doesn't seem to know either, because after a moment, he sighs. "Just be back by sunrise."

"Yes, sir," Heron says. Artemisia echoes him, a beat later and far more sarcastically.

There's a shuffling and the sounds of the stone doors sliding open and closed. Soft footsteps echo down the hall in opposite directions. And then it's only Blaise and me, and I am acutely aware of his presence. I can almost hear his breathing, his heartbeat.

"You don't have to go through with this," he says after a moment. "Say the word, Theo, and I'll take you out of this place. We can sail far away from here, make allies, gather forces, and attack when we know we're strong enough."

It's a tempting offer, but I shake my head.

"Have you heard of Goraki?" I ask. His silence tells me he hasn't, so I continue. "It's a small country east of here, smaller than Astrea. Or it was. That's where the Kalovaxians were before they came to Astrea. They don't talk about it much; I suppose most of them have all but forgotten its name by now. Crescentia remembers it a bit, though, and she's told me some things. It's where she was born—where the Prinz was, too, I'd expect. Cress said they didn't have any magic, but they were known for the quality of their silks. So the Kalovaxians came and they conquered, just like they did with us. They enslaved the people they didn't outright kill and made most of them harvest silk to sell around the world until there was nothing left to sell. When they left, they set fire to everything they could and found somewhere new to drive to ruins. They found us."

"Theo . . . ," Blaise starts.

"They know what they're doing, Blaise," I say, my voice shaking. "They've done this to other countries—more countries than I can name. And they'll do it to us. Goraki lasted ten years. How long do you think we'll last before the mines run dry and we become worthless to them?"

He doesn't answer.

"My plan is a good start. You know it is and you know it can work, and if it does, the Kalovaxians will be divided, fighting each other until another royal family comes out triumphant. When we put together an army and attack, they'll be the weak ones. It's our best chance, and it might be the only one we get."

He doesn't say anything for a moment, and I wonder if he's going to argue. "I'm coming in," he says instead.

I don't protest. I don't really want to. Dangerous as it is, having him near me is also reassuring. When I can see him and touch him, I'm somewhat more confident that he isn't something a mad part of me made up.

I can hear him slip from his guardroom, his sword clattering to the floor and his heavy boots stumbling over the stone floors. My door creaks open as he comes inside. I have no lock, but he closes it firmly behind him before turning to look at me.

"You're hiding something," he says.

I'm hiding so many things. The Kaiserin's warning, my growing feelings for Søren, the genuine nature of my friendship with Crescentia. Even if I wanted to tell him what was wrong, I would have no idea where to begin. It's easier for both of us if I keep lying.

I give a shaky laugh. "I'm just worried. Can you blame me for that? I feel like I'm balancing on the edge of a cliff and even a slight breeze will push me over." He opens his mouth and I know he's going to offer to pull me out again. I'm not sure I'll be able to say no twice. "I have it well in hand, though. You've seen it yourself. They all underestimate me and they won't see it coming until my knife is buried in their backs."

When we were children, we would play a game where we would each pinch each other on the soft underside of our arms to see who would react first, who would cry out or pull away or even blink. This feels like that. Which one of us will show our fear first? It won't be me. I hold his gaze and set my jaw, trying to radiate a confidence that I don't feel.

He sighs and drops his gaze. "You're doing well, but I can't help but think that if Ampelio were here, he would flay me alive for agreeing to this plan. I promised him I'd keep you safe, not send you into the arms of the enemy."

"Søren was your idea, Blaise, and it was a good one." I hesitate, focusing on the wall behind him. If I look at him, I'm sure he'll see my secrets laid bare. "He's not his father. He isn't cruel."

"I think you're right," he says after a breath. "But Artemisia is right, too. Your first kiss shouldn't be with him."

I look back at him, surprised. His eyes are suddenly locked on mine with such intensity that I can't look away. I don't want to.

"You said my first kiss was with you," I point out, surprised at how quickly my heart is beating all of a sudden.

"Well," he says, taking a step toward me. Then another one. He only stops when there are mere inches separating us. When he continues, his voice is barely louder than a whisper and I can feel his warm breath against my cheek. "I was told that didn't count."

His mouth moves closer to mine. I want to push him away, but I also want to pull him closer, though that desire surprises me. When did that happen? He's my friend—the oldest, and in some ways truest, one I have. But there's something more between us as well. Blaise terrifies me, but he also makes me feel safe. He reminds me of my life before, when I was cared for and protected and unscarred and surrounded by people I loved. How can a person be so many different things? How can he make me feel so many different things?

Before I can think myself out of it, I tilt my head up to brush my lips against his. Because he's right and Artemisia is right: my first kiss shouldn't be with Søren. Even if he is different from his father, he's still one of them and there are parts of me I won't give them.

For a second, Blaise doesn't move and it feels almost exactly like how we kissed as children, like we're going through the motions without any actual want. Just when I'm ready to pull away, his mouth softens against mine and he's kissing me back. His warm hands grip my waist and bring me closer to him, their heat seeping through the silk of my dress. When he draws back, he stays close enough that I can still feel his breath against my lips.

"I think even Artemisia would agree *that* counted," I say lightly, reaching up to touch his face.

He releases my waist and catches my hand in his. Something dark flickers over his expression and his grip tightens until it almost hurts.

"The Prinz will be here soon, I'm sure," he says, dropping my hand. "Don't do anything stupid tonight."

The words come out hard, but I'm beginning to understand Blaise enough to know that he means them teasingly, like he used to tease me when we were children. The years since then have robbed him of that lightness, instilled everything around him with a weight that feels suffocating if you get too close.

I laugh, but his expression remains unreadable, which is doubly unfair considering how my own doubt and hurt must be starkly written across my face. Cress and I have often talked about kisses—who we wanted them with, how we wanted them to go. She dreamed of a first kiss with the Prinz on their wedding day, like in one of her books. My imaginings were less picturesque, but they were certainly more than this. I never thought whoever I kissed would regret it the way Blaise seems to. He won't even look at me.

Embarrassment rises hot to my cheeks, but I force a smile and try not to let him see it.

"Not to worry, I was saving *stupid* for tomorrow, or maybe next week. I haven't decided yet," I reply.

He manages a smile, but he still doesn't look at me. When he turns to leave, I'm tempted to call after him, but his name dies in my throat. I doubt he would have listened anyway, whether I'm his queen or not.

VISITOR

———•———

Blaise used to hate having me trail after him everywhere when we were young. He ran, he hid, he called me names, but still I wouldn't leave him alone. We were exploring a tunnel in the abandoned dungeons below the palace when his patience finally ran out. He shut me in the tunnel and closed the door. I was in there only ten minutes when Birdie found me crying, but it was the most trouble he'd ever gotten in.

"She'll be your queen one day," his father told him later. I don't remember Blaise's father as an angry man. He was the rare sort of person who listened far more often than he spoke, and never raised his voice. That day, however, was the fiercest I'd seen him. "If you want to be a Guardian, you protect her with everything you have, because without her there is no Astrea."

I can't help but think about that day now, after Hoa has brought and whisked away both tea and dinner. Now the only thing left to do is wait to see if Søren will show up. Artemisia and Heron are still out, so it's only Blaise behind his wall, and we haven't spoken since he left my room hours ago. The quiet is awkward and heavy, like a wool cloak in the dead heat of summer. I feel like that child again, clinging to him when he wants nothing to do with me, even though I know that isn't true. He's here, he's helping me, he wouldn't do that if he didn't care. But maybe he's thinking of his father's decree to protect me. Maybe it's his loyalty to my royal blood that keeps him here, not me as a person.

The idea of it frustrates me.

He had been the one to come into my room—even sending the others away first. *He* had been the one to bring up our childhood kiss. *He* had started it. I want to say something about it, but it would only lead to another argument and I'm so tired of fighting with him.

My mother always shrugged off her romances, picking a new favorite for each season, though Ampelio was usually close and never fully out of favor.

Not for the first time, I wonder how she did it. I only have to worry about the feelings of two boys and I already feel like I'm being pulled apart at the seams. It should be simple: one is my ally, one is my enemy. In a perfect world, that's all either of them would ever be in order to keep things uncomplicated, but there doesn't seem to be any hope of that now. I can still feel Blaise's lips, warm and soft against mine, even as I look at my reflection in the mirror and wonder what Søren will think when he sees me.

If he sees me. It must be nearly midnight now and there's no sign that Søren is going to come after all. Blaise and the others must have been wrong.

"Why don't you like Dragonsbane?" I ask Blaise when the silence gets to be too much.

"I like her just fine," he says, clearly taken aback.

"You don't, though," I press. "Every time she's mentioned, you look uncomfortable. She's always your last option. You don't trust her, but she's saved so many lives—"

"If they could afford to be saved," he says before sighing. "I'm not . . . I get it. It's expensive, keeping her ship running and her crew fed. I can't begrudge her for needing reimbursement, but I've seen people die because they couldn't afford her help. And the attacks on the Kaiser—"

"She's been a thorn in his side since the siege, you can't deny that."

"Can't I?" he asks. "Ampelio did often enough over the years. Those ships she attacked, the cargo ships? Who do you think crewed them? A handful of Kalovaxians and ten times as many Astrean slaves. Who do you think took lifeboats out before the ships sank? Who do you think drowned in chains?" His voice has turned hard and angrier than I've ever heard it.

My stomach clenches at the idea of Astreans drowning in chains, helpless and afraid.

"I never thought about that," I admit quietly.

He gives a slow exhale. "She's done a lot of good, I won't deny that. But the price . . . Ampelio thought it was too high, and I agree with him."

Before I can reply, a knock comes, soft and tentative.

"Theo?" Blaise whispers, suddenly still behind his wall.

"I heard it," I say just as quietly, rolling out of bed and smoothing my dress down before walking toward my door. I'm halfway there when the knock sounds again, a little louder and not coming from the door at all. It's coming from my wardrobe. I grab the nearest thing—a brass candlestick set on the bedside table—with my heart pounding against my ribs. The other entrance. I realize Søren must have found it.

But how long has he been in there? And what did he hear? The thought sends me into a fresh panic, and I clutch the candlestick tighter.

The porcelain knob rattles; then the armoire door swings open and Søren tumbles out, barely managing to land on his feet. Clumsy as it is, there's a surprising amount of grace in the exit, especially considering that the wardrobe seems far from big enough to hold his broad frame. My dresses have been pushed to either side, and behind him, in the back of the armoire, I can just make out the opening of a tunnel.

A tunnel in my armoire is certainly helpful to know about, though I'm embarrassed that I've never found it myself. Not that there was ever much of an opportunity to snoop before, with my old Shadows always watching.

But how long has he been in there? If he overheard Blaise and me talking, I'll have a difficult time explaining that away.

"Søren?" I say, doing my best impression of being surprised. I drop my arm to my side and try to hide the panic coursing through me. "What are you doing here?"

He straightens up, and his bright blue eyes move from my face, to my dress, to the candlestick in my hand. There's no suspicion there, I notice. If he'd heard me talking about Dragonsbane as an ally, he wouldn't look nearly so amused. I almost sag with relief, but manage to keep my expression surprised.

"Sorry, I planned this to go a bit more smoothly." He scratches at the back of his neck and gives me a sheepish smile. "Were you talking to someone?"

I glance at Blaise's wall and give Søren a shrug. "My Shadows," I explain, gesturing to the walls. "I heard a noise and got a bit frightened."

He frowns and glances at the walls in turn. "Your Shadows are here? Even when you sleep?"

My laugh is light and flirtatious. "I'm a very dangerous girl, Your Highness. The Kaiser wants to make sure I don't incite rebellions or sneak off with crown prinzes."

"Ah," he says, and though the room is lit only by the moonlight coming through the window, I can almost swear I see his cheeks redden. "Do you think they can be persuaded to look the other way for a night?" he asks.

"Maybe if you ask nicely," I say before pitching my voice lower. "Why? Were you planning on inciting a rebellion tonight?"

Søren's eyes glint with amusement in the moonlight before he turns his attention back to the walls. "I'm taking Lady Thora on a stroll. We'll be back in a couple hours' time. I can manage to keep her out of trouble until then," he says in a voice I now recognize as his commanding Prinz voice.

"Are you certain?" I tease. "It's a pretty sizable job."

"Whose side are you on?" he asks.

I know he's joking, but the words send a jolt through me anyway, reminding me I need to be careful.

"The Kaiser won't like it," Blaise interrupts. He's pitched his voice lower and it sounds raspier. If I didn't know it was him, I would assume the voice belonged to someone older. Someone unused to speaking.

"The Kaiser doesn't have to know," Søren says. "And I'll see to it that you're handsomely rewarded."

Blaise hesitates, as if he's actually thinking it over. "Two hours," he says finally.

Søren nods, triumphant, and steps toward me, taking the candlestick from my hand and crossing to the dying fireplace, crouching with his back to me. When he stands up again, the candle is lit. "Come on, then," he says, coming toward me and slipping his hand around mine, pulling me toward the tunnel in the back of the wardrobe. "We don't have much time, and I want to show you something."

"Oh, what could it be?" I ask innocently. "Troops? Weapons? What else does a rebellion need?"

He glances at the walls before shooting me a warning look. "Careful, or they might change their minds," he says, but he hasn't lost the mirth in his eyes. Despite myself, I can feel a dose of giddiness coursing through me as well. His enthusiasm is contagious and his callused hand around mine is raising delightful goose bumps on my skin. I hope Blaise can't see the effect Søren is having on me, or if he can that he thinks it's just an act.

See? I want to say. *I can flirt with whomever I like, kiss whomever I like. It doesn't mean anything with him and it didn't mean anything with you.*

I need to get away from him as quickly as possible, so I follow Søren to the wardrobe. He holds the door open for me, but before I step inside, he draws me against him, shielding me from Blaise's gaze. His head ducks so that our foreheads are nearly touching.

"You look beautiful," he tells me, his voice barely louder than a breath.

He says it shyly, in a way that makes me wonder if he's ever said that to anyone before. A wave of triumph washes over me. After all, there is no mistaking a comment like that for something platonic. He does actually like me. I try to ignore the other reactions his words bring out in me—the heat that rises to my cheeks, the goose bumps that rise on my arms.

"Really?" I ask, tilting my head and raising an eyebrow. "And here I was just thinking I should have kept on that gray dress."

He gives a snort and motions me through the small doorway at the back of the wardrobe that's just big enough to crawl through.

AMINET

—◆•◆—

THE TUNNEL IS NARROW FOR a good five minutes of crawling before it becomes tall enough to walk hunched over, single file. Another ten after that, it becomes the size of a regular hallway, like the tunnel I used when I first met up with Blaise. Søren falls into step beside me. We pass entrances to more tunnels as we walk, spidering out to who knows where. Tunnels that Blaise and I never found when we were young but that might prove useful now.

Though the candle isn't bright enough to fill the whole tunnel, it casts a small circle of light around me and Søren. It's enough to see that Søren has grime smeared across his cheek and sprinkled through his fair hair. Judging by the way he smiles at me, I'm sure I'm in similar shape, but I don't mind. I prefer dirt to ashes, at least. I try to ignore the fluttering in my stomach that his smile sets off, but it's such a rare sight on him that I can't help but smile back.

"You have something . . . ," I start, reaching up to brush the dirt from his cheek. His skin is cool under my fingertips, and rough from the ghost of stubble that lingers there. His eyes meet mine and I suddenly feel shy. I drop my hand and quicken my pace. "How did you find this tunnel, anyway?" I ask him.

"The palace is full of tunnels," he says, catching up with me. "It's just a matter of looking for them. This one goes to my room as well, and a few other rooms in the north wing. There's one tunnel that I think goes to the dungeon, but I haven't tried that one."

"I'm a bit embarrassed I never realized there was a door in my wardrobe," I admit.

"Well, I suppose with your Shadows watching, you can hardly do much exploring," he points out. I can't very well tell him that I explored plenty before the siege, so I say nothing, and after a moment, he continues. "Are they always there? Your Shadows?"

"Always," I say with a sigh that I hope comes off as mournful but not whiny. "That's why they're called Shadows."

"Even when you sleep, though? Even when you change clothes?" He frowns.

"There's not much I can do about it," I say, hoping he doesn't take his chivalry to the next level and try to rid me of them. I'm not sure how I could talk him out of it without sounding suspicious. "Rumor has it that they're eunuchs, anyway. The Kaiser doesn't want to risk anyone damaging his property," I add with a meaningful look. Even in the warm candlelight, he looks a little green. I wonder if he's noticed his father's interest in me like the Kaiserin said he had, but I can't bring myself to ask.

"Where are we going, Søren?" I ask instead.

"A little farther," he says, walking ahead of me a few steps and feeling along the stone walls.

I frown. "Is that all you'll tell me?" I ask.

He glances back at me over his shoulder and smiles. "I thought the element of surprise would appeal to your sense of adventure," he says.

"What makes you so sure I have one?" I volley back.

"Call it a hunch." He finds the stone he's searching for and pushes it in. This one moves much more easily than the one I used when meeting with Blaise.

The outside air kisses my skin, surprisingly chilly and smelling of salt. "The harbor?" I ask, surprised. I step out of the tunnel. Beneath my feet, the ground shifts from stone to sand. Waves crash in the distance. "No. The beach," I realize, squinting to look out at the horizon.

I don't know what I'd been expecting, but it wasn't this. I hadn't even thought we'd be leaving the palace.

"You said you like the sea," he says, coming to stand next to me. He bends down, sticking the candle in the sand flame-first to extinguish it, leaving it there. "So do I. But that's not the surprise."

He takes my hand as easily as breathing, as if he's done it a thousand times before. My fingers are entwined with his, his callused palm pressing against mine as he pulls me after him. Though I know this is all a part of a game I'm orchestrating, a part of me wants to let go, not because his touch is repulsive, but because it *should* be and isn't. Just as Artemisia pointed out, this is the son of the man who destroyed everything and everyone I loved. The boy who slaughtered nine of my people because his father told him to. I shouldn't like the feel of his hand in mine, but I do.

He leads me over a dune and toward the shore, where the

waves lap at the sand and a small dark shape bobs just a few feet away. A boat, if it can truly be called that. It's not a drakkar or even a schooner. It's a sloop with a large mast, small hull, and a collapsed red sail.

"You did promise my Shadows I'd be back in two hours," I remind him. "What exactly did you have planned?"

"Just a short trip. Don't worry, she's surprisingly fast—we'll have time to spare," he says.

I have to gather my dress around my knees to keep it from getting wet as we wade into the water, but once we go deeper I give up and let it go. Søren doesn't seem to spare a second thought to his own clothes getting wet. The water is up to my hips by the time we reach the back of the rocking boat, and Søren has to place his hands on my waist to boost me up. The skirt of my dress is soaked, but I do my best to wring it out. A second later, Søren lifts himself onto the boat. When he sees my skirt, he gives me a sheepish smile.

"Sorry, I hadn't thought about that," he says. "I have a few sets of clothes downstairs if you want to change into something while that dries. They're my sailing clothes, so they won't be what you're used to, but . . ." He trails off, catching himself rambling.

He's nervous, I realize, though the idea is laughable. Søren is stoic and unflappable, a Kalovaxian warrior down to his bones. How can he be nervous around me, of all people?

"Thank you," I tell him. "Are you going to change, too?"

He nods. "In a minute," he says. "I'm going to get us moving first." He walks to the mast and lights two lanterns hanging there, flooding the area with a dim golden glow. He hands one to me before moving on to unfurl the sail.

I leave him to it and start toward the cabin. The boat is small and sparsely built, in typical Kalovaxian fashion, but there's a thick wool blanket spread out on the deck, with a wicker basket and another lantern on top to keep it from blowing away in the wind.

The door swings open with just a nudge and I carefully step down a short set of stairs into the dark cabin. With the light of my lantern to see by, I can make out a room as sparely decorated as the rest of the ship, with a single narrow bed and a rickety set of drawers. Little as there is in the cabin, it's a mess. The bed is rumpled and unmade, and there are clothes tossed haphazardly on the floor. I can't resist a smirk at another unexpected side of Søren. Back at court, he's always so impeccably put together, without a hair out of place or a single wrinkle in his clothes, but here at sea he's a slob.

I step gingerly over crumpled clothes and a few empty overturned tin cups and plates, making my way toward the set of drawers. Inside I find simple linen trousers and a white cotton shirt with buttons down the front. Both are far too big for me and I have to roll them up at the ankles and elbows to manage to move in them, but they're comfortable and, though they're clean, they still smell like Søren—salt water and fresh-cut wood.

When I emerge back onto the deck, the sail is fully open and Søren is at the helm, his back to me. When he hears me approach, he turns around and immediately laughs at the sight of me.

My cheeks warm. "It was the best I could do," I say, tugging uncomfortably at the too-big shirt and making sure the trousers haven't fallen too far down over my hips.

"No, it isn't that," he says, shaking his head. "It's just . . . strange to see you in my clothes."

"Not as strange as it feels," I point out, glancing down at the trousers. I don't think I could ever get used to wearing men's clothes.

His laughter subsides. "You still look beautiful," he tells me, making the heat in my cheeks double. "If you'd like, you can go back in the cabin, where it's a little warmer."

It's my turn to laugh. "I don't mean any offense, Søren, but I've never seen a room as messy as your cabin," I tease.

Now he's the one blushing.

"Besides," I continue, turning my face up to take in the open sky, "I like it up here."

When I glance back at him, he's watching me with a peculiar expression that sets my stomach fluttering. "Do you need help?" I ask him.

He shakes his head. "That's the beauty of *Wås*. She doesn't need a crew, just me," he says before tossing me a box of matches. Small as it is, it's the most dangerous thing I've been trusted with under such little supervision. I can't even use a steak knife when I eat alone in my rooms, though I don't know who they think I'll try to kill. Hoa? Or maybe they're worried I'll try to kill myself.

"Can you light that lantern?" he asks, nodding at the one set up on the blanket.

I tell him I can, though I'm not sure that's the truth. I've seen other people light matches, but I've never done it myself. My first attempts are clumsy; I snap a couple of sticks before one finally sparks and frightens me so much I nearly drop it. I just manage to light the wick before it burns my fingers.

"*Wås,*" I echo when it's lit. I stretch out next to the lantern and lie down on my back, staring up at the black velvet sky above, studded with thousands of diamonds. There's a chill in the air, but it's just enough to dull an otherwise warm evening. "You named your ship after the goddess of cats?"

"It's a long story."

"We still have about an hour and a half," I remind him, propping myself up on my elbows and watching as he adjusts the angle of the sail to catch the wind. His white shirt ripples and lifts in the breeze to show the hard muscles of his stomach. I try not to stare, but he catches my look and smiles.

"Fair enough. Give me one minute." He trims the sail once more and ensures we're heading in the right direction, then goes down to the cabin to change.

While he's gone, I lie down flat and stare up at the stars overhead. For the first time in a decade, I'm alone. I'm out of the palace, with the sky stretching out around me and fresh air in my lungs. It's feeling I never want to forget.

A few minutes later, Søren comes back and sits next to me, closer than I think he would dare if we were anywhere else. I sit up and lean back on my hands. There's still an inch between us, but even that space feels like the air in the second before lightning strikes.

"So. *Wås,*" I prompt.

His ears turn red. "My father gave it to me for my seventh birthday, but it was barely more than a hull then. It's tradition for a boy to build his own first ship. It took four years before she was seaworthy, and another two before she was anything to be proud of. Now she's the fastest ship in the harbor."

"Impressive," I say, smoothing my hand over the polished

wooden deck at the edge of the blanket. "But what does that have to do with cats?"

His fingers pick at a pill in the wool. "The docks are overrun with them, as I'm sure you've seen. Of course, the more experienced sailors knew to scatter orange peels on their decks to keep the cats off the boats, but no one thought to tell me that. I suppose they thought it was funny to see an arrogant prinzling step onto his embarrassment of a ship only to find dozens of cats lying in wait. What was worse, the cats took a liking to me. A few of them would follow me around the dock like ducklings trailing after their mother. The men started to call me *Wåskin*."

Child of Wås. Hardly the most ferocious of nicknames. I give a snort of laughter and try to hide it before I realize Søren is laughing as well. I don't think I've heard him laugh before, but something's changed in him since we left the palace. He's softer, more open here.

I wish he weren't, because it makes him easy to like.

He shakes his head and smiles. It's the first time I've seen him really smile, unguarded, and it sends all thoughts of plots and murder out of my head completely for an instant. For an instant, I let myself wonder what this would be like if I were just a girl having a secret rendezvous with a boy she might like. It's a dangerous path for my thoughts to walk, but if I'm going to get him to fall in love with me, he needs to believe I care about him, too. So I can let myself, just for tonight, believe it's that simple.

"It was a well-earned nickname, I'll admit," he says, cheeks reddening. "And I'd taken a liking to the little beasts. They weren't bothering anyone. The ship was just warm and smelled like fish." He shrugs. He tries to keep the story light, but there's a darkness in his eyes that won't lift.

"Your father didn't like his heir being associated with the goddess of cats," I guess.

His mouth tightens. "He thought it was unbecoming for any Kalovaxian, let alone a prinz. He told me that either I could take care of it or he would. I was nine, but I already knew what *that* meant. And I tried, but orange peels wouldn't work. They'd gotten so used to me, so attached, that there was nothing I could do to keep them away."

"So he had them killed?" I guess.

Søren hesitates before shaking his head. "I did it," he admits. "It seemed . . . nobler. They were my responsibility. And I made it as painless as I could. I poisoned the water I set out for them. No one called me *Wåskin* after that, at least not to my face."

He's staring straight ahead, blue eyes unfocused and expression back to its usual hard-edged frown.

It's the sad story of a sheltered child. Dead pets aren't so tragic when you've seen your mother slaughtered, when you've stabbed your own father in the back even as he sang you a lullaby. But still, Søren's pain was real. So was his disillusionment. It was the moment he stopped being a child. Who am I to say that it wasn't awful?

"I'm sorry," I tell him.

He shakes his head and forces a smile. "My father didn't get to be kaiser by being a kind man. You should know that better than anyone."

"And here I thought he got to be the Kaiser because he was born into the right family."

He gives me a sideways glance. "As a third son," he says. "You haven't heard the story?"

"Your mother told me about her wedding. Was that a part of it?" I ask, frowning. The Kaiserin had said he had killed his siblings, but for some reason I'd imagined them younger. I've seen the way second and third sons move through the world. They're hungry for attention and affection from anyone around them, or else they try their hardest to sink into the background. The Kaiser does neither. He owns the ground he walks on, the air he breathes. I suppose I assumed he'd been born like that.

Søren shrugs. "My father wants things and he takes them," he says. "Everyone else be damned."

The words send a shock through me. No one dares to speak like that about the Kaiser, and I didn't expect it from Søren of all people. They may not be close, but he's still his father. I'd thought it would take more effort to turn Søren against the Kaiser, but the Kaiser seems to have done a good enough job of that on his own.

"As captain of this fine vessel, I have the right to make a few rules," Søren says with a sigh, interrupting my thoughts.

"Rules?" I ask, raising an eyebrow.

"Well, one rule," he amends. "No more talk of my father."

I laugh, even though my mind is whirling, puzzling out how to push Søren's feelings about his father further, how to twist them more in my favor. But there is time for plotting later; tonight I need to just be a girl alone on a boat with a boy she likes. Tonight I need to be Thora.

"I like that rule," I tell him, surprised to find that it's the truth. I should be trying to coax more information out of him, but the prospect of a conversation that isn't darkened by the Kaiser's shadow is too much to pass up. "What happens if we break it?"

Søren softens, a small smile tugging at his lips. "Well, there *is* a plank," he says. He sits up and opens the wicker basket, pulling out a bottle of wine. "There aren't, however, any glasses."

I laugh, sitting up as well. "How barbaric," I tease.

"The plank or the lack of glasses?" he asks, uncorking the bottle with his teeth.

I consider it for a moment. "The lack of glasses. The plank is tolerable, I suppose, provided it's well polished." He passes me the open bottle of wine and I take a small swallow before passing it back to him. It's barely a sip, but I need to keep my wits about me. "What else did you bring?" I ask, nodding toward the basket.

He takes a significantly longer swig before passing the bottle back to me and digging through the basket. He pulls out a small chocolate cake, still warm from the oven, and two forks.

"Forks!" I say, clapping my hands in glee. "If you hadn't brought forks, I think I'd have gladly walked off the plank."

He holds one out to me, but pulls it back when I go to take it. "Just promise you won't stab me with it?" he says. His voice is teasing, but guilt ties my stomach into knots.

"Don't be silly," I say, keeping my voice light. "If I killed you here, however would I get back to shore?"

He smiles and passes me the fork. I'm not sure if it's the cake itself or everything else—the ocean, the sense of freedom, the way Søren's looking at me—but it's the best thing I've ever tasted. Though the cake is large enough for four people at least, it's only a matter of moments before there is nothing left but crumbs and both of us are overstuffed and lying on our backs with our heads angled together.

It's so easy, I realize, to pretend to be the sort of girl who likes him. It makes me wonder how much I'm actually pretending. I'm comfortable around him. Talking with him like this, saying things we shouldn't, feels as natural as breathing.

He must feel it, too, because he turns his face slightly toward me. "What's the Astrean word for cake?" he asks.

It's a dangerous question. After the siege, anytime I spoke Astrean, I would be hit. A sharp slap across the face, a fist to my ribs that would leave a bruise, a kick to my stomach that knocked the breath from me. I didn't speak a word of Kalovaxian back then, but I learned quickly. Speaking Astrean now with my Shadows is one thing, but it feels like a trap to speak it with a Kalovaxian prinz. When I turn to look at Søren, though, his face is open and guileless.

"Crâya," I say after a second, before frowning. "But no, that's not right. That refers to a lighter cake, usually lemon or some kind of citrus. Those were more common. This would have been called . . ." I trail off, struggling. We didn't have chocolate cakes very often, maybe once or twice that I remember. I close my eyes, trying to recall. "Darâya," I say finally.

"Darâya," he echoes, his accent abysmal. "And wine?"

I hold up the bottle. The wine is light and crisp, and though I've only had half of what Søren had, I can already feel it working its way through me, making my mind buzz.

"Vintá," I say. "This one would be a pala vintá. If it were red, it would be roej vintá."

"*Pala vintá.*" He takes the bottle from me and takes another gulp. "Ship?"

"*Baut.*"

"Wind?"

"*Ozamini.* Our air goddess was called Ozam, so it came from that," I explain.

"Hair?" He reaches out to touch mine, twirling a lock around his finger. I watch him, entranced. I inch closer without thinking. These are Thora's feelings. They cannot belong to me, can they?

"*Fólti,*" I say after a second.

"Ocean?" I can feel his breath against my cheek as he moves closer. His face takes up my entire view, blotting out the sky, the stars, the moon. All I see is him.

"*Sutana.*" The word is barely an exhale. "The same as *Ozamini,* but this time for the water goddess, Suta."

"Kiss?" His eyes never leave mine.

I swallow. "*Aminet.*"

"*Aminet,*" he repeats, savoring each syllable.

I should be prepared for his mouth drifting toward mine. Little experience as I have, I know it's coming; it's what I've been working toward, after all. But I'm not ready for how much I want him to do it. Not me as Thora, the broken girl, or Theodosia, the vengeful queen. Just Theo, both and neither. Just me. And maybe out here, with no one to see us but the stars, I can be that girl for just a moment.

So when he kisses me, I let myself kiss him back because I *want* to. I want to feel his mouth on mine and taste his breath. I want to feel his callused hands against my skin. I want to bury myself in his embrace until I forget Blaise and Ampelio and my mother and the tens of thousands of people who need me. Until we are two nameless people with no pasts, only a future.

But I can't forget, not even for a moment.

"Aminet," Søren murmurs again against my lips before rolling over onto his back. "I didn't bring you out here for that, you know."

"I know," I say, trying to get ahold of my wits. "If your goal was seduction, you wouldn't have led with the cat story."

He laughs and gives my shoulder a light shove. "I just . . . I realized I wasn't going to see you for a few weeks, at least. And I didn't like thinking about that." He pauses. "I hate being at court. Everyone there wears so many faces. They're all full of flattery and lies and manipulations, grabbing at whatever favor they can reach. It's exhausting. I think you're the only honest person in that godsforsaken palace. I'm going to miss you."

Guilt lumps in my throat, impossible to ignore. Despite what he thinks, I know I wear as many faces as most courtiers—more, probably. I've manipulated him as much as anyone. I'm doing it right now. But it's different, I suppose. I'm not grasping for favor or trying to get myself ahead. What I'm doing is necessary, but that knowledge doesn't make me feel any better.

I roll over onto my side to face him, propping myself up on my elbow. In the flickering lantern light, his features are softer, innocent.

"I'm going to miss you, too, Søren," I tell him quietly. That much, at least, isn't a lie.

He frowns. "Are you?" He reaches out to take my hand,

tracing the lines on my palm idly with his pointer finger. Slight a gesture as it is, it still makes me shiver. "How?"

"How what?"

"How can you look at me and not see him?" His mouth twists as he says the words. I don't have to ask who he means, but the blunt acknowledgment of his father makes me feel like I've been dunked in cold water. Søren seems to feel that way himself, his grip on my hand loosening.

He hates him, I realize. It isn't as simple as a son rebelling against his father or an egomaniacal father's resentment of his young, strong heir who will one day take his place. It's hate. Maybe not enough to match the hate I feel for the Kaiser, but it's something similar.

The realization twists my gut because it's one more thing that makes me understand Søren more—like him more. I can't afford to like him more.

"Well, now you have to walk the plank," I tell him, fully pulling my hand from his grasp. "You might be captain, but you can't go breaking your own rules—"

"Seriously, Thora," he says. Though the name is a stab in my gut, I'm grateful for it. I need the reminder that this bubble we've created isn't real, that the person he sees when he looks at me isn't real.

After a moment of thought, I decide to tell him the truth because I don't think he'll believe anything else right now.

"I used to," I admit. "All of you were indistinguishable— you, the Kaiser, the Theyn." I shake my head and take a deep breath. "Can you imagine what it was like to wake up in a world where you're safe and loved and happy and go to sleep in one where everyone you love is dead and you're surrounded by strangers who only let you live because it's convenient?"

"No."

"No," I repeat. "Because you were only a year older than I was when it happened. It wasn't your fault, and I know that." I pause for a breath. "You aren't your father."

"But—"

"You aren't your father," I say again, more firmly. It's the truth, but I can tell he doesn't believe it.

Still, his expression softens and I realize just how much he needed to hear those words, even if he doesn't believe them. Maybe his interest in me isn't just about saving the damsel. Part of him also wants to *be* saved. If he's stained by his father's sins, then maybe I'm the only person who can absolve them.

I inch closer to him and lift my hand, resting it against his cheek. His eyes are as dark as the water around us.

"*Yana Crebesti*," I say.

He swallows. "What does that mean?" he asks.

It could have meant anything, really, and he wouldn't have known any better. I could have told him that I was planning to kill him, that I hated every Kalovaxian in Astrea—including him—that I wouldn't stop until I saw them all dead. He wouldn't have known the difference.

"It means I trust you."

"*Yana Crebesti*," he repeats.

I close the slight distance between us and brush my lips against his, softly at first, but when his hand reaches up and knots in my loose hair, anchoring me against him, there is nothing soft about it. We kiss like we're trying to prove a point, though I can't quite say what it is. I can't quite remember who I am anymore. My edges blur. ThoraTheoTheodosia. Everything slips away until all that matters are mouths and tongues and hands and breath that is never quite enough. My hair falls around us like a curtain, shutting out the rest of the world. It's easier than ever to pretend that nothing else exists but this, but us.

He must feel it, too, because when we can't kiss anymore and he's just holding me against him with my face tucked in the crook of his neck, he murmurs in my ear: "We can keep sailing. In a day, we'll be near Esstena. A week we'll be past Timmoree. A month, Brakka. And then, who knows. We can sail until we get somewhere where no one knows us."

As traitorous as it makes me, I can imagine it. A life where a crown—gold or ash—doesn't weigh heavy on my head. A life where I'm not responsible for thousands of people who are hungry and weak and beaten every day. A life where I can just be a girl, kissing a boy because she wants to, instead of a queen kissing a prinz because he's the key to reclaiming her country. It would be an easier life in so many ways. But it wouldn't be mine, and though he might hate his father and his world, it wouldn't be his either.

Still, it's nice to pretend.

"I've heard that Brakka has a delicacy called *intu nakara*," I say.

He laughs. "Raw sea serpent. It's only a delicacy because it's so rare, not because it's any good, believe me. It tastes exactly how you would imagine."

I wrinkle my nose and kiss the small patch of exposed skin on his shoulder, just above his shirt collar. "And if I wanted to try it anyway?" I ask.

"Then you'll have all the *intu nakara* you want," he says. His fingers are tangled in my hair, combing through it idly. "Though I'm sorry to say there will be no *aminets*."

"*Amineti*," I correct him. "The plural is *amineti*." As in, I woke up this morning never having had a single *aminet* but now my count is up to three *amineti*. With two different boys. I push thoughts of Blaise and his confusing kiss out of my mind and focus on Søren. "But why is that?"

"Because *intu nakara* is notorious for causing terrible breath."

"Is that so?" I ask, propping myself up on my arm again to look down at him. "I don't think you'll be able to help yourself."

His hand leaves my hair and trails down to my waist. "I think you're underestimating the stench. They say you can smell it a quarter mile away."

"Disgusting," I tell him, wrinkling my nose.

He laughs and rolls us over so that he's looming over me, shoulder-length gold hair tickling my cheeks as he presses another lazy, lingering kiss to my mouth. When he pulls back, I follow him a couple of inches before breaking the kiss.

"Another day, I'll take you to Brakka and you can eat as much *intu nakara* as you like, but it's almost time to get you home."

I sit up and watch him walk back over to the helm, take the wheel, and turn the ship around, aiming us toward the shore. In the light of the full moon above, the hard lines of his face are softer, younger than they look in the day. He is not the same person to me that he was when we stepped onto this boat tonight, and I don't think there's any going back to how things were before.

I told my Shadows that I could kill him and start a civil war, and now I'm even more sure that the plan would work. There are already such high tensions between him and the Kaiser that I wouldn't have to do much to stoke them. But I also doubt that I'm going to be able to kill Søren when the time comes. I meant what I said to him: he isn't his father. And I don't think I can go back to pretending he is.

The season is turning and the night has gotten surprisingly cold, so I pull the blanket with me as I stand up, draping it around my shoulders and walking around behind him. Goose bumps rise along his bare forearms, so I wrap the blanket around him, too. If I stand on the tips of my toes, I'm tall enough to rest my chin on his shoulder.

"Do you promise?" I ask him.

"Do I promise what?" he asks, turning his head slightly so that his breath touches my lips.

"To take me away from here?" As I say it, I'm not sure which part of me is asking.

Something hard flickers across the sharp angles of his face and I worry suddenly that I've misread him, that I don't actually understand him at all. Speaking Astrean and this whole midnight sail might count as treasons, but they're little ones. Forgivable ones, though not without their own costs. Yet running away—not just halfhearted plans but an actual promise—that is something else entirely. Søren's smart enough to know that. He's smart enough to know that I'm really asking if he would put me above his duty as Prinz.

He sighs and presses a kiss to my forehead. "One day," he says.

It's not enough, but it's a start.

TEST

WE TRADE QUICK, DESPERATE KISSES the whole way back, barely making it within the two-hour time frame Blaise had set. Søren and I take the curfew seriously for different reasons—Søren's worried my Shadow guard will tattle to the Kaiser, but I'm worried Blaise will think I'm in trouble and do something reckless. Even when Søren kisses me outside the doorway that leads to my wardrobe, I can't help but think about Blaise's kiss earlier. They blur together in my mind until I can't quite keep straight who is who.

"I'll see you when I come back," Søren promises me. "I'll bring you a token."

A token from Vecturia, I remind myself. A token from a country not unlike mine that Søren and his men are going to conquer. Because that's who they are. That's who *he* is. I cannot let myself forget that.

I give him one last kiss before opening the passage door and crawling through, back into the wardrobe. My dress is still uncomfortably damp, but wearing it is preferable to what would happen if my dress was found on Søren's boat, or his clothes in my room.

My room is silent when I emerge, apart from loud snores coming from Heron's wall.

"I've got him," I say to whoever is listening. "Or nearly. He's half in love with me, and when he's back from Vecturia, I can finish it."

I don't add that I think I'm falling for him, too.

"Is everything else moving along?" I ask instead.

Blaise clears his throat. "Art's mother left tonight, and her ship is fast. She should get there a couple of days before they do. It won't be a lot of time to prepare anything, but the Vecturians will at least be warned. They can gather their combined troops on the nearest island and head them off there. The Kalovaxians will still likely outnumber them, but the Vecturians have the defensive advantage and they should be able to keep them at bay. The Kalovaxians think it'll be an easy siege; if it's more trouble than it's worth, they should turn around."

I nod. "The others are asleep?"

"Yes, it's nearly sunrise," he points out.

My body is exhausted, but my mind is buzzing, full of thoughts of Dragonsbane and freedom and the sound of Søren's rare laugh. I try not to think about Blaise and his kiss and the way he wouldn't look at me.

A yawn overtakes me and I realize just how tired I am.

"I think I'll join them," I tell him, crawling into bed without bothering to change my dress. "You ought to do the same."

"I'm not tired," he says. "Besides, someone ought to keep watch."

I'm about to protest, when I feel something hard beneath

my pillow. I reach under and feel not one but two items, and pull them out. The first is a thin, sheathed blade of polished silver. I hold it up to the weak moonlight pouring through the window next to my bed to admire it. I'd forgotten how elegant Astrean swords were, with filigreed hilts and narrow blades, so different from the cragged iron swords the Kalovaxians favor.

The second item is a small glass vial filled with no more than a spoonful of opalescent liquid.

"I'm assuming this isn't for my consumption?" I ask. Warmth seeps through the glass as I turn the vial over in my hands.

"Not unless *you* want to be turned to ash from the inside out," Blaise replies.

I nearly drop the vial, which would have been catastrophic. Encatrio. Liquid Fire. I'd heard rumors about it, but the recipe is a closely guarded secret that only a few know. Even the Kaiser hasn't managed to get his hands on it, though not for lack of trying.

"Something we thought you could pass on to your friend, and her charming father," he continues, drawing out the word *friend* sarcastically. "Another way to weaken the Kalovaxians, to make them fear us. If we can kill their strongest warrior, they'll think we can get to anyone *and* it'll make the Kaiser look weak."

My grip on the potion tightens with yearning and dread. He's right: if we could kill the Theyn, it would be almost as strong of a blow to the Kaiser as killing Søren. And besides, the Theyn haunts my nightmares as often as the Kaiser does. He's the man who killed my mother, who beat me and terrorized me and felt no guilt over any of it. I won't feel any guilt over him.

Cress, though . . . Despite what Blaise thinks, she's been a genuine friend to me, even when she shouldn't have been. She has shielded me time and time again, lifted me up when I couldn't stand on my own. She gave me a reason to get out of bed in the morning when I wanted so badly to die. Without Cress, there would have been nothing left of me by the time Blaise appeared. How can I possibly kill her?

I knew it would come to this, to betraying her for my country. But I never imagined it would go this far. I think of the way the light left my mother's eyes, the way her grip on my hand went slack. I think of the sword slicing through Ampelio's back, the way he shuddered out one last breath before going still. Cress replaces them in my mind. I see her eyes, feel her hand, watch her soul get wrenched from her body.

More than once, she's called me her heart's sister, a Kalovaxian expression for a friendship that goes deeper than family, so deep that two people share one heart. I used to think it silly, considering Cress's father was the reason I didn't have a family anymore, but now it feels painfully accurate. Losing Cress, *killing* her, would carve a rotting hole in my heart that would never heal.

It's Thora's weakness, I tell myself, but it isn't. Not completely.

"Theo," Blaise says, his voice a warning I don't need. Don't want. My grip on the poison tightens and I'm tempted to hurl it at the wall Blaise sits behind.

He gave me hope when I had none and he is my lifeline in this storm, but right now I wish he had never come back. I wish I were alone in this room, surrounded by my real Shadows and blissfully ignorant of everything outside the palace. I wish I were Thora again, because Thora never had choices to make.

But I don't have a choice now either. Not really. That's what hurts the worst.

"I'm tired, I'm going to sleep," I say, shoving the poison and the blade back under my pillow.

"*Theo*." His voice snaps like a sail in the wind.

"I heard you," I say, matching his tone. "I can hardly do it tonight, can I? Striking out at the Theyn is risky and we need a plan if we're going to do it."

His silence hangs heavy for a long moment. "But you will do it," he says. I hate the doubt there, how clear it is that he still doesn't fully trust me. But then, I can't really blame him. I'm not sure I trust myself either.

I don't answer and he doesn't press me, but I know his patience won't last. He'll want an answer soon, and I don't know if I can give him one.

DOUBT

❖ • ❖

THE THEYN RETURNS FROM THE mines the day after Søren leaves, but the poison stays stuffed in my mattress, along with the ruined nightgown from when I first met Blaise. Even so, I feel its weight constantly, pressing in on all sides.

Killing the Theyn is right; it is necessary, I have no doubts about that. Even from a distance, I can almost smell fresh blood on him. Astrean blood. If it were only him, I wouldn't hesitate. I could pour the poison down his throat without a scrap of guilt. I could watch the light leave his eyes and smile. Maybe it would even bring me a measure of peace to kill him.

But the longer I think about it, the more certain I am: I can't kill Cress any more than I could cut out my own heart.

A week passes and my Shadows must notice my hesitation to strike. They make no comment, but I hear their judgments all the same, lingering in every conversation, hiding in each beat of silence. They are waiting, and each day I hesitate costs me a bit more of their respect.

She's not your friend, I tell myself again and again, but I know it isn't true. I remember the girl who saved me from bullies, who turned the shame of the ash crown into war paint when she knew she would be punished for it, who distracted me from the pain of my welts by reading to me from her favorite books. The girl who has been my friend even when she's had a thousand reasons to shun me.

She is your enemy. But she isn't. Crescentia might be a lot of things—selfish and calculating among them—but she isn't cruel. She has no blood on her hands and has committed no crime but being born to the wrong country, to the wrong man. Is that something worth killing her for? Wouldn't that make me the same as the Kaiser?

More than once over the past several days, I've woken up drenched in cold sweat, though now it isn't the Theyn's scarred face haunting me, or even the Kaiser's cruel eyes, but Crescentia's smile. She holds a hand out toward me like she did all those years ago. *"We're friends now,"* she says, only in my dreams her rosy skin turns gray as her mouth gapes open in a silent scream. Her eyes, blood-red around gray irises, are locked on mine, accusing, frightened, betrayed. I want to help her, but I'm frozen in place, and all I can do is watch while the life leaves her eyes, just as it left my mother's.

When my screams wake up my Shadows, I feed them lies that are all too easy to believe: that I dreamt of the Theyn killing my mother, or of the Kaiser's punishments. They don't believe me.

Even though I can't see his face, I can hear doubt in the way Blaise breathes, warnings in the idle shuffle of his feet. It's the pinching game all over again—which one of us will acknowledge it first? For once, I'm glad for the wall that keeps us apart, because I know that if he looked me in the eye and asked what was wrong, I would turn into a mess. Over one Kalovaxian girl.

They might leave me for that, declare me a lost cause and walk away. They could let the Kaiser have the broken parts of me and wage their war elsewhere. I don't know that I would blame them if they did. What kind of queen am I if I put my enemy before my people?

I try to avoid Cress as well. The morning Søren left, I woke up to her melodic knocking at my door.

"You look awful," she chirped playfully when she flounced in before breakfast. She didn't mean it cruelly and I couldn't deny the truth in her words. I *felt* awful. I'd gotten in from my meeting with Søren only five hours before, and most of those hours I'd spent tossing and turning in bed, thoughts of the poison and Blaise's words weighing heavily on my mind.

"I'm not feeling well," I told her, which was true enough. "I don't think I can join you for breakfast this morning."

Her smile faltered. "Then I'll have breakfast brought to you," she insisted. "And I'll stay to keep you company. My father brought me a new book of Astrean folklore that I'm sure you'll love, and—"

"No." The word came out harsher than I'd meant it to, sharpened by the mention of the Theyn and the idea of her reading a book about my people's history that I myself was no longer allowed to possess and the knowledge that the poison tucked safely away in my mattress was destined for her.

Cress's eyes went wide as a child's and her chin warbled. She looked so hurt that I nearly apologized, nearly begged her to stay and keep me company, anything to keep her happy, but I resisted and after a moment she nodded.

"I understand," she said, though it was clear she didn't.

I sighed. "I just don't want to get you sick, Cress. I would never forgive myself. I'll find you when I'm feeling better."

She nodded, but I could tell she didn't believe me. She opened her mouth to say something but quickly shut it again.

"I hope you feel better soon, Thora," she said softly before leaving me alone.

Two days after that, she sent a letter asking me to join her on a trip to the dressmaker, and I replied that I had a dancing lesson I couldn't miss. She came to see me again yesterday, but I begged Hoa not to answer the door and to pretend we were out. She gave me a wary look, but acquiesced.

But if there's anything I know about Crescentia, it's that she's stubborn and she always finds a way to get what she wants.

Her next attempt comes today while I'm eating breakfast, in the form of an invitation to a *maskentanz*—a masked ball—she's throwing to celebrate her father's return from the mines. I don't think I'm allowed to refuse, even though it means wearing that godsforsaken ash crown again, which will render any mask useless.

I show the invitation to Hoa and her dark eyes scan it, the space between her eyebrows pleating. She looks up at me, her expression muddled, before nodding once and hurrying from the room. There's a lot of preparation for a maskentanz, I'm sure, and not a lot of time to do it. It's typical of Crescentia to throw something together at the last minute without thinking about who would actually end up doing all the work. But even that show of thoughtlessness doesn't irritate me the way it usually would. All I can think of is the poison.

"Anything exciting?" Blaise asks when Hoa is gone.

"A maskentanz Cress is throwing tonight to celebrate the return of the Theyn from his *inspection* of the mines," I say, folding the letter up again. They don't reply and I realize that they likely have never heard the word *maskentanz* before. I doubt they held parties in the mines. "A masquerade, a party," I explain.

Still they say nothing, but their expectation is suffocating.

"There will be too many people around to use the poison," I say, before anyone can suggest what I know they're thinking. "It'll be too easy to make a mistake and kill the wrong person."

"They're all Kalovaxians, there is no wrong person," Artemisia says, venom in her voice. "And with so many people, no one would know who was the poisoner."

I understand the bite in her words, even though I'm not sure I really agree with them as much as I used to. If I could poison every Kalovaxian in the palace tonight, would I? I'm almost glad not to have that option, because I don't know what choice I would make. Yes, it would mean getting rid of the Kaiser and the Theyn and all the other warriors with their bloodstained hands and cold eyes, but there are also children here whose only crime is that they were born to the wrong country.

I know better than to tell Artemisia that.

"An *Astrean* poison? That alone would cast blame on me, and the Theyn is the Kaiser's closest friend—he might be distraught enough to kill me for it. And if the poison *does* reach the wrong Kalovaxian, I doubt you would be able to find more for the Theyn so easily or you would have already poisoned the entire castle," I reply, which quiets her. I rub my temples; the conversation—and what I know it will lead to—is already making my head ache.

"I'll do it soon, but we need a plan first and we haven't been able to form one yet," I say.

"*You* haven't been able to form one yet," Artemisia says. "And we all know you haven't actually been trying to, have you?"

I can't answer. Even through the wall, I can feel her resentment. She's hotheaded, but this feels like something else.

"We got word from a spy in the Earth Mine," Heron says after a second. "The Theyn halved their rations and they've begun sending children into the mines to work earlier than ever. Some as young as eight. No word from the other mines yet, but it's hard to imagine it's only the Earth Mine."

"Punishments for the riot?" I ask.

"Yes and no," Blaise says, voice heavy and tired. I wonder when the last time he really slept was. "That didn't help matters, and it's certainly the reason for the rations, but the children . . . The Kalovaxians are running out of slaves to work, and gem turnout isn't what it used to be. It's probably another reason for the attack on the Vecturia Islands. They need more slaves."

I can't help but think about Goraki and how the Kalovaxians burned the entire country and left when they ran out of resources. I wonder if Blaise is thinking the same thing. We're running out of time.

My stomach clenches. "And the Theyn gave the order as part of his inspections," I guess out loud. They don't contradict me. "Believe me, I would like nothing better than to kill him tonight, but it would be a foolish move and it'll only make things worse when we fail."

"Are you sure that's what makes you hesitate?" Artemisia asks, her acidic voice so quiet I almost don't hear her.

"Artemisia!" Heron hisses.

"No, it's fine," I say, taking a step closer to Artemisia's wall, matching her tone. I can't show doubt; I can't show fear. "If you have something you would like to say, Artemisia, please don't hide it. I'm very interested in what you think."

I'm greeted only by silence, but that doesn't make me feel any better, because *I* have doubts. Not about my loyalties, exactly, but in myself. These are people who took everything from me—my mother, my country, my mind. Ever since Ampelio died, I've been waiting for the moment I'll be able to take my revenge and bury Thora for good. Now that moment is here and I'm not sure I can really do it.

After a lunch alone—or as alone as I ever am—in my rooms, I hear a quick, soft knock on my door. It isn't Crescentia's melodic knock or the forceful rapping of the guards, and I can't imagine who else it might be. Hoa is clearing my lunch plates, so I go to answer it.

Warily I open the door, only to find no one on the other side. I lean out and peer down the hall in either direction, but the hall is empty. I almost close the door again before I notice the rolled piece of parchment on the ground in front of the door.

I pick it up and bring it back inside with me, closing the door firmly behind me. The letter is sealed with Søren's sigil of a drakkon breathing fire, so I slip it into the pocket of my dress.

"It must have been the wind," I tell Hoa.

She doesn't seem to believe me, though. When she leaves the room a moment later, balancing the tray of leftover lunch food in her arms, she gives me a suspicious glance. I smile at her like it's any other day, but I don't think it fools her.

Not for the first time, I wonder how she sees me. She's known me since I was six years old, she's held me when I've cried, she used to tuck me into bed. I don't trust her—I think the part of me that trusts people has been irreparably broken—but I do love her, in a way. It's a shadow of the love I feel for my mother, roughly the same shape but without the color or warmth. Hoa looks at me sometimes like she's seeing her own shadow of a ghost. But I can't ask her anything about it, and she certainly couldn't tell me anything if I did.

When the door clicks shut behind her, I take the letter from my pocket and break the seal with my pinky nail before unrolling it.

"The Prinz?" Blaise asks.

I don't answer him except to nod. Søren's handwriting is a sloppy, rushed scrawl that makes it difficult to read.

Dear Thora,

I dreamt of you last night and when I woke this morning, I could have sworn your scent lingered in the air around me. It's been like this all week.

You haunt my mind both sleeping and waking. I keep wanting to share my thoughts with you, or ask you for your opinion on things. Usually I look forward to time away from court, when it's only my crew and me at sea. There are no pressures, no formalities, no games apart from those played with cards and ale. But now I would give anything to be back in that godsforsaken palace because you would be with me.

The short of it is: I miss you terribly, and I'm wondering if you miss me as well.

Erik has been teasing me relentlessly about you, though I suspect he's a bit envious. If I were a better man, I would encourage him to pursue you and I would let you go, because I know he's a safer choice for you. We both know what my father's wrath would be if he learned how much I care for you. I'm not selfless enough to step aside, though if you asked me to, I would certainly try. You could ask me for the ocean itself and I would find a way to give it to you.

The seas are smooth and if everything goes as easily as it should, I'll be back before the new moon with good tidings that should make my father a very happy man. If you would like to send me a letter, and I hope that you do, leave it where you found this one and trust that it will find me.

Yours,
Søren

I read the letter twice, trying to smother the giddiness his words bring out in me. If I were alone, I might smile. I might press the letter to my heart, my lips. I might imagine him, in his cabin with only a candle for light, laboring over the words and chewing on the end of his quill as he tries to put his thoughts on the paper. I might wonder what, exactly, he dreamt about me.

But I'm never alone, and for once, I'm grateful for it. My Shadows' eyes dissect every twitch in my expression, reminding me who I am and what's at stake. Especially after our argument earlier, I'm sure they are looking for signs that I'm having doubts, and I can't let them know that I am.

I can't let them know that there is a part of me falling for the Prinz they want me to kill.

"He doesn't say anything interesting, no mention of Vecturia," I say, crumpling the paper in my hands and beginning to rip it into shreds. "It's a love letter, nothing about what he's doing. The seas are smooth, he expects the trip to be easy and quick. Of course, this was a few days ago. He said he'd be back before the new moon. That's only two weeks away."

"He should be getting to Vecturia today, if the seas are calm," Artemisia says. Her voice is still sharp at the edges, our earlier argument unforgotten.

"It's a shame none of you are Fire Guardians," I say, looking down at the scraps of paper cradled in my hands and wishing I could burn them. The pieces are no bigger than my pinky nails, but I wouldn't put it past the Kaiser to have someone rifle through my rubbish and reassemble them.

Not for the first time, I wonder if I could start a fire. If the legend is true and Houzzah's blood truly runs through my veins, it should be simple, even without training or a gem. I've felt the draw of the Fire Gem more intensely than any of the others, the strong temptation to call on it and use whatever power I can summon. But I won't test that theory. Not ever. Before the siege, I'd often heard stories of humans who thought themselves worthy of power they weren't blessed with in the mines. I remember how the gods punished them for their pride or recklessness. I can't risk their wrath, now more than ever, when one mistake could ruin me. Could ruin Astrea forever.

I hear Artemisia's words again, her doubt in the gods and their power. It's been nagging at me, this suspicion that maybe she has a point. Why haven't the gods saved Astrea if they love us so much? If I'm truly descended from Houzzah, how could he have let the Kalovaxians treat me this way and done nothing? I don't like to think about that or ask those questions, but I can't help it.

But my mother is waiting for me in the After, I have to believe that. If she's not—if there is no After—I don't know what I'll do. The idea of seeing her again one day is the only thing that's gotten me out of bed some mornings. Legend says that using a gem without the gods' blessing is sacrilege and sacrilegious souls aren't allowed into the After. As much as I want to feel fire at my fingertips and bring the world around me to ash, I won't jeopardize the After for it.

"Art," Blaise prompts, drawing me out of my thoughts.

"I can help with that," she says.

I hear the sliding of a door opening and closing before my own door opens and Artemisia slips in, drawing her hood back and showing me her face for the first time. I swallow my surprise—she doesn't look at all how I expected her to.

She's so slight she could almost pass for a child, though I would guess she's close to my own age, maybe a little older. Much to my surprise, she isn't Astrean, or at least not completely. She has the same tan skin and dark eyes, but hers are hooded. Her heart-shaped face is sharply angled with high, freckled cheekbones, and her mouth is small and round. Since I know Dragonsbane is Astrean, I would have to assume that Artemisia's father is from somewhere in the East, though I haven't met enough people from those lands to hazard a more specific guess.

The most extraordinary thing about her is her hair. It hangs down to her shoulder blades in a straight, thick sheet, white at the roots and a shocking cerulean blue at the ends. It shifts and changes in the light, like water, mirroring the Water Gem pin embedded in it.

Some Guardians show physical manifestations of their gifts. There was an old story of an Earth Guardian whose skin turned gray and hard, but most of the markings are subtle, like scars. Ampelio once showed me his: a bright red burn over his heart that looked fresh, but he said it had been with him since he finished his training.

She gives me an irritated look, and I realize I've been staring. She shakes her hair back over her shoulders and it fades to a dark auburn the same color as mine. Is she mimicking me intentionally? I want to ask her, but she's already annoyed with me. I don't want to anger her further.

"I'm sorry," I say. "Your hair—it just took me by surprise."

"You should try waking up with it," she says, her expression unwavering. I don't know her well enough to be able to tell if she's still angry or if this is simply how she is.

"It's beautiful," I say, hoping for a smile. She only shrugs.

"It's a burden," she replies. "When I escaped the mines, everyone was looking for a girl with blue hair, and I didn't have enough power without a Water Gem to change it for more than a few minutes. Do you have a bowl to put the pieces in?"

I nod toward my vanity, where an empty bowl sits, ready for Hoa to mix cosmetics in. Artemisia brings it to me and I drop the scraps into it. She holds one hand over the bowl, covering the top completely. The gems in her hairpin wink and glitter as her eyes close tight, and the air around us begins to hum with energy. It stops as quickly as it starts and her eyes fly open again, flashing blue for a second before turning back to dark brown. She lifts her hand from the surface of the bowl and we both peer into it.

The scraps of paper are gone, reduced to a thick liquid the same color as the parchment.

"You turned them to water?" I ask.

"Not quite," she says pursing her lips. "I rushed the dissolving process. It would have happened on its own, eventually. Now you only have to get rid of this, which should be much easier. I recommend dumping it into your chamber pot."

She passes the bowl to me, and when our fingers brush, her skin is cool and smooth.

"Thank you," I say.

"Now we have to think about the reply," she says, clasping her hands together in front of her. "Blaise, Heron, I'm sure this will be boring for you. Take a lap around the palace. See if you can learn anything new."

Blaise hesitates. "Art . . . ," he warns.

"Oh, don't worry, I'll play nice," she says with a smile so sweet I know it must be fake.

The others know it, too, because Heron gives a loud snort and Blaise sighs. Still, they relent, boots clacking against the stones, doors opening and shutting again. As soon as they're gone, Art's smile turns feral. I busy myself by sitting at my desk and bringing out a sheet of parchment and my quill, but her presence is heavy at my shoulder.

She wants to make me nervous, to remind me I need her more than she needs me, but I won't give her the satisfaction. I am done with being bullied.

"I can't write if you're going to linger like that," I snap.

"You should welcome an audience for your act," she replies evenly.

"If he's going to believe it, I have to believe it," I say. "But at the end of the day, I know what is real and what is fake."

"Do you?" she asks, tilting her head to one side. "Is that why you're putting Kalovaxian murderers before your own people?"

So she hasn't put aside our earlier argument, she's just been biding her time, waiting until I am alone and defenseless. But I don't need Blaise to stand up for me.

"I am not going to risk our lives and act hastily just so you can test my loyalties."

She laughs, but it's a joyless sound. "You think this is just a test? Have you forgotten what the Theyn has done to our people? To your mother?"

Her words sting, but I won't let her see me falter.

"I wasn't talking about the Theyn," I say. "You want to know if I'm loyal to Crescentia over you."

She shrugs. "Oh, I've known better than to trust you from the start," she says. "The girl was Blaise's idea."

"I have nothing to prove. Not to them, or to you," I say, lifting my chin. "And I'm not about to destroy everything we're working for, for a hastily thrown-together plan. When the moment is ready, I'll strike."

Her smile is cruel and mocking. "Of course, *Your Highness*."

I turn away from her and back to my letter, struggling to ignore the feeling of her reading over my shoulder.

Dear Søren,

I find it difficult to believe that your thoughts are as consumed by me as mine are by you, if only because I can't imagine how you are managing to command a ship in such a condition. I envy you that you have Erik to speak to about this, because I have no one. Crescentia wouldn't understand or forgive me, and I don't understand it myself, but I can't deny that my heart is yours—no matter how inconvenient or dangerous it is.

Over my shoulder, Artemisia gives a derisive snort that makes my cheeks warm. Yes, it's over the top, but isn't that the idea of a love letter? I ignore her and continue.

You have me distressingly curious: what exactly
was this dream of yours about? I look forward to
your return so that we can make it come to life.

Art makes another noise, but this time she sounds more
approving, so I suppose I must be doing something right, even
though I feel foolish writing these things down. I hesitate before continuing, knowing what I want to say to him now, but
acutely aware of Artemisia behind me, silently—and not so
silently—judging every word I write. In the end, though, I decide to write the truth. A part of me worries that someone
might find it, but Søren wrote plenty of dangerous things in
his letter to me; if he wasn't worried about it being found, I
shouldn't be either.

As to what I want from you, it's nothing as
extravagant as the sea, though it feels just as vast
and impossible. I want you; I want to be able to
walk in broad daylight with my hand in yours; I
want to kiss you and not have to worry who sees
it. And when I dream of you—which I do all too
often—I dream of a world in which that is possible.

To that, Artemisia says nothing, which is almost worse.
I press forward, writing something I know she'll have to approve of.

Please, tell me about your days and what
occupies them. Mine are as simple and dull as they

usually are, often spent reading in my rooms or listening to idle gossip. The most interesting thing that happened was when the late Lord Gibraltr left his fortune to his bastard instead of his wife and daughters. Please tell me something more engrossing than that, I beg of you.

I count the days to the new moon eagerly and look forward to having you in my arms again.

Yours,
Thora

MASKENTANZ

———•◆•———

A N HOUR BEFORE THE MASKENTANZ, there's a knock at my door. It isn't a knock I recognize, but when I open the door I find one of Crescentia's family's attendants on the other side—an older Astrean man with weathered skin and clouded eyes. He passes me the large box he holds without a word before dipping his head in acknowledgment. He's gone before I can thank him.

I bring it inside and set it on my small dining table. When I open the lid, my heart clutches painfully in my chest, though I hope my Shadows don't notice.

Inside is a gown of layered turquoise chiffon, and when I lift it out and hold it up, the material is as light as a breath against my skin. It would be completely weightless if the outer layer of the skirt weren't covered in thin gold disks shaped like fish scales. Or, more accurately, siren scales.

Cress and I have always loved sirens. As children, we read every book on them we could find in her father's library, doodled pictures of them instead of taking notes during lessons— Cress even agreed to a few nausea-inducing boat rides in the hope of finding one. It didn't matter that they were dangerous, or that sailors never managed to survive seeing them. We didn't want to see them, anyway; we wanted to *be* them.

Give me fins instead of legs and I could swim to depths where the Kaiser's men would never be able to find me. I could sing a song to drown anyone who tried to hurt me. I could be safe. For Crescentia, who had been raised to be soft and quiet and sweet, sirens were something ferocious and loud and still irresistibly lovable. That's the difference between us, I suppose: Crescentia yearns for love, and I prefer destruction.

On chilly winter days, when Cress's nanny would take us down to the heated pools below the palace, we spent the bulk of our time splashing in the water, pretending our legs were turning into fins. In years stained with blood and pain, those were the moments that made the rest bearable. Crescentia reminding me of them now feels like an apology for her behavior over Søren. She must think that's why I've been avoiding her. If only it were that simple.

Moments after the dress arrives, Hoa enters to help me into it, her nimble fingers dancing over the minuscule hook-and-eye closures that line the back, starting below my shoulder blades and working their way down my spine. The tops of my scars will be visible above the bodice, but for the first time I refuse to be ashamed of them. They are ugly, yes, but they mean I've survived.

You're a lamb in the lion's den, child, the Kaiserin said to me. *You're surviving.*

But surviving isn't enough. Not anymore.

Hoa wraps my neck and wrists with strands of pearls, weaving a few more into my hair. The gold half-mask Crescentia sent with the dress is studded with them as well, in ornate curlicues that wrap around the eyes.

Hoa gives a hum of approval as she looks me over before turning me to face the mirror.

The ensemble is perfect, so lovely I almost feel like I'm just another courtier going to a party instead of the way I feel when the Kaiser dresses me—like a trophy on display.

Of course, I'll still have to wear the ash crown, which will ruin the dress in a matter of moments, but just now I feel beautiful.

Another knock at the door sounds, but this time I know who it is. Hoa does as well and she bustles over to answer it. One of the Kaiser's attendants is standing there with another box. The ash crown.

Hoa gingerly takes the box, sets it down on my vanity, and starts to open it. While her back is turned, I scramble for the dagger hidden in the secret pocket of my cloak. As Hoa takes great pains to carefully lift the crown from the box, I wedge the dagger into the bodice of my dress. I can't imagine needing it, but keeping it close gives me the illusion of safety, at least.

"Careful," Blaise whispers, so quietly I barely hear him.

"I know what I'm doing," I hiss back, which might be the biggest lie I've ever told.

As my Shadows follow me down the hall, I'm more aware than ever of the ash crown shedding flakes with each step I take. I can't count the number of times the Kaiser has made me wear one of these awful things, but this time is worse because I know they're watching. I know it's an insult to them as much as me. More than ever, I want to rip it from my head and crumble it to dust in my hands, but that won't help anyone.

Footsteps fall in next to me. When I turn, only two Shadows are behind me.

"Heron," I warn. I'm careful to move my mouth as little as possible. The hall is deserted, but the Kaiser is always watching, waiting for me to slip.

"I'll be careful," he replies, voice soft as ever. "I'm sorry about Art earlier, really. She has friends in the mines."

"You must as well," I point out.

For a moment, he's quiet. If it weren't for the rustle of his cloak, I would think he'd fallen back in line with the others.

"No," he says finally. "They've already taken everyone I loved. My parents, my sister, my friends. My love. His name was Leonidas. You would have liked him, he had a sharp mind." He pauses again and I know this must be difficult for him to talk about. I'm suddenly struck by the fact that I don't know much about Heron at all. He rarely speaks up, and usually only about practical things. I thought he kept to himself because he didn't care as much as Blaise and me, and even Art, but that isn't true, I realize now. It's because he's cared too much in the past and paid for it. I open my mouth to tell him I'm sorry, to promise vengeance the same way I promised it to Blaise when he told me about his parents, but nothing comes out.

After a moment, he continues and I do the only thing I can. I listen.

"I watched while the guards killed them or took them away

when they went mad. I saw it all, and I can only imagine how it could get worse now. But you've seen horrors, too."

I can't think of anything to say at first. "I've been thinking more and more that Artemisia has a point," I say finally. "The gods from my mother's stories wouldn't let these things keep happening. They wouldn't let the Kalovaxians win."

Heron makes a sound in the back of his throat. "I wanted to be a priest before, you know. It was the only thing I ever wanted, even as a child, and there have been times over the last decade when I've wondered that as well, when I've been angry with the gods."

I glance sideways at him, forgetting for an instant that he's invisible. I look forward again. "Are you still?"

He doesn't answer for a moment. "I believe that if the gods could interfere they would, but maybe that's beyond their reach. Maybe, instead, they can give us what we need to succeed on our own."

"Like your gift," I say. "And Blaise's and Art's."

I can't see Heron, but I get the feeling he's nodding. "And you," he says.

I almost laugh but manage to hold it back. "I don't have a gift," I say. No one is in this hall, but I'm still careful to speak under my breath and move my mouth as little as possible.

"Maybe you *are* the gift," he says. "Descended from Houzzah, the rightful queen."

There's that word again, *queen*. It doesn't feel like a title that belongs to me, and hearing Heron describe me as a gift to my country also adds more weight to my shoulders. I know he means the words as a comfort, but they feel more like a condemnation. It hurts worse than Artemisia's carefully thrown barbs or Blaise's doubtful looks. He believes in me, and I'm sure I'm going to let him down somehow.

He squeezes my arm one last time before slowing his steps to fall back with the others. I turn down the corridor to the banquet hall alone.

For a ball thrown on a day's notice, Crescentia accomplished an awful lot—not the least of which is the crowd itself. The crush of bodies glitters in the light of the grand chandelier as if the lot of them were dipped in a vat of tar and rolled through Spiritgems. They have all gathered because they admire the Theyn—or because they fear him. It's hard to say for certain, and it matters little in the end. The result is the same: awed devotion.

They are all masked, like me, but I can tell most of them apart easily after years of paying attention to details.

The woman dressed as a peacock is the Baroness Frandhold, who carries herself like a woman ten years younger and twice as beautiful, chatting with her most recent paramour, Lord Jakob, who is only a scant few years older than me and who made an unsuccessful play for Cress's hand shortly after she turned sixteen. The baron is nearby, but seems as unconcerned with his wife's behavior as ever. He's too busy flirting with a soldier.

Even though I'm not looking for her, my eyes find Lady Dagmær—but now that she's married she's Lady Dalgaard, as only maidens and royals use their given names. The wedding was a hasty affair, the quicker for her father to get his payment and Lord Dalgaard to get his new plaything. Only a few days wed and there are already bruises mottling her exposed arms that everyone pretends not to see. She stands alone, the crowd giving her a wide berth as if her misery is contagious. The Dagmær I remember was the brightest spot at any gathering, always laughing the loudest, dancing the most, flirting outrageously enough to keep everyone talking for weeks. But now her eyes have gone dull behind her mask, and she flinches from the light and noise like a frightened rabbit.

I shouldn't feel guilty. My people have endured so much worse. I have endured so much worse. I shouldn't feel guilty, but I do. I did that to her, and the knowledge weighs heavy on my shoulders.

I force my eyes away from her and search the crowd for Crescentia. She isn't difficult to spot—all I have to do is look for the Kaiser at the center of it all, the gold crown standing as tall and proud on his head as ever. He doesn't bother trying to disguise himself in the spirit of the maskentanz, and why would he? He's far too in love with his own power to pretend to be anyone else for even a night.

I keep my distance, not wanting to draw his attention. Deep in conversation with him, Crescentia looks beautiful. Her own costume matches mine, except that it's a soft lavender on top, and the scales on the bottom are silver. Instead of pearls, she wears coral, the better to bring out the roses in her cheeks. She might be a girl, and worth little to the Kalovaxians beyond marriage and motherhood, but no one can watch her work the Kaiser and not admire her head for strategy. She wraps him around her finger without ever letting him realize, giving him a dimpled smile here, a shy look there, holding herself tall and proud—every part the prinzessin she wants so badly to be. All she really needs is the Prinz.

The Kaiser's attention lingers on her longer than I'm

comfortable with, but at least it isn't the way he looks at me. There's no leer in his gaze, just cold calculation. It's a shame that Søren isn't here to see his future paved out in front of him, but he doesn't need to be. I feel only a trickle of pity before I remind myself that Søren will never marry Crescentia. If my Shadows have any say, they'll both be dead long before that day ever comes.

The thought sours my stomach.

"I'm half sure Crescentia went to all this trouble more to draw you out than to celebrate me," a stiff voice says from just behind my left shoulder. "She's been very put out these last few days without you."

My worst nightmares swim before my eyes, and I have to stop myself from shuddering. I'm grateful to have my dagger so close, even if I can't imagine actually using it. Being in the Theyn's presence always feels like suffocating. It sends me into a panic of rapid heartbeats, blurred thoughts, and cold sweat, though I try not to show it. I am suddenly six years old again and watching him slaughter my mother. I am seven and he's holding the whip while the Kaiser pries my name from my mind. I am eight, nine, ten, and he's standing over me with a bucket of ice water, a fire poker—whatever the Kaiser instructs him to use to drive Theodosia out of me so that Thora is all that's left.

He wouldn't hurt me here. I know that. Still, I can't help but run through all my secrets, all my plots, sure that he can read them as clearly as words on a page.

"She's very kind," I force myself to say. "I'm lucky to have her as a friend."

"You are," he agrees, but there's a threat in his tone that I don't miss. Of course, everything the Theyn says to me sounds like a threat. *The Theyn* is a threat, whether he speaks or not.

"I'm very sorry for all the trouble in the mines," I continue, as if I had anything to do with that. I *wish* I did. I wish I had been able to accomplish something so large. "I know Crescentia missed you terribly." I'm not sure that's true, since Cress never really talks with me about her feelings about her father. Still, it seems like the right thing to say.

"And I missed her," he replies after a beat.

"She'll make a wonderful prinzessin, I think." It's a struggle to keep my voice light and conversational, to keep my hands from shaking, but I manage. The Theyn thrives on fear; he can smell it like a hunting dog.

For a moment, we both watch Crescentia as she gives the Kaiser a dimpled smile, wrapping him tighter around her finger.

"She was born to be," the Theyn says finally.

I sneak a glance at him and immediately wish I hadn't. The way he's watching Crescentia makes my chest ache, because how dare he? How dare he love his daughter when he took my mother away? Because of him, I will never see my mother look at me like that. He is a stone, incapable of feeling anything, and I don't like being reminded that he's also human. I don't like being reminded that we both love the same person.

Crescentia turns our way and her blinding smile grows wider. She excuses herself from the Kaiser with a softly spoken word and a brief touch of her hand to his arm. The Kaiser follows her gaze and the look in his eyes presses in around my chest until I can scarcely breathe.

"Excuse me, please," I say to the Theyn, ducking away.

Even as I retreat, I feel the Kaiser watching me, always watching me. His gaze spreads decay on my skin and I yearn for a bath to scrub it off.

I am a lamb in the lion's den. How can I be any kind of queen when I am so easily frightened? Artemisia wouldn't cower from the Kaiser; she wouldn't hesitate to plunge the dagger into his chest here and now, no matter what it cost her.

"Thora!" Crescentia calls after me. I slow my steps but I don't turn back, too frightened of meeting the Kaiser's gaze again. Too frightened of what I'll find there.

Cress falls into step next to me and loops her arm through mine. "I'm so glad you came. You look lovely."

Her quick gray eyes dart up to take in the crumbling crown, the ash I can feel covering my face, neck, and shoulders. It itches terribly, but I don't dare scratch. Better to pretend it isn't there at all.

"Thank you," I tell her with a forced smile I hope seems natural. "It was so kind of you to send the dress. We could be sisters tonight." I squeeze her arm and try to ignore the guilt seeping into my gut.

"We are," she replies with a smile that feels like a blow to my heart.

There is nothing to say to that. All I can give her are lies, and I can't do that tonight, not to her.

All I am is a lie, I remind myself. *Thora is a lie*. But that isn't the whole truth.

My mouth opens and I'm not entirely sure what will come out, but before I can say a word, a boy with a golden-horned ram half-mask approaches. Even with his scar gone and his features blurred to give him a more northern look, I'd recognize Blaise anywhere. I glance around the room warily, knowing that Artemisia must be nearby as well, to hold this illusion, but if she is, I can't see her. There are too many people, too many masks.

"A dance, Lady Thora?" Even beneath the mask, I can see his mouth twist unpleasantly around my false name like it's a curse. He's never had to call me that before, and I can tell he hates himself a bit for it, even if it is unavoidable.

Crescentia's blond eyebrows arch so high they nearly disappear into her hair, but her mouth is smiling as she nudges me toward him. Though he is the last person I want to talk to, I have no choice but to take his hand and let him lead me onto the dance floor.

"Are you insane?" I hiss, sticking to Kalovaxian and moving my lips as little as possible. "If you're caught—"

"It's a *maskentanz*," he says, overemphasizing the hard edges of the Kalovaxian word so that it sounds more like a hacking cough. "There's little chance of that."

"Little, but not *none*," I point out, fighting to keep my tone level. "Besides, you don't even know how to dance."

"I watched a few of them," he says with a shrug, resting his hand on the small of my back and taking my free hand in his. It's the proper placement for the *glissadant* that the orchestra is playing, but his steps are clumsy. The warmth of his touch seeps through the metal and silk of my dress.

"Not enough," I say, wincing as his foot comes down hard on mine. "Follow my lead."

He sighs, but does as I say, letting me guide him into something resembling the complex steps of the dance. We almost blend into the twirl of the other dancers around us, but I'm not foolish enough to believe that people aren't watching me, wondering who the newcomer is who chose to dance with the Ash Princess, of all people.

I wonder if he's thinking about how this ballroom felt before the siege, though we were far too young to ever attend balls when they were held here. Our parents must have, though. They would have danced together and laughed in this room, sipping wine from the same gilded goblets the Kalovaxians use now, raising toasts to my mother and the gods and goddesses, to Astrea.

I try to remember that I'm supposed to be angry with him for what Artemisia said, but having him this close is disconcerting. The last time we were this close, he was kissing me. He was holding my wrists tightly in his grasp, refusing to meet my eyes. He won't look at me now either, but I think that's less to do with rejection this time and more because he can feel the anger rolling off me.

He doesn't know what to do with it, and I'm worried that if I open my mouth, I'll snap at him and everyone will stare, so we fall into an uncomfortable silence that feels like a different version of the pinching game. Which of us will break first?

This time, I win. He starts rambling, eyes darting around the room like he's afraid to look at me.

"This seemed too good an opportunity to pass up, and we couldn't hear anything from the Shadow spots. Artemisia conjured the illusions: I'm a visiting duke's son from Elcourt, Artemisia is a reclusive country lady, and Heron decided it was best for him to stay invisible and mill around the open sun—or rather, *moon*—pavilions—"

"Do you trust me?" I interrupt, because the more he talks around the argument we're pointedly not having, the bigger it feels.

His brow furrows and he twirls me under his arm, giving me a chance to survey the room.

I'm relieved to realize that most people aren't watching us; they're too busy with their own private dramas to care about mine. But some people still are, including the Kaiser. When my eyes meet his mid-twirl, my stomach turns to lead.

"I . . . Why would you ask that?" Blaise says when the twirl ends and he steadies me again with his hand on my back.

It's not an answer, but it might as well be. I lower my voice to a whisper. "I'm not risking everything to play games, Blaise. I'm not a monkey trained to do tricks for your amusement—"

"I never said—" His voice rises before he catches himself, glancing around to see if anyone noticed, but the other dancers all seem engrossed in their own conversations. Still, he lowers his voice. "Where is this coming from?"

"Art said it was your idea to have me poison Crescentia. There's enough Encatrio for two people and there are plenty of others in this castle who prove much more of a threat than one spoiled girl. So tell me it's not just another fire you want me to walk through to prove my loyalty."

His shoulder muscle tightens under my hand and his skin almost feels warmer.

"It's not your loyalty I'm worried about," he says after a moment. "It's your mind. The Kalovaxians have had you for ten years, Theo. That isn't something that's easy to leave behind."

He's only giving voice to my own fears, but the words still

sting. "I told you, I'm fine. And you're in no position to be judging someone's sanity. Don't tell me five years in the mines didn't leave their mark on you."

I can feel his temper roiling, but I don't flinch from it.

"Every move we make is dangerous, Blaise," I continue. "And I need people who I can trust. Who trust me."

He laughs, but it's a joyless sound. "And yet you clearly don't trust me, Theo."

I want to deny it, but he's right. I believe we want the same things; I believe he would lay down his life to protect me. But I also believe it's a secondhand loyalty, filtered through his promise to Ampelio. It's diluted, bound by duty, not necessarily by choice. I thought maybe he cared about me when we kissed, as a person instead of a symbol, but I can still feel his hands around my wrists holding me away, the awkward way he wouldn't meet my eyes. I'm a duty to him, and that is all.

He's right: I can't put my trust in him any more than he can put his trust in me.

"Give me a reason," I say. "One real reason to poison Cress."

He licks his lips, eyes darting around, searching for an answer. "They say she'll be a prinzessin soon enough."

"We both know she'll never be a prinzessin. Søren will be dead long before she has a chance to marry him," I point out. "Give me a real reason and I'll do it."

His mouth tightens. "She's a Kalovaxian. She's the Theyn's daughter. Those should be reasons enough," he snaps. "Why don't you give me a reason *not* to kill her?"

"She has no blood on her hands," I tell him. "She likes to read books and flirt with boys. She isn't a threat."

A battle rages behind his eyes and he tightens one hand on my waist. "Captive animals grow to love their captors all the time, even when they beat them. It's not surprising that you love one of yours."

The words light a fire in me, though I know in his own way, he means them as a comfort. "I'm not an animal, Blaise. I'm a queen, and I know who my enemies are. Being born to the wrong man doesn't make her one of them."

I pull back from him as the song comes to its end and I walk away, half expecting him to follow me. But I suppose he knows me well enough not to.

I'm not halfway across the ballroom when the Kaiser's broad form cuts into my path, effectively blocking me. I drop to a curtsy, but when I rise he's still there, still watching me the way he has been all night. My stomach sours.

"Your Highness," I say.

I keep my eyes averted. *I am Thora, docile and broken,* I tell myself. *I will not anger the Kaiser and he will keep me alive.*

"Ash Princess," he replies, an ugly curve to his mouth. "I hope you thanked the Theyn for his services in the mines these past weeks, subduing the riffraff."

"Of course, Your Highness," I reply, though the thought of it makes me sick. How many more of my people did the Theyn kill in his *inspections*?

He moves aside to let me pass, but when I do, he brushes against me and runs a hand along the curve of my waist and over my hip. Shock floods through me, followed by repulsion. I force myself not to shudder or jerk away, because I know that's what he wants and it would only make things that much worse. The dagger in my bodice is within reach, and for a moment I let myself imagine pulling it out and drawing it across his throat before he could even realize what was happening. I want to do it so badly it's painful to hold back. My hands shake, and I struggle to keep them still and at my sides. Guards would be on me in a moment if I tried, and our rising rebellion would be cut short.

It isn't worth it. Not yet.

He bends his face to mine, close enough that I can smell wine, sour on his breath. Bile rises in my throat, but I swallow it down.

"You've grown awfully pretty, for a heathen," he says, low in my ear.

I keep my expression neutral even while his words feel like grime coating my skin. *Soon,* I promise myself. Soon I will kill him, but not tonight. Tonight I have to play a different part.

"Thank you, Your Highness." The words aren't mine, they're Thora's, but they still burn my throat.

My heart is hammering so loudly it feels like the whole room can hear it, even over the orchestra. He lingers a moment longer, his grip on my hip tightening, before he is gone. I let out a long, shaky breath and hurry in the opposite direction as quickly as I can.

Blaise stares after the Kaiser, fury clearly etched in his expression. He doesn't know how to hide it like I do, so it shows in the hard line of his mouth, the crease in his forehead above the mask. When his eyes meet mine, they soften. We remember who our real enemy is.

He makes a move toward me, but I give a minute shake of my head. He already drew attention to himself by dancing with me, and his lies about his identity will hold only until someone asks him the wrong question.

There's too much at stake to risk a moment of comfort, and I'm not sure I want it from him anyway.

The crowd parts for me, not out of any kind of deference but because no one wants to get ash on their pretty clothes. I cling to the edge of the room, as far from the crowd as I can get. The ghost of the Kaiser's hand is still on me, his sour breath lingering in my nose. The memory will haunt my nightmares tonight, and probably for a long time to come.

"Still playing games, my little lamb?" a soft voice says from the shadowed alcove behind me.

The Kaiserin waits there, her skeletal frame nearly disappearing in a gray dress that swamps her. Her mask is a strip of black organza that wraps around her temples, with holes cut for her eyes. She is more ghost than woman.

"I've never enjoyed games," I tell her, surprised that my voice comes out level.

She laughs. "Everyone has their games, little lamb. The Kaiser plays them in the palace, the Theyn plays them on the battlefield, Søren plays them on his ships. Even your friend plays them—quite well, too."

For a heart-stopping second, I think she means Blaise, but it's Crescentia she's talking about.

"She'll make a beautiful prinzessin," I say.

"That's all a prinzessin has to be," the Kaiserin says with a scoff. "No one expects more from them than beauty and grace. You know all about that, though. You've been playing that part since you were a child. The pretty little Ash Princess with her sad eyes and broken spirit. Or maybe not so broken."

The Kaiserin's words send a jolt through me that I try to ignore. I pretend to misunderstand them. "The Kaiser was kind to let me keep my title," I say.

She laughs. "The Kaiser is many things, but we both know *kind* is not one of them." When she takes my hand, her touch is ice cold. There is little more to her than bones and thin skin. "He always wins his games. That is why he is the Kaiser."

Because he cheats, I want to say, but that isn't the right response. There isn't one, but she seems to know that.

"Surviving is enough, little lamb."

She presses a chilled kiss to my forehead before walking back into the crush of courtiers, her lips black with ash.

BODY

———— • ————

THOUGH THE MASKENTANZ STRETCHES ON until the eastern
sky is bleeding pastels and the moon is rapidly fading in
the west, I spend the rest of it clinging to the edges of the
room, hoping to avoid the Kaiser's gaze. I'm not sure whether
it's the energy from the ball itself or the Kaiser's threat hanging over my head, but sleep feels miles away, even when my
body grows heavy and lethargic. When the last guests begin to
file out through the main entrance, I reluctantly follow, ready
to turn in for what I'm sure will be a restless couple of hours
in bed, but when I reach the doors, Cress is waiting, holding
two steaming mugs of spiced honey coffee.

Relief seeps through me at the sight of her, my friend, but
it's quickly quashed by the sharp memory of the poison hidden in my room and what I'm meant to do with it. My conversation with Blaise echoes in my mind, but I push it aside.

"The night is young," she tells me with a grin, passing one
mug to me.

I thank her and take a small sip. In the Astrean tradition,
the coffee has been mixed with honey, cinnamon, and milk.
It's too sweet for most Kalovaxians, but it's the way Crescentia

always orders it. Not for the first time, I wonder whether it's because she has a sweet tooth or because she understands how much the small gesture means to me.

The coffee tastes like my mother's breath when she kissed me good morning, and the memory soothes me and breaks me all over again.

Crescentia links her arm with mine and steers me not through the crowded entrance hall, but through a smaller one that shoots off to the side. Having her so close and knowing what I'm expected to do feels like a splinter in my heart, sharp and nagging, no matter how I try to ignore it.

"I should go to bed, Cress," I tell her. "I'm exhausted."

"That's what the coffee's for," she says cheerfully, squeezing my arm. "We hardly had a chance to talk the entire night, Thora."

"I know. You were such a wonderful hostess and I didn't want to steal you away. But we'll talk tomorrow, I promise."

Crescentia glances sideways at me as we walk, though she doesn't let go of my arm.

"Are you angry with me?" she asks after a long moment of quiet. She sounds wounded and, despite myself, my heart lurches.

"No," I say with a laugh. "Of course I'm not."

"You've been avoiding me," she insists. "This week. Tonight. Now, even."

"I told you, I was sick." The words sound hollow even to me.

"Just one hour, Thora. Please."

She sounds so hurt that my soul cracks and I'm tempted to say yes. And why *shouldn't* I say yes? What's waiting for me back in my room? Another argument with Blaise and Artemisia, with Heron trying to play the mediator? And Blaise will want to talk about the Kaiser, what he saw, and I can't do that. I shudder thinking of the Kaiser's hand on me, his breath against my skin.

If Blaise asks me about it, I will fall apart and I will lose what little respect they have for me.

Crescentia is easier because being around her means becoming Thora, and Thora doesn't think about things too much. Right now, Thora feels like a blessing.

"All right. I'll stay up a little longer." I hesitate for a breath. "I've missed you, Cress."

She beams at me, almost glowing with her own light in the dim hallway. "I've missed you, too," she says before pushing a door open with her shoulder.

I realize her intended destination just as the brisk early-morning air hits me. The gray garden. It could never be as beautiful as it was under my mother's care, but in this light there's something eerily lovely about it. It's a ghost of a place, filled with ghosts of its own. Skeleton fingers of the bald tree branches stretch out high overhead, casting smoky shadows against the stone in the dawn light.

Next to me, Cress wrinkles her nose in distaste as she looks around at the garden. It isn't her sort of place. She prefers color and music and crowds and life, but still, when her eyes find mine, she smiles. Another thing she does for me, because she knows what this place means to me. Because she also knows what it is to lose a mother.

The realization causes another stone of guilt to fall into my already heavy gut.

"It's because of the luncheon, isn't it?" she asks me. "I made you wear that hideous dress and then I acted so jealous when you spoke with the Prinz. I shouldn't have acted that way. It was . . . unbecoming. I'm sorry."

The apology takes me by surprise. I'm not sure I've ever heard Cress apologize to anyone before, at least not genuinely. Not when it wasn't simply a way to get what she wants. But there's no mistaking the regret in her voice now. I smile and shake my head.

"Nothing you do could ever be unbecoming, Cress. I promise, I'm not angry with you." She doesn't look convinced, so I give her arm a squeeze and look her straight in the eye when I lie, hoping that will make it seem true. "I'm not interested in the Prinz. I promise you that."

She bites her lip and looks down at her coffee. "Maybe not. But he likes you."

I force a laugh, as if the idea were ridiculous. "As a *friend*," I tell her, surprised by how smoothly the lie rolls off my tongue. I nearly believe it myself, even with the fresh memory of Søren's mouth against mine. "Of course a boy considering marriage with a girl will seek out the friendship of her closest friend. When we talk, it's always about you."

She smiles slightly, her shoulders relaxing. "I do want to be a prinzessin," she admits.

"You would make a good one," I tell her, and I mean it. The Kaiserin's words come back to me: all a prinzessin has to be is beautiful.

She's quiet for a moment, crossing to sit down on the stone bench beneath the largest tree, motioning for me to join her. When I do, she takes a deep, wavering breath before she speaks. "When I am Kaiserin, Thora, you'll never have to wear that horrible crown again," she says quietly, staring straight ahead at the garden, now awash in pastel light from the rising sun.

Her words take me by surprise. Ever since the incident with the war paint, she's never mentioned the ash crown, or even looked at it. I thought she'd grown used to it, stopped seeing it altogether. Again, I've underestimated her.

"Cress," I start, but she interrupts me, turning to face me fully and taking my hands in hers and smiling.

"When I'm Kaiserin, I'll change everything, Thora," she says, voice growing stronger. "It isn't fair, the way he treats you. I'm sure the Prinz thinks so, too. It breaks my heart, you know." She gives me a smile so sad that for a moment I forget that I'm the one she's pitying and not the other way around. "I'll marry the Prinz and then I'll take care of you. I'll find a handsome husband for you and we'll raise our children together, like we always wanted. They'll be the best of friends, I know it. Just like us. Heart's sisters."

A lump hardens in my throat. I know that if I put my life in Crescentia's hands, she would shape it into something pretty for me, something simple and easy. But I also know that's a childish hope for sheltered girls with the world at their feet. Even before the siege, my mother impressed upon me the difficulties of ruling, how a queen's life was never hers—it was her people's. And my people are hungry and beaten and waiting for someone to save them.

"Heart's sisters," I repeat, feeling the weight of that vow. It isn't something made lightly; it's a promise to not just love another person but trust them. I thought I didn't trust anyone, that I wasn't capable of it anymore, but I do trust Cress and I always have and in almost ten years of friendship she has never once made me regret that. She is my heart's sister.

My Shadows are watching, I know. I can make out the outlines of their figures in the second-story windows, peering down at us. But they won't be able to hear anything.

"Cress," I say, tentatively.

She must hear the hitch in my voice, because she stiffens, turning toward me, fair eyebrows arched over a bemused smile. My heart hammers in my chest. Words surge forward, and part of me knows I should hold them back, but Cress has never been anything but honest with me. We are heart's sisters, she said it herself. She has to love me enough to put me first.

"We could change things. Not just for me, but for the rest of them as well."

Her brow furrows. "The rest of who?" she asks. An uncertain smile tugs at her lips, like she thinks I'm telling a joke she doesn't understand yet.

I want to turn back, to pull the words from the air between us and pretend they were never said, but it's too late for that. And yes, Cress is the daughter of the Theyn and that makes her a perfect target, but it could make her an even more invaluable asset. Could I bring her in? I think of how I changed my Shadows' minds about Vecturia. I can sell this to them as well. I can save her.

"The Astreans," I tell her slowly, watching her expression. "The slaves."

Her smile lingers for a moment, a ghost of its former self, before fading to nothing.

"There is no changing that," she says, her voice low.

It's a warning. I ignore it. I reach out with my free hand to take hers. She doesn't pull away, but her hand stays limp in mine.

"But we could," I say, desperation creeping in. "The Kaiser is a cruel man. You know this."

"He is the Kaiser, he can be as cruel as he likes," she replies. She glances around, as if there's someone listening nearby. When her eyes find mine again, she looks at me like I'm a stranger, someone to be wary of. In all our years of friendship, she's never looked at me that way.

I'm dimly aware of how tightly I'm clutching her hand, but she doesn't flinch. She doesn't try to pull away. "If you could be Kaiserin. If . . . if you could marry Søren. You could change things. The people would love you, they would rally to you over the Kaiser, you could take the country from him easily."

"That's treason," she hisses. "Stop it, Thora."

I open my mouth to argue, to tell her my name is not Thora, but before I can speak, something over Cress's shoulder catches my gaze in one of the high windows that borders the garden to the west. I see a pale figure in a gray dress. I see yellow hair trailing behind her like the tail of a comet as she falls. I hear a scream that echoes in my bones and ends with a sickening thud on the other side of the garden, a hundred feet away.

Both of our mugs fall from our hands and break on the stones before Crescentia and I run toward it, but I know when we get there it will be too late. There is no surviving a fall like that.

The blood is the first thing I see. It pools out around her body—so much, so quickly. It's the only color I can see against the gray of her dress, the gray of the stones, the colorless pallor of her skin. Her body is broken, limbs twisted at unnatural angles, like a marionette whose strings have been cut.

In my gut, I know who it is, but when her face comes into focus, shock still shakes me to my core. I'm so lost in it that I almost don't hear Crescentia's panicked cries next to me. I almost don't feel her clutching my arm in shock and fear, our previous discussion forgotten, as if I can protect her from the Kaiserin's corpse.

I untangle myself from Cress and inch closer to the body, stepping around the blood. I crouch down and press my hand to the Kaiserin's cheek. Even in life her skin was cold, but it seems different now that she's truly dead. Her eyes stare off at nothing and I close them, even though I'm sure they'll follow me into my nightmares.

In the end, though, it's her mouth that unravels me. Her dry lips are still caked in ash from when she kissed my forehead with something resembling love, and she's smiling more broadly than I ever saw her when she was alive. She has the same smile as Søren.

"Thora." Crescentia shakes my shoulder. "Look up."

In the window the Kaiserin fell from, a figure watches us. It's too dark to make out his face, but his golden crown glints in the early-morning sunlight.

GRIEF

———◆ • ◆———

CRESCENTIA AND I DON'T SPEAK about what we saw in the week that follows the Kaiserin's death. We also don't talk about the conversation that preceded it, and I can't help but wonder if it was all some kind of twisted nightmare. But that can't be, because every morning I wake up and the Kaiserin is truly dead.

Only seconds after we found her, the guards came and questioned us, but we both knew better than to point fingers at the Kaiser.

We saw nothing, we told them, and they believed us without hesitation.

The court whispers that the Kaiserin finally succumbed to her madness and jumped, something most had been speculating about for years and a few had even been crass enough to place wagers on.

I heard that the Kaiser made the winning bet, but that's only a rumor, albeit one that's easy for me to believe.

The funeral was a quiet affair, one I wasn't even invited to, though Cress was. She came to visit after and told me about how the Kaiserin's body was displayed—clean, but just as broken as we'd found it. She told me that the Kaiser sat in the back of the chapel but left after only a few moments without giving the customary speech. Kalovaxian tradition says that those in mourning should shave their head, but he still wears his hair long, in the tradition of warriors, though it's been decades since he was last in battle.

I try to hear any bitterness in Cress's voice, any hint that the things we spoke of before have taken hold, but it's as if she's forgotten them completely. It may be a good thing. It may be that I was a fool to trust Cress, not because of who she is but because of how she was raised. This is the only world she knows, and though it's a nightmare to me, it's a world she is at home in. I suppose it's easy to be at home in a world where you are on top. It's easy not to notice those whose backs you stand on to stay there. One doesn't even see them.

Blaise tries to ask me about what happened in the garden, but even though I can't manage to be angry about our conversation at the maskentanz anymore, I'm not ready to talk to him again either. If I do, it will all come flooding out—the Kaiserin's warning, the Kaiser's leers, my feelings for Søren, my almost-confession to Cress. It's better if he doesn't know any of those things. Blaise protects me in his way, and I protect him in mine.

There is no word from the Kaiser, though I expect something is coming, some new game that I will have to learn the rules to before he begins to cheat. If the Kaiserin was right about the Kaiser wanting to marry me to cement his hold over Astrea, I can only think the proposal will be coming soon. The idea creeps into my nightmares and many of my waking thoughts. No matter how many times I bathe, how hard I scrub my skin with sponges and oils, I can't erase the feel of his hands on me. Sometimes just before I drift off to sleep, I'm suddenly jerked awake, certain that I smell his sour breath again.

One day, when I wake up, my fingers close around something hard and hot under my pillow. The bottle of Encatrio, I realize, pulling it out. I left it in its usual place in my mattress, but someone must have moved it to remind me—as if I could have forgotten. I feel my Shadows watching but no one says anything. No one is surprised it's there.

I should say something, I know I should, but I can't muster a defense again. I know as well as they must that I'm running out of excuses.

Instead, I get out of bed, Encatrio in hand, and kneel down to push it back into the hole in the mattress, not saying a word about it.

It would be imprudent to poison Cress and the Theyn too hastily, I tell myself, just as I've told my Shadows countless times. If we slip up, the Kaiser will blame me and I'll likely lose my head before Søren returns. Our plan will fall to pieces and it isn't worth that. But I know that's only a fraction of the truth. There is a much larger part of me that keeps playing my conversation with Cress in the garden over and over in my head, trying to imagine what might have happened if the Kaiserin hadn't fallen at that moment, what Cress might have said.

I'm too afraid to bring it up again with her. I keep seeing the wary look on her face; I still hear her telling me that there is no changing the enslavement of the other Astreans. Still, there is a part of me that hasn't yet given up hope that I'm wrong.

Every morning before Hoa comes in, I check the doorway for another note from Søren, but there is never one to find. He was due back a couple of days ago now, and while I figure this must mean Vecturia is still fighting, I can't help but worry that he might not come back at all.

And what will he come back to if he does? A world suddenly bereft of his mother, the only person in this palace he loved. He never even got to say goodbye to her. I understand that more than I care to, which is why I decide to write him another letter.

I don't tell my Shadows what I'm doing when I sit down at my desk—I can't stand to have Artemisia breathe down my neck again. Not this time, when there is no hidden strategy to my words, no deceptions or subterfuge, just honesty.

Dear Søren,

I'm sure, by now, that word of your mother has reached you. I wish I could be there with you to provide whatever comfort I could. Your mother was a good woman and much stronger than I think most gave her credit for. We spoke for a few minutes that night, and she told me how proud she was of you and the man you had become. I know it isn't much, but I hope that you take some measure of comfort in that. She loved you dearly, Søren.

If this letter is found, I'm sure the Kaiser will punish me severely for what I am about to say, but I think you need to hear it.

My mother was killed ten years ago, and I wish that I could tell you that it becomes easier over time, but that wouldn't be the truth. I don't think I will ever grow used to breathing in a world where my mother no longer does. I don't think I will ever close my eyes at night without seeing her death all over again. I don't think I will ever stop wanting to turn to her when I need advice or have questions. I don't think I will ever stop feeling like there is a part of me missing.

First, you will not believe it. You'll have to remind yourself often that she's gone. And though you know better, part of you will still expect to see her greet your ship when you come home. She won't, and I'm so sorry for that.

Next, you'll grieve. It will take everything you have to get out of bed in the morning and continue with your life, but you'll do it because that's the kind of man you are. There are thousands depending on you right now, and you're too good a leader to let this ruin you.

After that—or maybe even during it—you'll become angry. You'll be angry at the gods for taking her, you'll be angry at your father and the court for driving her to madness in the first place, you may even be angry at me for witnessing it and being unable to stop it. It's all right if you are, I understand.

If there is a step after anger, I haven't yet found it.

Yours,
Thora

I start to roll the letter up, but as I do an idea strikes me and I freeze.

"If I tell Søren that the Kaiser killed his mother, it would be enough to make the divide between them permanent," I say aloud, partially so my Shadows can hear me and partially so I can hear the words out loud myself. "He would be furious, enough so to act out against the Kaiser publicly."

For a moment, no one says anything.

"How can you be sure?" Blaise asks finally.

"Because I'll make him feel that he has no choice."

I unfold the letter and dip my quill into the inkpot once more, the pieces of the plan falling into place. It feels inevitable, in a way, as easy as toppling a pyramid of fruit by removing just one piece.

As easy as driving a dagger through his heart? A voice whispers through my mind, but I try to ignore it. I knew it would come to this; it was my idea, even. It's the only way I can see to retake Astrea, and I am not going to change my mind now because I care for Søren more than I thought I would.

* * *

The next day, I answer the door to find Elpis, sent to bring me to meet Crescentia for coffee. For a moment, I think about saying no, because every time I'm around her the guilt in my gut becomes too much to bear, but there is a part of me that always hopes and dreads that this will be the time we acknowledge what was said the night of the maskentanz.

"Just a moment," I tell Elpis, my heart thudding in my chest. I leave her in the doorway before going back into my room, to my hiding place in the mattress to retrieve the vial of Encatrio. I'm not going to use it, but taking it should buy me some time with my Shadows, should show them that I'm willing to use it. I feel their eyes on me as I tuck it into the pocket of my gray brocade mourning gown. They give no sign of warning or encouragement—even Artemisia stays mercifully silent. Maybe they know as well as I do that it's an empty gesture.

Elpis gives me a small smile when I meet her back at the door, and we start down the hall to the pavilion. There is little that can be said, since the halls are crowded with people. Still, having her close helps me focus. Elpis is why I'm doing all of this, why I'm playing a game I have a hard time imagining I can win, why I'm carrying a vial of poison in my pocket intended for my closest friend. Elpis, and all the people she represents, all the others who have been enslaved for as long as they can remember. All the others who are chained and beaten and hungry but still have the gall to dream of a better world. I will build it for them, but not with the bones of innocents.

We turn down an empty hallway that leads to the east wing of the palace. Talking is still too much of a risk, but as soon as she's sure we're alone, Elpis grabs my hand. Her fingers are all bone and another wave of guilt slams through me. I ate a five-course meal last night, but when was the last time she ate more than a bowl of broth?

She presses something into my palm before dropping her hand. When I look, there is a small, crumpled flower made of scraps of pink silk I recognize from one of Cress's gowns. Each petal has been painstakingly cut and arranged around a single pearl no bigger than a freckle. The memory is there, but it slips through my fingers like smoke.

"Happy Belsiméra, Your Highness," she murmurs, her smile rare and wide.

I close my palm over the flower and tuck it into my pocket and out of sight. My mother and I used to make dozens of silk flowers together for Belsiméra for those closest to us, though my tiny fingers were clumsy and most of my flowers turned out shapeless and unusable. She enlisted seamstresses to make hundreds more, enough for all the Guardians and the palace staff.

Belsiméra—the birthday of Belsimia, goddess of love and beauty. In the story my mother used to tell me, the earth goddess, Glaidi, always loathed the fall, when her flowers would die and her trees would grow skeletal. She mourned the loss of color in the world, the loss of beauty.

One year, when the season turned and Glaidi grew melancholy and distant, the water goddess, Suta, cheered her up by crafting a hundred flowers from silk and presenting them to her friend. When Glaidi saw them, she was so moved by the display of love and beauty that she began to weep tears of joy.

One of the tears landed on one of the silk flowers, and from that bloom, Belsimia was born.

To celebrate Belsimia and the deep friendship that created her, we used to craft silk flowers and give them to friends and loved ones throughout the day. At night, there was a celebration in the capital, with dancing and sweets and silk flowers everywhere.

I remember making the flowers with my mother and passing them out to everyone who worked and lived in the palace. I remember the festival, when Ampelio scooped me up in his arms and swung me around in a dance until I was delirious with giggles. I remember it was my favorite night of the year, even more so than the ones with gifts.

"Thank you, Elpis," I say, looking at the younger girl, whose cheeks flush pink. "I'm sorry, I don't . . ." I trail off, biting my lip, embarrassed. "I'd forgotten."

She nods, her eyes solemn. "We celebrate in the slave quarter still, but we have to do it very quietly. If anyone knew . . ." She shakes her head. "I wanted to give one to you. You'll keep it hidden, won't you?"

"Of course," I say, smiling. "Thank you."

I turn to start down the hall again, but Elpis touches my arm, stopping me.

"I need to do something," she whispers.

"Elpis—" I start, but she interrupts.

"*Anything*, please," she says. "I can help, if you'll let me."

Her dark eyes are so earnest that it's easy to forget she's only thirteen. In the old Astrea, she would still be considered a child.

"I need you to stay safe," I tell her gently.

"But—"

"The time is coming," I murmur in Astrean, casting a glance down the hall for anyone who might be listening. "I need your patience."

She bites her lip and releases my arm. "I just want to help," she says, sounding even younger than she is.

The desperation in her voice clutches at my heart. "You are helping," I assure her. "You've already done so much."

Her eyes dart up to mine, searching for any sign that I'm patronizing her. Finally she bows her head slightly.

"Thank you, Your Highness," she says.

She doesn't say the title the way the others do; there are no strings attached. I hold her full trust in my hands and it is a terribly fragile thing. I will not break it.

THREAT

COFFEE HAS BEEN SET UP at one of the wrought-iron tables on the public sun pavilion. Striped violet and white silk awnings hang over the large veranda, flapping in the wind, while gold candles lend warmth to each table, aided by the Fire Gems studding the holders. Though winter is fast approaching and the sun is becoming a rarer and rarer sight, the space is still alive with court activity. If anything, the Kaiserin's death has reanimated the courtiers. They are bursting with fresh gossip now about who the Kaiser will marry next, and each great family has a daughter they are eager to sacrifice for an extra helping of favor.

I count twelve of them now, some younger than me, and each in a dress far too revealing for the weather. Everyone but me, it seems, has already moved on from mourning gray though there are three weeks left of the traditional Kalovaxian mourning period. They all shiver in their silks and sip coffee with shaking hands, surrounded by circles of fussing family members as they wait, just in case the Kaiser decides to make an appearance.

Across from me, Cress studies a book of poems, rarely

looking up even though she invited me today. We still haven't spoken of our conversation in the garden, but I can feel it wedging between us and casting a shadow over every word we speak. I want to bring it up again now, to push her the way I didn't have the chance to then, but every time I try, the words die in my throat.

"Poor girls," Cress murmurs, barely looking up from her book of Lyrian poems, quill in hand. "All that work for nothing. My father says the Kaiser already has his bride picked out. He thinks the betrothal will be official by the time my father leaves for Elcourt in four days."

I freeze, cup to my mouth, dread pooling in the pit of my stomach.

"I don't suppose you heard who?" I ask casually, setting the coffee cup down on the saucer.

She shakes her head with a huff and scribbles something out. "He wouldn't tell me, as usual. He seems to think I can't be trusted with his secrets."

I force a laugh. "Well, he's right, isn't he?" I tease.

I expect her to laugh as well, but when she looks up at me, her eyes are somber. "I can keep secrets, Thora."

The words are innocuous enough, but they feel heavy. What I said in the garden was treason, and she could have used that to secure herself a crown. But she didn't and that means something, doesn't it?

"Of course you can," I tell her quietly. "You're my heart's sister, Cress. I'd trust you with my life."

The vial of poison is warm against my skin.

She nods once and goes back to her poem. *"Ch'bur,"* she

says, twisting the feather of her quill as she thinks. "Do you suppose that's related to the Oriamic word *chabor*? Clawed?"

"I don't know," I admit. "Try it out loud."

She bites her bottom lip for a moment. "*In the valley of Gredane*—that's their term for the underworld—*my love waits for me, still wrapped in Death's clawed embrace.* No. That can't be right, can it?"

I try to answer, but all I can see is Cress's limp, gray body held in a giant bird's claw.

"Besides, I don't see what it matters," she says, dragging me out of my thoughts and scribbling something else in her book. "It isn't as though the girl—whoever she is—will say no, is it?"

It takes me a moment to realize she isn't talking about the poem anymore, or alluding to my treason. We've circled back to the Kaiser now, and she seems awfully cavalier about it, considering she's as eligible for the role as any other girl. But it won't be her and I suppose she knows it. Her father wouldn't let that happen. He might be the Kaiser's attack dog, but even he has a line and that line has always been Cress.

"It isn't as though she *can* say no," I point out, earning me a warning look from Cress.

"Don't pity her too much, Thora," she says. "I think I could put up with the Kaiser if the crown came with it."

Kaiserin Anke might disagree with you, I want to say, but I manage to hold myself back. Cress and I have a silent agreement not to mention what we saw that night, and I'm not about to break it. She knows the Kaiser pushed the Kaiserin out that window as well as I do, but neither of us has the courage to say it out loud, as if not speaking the words is enough to quell the danger of what we saw. After all, if the Kaiser murdered his wife because she was an inconvenience, what's to stop him from doing the same to us?

Still, I want to confide in someone about the things the Kaiserin said before she died—before she was killed. I want to tell someone about my feelings for Søren and how that complicates the plan I hatched with my Shadows. I want to talk about that plan and how fragile it feels sometimes.

But I can hear her voice whisper through my mind. *"That's treason. Stop it, Thora."* And I can't even bear to think what her reaction would be if she knew about Søren and me.

But I don't know if I can even be angry at her for her reaction in the garden. I asked her to choose between me and her country—not to mention her father. I should have known what she would choose. I know what *I'm* choosing, after all.

The poison weighs heavier than ever in my pocket.

"And," Cress continues without looking up from her poem, "it'll be a better match than you could have hoped for otherwise."

I freeze, my cup halfway to my lips. With shaking hands, I place it back in its saucer.

"What did you say?" I ask.

She lifts one shoulder in a blasé shrug. "No one had to tell me the Kaiser's plans, Thora. It just makes sense. I heard a few whispers about the riots, how there are still countries who refuse to acknowledge the Kaiser's claim on Astrea. His marriage to you would solve that problem nicely. Also, he had no use for the Kaiserin anymore—she gave him his heir, served her purpose. And I always wondered, I suppose, why he kept you alive."

She says it all so calmly, her eyes still fixed on her book. But it's not because she doesn't care. I can hear it in her voice. It's because she's afraid to look at me.

"So when you saw him push her out that window, it must have confirmed your suspicions," I reply, matching her easy tone, as if we were talking about dinner plans instead of murder.

She flinches at that, but it's so slight I nearly miss it. After a breath, she finally looks up at me, placing her quill down on the table.

"It'll be for the best, Thora," she says firmly. "You'll be the Kaiserin. You'll have power."

"Like Kaiserin Anke had power?" I ask her. "You say I am your heart's sister and that's what you want for me? To end up like her?"

The flinch is more pronounced this time and her gray eyes dart around. She exhales.

"Better that than a traitor on the executioner's block," she says, her voice low.

The venom in the words feels like a slap and I struggle not to recoil from her. I swallow. "I don't know what you're talking about, Cress," I say, but my voice shakes and I know it doesn't fool her. No matter how she tries to pretend otherwise, Cress is no fool.

"Don't insult me," she says, leaning back in her chair. She reaches into her pocket and withdraws a folded piece of paper. The seal has been broken, but it once was a drakkon breathing fire. Søren's sigil. The sight of it hollows my stomach, and a thousand excuses rise to my lips, but I already know there is no excuse for what is in that letter.

"Where did you get that?" I ask instead, as if I can somehow turn this on her, make her the one who betrayed me.

She ignores me, opening the letter slowly. Hurt flickers across her expression as she begins to read.

"'Dear Thora.'" Her voice remains flat and emotionless. "'I can't find the words to express how happy your letter made me. I know that I didn't say it so plainly in my last letter, though I'm sure you could have surmised as much, but my heart is yours as well.

"'In your letter, you said that you wanted a way for us to be together without having to hide it. I want the same. I want to tell everyone; I want to brag about your letters the way my men brag about the letters their sweethearts send them; I want a world where there is a future for us that is not sneaking through dark tunnels (as enjoyable as that sneaking might be). But I think, more than anything else, I want to live in a better world than the one my father has created. I have hope that one day, when I am kaiser, I can create that world. And now I have hope that when I do, you'll be at my side.'"

She looks back at me as she folds the letter again. "There's more, of course. Bits about his ship's activities, how the battle is going—painfully boring, really, though I'd imagine that's the part you're interested in."

I can't say anything, only watch as she tucks the letter away. It must have come recently. I'd assumed he'd been too busy in battle to write me back, but Cress must have found it under my doormat.

"It isn't what you think," I manage finally, though it's ridiculous how untrue that is.

"I think you lied to me, Thora," she says softly, but all traces of softness are gone from her expression. She is all hard angles and furious eyes. She looks, for the first time, like her father. "I think you stole my Spiritgems, which means you're working with others. You wouldn't have grown this rebellious on your own. Three, I would imagine, given how many of my pieces you took?"

Ice trickles down my spine and my heart thunders. She can't know about my Shadows, not like this. I cast my eyes around and spot them off to the side of the sun pavilion, watching but too far away to hear anything. They're still there, which means she hasn't told anyone about her suspicions yet. I can't let her.

"I'm sorry," I tell her, leaning forward. "I'm so sorry, Cress, but it isn't what you think."

"What I *think* is that it's too convenient," she says, pursing her lips. There's a dangerous glint in her eyes that reminds me of her father. "These others that you're working with show up and you get them Spiritgems and at the same time you decide to start romancing the Prinz. You have to know that a match between him and you would never be allowed, and you're too smart to pretend otherwise. Which means you were aiming for something else."

She glances back down at the letter in her hands.

" '*I misled you before, when I said we were leaving to solve some issues with Dragonsbane in the trade route, but if you're truly so bored that you want to know what's happening here, I'll tell you.*' "

She breaks off again and looks back up at me. There is no emotion in her eyes, which is just as well. My whole body is numb.

"You don't care about whatever mission the Kaiser sent him on. I have a hard time believing you wanted to hear about it, but I suppose these people—whoever you're working with—did, though, and they told you to seduce the Prinz to get as much information as you could for them. Am I wrong?" she asks, tilting her head to one side as she watches me.

Yes, I want to say. *But not about what really matters.*

She must take my silence for a no because she continues. "I understand it, Thora," she says, her voice shifting to what I'm used to from her, gentle and kind. It reminds me of the way the Theyn spoke to me after he killed my mother, asking if I was hungry or thirsty while her blood was still wet on his hands. "I meant it when I said that your life is unfair. The way he treats you is unfair. But this isn't the way to fix it."

I want to scream that it isn't about me at all, that the unfairness of my life is nothing compared to the miseries endured by the other Astreans in the city, the other Astreans in the mines, the other Astreans who fled to become third-class citizens in other countries.

I take a breath, force myself to hold her gaze instead of screaming the way I so badly want to. Because I am not her friend and I never have been. I am her pet and she loves me like I'm something less than her, and the realization of that feels like I drank the vial of Encatrio myself. Like I'm turning to ash from the inside out.

When I speak, my voice is soft and level. It is remorseful, despite the resentment coursing through me. "How do I fix it, then?" I ask her.

It's exactly what she wants to hear. Her smile is genuine, relieved. She reaches across the table to take my hands in hers.

"You do what's expected of you," she says, as if it's simple. To Cress, it is. She's always done what is expected of her and she's going to get a crown because of it. But we are not the same. We live in two different worlds, and different things are expected of us. "You give the Kaiser what he wants. You stay alive until I can save you."

I swallow down the bile rising in my throat. She means well, which makes it so much worse.

"Will you tell the Kaiser?" I ask.

She draws her hands back and clears her throat. "I don't see why he needs to know. You faltered, it's to be expected. But no real harm has been done, has it?" she says, as if I broke a piece of china instead of plotted treason.

"No," I say.

She nods, pressing her lips together thoughtfully. After a second, she gives me a smile, but it's sharp enough to cut through steel.

"Well, then I suppose I can keep it to myself, given that it stops." She pauses, taking a sip of her coffee. She is playing a game where she holds all the cards, and she knows it. She's weighing how much she stands to gain from her win. "You'll end things with the Prinz when he returns. The Kaiser is going to arrange our betrothal when Søren gets back, and I don't want him to refuse because of your meddling."

"Of course," I say obediently.

"And the others? The ones you gave my gems to?" she says. "They're the ones who put you up to all of this, I know. You would never have done this on your own. They led you astray, and we'll have to turn them over to the Kaiser."

Cress has written her own version of this story, and it's an easy enough one to play along with. Better, by far, than the truth. She wouldn't have forgiven me so easily if she knew my feelings for Søren were genuine, or that I acted of my own volition. But if she thinks of me as a pet, trained to do tricks for her amusement, why would she expect anyone else to see me differently?

"They're gone," I tell her. It's getting easier to lie to Cress. This one doesn't even cause my stomach to clench. I know I need to convince her, though, to keep the others safe, so I continue. "They knew a hopeless cause when they saw one. After I gave them the gems, they left. They said they would barter passage on a ship to Grania. They offered to take me with them, but I . . . I couldn't leave."

Cress's smile softens into something more natural. "I'm glad you didn't go," she says. "I would have missed you." She picks up her quill again and glances at her book before looking back at me again. She hesitates for a second. "This is what's best for you, Thora. He'll kill you otherwise. You know that."

The words stick in my throat, but I force them out. "I know."

She reaches across the table to pat my hand before returning to her poem. Her mind is easy once more, the one wrinkle in her life smoothed out. It is simple to her, like the chess games she and her father play. She has me in checkmate, so the game is over and done. She's won.

But it is not simple. Everything in me feels torn to pieces, and I know there will be no mending me.

I focus on the candle between us, the steady dancing of the flame as it shrinks and grows at the same pace as my quick heartbeat. I watch as it slows and a strange calm spreads over me. I shouldn't be calm. I should want to rage and scream and slap her across her pretty face.

I should not be calm, but I am. There is one path ahead of me now, and I can see it clearly lit. It is an awful path, one I hate. I will never forgive myself for walking down it. I will not come out the other side the same.

But it is the only path I can take.

Cress glances up and opens her mouth to speak, but then she catches sight of something over my shoulder and shoots to her feet, posture ramrod straight. A second too late, I realize everyone else has stood as well, and I hurry to follow, even as my stomach sinks. With the Kaiserin dead and Søren still at sea, there is only one person whose presence could cause such a reaction.

In the instant before I fall into a curtsy, I see the Kaiser standing by the double-door entrance, dressed in a velvet suit with gold buttons that strain over his round stomach. As if that weren't bad enough, the Theyn is at his side, which can only mean one thing.

Sure enough, they are coming our way. The Theyn is as stone-faced as ever, but the Kaiser's eyes are bright with the kind of malicious glee that haunts my nightmares. Already, I am struggling not to shudder under the weight of his gaze.

Soon, I remind myself. Soon I will have nothing to fear from either of them. Soon I will be far away from them both. Soon, hopefully, they will be dead. Soon they will never be able to touch me again. But *soon* is not *now*. Now, they can still hurt me. Now, I still have to play the Kaiser's games.

Again my eyes find the candle, because it's easier to look there than at them. Though my heartbeat is quickening again, the flickering of the candle still matches it.

"Lady Crescentia, Lady Thora," the Kaiser says, giving me no choice but to look at him.

His next move is coming, his latest game, but for the first time I am a step ahead of him, and I will use that to my advantage.

In my mind, Thora is a huddled mess of panic and fear. She remembers his hands, she remembers the whip, she remembers his sickening smile when he called her a good girl. But I will not be afraid, because I have a vial of the deadliest poison known to man in my pocket and I can end his life with half of it.

"Your Highness, Theyn," I say, keeping my voice soft and level. *I am a simple girl who thinks only simple things.* "It's so lovely to see you both. Won't you join us for coffee?" I ask, gesturing to the table. As if I have any say in the matter.

The Kaiser's gaze flickers to Crescentia.

"Actually, Lady Crescentia, if you don't mind, I'd like to have a few words alone with Lady Thora," he says, and though the words are polite enough, they are a pointed command. Cress must hear it as well, because she hesitates for a breath and her eyes find mine, a reminder there that I do not need. Her threats from a moment ago are still echoing in my mind.

"Cress," her father says. He holds an arm out to her, and after a last glance my way, she links her arm through his and lets him lead her away.

The Kaiser takes her seat and I retake mine, trying to calm my racing heartbeat. The candle is still matching it, though a quick glance at the other tables tells me that theirs are calm and solid. Only mine is erratic, and I cannot think about why that is, not now with the Kaiser staring at me like he is. I'm painfully aware of the other courtiers watching and whispering. I push them out of my mind, focusing on the Kaiser, on the pot of coffee between us and the vial in my pocket. If I can manage to kill the Kaiser, Blaise and the others will call it a success even if Cress and the Theyn are still alive. Maybe I can even get out before Cress discovers what I did, before she tells her father everything and they arrest me. But even if I am killed for this, it will be enough. My mother and Ampelio will greet me in the After with pride.

I slide the vial from my pocket and into the long sleeve of my dress so that the corked top is wedged between the skin of my wrist and the cuff. When I slipped it into my pocket this morning, I never imagined I would actually use it. It was a gesture to placate my Shadows, but now I can actually see myself pouring the poison into the Kaiser's cup when he isn't paying attention. I see him drinking it. I see him burning alive from the inside out. And I don't flinch from those thoughts, murderous as they might be. If anyone deserves to die from Encatrio, it's the Kaiser.

"Coffee, Your Highness?" I ask with a bland smile, lifting the pot. If I just pretend to scratch my wrist, I can uncork the top and slip the poison in without anyone noticing. . . .

But his nose wrinkles. "I never developed a taste for the stuff," he says, waving a hand dismissively.

Frustration rises in my chest but I force it aside. So close, but I can't very well shove the poison down his throat.

"Very well," I say, setting the pot back on the table. "What can I do for you, Your Highness?"

Though it nauseates me, I glance up at him through my eyelashes and summon my sweetest smile.

His smile broadens and he leans back in the chair, which creaks under his girth.

"The Theyn and I have been discussing your future, Ash Princess, and I thought you might like a say in it."

I have to choke back a laugh. He already has my future plotted, and nothing I say could change that. It's the illusion of a choice, just like the one he gave me when he asked me to kill Ampelio.

"I'm sure you know what is best for me, Your Highness," I reply. "You have been so kind to me so far. You must know how grateful I am."

His hand slides across the table toward mine and I force myself not to pull mine back. I let him place his thick, clammy fingers over mine, and I pretend his touch doesn't revolt me. I pretend I welcome it, even as bile rises in my throat.

"Perhaps you could show me just how grateful you are," he murmurs, leaning toward me.

I can't look at him, so I watch his hand instead. His sleeve is touching the base of the candle, only inches away from the flame. If it isn't my imagination or a coincidence—if I really am controlling the flame without meaning to—what else can I do? How difficult would it be, really, to make a spark jump and catch his sleeve on fire? It would look innocuous enough, but it would make him stop touching me.

I would give anything for him to stop touching me. Anything.

Even your chance at the After? Even your mother? Even the future of your country?

The questions give me pause.

Suddenly a crack slices through the air and the Kaiser is yanked back, falling to the ground in a graceless heap, the chair splintered beneath him, the iron frame snapped cleanly in half. Shocked, I leap to my feet, along with everyone else on the pavilion.

Lying on his back, he reminds me of a turtle flipped over onto its shell. His bloated stomach strains at his shirt as he writhes, struggling to sit up to no avail. His guards rush forward to protect him, but when it becomes clear there was no attack, only the Kaiser's girth breaking the chair, even they have to struggle to keep straight faces as they help him up to his feet. The courtiers crowded on the pavilion are less able to hide their giggles, which makes the Kaiser's face grow redder and redder with fury and embarrassment.

I search for my Shadows lurking in the corners, and for Blaise in particular. The Kaiser's weight alone wasn't enough to break the wrought-iron chair, not without a touch of Earth magic. But it's hard to believe Blaise would have done something so reckless on purpose.

There are only two figures standing in a dark corner, one

tall and one short. Blaise isn't there, though I know he was a few seconds ago.

All I can do is hurry around the table to where the Kaiser is being helped up by his guards.

"Your Highness, are you all right?" I ask.

He pushes his guards away and brushes off his clothes before taking a step toward me. His blue eyes—the same color as Søren's—dart around the pavilion. No one dares laugh out loud, and many avert their gaze, pretending not to have seen the blunder at all. But he must know it's a lie. He must know that they are all mocking him. He pushes his guards away from him, setting his jaw in a firm line and coming toward me. The smell of sweat and metal is overwhelming.

"We'll speak again soon, Ash Princess," he says, reaching his hand up to touch my cheek. Søren did the same thing when we were on his boat, but this is so much different. It is not a touch of affection, it is a claim staked in front of dozens of courtiers, and in an hour's time, the whole city will know about it.

When he turns to go and finally takes those cold eyes off me, my knees all but buckle and I have to grip the edge of the table for support, though I try to hide it. Now more than ever, everyone is watching me, praying for me to fall so that one of their girls can take my place.

I am a lamb in the lion's den, and I don't know that I can survive.

BELSIMÉRA

———•———

WHEN I GET BACK TO my room, I'm relieved that Hoa isn't there. It's all I can do to keep the storm of fear and doubt buried deep in me. Screams and tears and fire scratch at my throat, but I swallow them all down, down, down. I cannot appear weak, not with my Shadows watching me. But someone is always watching me, aren't they? Always expecting something of me, always waiting for me to slip.

With calm, measured steps, I cross to the water basin sitting on my vanity and dip my hands into it. The hands he touched. I scrub them until they are red and raw, but it doesn't do any good. I still feel the Kaiser's touch. I still feel the threat of him wrapped around my neck like a noose.

There is a pumice stone next to the basin, so I use that, digging it into every part of my hands, the palms, the backs, my fingers, even the spaces in between. It doesn't matter, it's never enough. Even when my knuckles bleed and turn the water pink. Even when my skin turns numb.

Good girl. You've grown awfully pretty, for a heathen. Perhaps you could show me just how grateful you are.

A strangled cry breaks the silence and I look around for

the source before realizing that it's coming from me, that I'm the one crying, and now that it's finally started, I can't make it stop. My legs give out and I fall to the floor, bringing the basin down with me and drenching the skirt of my dress with bloodied water.

I don't care. I don't even care when the door opens, even if it's Hoa, ready to run to the Kaiser. Let her. It's too much. I can't do this. I am not enough.

Footsteps come toward me and I look up to see Artemisia in her black cloak, indigo hair spilling over her shoulders and something that might be pity in her hard eyes.

"Stand up," she says, her voice soft.

I should listen to her, I shouldn't let her see me like this. She thinks I'm useless already, and I don't want to prove her right. Still, I can't move. I can't do anything but cry.

With a sigh, she drops to her knees in front of me and reaches for my bloodied hands, but I pull them back and cradle them against my stomach.

"I'm not going to hurt you," she snaps. "Let me see how bad it is."

Hesitantly I hold them out to her, flinching when she none too gently turns them over.

"Heron?" she says over her shoulder to where a tall boy with overgrown black hair and thick eyebrows lingers in the doorway, looking like he might be sick. "A little help?"

Her words send a bolt of energy through him, and he shakes himself out of his stupor, coming to sit on my other side. He towers over me by at least a head, and though he looks stricken, I can see signs of the mysterious boy who's been behind my wall for the last couple of months, the voice of reason. It's there in the softness of his hazel eyes, in the lopsided quirk of his mouth.

He takes one of my hands from her, inspecting the damage himself. His hand dwarfs mine, but it's comforting. "It's not too bad," he says after a moment. "I can fix it."

My throat is so raw from crying, but I still can't stop. "Where's Blaise? Is he all right?" I manage to ask between sobs.

"He's fine. We thought it best he take a walk and calm down after that outburst," Artemisia says.

The chair. The Kaiser falling. It *was* Blaise's power, and not an intentional use of it, apparently. I nod and try to take deep breaths, but they come out ragged.

"I can't . . . I can't do this anymore." I don't mean to say the words, but the dam inside me has broken, and there is no controlling what comes out with the tears.

"Then don't." Artemisia's voice is all hard edges.

"Art," Heron warns, but she ignores him.

"Give up. Go as mad as their Kaiserin. What's stopping you?"

Her words burn through me, but at least they've dried up my tears.

"There are twenty thousand people counting on me," I whisper, more to myself than them. "If I give up . . ."

"Most of them won't know the difference," she says. The words are cruel, but the fight has gone out of her voice. She sounds as tired as I feel. "You might be the queen, but you're just one girl. The revolution won't stop because you do. It didn't stop when Ampelio died, and he'd done far more than you have. If you died, or I died, or Heron, or Blaise . . . We're all just pieces. We do what we can, but at the end of the day, we're all expendable. Even you."

"Then why do it at all?" I ask her. The words come out bitter, but I don't mean them that way. I really do want to know.

She doesn't say anything for a long moment. It's only when I've given up hope of getting an answer that she speaks, her voice low and steady and so unlike the brash, loud Artemisia I've gotten to know.

"Because that's how water works. The river flows, pushing against a stone, even as it knows it won't move it. It doesn't have to. Enough currents go by, over enough time, and even the strongest stone gives in. It might take a lifetime or more, but water doesn't give up."

"Nothing will stop him. I can't win against him," I say.

"No," she says. "You likely can't."

"*Art,*" Heron warns again. The hand he's holding has turned to pins and needles, like it's fallen asleep. It doesn't feel the way it does when Ion heals me after the Kaiser's punishments. His touch always leaves my skin feeling tacky and slick and grimy, but Heron's touch is comforting, warming, as his power travels over my skin.

"I won't lie to her," Artemisia scoffs.

Her words are harsh, but there's something refreshing about her honesty. I think I prefer it to Heron's kind fibs.

"We won't let anything happen to you," Heron says. "As soon as the Prinz is back, we'll get you out."

"After I kill him, you mean. And the Theyn, and Cress."

If Blaise were here, he would probably tell me that my safety was the priority. He would begin making plans for all of us to leave immediately, and I don't know that I would have the courage to turn him down. But he isn't here.

Heron and Artemisia exchange a look that I can't read.

"Yes," Artemisia says.

Heron releases my hand and the skin of my palm is smooth and clear, as if I never fell apart. He takes the other and begins again.

"In the mines," Artemisia says, drawing my attention back to her. She isn't looking at me, instead staring at the patterned tile floor, tracing the lines with her little finger. "I learned quickly how to use the only leverage I had with one of the guards. It . . . was its own kind of torture, but he gave me extra rations in return, and the easiest shifts. He looked the other way when my little brother didn't pull his weight. I told myself . . . I told myself he cared for me, that I cared for him even. It's easier to lie to yourself, isn't it?"

No, I want to say. *It's not the same thing.* But I can't help thinking that maybe it is. Maybe lying to yourself is the only way to survive.

When she speaks again, the softness is gone. "But when my brother went mine-mad and that same guard smashed his head against a boulder five feet from me, I saw the truth of it." Her breath shakes. "For months after, I would fall asleep next to my brother's murderer and pray that death take me as well." She laughs, but it's an ugly sound. "I never prayed before, never saw any use for it. I didn't believe any of it, even as I thought the words; I just needed to talk to *someone,* even if it was only in my mind. I still don't believe in your gods, but I do know that I grew stronger and stronger, until I had the strength to slit the guard's throat while he slept."

Her dark eyes flash up to meet mine and there is a kind of understanding there I never expected from her. I realize suddenly that I don't know her at all, or Heron, or even Blaise anymore. They all must have stories like this, stories I haven't heard, about horrors I can never really understand.

"We are not defined by the things we do in order to survive. We do not apologize for them," she says quietly, eyes never leaving mine. "Maybe they have broken you, but you are a sharper weapon because of it. And it is time to strike."

When Artemisia and Heron leave, I can't sit still. It isn't the same panicked energy from earlier—there is a calm to my thoughts, a distance. I see the situation as if it were happening to someone else. My mind is busy, and so my hands yearn for something to do as well.

I go to my hiding place in the mattress and dig around until I find the nightgown I ruined when I first met with Blaise what feels like a lifetime ago. The once-white material is gray with dirt and grime.

It tears easily into strips, though they're sloppy and frayed at the edges, not like they would be if I were allowed a pair of scissors. But it will do.

Artemisia and Heron say nothing as they watch me roll each strip into a shoddy rosette, bound with pieces of straw from inside the mattress. After a few moments, Blaise settles back into his room without a word, but I barely hear him.

I'm barely aware of any of them. All that exists are my fingers, the rosettes, and my mind turning over every possible outcome.

Though I know what I have to do, I can't help but wonder if my mother would make the same choice in my position. The truth is, though, I don't know what my mother would do. She is half memory, half imagination to me.

I tie the last of the four rosettes and gather them in my hands.

"Happy Belsiméra," I say into the silence.

Heron shifts behind his wall. "It isn't—" he starts, but breaks off.

"Is it?" Blaise asks.

I shrug. "Elpis says it is, and I trust her to know."

I thread a rosette through each wall in turn, squishing them a bit to fit through the holes. "I know it isn't much," I say when I have only one left—for Elpis the next time I see her. "But I want you all to know that even when we disagree on things, you are my friends—no, my family. I trust you, though I know I don't always know how to show it. And I hope you all know that I would give my own life for yours without hesitation. I will never be able to properly express how grateful I am not only that you came here to help me, but that you've stayed when I haven't made it easy. Thank you."

For a long moment, none of them speak, and I worry I've gone too far, said too much. They'll think me a sentimental fool who has no business being anyone's queen.

Finally Heron clears his throat.

"You're family," he says, which is somehow so much better than him saying I'm his queen. "Family doesn't walk away."

"Besides," Art adds, "I find it amusing when you try to argue. That's when I like you best."

My laugh takes me by surprise, but hers comes a second later. She is my friend, I realize. Not the same way Cress was, not the kind I enjoy light conversations with, not the kind I dance with or try on dresses with. I might not always like her, but she is here when I need her in a way Cress couldn't be. The thought of it causes a lump to rise in my throat, but I try to ignore it. Belsiméra is a happy occasion.

"When we were children," Blaise says, a smile in his voice, "you used to always try to give me a flower, do you remember?"

"No," I admit, sitting down on my bed and looking at the flower in my hand. It's not as pretty as the one Elpis gave me, but I hope she'll like it. "It was so long ago, it's a bit fuzzy. I remember making them with my mother, though, much prettier than these."

"They were," he agrees. "And in the two years before the siege, you would always try to give me the prettiest one you had and I would always run from you."

"I don't remember that," I say, looking at his wall. "Why?"

"Because your flowers always came with strings attached," he says. "You kissed everyone you gave one to."

"I did not," I say with a laugh.

"You did," he insists. "Every Belsiméra, you would prance through the castle with your basket of flowers, passing them out to everyone you saw and demanding a kiss in return. Everyone thought you were the funniest thing, but they all obliged. No one could ever say no to you. Not because of her title," he adds quickly, to the others. "Everyone loved her."

"I grew up in this tiny village on the eastern coast," Heron says. "Even we heard about you there, how everyone who met you cherished you."

The words warm me and bring out a hazy memory, though I'm not sure how much of it is real. I remember the wicker basket hanging on my arm. I remember maids and cooks and Guardians crouching in front of me or lifting me up to kiss my cheek or my forehead and saying *Thank you, Princess. I'll treasure it always. Happy Belsiméra.*

"Blaise clearly didn't," I say, teasing.

He hesitates for a minute. "I did," he says. "But you were still a girl chasing me around and demanding a kiss. It wasn't anything personal. At that age, I was refusing to kiss even my mother."

"We never really celebrated on the ship," Artemisia admits. "My mother is Astrean, but the crew comes from everywhere. If we celebrated every holiday, we never would have gotten anything done. This is my first."

"Do you not know the story, then?" I ask her.

"I don't think so. My mother taught me the names of the gods, but she isn't one for stories," she admits.

I stumble over the beginning, but by the time I reach the part where Suta makes the flowers for Glaidi, my mother's voice has taken over and the story spills out without me thinking about it. I'm more audience than I am speaker, and when I tell her about Belsimia growing from the love and friendship between the two gods, tears are leaking from my own eyes.

"In the version I heard," Heron says quietly, "it wasn't Glaidi's tear that caused Belsimia to grow from the flower, it was when she kissed Suta."

"My parents used to argue about whether Belsimia grew from the flower or was transformed from the flower itself," Blaise says.

"I can't imagine your parents arguing about anything," I tell him. "They were always so happy."

Blaise is quiet for so long I worry I've upset him. "My father used to say they argued because they cared too much. He said I would understand when I was older."

The words feel more like a confession than a memory, and even with the others present, I know it's meant for me. Warmth rises to my cheeks and I turn my face away so he can't see.

He clears his throat.

"While I was out . . . calming down after the accident with the Kaiser, I did some thinking," he says. "About the Theyn's daughter . . ." He hesitates. "It isn't necessary. You were right." It pains him to say the words, I can tell, but it doesn't bring me any joy to hear them now that Cress showed me who she really is.

"Blaise," Artemisia snaps.

"Art," Heron adds, a soft warning in his voice.

"If either of you can think of a reason to kill the girl that has nothing to do with Theo's feelings for her, I'm happy to hear it. But we all know the Theyn can be killed alone." Blaise sounds so much like his father that my heart lurches in my chest.

Artemisia must have a retort; even Heron must have something to say to that, some argument for killing Cress. I wait for it. I yearn for it, for some other reason besides my own foolishness in trusting her in the first place. But they both stay quiet. I close my eyes tight before forcing myself to tell them the truth.

"She thinks I was seducing the Prinz to get information," I confess. "She hasn't figured anything out past that, but she knows I'm working against the Kaiser, she knows about Søren and me, and she knows I stole her gems because I was working with others. She isn't going to tell the Kaiser, so long as she thinks I'm just a pawn and that I'm repentant. I told her I was. But I don't know how long she'll think that. She wants to be a prinzessin, and if she still thinks I'm standing in the way of that—" I break off, a heaving sob tearing through me.

Saying it out loud hurts. Not just emotionally—it's a physical pain in my chest, dagger-sharp. Because no matter what I want to tell myself about loyalty or friendship or duty, the truth is startlingly simple: I put Cress before my people and she put her ambition before me. I made a mistake and it isn't one I'll repeat.

I wait for their condemnation, for them to call me a fool, but the words never come. Not even from Artemisia. Instead, they stay quiet until I speak again.

"There's your reason," I tell Blaise, hard resolve coming into my voice. "I'll do what I need to do, but not yet. The Kaiser will find a way to blame me, even if there's no proof of it. The Encatrio will make it clear it's an Astrean attack—which we *want*—but if I'm still here, he'll blame it on me. The Theyn is his closest friend; he might even kill me for his and Crescentia's deaths, no matter what it costs him. We should wait for Søren to get back, for him to speak out publicly against his father. Then we'll end it all, strike out at the Theyn and Cress and Søren at once. They'll never see it coming."

I take a deep breath, surprised at how sure I suddenly feel about all of this. There is no room in me anymore for uncertainty or guilt. I sound older than I am, harder than I am. I don't sound like my mother—not quite—but I think I might sound like a queen.

"And then we'll leave. I know we can't free the slaves in the palace on our way out, there are too many and it would slow us down too much, but we can't leave without Elpis and her family. I think we owe her that after everything she's done. Will that be a problem?" I ask.

"No," Blaise says after a moment. "No problem at all."

PUNISHMENT

‖ ’M JERKED AWAKE IN THE middle of the night by my door
being forced open and a cacophony of heavy boots thundering toward me. It’s a sound that often haunts my nightmares, and at first I think this is just that, but the rough hands
that grab my arms and haul me from bed can’t be imagined.
The guards are silent and I think my pounding heart is loud
enough for all six of them to hear. I want to scream and thrash
against them, but I know well enough that that doesn’t do me
any good, so I swallow my terror and try to focus.

The Kaiser sent six guards to escort me, more than he usually does when this happens—when he wants to punish me.
I would be flattered if I weren’t so afraid. Still, I gather myself enough to cast a gaze to the walls where my Shadows are
watching, praying to all the gods that they don’t do anything
foolish.

“Would you mind telling me what it’s about this time?”
I ask, snapping like Crescentia does when one of her slaves
combs her hair too roughly or doesn’t cook her morning egg
long enough. Like it’s only a mild annoyance and I’m not
facing a whipping. No matter how many times I’m dragged

before the Kaiser and beaten to the edge of death, the horror of it never lessens.

I have to struggle not to tremble, not to retreat so deep into my mind that I'll never find my way out again. But I know my people have endured so much worse than this. I think of Blaise and his scar. Of Heron's losses. Of what Artemisia told me yesterday. I have to endure.

"Kaiser's orders," one guard barks at me. I don't know his name, though I should by now. He's one of the Kaiser's favorites, a former warrior with a scarred face and a nose that looks like it's been broken too many times to count. He has a meaner streak than most, which is truly saying something, and I know better than to push him.

"I'll come willingly," I say, struggling to keep my voice level. "We've gone through this enough times that you know I'm no threat. Whatever it is that's happened, I'll take the Kaiser's punishment without complaint. Just as I have in the past."

The words are less for them than they are for Blaise and the others. Then the thought hits me—*What if they're not there?* What if *that*'s what this is all about, and I'm walking not toward a punishment, but toward an execution?

What if Cress went to the Kaiser anyway and told him everything?

Those thoughts echo through my mind as the guards haul me from my room in my thin nightgown, not even letting me put on shoes. I stumble barefoot on the cold stone floor, stubbing my toes as two guards pull me along by my arms, not slowing down even when the scrapes and scratches of the stones beneath my feet draw blood and they're more dragging than escorting me. I barely even notice the pain. All I can think is that Cress went to the Kaiser after all and that he has found my Shadows. He's killed them and now he'll kill me and all will be lost.

When we finally round a corner, I nearly let out a sigh of relief. They're taking me to the throne room, not out to the capital square, which means it won't be a public punishment, as they usually are. The only times punishments happen in the throne room are when the Kaiser doesn't want word of what caused them to spread outside the palace. If he were executing me for treason, he would need an audience. This is something else, something embarrassing that's happened that he wants to keep quiet.

The throne room is less crowded than usual, but everyone who matters to the Kaiser is present. The high dukes and duchesses cluster near the throne, the barons and baronesses, the counts and countesses. All the usual joy and merriment has gone out of them; there is only blood in their eyes. Standing in the shadow of the throne is Ion, the traitor Guardian. His eyes are focused on the ground, as they usually are when I'm called before the Kaiser like this. His cowardice won't let him look at me, not even at the end, when the Kaiser will instruct him to heal my wounds just enough that I can function with them.

"Lady Thora," the Kaiser says from his seat on my mother's throne. He leans forward, the Spiritgems that all but blanket him clinking as he moves.

"You summoned me, Your Highness?" I ask, letting my fear show in my voice. It's no fun for him if I'm not afraid.

For a long moment, he doesn't speak; he only watches me.

His eyes cross my skin, making me too conscious of the thin nightgown I wear, of my exposed calves and feet. I want to cover myself, but that would only anger him and I cannot afford that right now, so I do nothing. I let him look, which feels worse than any whipping.

Finally he speaks. "Three weeks ago, my son led a battalion of four thousand men to Vecturia. Two weeks ago, I received word that they were met with troops that had been expecting them, but my son assured me that victory was still possible. He and his warriors fought valiantly until days ago, when his ships were attacked from the other side by a fleet believed to be under the command of the notorious pirate Dragonsbane. What was supposed to be a simple Conquering became an ambush that cost many of our men's lives."

Many of the courtiers gathered have sons who would have been in Søren's crew, I realize, young men who had been sent on an easy Conquering that should have bolstered their reputations with minimal risk to their safety. At least until I evened the field.

But these people don't know that. They can't. If the Kaiser knew I'd sent a warning to Vecturia with Dragonsbane, it would mean he knew about my Shadows as well, and I would be taken straight to my execution.

No, this is merely a show, a way to make the Kaiser and his dearest supporters feel better about their embarrassment. Most of them must have daughters they would like to see made kaiserin as well, another strike against me. They called for this, and the Kaiser was all too eager to agree. After all, this is how he likes me best: beaten and broken.

"I'm sorry, Your Highness. That is terrible news."

His eyes narrow and he shifts again in his seat.

"Your people were behind this," he says.

It isn't the first time he's accused me of this, but this time I actually am responsible, and I am proud of that. These will be scars I will wear with pride.

But the war isn't won yet, and we have much farther to go. So I drop to my knees and let Thora come forward to do what she does best: beg.

"Please, I have no people, Your Highness. I haven't spoken to another Astrean in years, on your orders. I had no hand in this, you know that."

His games grow boring when he wins them too easily.

"Theyn," he says, snapping his fingers.

The crush of nobles parts for the Theyn, scarred face drawn and stoic, a whip in hand. He doesn't look at me, but then, he never does. Not like the Kaiser, who enjoys every grimace, every scream, like a child watching a puppet show. The Theyn does this out of duty, which somehow makes me hate him more.

One of the guards rips my nightgown so that my back is bare, but thankfully everything else remains covered this time. The two who hold each of my arms brace themselves, as if I could possibly overpower them. But I don't even try. Fighting only makes it worse. I learned that lesson a long time ago. Better to save my fighting for when it can actually make a difference.

"Twenty lashes," the Kaiser says, his voice so soft I almost don't hear it. "One for each family here who lost a son due to the foolishness of Astreans."

Twenty. It doesn't seem like a lot of men, all things

considered, but if they are this highborn, this close to the Kaiser, they would have been farthest from the actual battle and better protected than anyone else. If twenty of them were killed, the overall numbers must be much higher.

This is worth it, I repeat again and again in my mind, hoping that will lessen the sting.

The Theyn's boots click on the stone floor as he approaches from behind. I keep my head down so that it will be harder for them to see me cry. The first strike is always both the hardest and easiest to take. When it comes, I lurch forward, held in place only by the guards gripping my arms. The shock of it alone is almost worse than the pain, but at least it lands on unbroken skin. The next ones do not. They layer over one another until I could swear the tail of the whip is cutting through skin and flesh to kiss my very bones. Until it feels like it's slicing through my bones instead.

On the fourth strike, I can't hold back a scream. On the fifth, my knees buckle but the guards force me to stay upright. On the sixth, the tears finally come, streaming hot down my cheeks. By the time the tenth hits, I make it to that place where I am only half in my body. The other half floats somewhere above, feeling nothing, only watching. My mind grows fuzzy and dark spots dance in front of my eyes. I want to pass out to make the pain stop, but the last time I did, the Kaiser waited for me to wake up before finishing the punishment himself and adding another five lashes.

My hair is plastered to my forehead with sweat, despite the cold. The room is still, the jeers and shouts from the audience falling silent—at least to me. Nothing exists outside of my body, outside of this pain that I know will consume me.

My name is Theodosia Eirene Houzzara, Queen of Astrea, and I will endure this.

The whip cracks again and I feel it all the way to my toes. My arms ache from the guards' grip. I can't stand up, can't stand tall the way my mother would have wanted me to. All I can do is scream and cry.

My name is Theodosia Eirene Houzzara, Queen of Astrea.

Another crack that bites through skin and muscle and bone. Another wound that will never heal.

My name is Theodosia Eirene Houzzara.

The next one hits my spine, sending a wave of shock that makes my whole body spasm. The guards don't loosen their grip, so I only hurt myself worse.

My name is Theodosia.

Lost count now. It will never end. The guards release me and I fall to the hard floor in a huddle as another blow hits.

My name is . . .

My name is . . .

I focus on the tiles beneath my feet. I took my first steps on these tiles, my mother's hand clasped tightly around mine to keep me up. If I concentrate hard enough, I can almost feel her now, urging me to be strong, promising me that it will be over soon.

My name is . . .

One of the tiles is cracked. Unsurprising, considering how old they are and how little care the Kalovaxians take. But as I stare at the tiles and the Theyn brings the whip down again, another tile splinters, thin cracks bursting out from the center like spider's legs.

I am imagining things. It isn't the first time the pain has

gone to my head. But even as I think it, I know it isn't in my head.

I look up, past the gathered courtiers to the back of the room where my Shadows watch, their faces hidden by drawn hoods. *Blaise.* Energy pours off him in waves, though no one else seems to notice.

Even in the shadow of his hood, I can make out the green of his eyes, locked onto mine. He's struggling to hold back, but it's a struggle he's losing. Artemisia and Heron are trying to calm him, but it isn't any good, he's about to erupt.

I do the only thing I can: I meet his gaze and hold it, even as the whip bites into my back again. I'm not sure if he's soothing me or I'm soothing him, but the tenuous tie between us feels like all that's keeping either of us alive, and I don't dare break it.

LULLABY

—◆·◆—

W HEN IT'S OVER, THE KAISER and the courtiers file out, leaving me crumpled on the bloody floor. My Shadows wait in the back of the room, unsure what to do, but Ion makes his way toward me the way he always does, his Air magic making his steps light and soundless.

I can't help but flinch when he crouches down next to me and his cold, dry hand comes to rest on my back where most of the blows hit, sending a wave of pain so strong it makes me dizzy. I clench my fists, digging my nails into my palms to stay alert, and chew hard on my lip to keep from screaming. The pain only lasts a second before his power begins to seep through me, sealing the wounds. The skin of my back feels like ice.

When Ion removes his hand, the wounds still hurt, but it isn't enough to incapacitate me. With a shuddering breath, I struggle to my feet, wincing as I do. It'll be another few days and a few doses of the salve Ion gives Hoa before the pain goes away completely.

The pain is less when I'm hunched over, but I force my shoulders back and stand up tall. Ion still doesn't look at me, but the hate simmering in my stomach refuses to be ignored. It's only my Shadows who can see us, so I do what I've wanted to for ten years.

I touch his shoulder so that he has to look at me, dark eyes empty and numb.

"Your ancestors are watching you from the After with shame," I bite out in Astrean, relishing his shocked expression. "When your days are over, they will not let you in."

I turn away from him before he can respond. I doubt he'll tell the Kaiser—he'll assume my Shadows will.

I hasten to close the back of my nightgown as I walk, wincing when the cotton brushes against the tender wounds and sticks to the blood that paints my back. The nightgown was white when I put it on, but now most of it has been stained red.

My Shadows fall in behind me as I leave the throne room. They don't touch me and I don't want them to. I'll break if they do, crumble to pieces like my ersatz crown. I am a princess made of ashes, after all. I can't help but fall apart.

Walking back to my room takes almost three times as long as it should, because each step makes my whole body ache and every few seconds I stumble. Once, Heron catches me by my elbow before remembering the role he's playing. I have to stop myself from leaning on him.

Hoa is waiting in my room with a bowl of hot water, rags, and bandages ready. She won't look at me, but she always has trouble after my punishments—sometimes I could swear they hurt her even more than they hurt me, though I'm not sure how that's possible.

The silence is almost a comfort as she washes the new

wounds and dresses them with the ointment Ion gave her. It's nearly as painful as the whip itself, but when it's over the pain has dulled to a constant thrum. With guarded tenderness, she washes the blood from the rest of my skin and my hair before dressing me in a fresh nightgown. She knows by now that I won't be wearing anything else today. Or tomorrow, more than likely. I wince as the fabric brushes my back, and her hand lingers for a brief second on my shoulder. She turns to go.

"Thank you." The words come out a choked whisper, but she hears them and turns to look at me for a moment before nodding and slipping out the door.

I don't think I've ever heard my Shadows this silent. There is always something—breathing, whispers, movement—but now there is nothing.

"I'm fine," I say when I can't stand it anymore. It's a lie, we all know it, but if I say it enough times maybe it'll turn true.

They don't reply, though I hear one of them shift in their seat. I hear another one—Heron, I think—let out a loud exhale. There is nothing for them to say. Nothing will take away my pain; nothing will change what happened. Silence is easiest for all of us.

I slip into bed, careful to stay on my side, curled up in a ball like an infant. I bury my face in one of my pillows and let myself cry as quietly as I can, but I know they can still hear me.

Artemisia's voice comes first, softer than I've ever heard it. It wraps around me like a silk shawl, light and cool.

"Walk through the fog with me,
My beautiful child.
We're off to dreamland, my dear,
Where the world turns wild."

Her voice breaks as she sings the old Astrean lullaby, and I know she's crying, too. The thought of Artemisia crying is ludicrous. She's always so strong, so sure of everything. Is she thinking of her mother singing the song to her, as I am? I can almost feel my mother's fingers stroke through my hair, almost smell the garden scents that clung to her.

Heron's deep baritone joins in like a gentle hand on my shoulder, calm and reassuring.

"Today is done, the time has come
For little birds to fly.
Tomorrow is near, the time is here
For old crows to die."

The words wrench a sob from me that I can't control. My Shadows don't mean anything by it, I know. They don't—can't—know that they were some of the last words Ampelio whispered to me before I killed him. Did he ever sing the lullaby to me before? Did he hold me in his arms once and rock me to sleep? I want to believe he did.

Blaise adds his voice next, and it's so terrible that I almost laugh, despite everything. It warbles at the edges and is horribly off-pitch, but he sings anyway because he knows I need to hear it.

"Dream a dream of a world unknown,
Where anything can be.
Tomorrow you'll make your dreams come true,
But tonight, child, dream with me."

Theodosia Eirene Houzzara. The name sings through my body, softening me. I repeat it over and over, clutching it the way a child holds on to her favorite blanket.

My tears stop, though my shaking doesn't. It won't anytime soon.

"Søren can't be far behind the letter. A day or two at most," I say after a moment. My voice sounds stronger than I feel. "As soon as he's back, the plan is in motion. After what I told him about his mother in that letter, he won't want to wait before confronting his father. Even if he doesn't do so publicly, the whole palace will know about it within the hour. You'll need to pick a guard to frame for the murder, one of the Kaiser's closest. Heron, you'll tear a piece of his shirt, take his blade, his hair tie, any clue that could lead back to him and the Kaiser."

"I think I liked the look of the one who led the men dragging you out of bed today," Heron says, and though his voice is quiet and gentle, there's a hard edge beneath it.

"I heartily agree with that choice," I tell him before turning to Artemisia's wall. "Artemisia, go down to the cypress grove and see if your mother has returned from Vecturia yet."

Silence follows my words for a few breaths, leading me to expect a retort or a scoff.

"Yes, My Queen," she says instead.

It's the first time she's called me that without a hint of sarcasm.

I take a steadying breath. "Then, as soon as Søren moves against his father, I'll kill him." My voice doesn't waver when I say the words, though they still twist my stomach. With the pain from the Kaiser's punishment fresh, my feelings for Søren feel less important. I can do it, I tell myself, and I almost believe it.

"How?" Blaise asks quietly. The word isn't laced with doubt like it might have been even yesterday; it's a genuine inquiry.

I bite my lip and burrow farther under the covers, as if I can escape the thought of Søren's open smile on the boat, the way he held me, making me feel safe for the first time in a decade, the way he looked at me as if he understood me.

"He trusts me," I say finally, hating the words as I speak them. "He'll never see it coming."

Slowly, one by one, their breathing turns long and even, but try as I might, I can't join them in dreamland. I'm sure that nothing pleasant awaits me there, no better world, certainly. Only nightmares, plagued by the Kaiser's hands, the Theyn's whip, Ampelio's blood, my mother's lifeless eyes.

My door opens quietly and I turn to see Blaise slip inside and draw his hood back. I should tell him to leave, because if he's discovered here, *now,* everything will be ruined. He must know it as well, but neither of us says a word as he shrugs off his cloak and slides into the bed next to me. He opens his arms and I hesitate only a second before curling into him, resting my head on his chest and holding on to him like he's the only thing anchoring me to this world. His arms come around me as best they can, careful to avoid touching my back.

"Thank you," I whisper.

His sigh ruffles my hair, but he doesn't reply. I tilt my head up to look at his face. In the fading moonlight, his dark green eyes are spectral and his scar stands out sharply, pale white against dusky fawn skin. I brush my thumb over it, feeling him flinch before his eyes flutter closed and he leans into my touch.

"What happened?" I ask.

He shakes his head. "You don't want to hear that story. Not now, after . . ." He trails off, unable to say it.

"Please."

Blaise shifts slightly, his eyes moving past me to stare at the space over my shoulder. "In the mines, there are quotas," he says after a moment. "You need to bring in a set weight of gems a day, otherwise they withhold your dinner rations. Which only makes you weaker and means that the next day you're even more likely to miss quota. Not a very fair system, but it keeps everyone on edge, makes us determined not to come up short even once. If you miss it three days in a row, they put you in a cell deep in the mines, so far below ground you forget what fresh air tastes like." His voice begins to waver, but he clears his throat and continues. "Most people who go into the cell don't come out sane. Being that deep . . . it does something to people. It's like spending years in the mines, but in the space of a day or two. Usually the people who are sent there are taken straight to their execution afterward."

"But you weren't," I say quietly.

He shakes his head. "I was ten or so, and there was a man who slept on the cot next to mine. Yarin. He was about my father's age before he . . . Anyway, he wasn't well. The dust from the mines gave him a terrible cough and made him weak. He missed a lot of quotas, but never three in a row. He was careful about that, and our group always shared rations with him when he lost his. It wasn't easy—the rations were meager already—but . . . what else could we do? We all knew that if he was sent to the cell, he would never come back to us.

"The guards knew it, too. They weren't right, those men. They enjoyed watching us fail, they enjoyed beating us for it. And, maybe more than anything, they enjoyed taking people away for executions. And Yarin was an easy target. More than once, I saw them knock a handful of gems off the scale when they weighed his so that he came up short. The Kalovaxians are monsters, you've seen it as surely as I have."

I think of the Kaiser and can't disagree, even as thoughts of Søren and even Cress protest.

Blaise continues. "Yarin was on his third day, and I knew there was no possible way he would make his quota. His cough was worse than it usually was, and he had to stop every few minutes to catch his breath. When the day started to draw to an end, he didn't even have half of what he needed." He stops to swallow, the lump in his throat bobbing. "But I did. The guards didn't stay down there with us—they didn't want to risk mine-madness—so they only entered for a few moments at the beginning of the day and the end. Before they came to fetch us after sundown, I switched my pail with Yarin's. Yarin tried to stop me, of course, but it was done.

"When the time came to measure, Yarin passed, even

when the guards took a handful out. And I didn't come close to making it. But the guards had been overseeing us for as long as I could remember. They knew that since my first day in the mines, I never missed quota. They knew what I'd done, even if they couldn't prove it. I thought I would die that day, but they had worse in mind. They killed Yarin with just a swipe of a dagger across his throat, right in front of the whole group, and then they took me down to the cell.

"I found out later that they left me there for a week, but I didn't know that at the time. Down there, alone in the dark, a day feels like a year and a minute at the same time. When they finally came for me, I was huddled in the corner, my fingers shredded. I'd tried to claw my way through the stone, I think, but I don't remember any of it. And I had this." He gestures to the scar. "A mark, like Art's hair."

I trace my fingers over his cheek. Despite the chill in the air, the scar itself is hot to the touch, and it pulses through me like a second heartbeat. It draws me closer and drowns my thoughts in a pleasant hum, like when I hold a Spiritgem. The power of it frightens me, and though I don't want to let go, I start to pull my hand away. Blaise's hand covers mine, holding my hand over his skin, his scar. His eyes are so intent on mine that I can't look away.

"You feel it, don't you?" he asks.

"It's strong," I say, trying to hide my unease. I don't remember Ampelio's scar having that kind of power, nor did the markings on any other Guardian I'd heard of. I try to force confidence into my voice. "Glaidi blessed you. She knew how strong you were, even then. Your father would be proud."

The muscle in his jaw tightens as he swallows. "It doesn't

feel like a blessing, Theo." His voice is more of a breath than anything. "I can't control the power. You saw what I did to the Kaiser's chair, what happened in the throne room today. Ampelio helped as much as he could, but it wasn't enough. I scared him, I think. I scare myself. It's my fault they caught him. If I hadn't lost control . . ."

"The earthquake at the mines," I realize. "The one that sparked the riot."

He nods, eyes dropping. "The one that killed a hundred people," he adds. "And led to Ampelio being caught."

I've never heard of someone wielding that much power without a gem, uncontrollable as it might have been. I hadn't even thought it was possible, but I have no reason not to believe Blaise. The anguish written plainly on his face twists at my heart; it's a feeling I know too well. I open my mouth to tell him it wasn't his fault, that it was an accident, that Ampelio wouldn't have blamed him. But as true as all those things might be, they won't do any good. I know because even though I'm sure executing Ampelio was the only thing I could have done—even though he asked me to do it—I still feel guilty. Blaise's guilt is just as bad, and there is nothing I can possibly say that will take even a small part away.

So I don't say anything at all. Instead, I wrap my arms around him and just hold him while we both cry. His heart presses against mine, in tune, and when our tears slow, his lips press against my hair, my forehead, my tearstained cheeks. He begins to pull back, but I root him in place, drawing his lips to mine.

It's a different kiss entirely from the uncertain one we shared three weeks ago, the one we haven't spoken of since.

The one I thought he rejected me after, though now I wonder if I misread that. It's different, too, from the way Søren and I kissed. Our kisses were filled with hope and giddiness, with the exploration of something new and beautiful.

This is a kiss of acceptance, for him as well as me. It's forgiveness for things we've done that are unforgivable. I love him, but the realization doesn't feel like plunging into ice water the way it does when I try to pull apart my feelings for Søren. Because falling in love with Blaise was always going to happen, even if we lived in a simpler world where the siege never happened. Even if we were both unscarred. We were always going to end up here.

I can see it before me as clearly as if I'm looking through a window: our parents still alive and happy and teasing us for every tiny show of affection, Blaise and I walking through my mother's garden hand in hand, kissing him goodbye when he leaves for his Guardian trials, kissing him hello again when he finally returns. I want that life so badly that my chest aches, and there is nothing I wouldn't give to have it.

He holds me until I fall asleep, but when I wake up to the sun streaming through my window, I'm reminded that we don't live in that simpler world. Because he's gone, the others are watching me, and my back is screaming.

ENCATRIO

———— ◆ ————

Hoa was merciful enough to let me sleep in—she knew I needed it. It must be past noon. For a moment, I forget what happened last night, but as soon as I move, the welts on my back send a lightning bolt of pain through me and I let out a hiss.

"The Prinz is back," Artemisia says immediately, like she's been waiting for hours for me to wake up. She likely has been. I slowly force myself into a sitting position.

"Did you hear me?" she asks when I don't answer right away.

"I did," I say. My wounds ache as I stretch my arms over my head. "Give me a moment."

I carefully climb out of bed, crossing to my wardrobe to keep my back to her. My heart is racing, and it's difficult to hide my sense of panic. Though I still remember the feel of Blaise's arms around me, his lips against mine, I can't deny that I have feelings for Søren as well, and if he's back, that means the time is coming for me to kill him. I don't want to; the thought of burying my dagger in his flesh, the way I killed Ampelio, makes me want to vomit, and I don't think it's something I'll ever be able to forgive myself for.

But with the Kalovaxians divided and fighting among themselves, they'll be weakened to an outside attack. It's the best chance we have to start to reclaim our country and free my people. I can't afford not to take it.

I find an amethyst chiton dress that I don't need Hoa's help to put on and pull it out of the wardrobe. "Who told you that Søren's back?" I ask Artemisia, silently chiding myself for using his name instead of just his title. I can't help but think of *the Prinz* and *Søren* as different entities altogether. It makes it easier that way.

"No offense, Theo, but watching you sleep is boring," Heron says. "I cloaked myself and took a walk around the castle a couple of hours ago. It was all anyone was talking about."

"Any word on how badly his troops fared?" I ask, wincing as I stretch my back, causing the fresh wounds to stretch as well. "I'd like to know that whipping came with a silver lining."

"He left with four thousand men; he came back with less than two thousand," Heron says, and I can practically hear him smiling. "Dragonsbane came through."

"Albeit reluctantly," Art adds. "According to the crew members I talked with this morning, she only wanted to warn the Vecturians. They gathered enough forces from all of the Vecturian Islands to put up a fight against the four thousand Kalovaxians. My mother's ship was on its way back here when the Vecturian members of her crew rebelled and convinced most of the crew to return and help tip the scales. The Kalovaxians didn't expect it to be much of a fight. They weren't prepared and had no choice but to retreat."

"Still, give her my thanks," I say to Artemisia. "It's no wonder the Kaiser was so angry." I can't help but smile. It was worth it, I tell myself, even as my back aches.

"Tell her the rest," Blaise says, his voice soft.

"Blaise," Artemisia says, a warning in her voice.

Panic seizes my chest. If Artemisia is the one trying to spare my feelings, it can't be good. "Tell me," I say.

Heron sighs. "They didn't leave without a parting gift. A thousand flaming arrows with Fire Gem heads, shot into the forest by the shore. There was a village there, a small one."

"It was also the location of most of Vecturia's food sources," Artemisia adds. "They couldn't put the fire out until three-quarters of it was gone. With winter coming . . ." She doesn't finish, but she doesn't have to.

Most of the people there will starve. I don't have to ask to know that it was Søren who gave that command. It's a brilliant move, disgusting as it is. Would I do the same, if it came down to it? I tell myself I would never doom thousands of innocent people to die for my country. But as soon as I think it, I know it isn't true. Manipulative as she might be, Crescentia has no blood on her hands, and by the time the sun rises tomorrow, I'll have killed her. It's a smaller scale, yes, but it isn't so different. *I'm* not so different.

I am my mother's daughter, but she only raised me for six years. The Kaiser's had the other ten, and whether I like it or not, he's had a hand in shaping me.

I clear my throat, aware of them all watching me, waiting for a reaction. "They'll still eat better than they would have if the Kalovaxians had won," I say, struggling to sound certain when I'm anything but. There is no right answer, no right path. People die no matter what I do. But *fewer* people, which is something, isn't it? Of course, more than two thousand Kalovaxians were killed as well, and though their deaths are a victory for us, they were all someone's child, someone's sweetheart, someone's friend. Someone will be torn apart mourning them.

"We made the right move," Blaise says, his voice firm. "I just thought you should know."

My throat is tight when I speak again, but I manage to get the words out. "I always want to know."

I busy myself by crouching down next to my bed and reaching under the sheets to the small hole in the mattress. With my face hidden, I take the chance to let my guilt rack me, but by the time I rise again, Encatrio in hand, there is no sign of it. I can't afford weakness, especially not now.

The time has come for little birds to fly. The words echo in my mind, in Ampelio's voice and in my mother's. The time has come to avenge them, finally. The time has come to reclaim what is mine, no matter what it costs me.

"The Kaiser will have a dinner in Søren's honor tonight," I say. "He always does when a crew returns from battle, and I'm sure he'll find some way to spin it into a victory. Søren won't be able to make it through the night without lashing out at the Kaiser. I'll push him to it if I need to."

"But if Cress sees you talking to him, she'll tell the Kaiser about you—" Blaise starts, but I interrupt.

"Cress won't be there," I say, the pieces of a plan falling

into place. "She'll miss the banquet, and since he's due to leave tomorrow, the Theyn will insist on staying to dine with her. He'd rather spend time with his daughter than attend a banquet celebrating a battle he had nothing to do with. The poison will be in the dessert wine, which they should drink close to midnight. And I'll make plans with Søren to see him after the banquet and then I'll finish it. We need to send word to Dragonsbane that we're leaving before morning."

"What about the girl?" Heron asks. "We're taking her with us, aren't we?"

"Yes, and her family." I press my lips together. "Her mother and brother should be in the slave quarter. Get them on Dragonsbane's ship this afternoon," I say after a moment. "But you can't take Elpis until tonight."

The Theyn is the last person I want to see today, but I console myself with the knowledge that he'll be dead soon and unable to hurt me—or anyone—ever again. I won't wake up screaming from nightmares about him. I won't cower when he enters a room. I won't have to look into the face of my mother's murderer and smile.

The Encatrio is warm in the pocket of my dress, a constant reminder of its presence and its power. I don't think about Crescentia. As difficult a choice as this is, I am doing the right thing. The only thing.

I knock on the door to Crescentia and the Theyn's quarters, and only a moment passes before the door opens to reveal Elpis's round face.

"Lady Thora," she says. She's surprised, but she's careful to keep her face blank. She has the makings of a good little spy, though I hate that I made her into that. I hate that I now have to ask more of her.

"Is Crescentia here?" I ask her.

She glances behind her to make sure no one is listening nearby. "Lady Crescentia is having lunch with the Prinz," she tells me in a hushed tone.

"Oh?" I ask. I shouldn't be surprised. It's an arrangement, of course, orchestrated by the Kaiser and the Theyn. "Well, I can't blame her for finding his company preferable to mine, but please tell her I stopped by."

I don't make a move to leave and she casts a glance behind her to make sure we're alone. "Is there anything *else*?" she asks meaningfully. "The Theyn is out as well."

"You said your mother was a botanist before the siege. I don't suppose you know your way around plants and herbs as well?"

Elpis's forehead creases, but she nods. "Passably, yes."

"Can you think of something that might make Crescentia ill enough to miss the banquet for the Prinz tonight, but not too ill to partake in her evening meal?"

She chews on her lip for a moment. "I don't think there *is* an ill enough that would make Lady Crescentia miss this banquet."

Elpis has a point. Tonight will bring Cress one step closer to becoming a prinzessin. She'll spend the whole night at Søren's side and the entire court will be whispering about it. She wouldn't miss it if she were dying. But . . .

"What if you put something in her powders that would affect her appearance?" I suggest. "She wouldn't want to go to the banquet then."

A small smile works its way to Elpis's mouth, growing wider. "Ground treska seeds. That would irritate her skin, even cause it to swell if I use enough."

"Use enough," I tell her, not wanting to take any chances. And though I'm not proud of it, the idea of Cress's lovely face red and swollen gives me some satisfaction. "Do you have access to it?"

"Yes, we keep some whole seeds in the pantry to use as a spice. Grinding them up will be easy," she says, rocking back and forth on the balls of her feet in excitement. "I can do it tonight when she's preparing for the banquet."

"Perfect," I say. "Thank you, Elpis."

I should leave it at that, but I linger for a moment more, another favor weighing heavy on my tongue. I search for a different way even as I know there isn't one. I will never have the strength to poison Cress myself. I know that now. But looking at Elpis, seeing the uncomplicated hate she feels for Cress and the Theyn, I know she does. "Would you like to do more?" I ask her.

Elpis's eyes widen. "Please," she breathes.

I only let myself hesitate for a second before I draw the Encatrio vial from my pocket. "Then I have another job for you. You're welcome to say no, Elpis. I won't be angry. We'll find another way. One of my Shadows is fetching your mother and brother now, putting them on a ship to safety. You'll be with them by tonight, I promise, no matter what you choose."

Elpis listens intently as I outline my plan, nodding along

with her mouth twisted and her brow furrowed. Even as I ask it of her, I know it's too much. She's a child, and I'm trying to make her a murderer—*like me,* I think. This is not a job for a child, and I can almost feel Blaise's disapproval from wherever he's watching me.

Though, really, I'm not making Elpis anything the Kaiser and the Theyn and even Crescentia haven't already made her. In a way, the Kalovaxians raised her, too.

So of course, she says yes.

ERIK

— • —

ERIK IS WAITING IN FRONT of my door when I return, one hand on the pommel of the sword sheathed at his hip. He doesn't look like he's even taken the time to change since he left his ship—he's still dressed in rough-spun breeches and a white shirt in need of a good cleaning. Coal is smeared along his cheekbones to direct the sun away from his eyes. I'm a few feet away from him when the smell of sweat and fish hits me so hard it makes me dizzy.

He breaks into a lopsided smile when he sees me, and he pushes off the wall he was leaning against, meeting me half-way down the hall.

"I'm so glad you're safe, Erik," I tell him, surprised to find that it's true. Maybe it's because he isn't fully Kalovaxian, and I have a difficult time thinking of him as one of them.

"It takes more than a few pirates to kill me," he says, shaking his head.

I hesitate. "How is he?"

Erik's face clouds, and he doesn't have to ask who I'm referring to. "Søren's . . . as you would expect him to be. What-ever you said in your letter seemed to comfort him, though. He read it at least a dozen times before he burned it. Of course, the Kaiser blames him for the failure of the siege. This was his first major command and it should have been an easy one. But I was there, Thora. There was nothing he could have done. We were ambushed."

An ambush to stop an ambush. These are not people who deserve my pity.

"I know," I tell him instead. "It must have been awful. I'm glad you both are safe, though."

He nods, but his eyes dart around and he lowers his voice to a murmur. "I was hoping we could speak privately. Well . . ." He breaks off, glancing behind me where I'm sure my Shadows are waiting. "As privately as we can."

I lower my own voice to match his, even though my heart is thundering. "Is everything all right?"

He pauses, blue eyes flickering around the empty hall. "When we first met, you asked me about berserkers. . . ." He trails off, but raises his dark eyebrows pointedly.

My hand slips on his arm at the sound of the word, but I'm careful to keep my expression nonchalant. Lady Thora doesn't *really* care about anything as boring as berserkers, whatever they might be. She only asked him out of mild curiosity. I can't let him see how desperately I want to know.

"I know the perfect place," I say.

The garden is empty, as it usually is, and as soon as we've taken a lap around the perimeter to ensure no one is listening, Erik drops my arm and turns to me. All pretense of friendliness dissolves immediately. His eyes go cold in a way that reminds me of the Kaiser so much it's jarring. I unconsciously take a step back.

"Did you tell anyone about Vecturia?" He asks the question quietly, but like he already knows the answer.

The accusation stops my heart and panic seizes me, but I struggle not to show it, to keep my expression surprised and perplexed, but not afraid.

I meet his gaze. "Of course not." I manage to laugh at the ridiculousness of the question, even as my heart hammers loudly in my chest.

"It was a quiet mission; trade-route pirates were our official story. I was the only one besides Søren who knew otherwise before we left, and I didn't tell anyone except you. But Dragonsbane knew, the Vecturians knew."

I glance up at the windows, counting one, two, three Shadows watching. If the accusations go any further, they can make sure Erik ends up at the bottom of the sea with my former Shadows. No one is around to see, he made sure of it himself. Still, I would rather it not come to that.

"I have no idea, Erik," I say, keeping my voice level. "I'd all but forgotten you even mentioned Vecturia until now. Besides, I'm watched always, even now—do you think I had any opportunity to waltz out of the palace, find Dragonsbane, and tell him what you had planned? I don't even *know* what you had planned. The Kaiser already made me answer for your failure. Are you going to make me answer for it again now?"

For a beat, he looks uncertain, his eyes flitting away before landing on me again.

"Nothing else makes sense, Thora," he says, but his voice wavers.

"And this does?" I ask him. "That I'm a *spy*, giving information to pirates? How does that benefit me at all?"

He lifts a shoulder in a defiant shrug, but it's halfhearted. "Dragonsbane is known to work with Astrean rebels. It's a way of striking back, a way of weakening our troops, even a way of getting rid of Søren—"

"I would never," I say, letting my voice rise to a shout before I hasten to lower it, stepping closer to Erik. "I . . ." I trail off, making a show of biting my lip and looking troubled. "I *love* Søren."

It's not the truth, but it isn't as much of a lie as it should be. I give a mournful sigh and sit down on the stone bench at the garden's center, letting my shoulders slump forward.

"I've been raised here among Kalovaxians," I continue, making my voice fray like I'm on the verge of tears. "After everything I've done, everything I've endured, I can't believe you would still question my loyalty."

I hear him huff out a breath before sitting down next to me. "I'm sorry," he says after a minute, and it takes all I have to hide the relief coursing through me.

He clears his throat. "When you said the Kaiser made you answer for our failure . . ." He trails off.

I sigh and turn my back to him, tugging down my collar just low enough that he can see the tops of some of the fresh scars. Even with Ion speeding up the healing process, they're raw. They look a few days old instead of a few hours, but are still red and raised and painful. He lets out a curse under his breath, and when I turn back I see he's gone a few shades paler, so that he almost looks like a full-blooded Kalovaxian.

He'll tell Søren about this, I realize, and I can use that to my advantage. I can fuel Søren's anger at his father even more.

"It's not the first time, and I doubt it will be the last," I say, pulling the collar of my dress back up so that the wounds are covered once more.

"When Søren finds out—"

"He'll do what, Erik?" I ask, choking out a bitter laugh. He'll repeat this to Søren, so I need to make it count. "He won't stand up to his father. He won't take me away from here. He'll marry Crescentia, just like the Kaiser wants him to, and keep me as, what? His mistress? Or his stepmother, if the Kaiser gets his way. And we both know he always does."

The idea is so ridiculous that I can't help but laugh, as much as it sickens me. I glance at Erik, expecting surprise, but he shows none.

"You've heard the rumors," I say. "He hasn't been very subtle. Does Søren know?"

He shakes his head. "Søren prefers to ignore rumors, even ones he knows are true," he says. "In our many years of friendship, he's never once asked me if I'm really his father's bastard."

The revelation shocks me, but at the same time, it makes sense. I assumed Erik was someone important's half-Gorakian bastard, though I'd thought it was a baron or a count. I never even considered the Kaiser, which was foolish. Now that he's said it, I see the similarities in their features—the jawline, the nose. He and Søren even have the same eyes, the Kaiser's eyes.

He must see my surprise, because he laughs. "Come now,

Thora. Here I thought you were brighter than you pretended. I thought you'd have figured it out by now, especially since you see more of my mother than I do."

"Your . . . ," I start, but trail off. There are very few people I see regularly, and since Crescentia can't be his mother, that only leaves one other woman. Hoa. He's talking about Hoa.

Erik gives me a level look and for a second I could swear he knows all my secrets. But that's impossible. "My mother plotted against the Kaiser from his bed after the Conquering of Goraki. He was kind enough to spare her life, even though she's a traitor."

He says the words too easily, the way I do when I'm reciting one of the lies the Kaiser has burned into my mind. I want to challenge him on it, but I can't without losing part of my mask as well, and I cannot risk that. His eyes scan my face, watching for a reaction I'm careful not to give. After a moment, he sighs and pushes himself off the bench.

"It's a person," he tells me.

"Pardon?" I ask, bewildered.

"A berserker," he says. "It's an Astrean, to be exact. I'm assuming you know what happens when most people spend too long in the mines."

"They go mad and are put to death," I say.

He avoids my gaze, staring at the stone floor instead. "Yes to the first, no to the second. The madness, I'm sure you know, is caused by the concentration of too much magic from the mines. It's what gives the gems their power. Over time, it makes its way into the blood of people who work there. Some people can handle it, most can't. You know the symptoms," he says.

I frown. "No. People still went mine-mad before, occasionally, but the details weren't the kind of thing anyone talked about in front of a child, and after the Conquering . . . well, no one discusses anything like that with me."

Erik lists them off on his fingers. "Feverish skin, erratic bursts of magic, emotional instability, insomnia. The short of it is, they become dangerous," he says.

A thought rises in my mind, but I push it down before it takes shape. *No.*

He continues. "Human powder kegs. Send them to the front lines with a gem to nudge them over the edge and it's only a matter of minutes before their power is unleashed, uncontrollable and strong enough to take out everything within a twenty-foot radius. In fire, water, earth, or air. It doesn't matter much, the result is the same: ruination."

"You're lying," I say, though I don't think he is. Try as I might, I can't imagine it. Corbinian is evil, I have never doubted that, but this? This is beyond anything I thought even he was capable of. "How do you know?"

The look he gives me is one I'm not used to, almost tender. It puts me on edge. It is the kind of look you give a person before you shatter them.

"Because I saw it. In Vecturia. Søren used ships full of a few hundred of them, but even that wasn't enough. Søren put off using them until the last minute. It was too late—the battle was already lost."

All my breath leaves me. No. The Kaiser may be capable of this, but not Søren. Not the boy who ate chocolate cake with me and asked me the Astrean word for it. Not the boy who promised to take me away from this godsforsaken place.

Not the boy who kissed me like maybe we could save each other.

But of course he did. Because that is who he is: a Kalovaxian warrior to his last breath. He is not the chivalrous prinz and I am not lovesick Lady Thora, no matter how we try to pretend otherwise.

"He refused at first," Erik says after a moment, as if that makes it any better. "The Kaiser insisted."

I swallow the rage burning through me. I can't let it show. Not yet. "I'm sure Søren did what was required of him," I say as calmly as I can, though I know I don't sound convincing. Tears blur my vision, but I will not let them fall.

"Thora," Erik says after a moment. "Are you all right?"

How can I possibly be all right? I want to scream and hit something and maybe vomit at the thought of hundreds of my people being used like that, dying like that.

With a concentrated effort, I get to my feet and smooth out my skirt. When I look up at Erik again, I keep my expression neutral.

"Is your mother loyal to the Kaiser, Erik?" I ask him.

He watches me warily, like I've become a tiger who could pounce at any moment.

"As loyal as you are," he says finally. "She doesn't want trouble. She's had enough of that in her life."

It isn't an answer, really. I can interpret those words any number of ways, and after my misstep with Cress, I should be more careful. I should trust no one. Yet I can't help but remember Hoa tucking me into bed when I was a child, how she held me when the Kaiser had this garden burned. I don't know what the Kaiser will do when he finds out I've escaped—when he finds out I've killed his friend and his son—but I know I can't leave her here to face the brunt of it.

"Take her and get out of the city tonight," I tell him.

I expect a protest, or at least a question, but Erik only searches my expression for a few seconds and nods tersely.

"Thank you," he says with a slight bow. "May our paths meet again, Theodosia."

It isn't until he's left me alone in the garden that I realize he called me by my true name.

SISTER

———•———

I ALMOST DON'T TELL MY SHADOWS about the berserkers. The
idea of them is so horrifying, part of me wishes I didn't
know what they were myself—not to mention the fact that
it likely happened to people they actually knew and loved.
I think of what Heron told me about the boy he was in love
with, Leonidas, and how he was taken away for his execution
after he went mine-mad. Isn't it better that he thinks that of
him, that he was given a quick death instead of turned into
a weapon? But they deserve to know what became of their
friends and family, and they need to know what we're up
against.

"There were rumors," Artemisia says after the moment
of shocked silence that follows my explanation. "I heard
that the mad ones were taken away for testing. There were
even whispers about Kalovaxian physicians harvesting magic
from their body parts, selling their blood overseas. But I never
thought . . ." She trails off.

My voice breaks despite my best efforts to keep it strong.
"Elpis has the poison. She's giving Cress a powder that will
cause her face to redden and swell so that she'll have to miss

the banquet tonight. If she doesn't attend, the Theyn will have no reason to either, since he detests parties. They'll dine together, alone, since the Theyn is due to ship out again soon. Søren is already furious with his father, and tonight I can push him over the edge and get him to confront him publicly. Then I'll convince him to come for another late-night sail, and when we're on the boat alone, I'll kill him with the dagger." I don't hesitate or stumble over the words like I might have only a few hours ago. I'm an altogether different person now, and so is he. "Artemisia, is your mother ready for us to leave?"

"She's been waiting on the order," she replies. Even with the wall between us, I know she's smiling. "I'll go now and make sure everything is ready. Any destination in particular?"

I lick my lips, turning over options. There are precious few of them. "The Anglamar ruins. It's the perfect place to regroup and strategize before we liberate the mines."

The answer is met with protests. All three of them speak over one another to tell me the same things: liberating the mines is a bad idea, there are too many guards, it's impossible. I wait for their protests to die down.

"It's the only way," I say. "With our current numbers, we can't make a real stand. Help from other countries will come with strings, but there are thousands of Astreans in the mines. And knowing what we do now . . . I can't let my people—many of them children—stay there a day longer than necessary. It's the only thing to do. And with the Prinz dead and the court fighting among themselves over what to do about it, they won't be at their full strength. If there was ever a time to try to take the mines back, it's now."

I wait for more protests, but they don't come.

"My mother will say it's too risky," Artemisia says finally. I open my mouth to argue. "But I can convince her."

I nod, fighting a smile. Having Artemisia on my side is new and welcome. "Heron, go gather evidence to frame the guard. I'll need it by the time I return from the banquet."

"Yes, Your Highness," he says.

The knock at my door takes me by surprise. It's only mid-afternoon and the banquet isn't due to start until dusk, so it can't be Hoa or an attendant bringing my dress and crown. At first I think it might be Søren, but it's a far too conventional entrance for him. Hesitantly I set aside the book of Elcourtian histories—reading is the only way to calm my anxious mind—but before I can get out of bed to answer, the door opens and Cress glides in, pink silk dress flaring behind her. She hasn't started getting ready for the banquet yet, and her fair skin is still unblemished and smooth.

When she sees me, her steps grow slow and hesitant, her gray eyes finding mine before quickly darting away. Though she must still be giddy from her lunch with Søren, her expression is somber.

"I . . . ," she begins, dropping her eyes to the floor. She brings her hands together in front of her, wringing them. "I heard about what happened. The . . . ." She can't say the words, but I know she means my punishment, which is surprising on its own. In ten years, she's never brought up my beatings. She pretends they don't happen at all.

But after our last conversation, she must feel guilty. It

shouldn't soften me; it shouldn't make my heart clench in my chest. But it does. I try to think of the things she said to me yesterday, the coldness in her voice, the unveiled threat she poses even now. The girl who put her ambitions over my life. That is not a friend, I tell myself, but the way she's looking at me now, shamefaced and concerned—I could almost forget what I now know to be true.

I should tell her to go, I should give some excuse or other—I'm not feeling well, I want to sleep, I'm in too much pain. I could tell her I will see her at the banquet tonight, make some plan that will never come to fruition. Because having her here, I know I will waver again and I can't afford to do that.

"Come on," I say to her instead, scooting over on the bed to make room for her to lie down next to me. My back aches as I move, but I'm only dimly aware of it now.

Cress's smile is beatific as she does just that, picking up the book of Elcourtian histories.

I'm going to miss her smile. The thought is like the Theyn's whip, a pain I feel to my bones.

"It's good," I tell her, nodding to the book.

"Have you gotten to the Fishmongers' War?" she asks eagerly, flipping through the pages until she finds the right chapter.

I have, but I let her read it to me anyway, her voice soft and melodious as she discusses the peasant fishmongers who rose up against the Elcourtian royalty almost five hundred years ago. It wasn't a fight they had any right to win, they were inexperienced and outnumbered, but it wasn't long before peasants across the country joined their cause, fed up with the current corrupt regime. That, combined with the fishmongers' better mastery of the surrounding seas, led them to execute the entire royal family and strip the nobility of their titles and wealth, redistributing them among themselves.

It's practically a fairy tale, but the real thorn is in the ending. The current King of Elcourt, generations removed from his fishmonger forefather, is as awful as the one the country rebelled against in the first place.

That bit isn't in Crescentia's book, of course, but I've heard the rumors all the same.

After reading for only a few moments, Crescentia puts the book aside and takes hold of my hand.

"I'm sorry. I understand now," she says, voice heavy. The words twist at my stomach because she doesn't understand, as much as I wish she did. She thinks she understands why I tried to rebel against the Kaiser, but only because of the punishment, only because of the recent reminder of how terrible *my* circumstances are. She thinks that is why I acted. She understands *my* pain because she loves me, but her compassion ends there.

She takes a shaky breath. "I told you I didn't remember my mother, but that isn't true. I remember some things, though I wish I didn't."

I sit up, though my welts scream at the movement. In the ten years I've known her, Cress has mentioned her mother exactly once, when she told me she'd died when she was very young. I don't even know her name.

"You know we were in Goraki before we were here. I was born there. So was Søren," she continues before her voice turns bitter. "My mother was said to be one of the most beautiful women in the world. Everyone was in love with her. She could have married a duke or an earl if she'd wanted, but for some reason, she chose my father, an upstart warrior at the time, the son of a shipsmith. I suppose she must have loved him."

Her smile is a brittle, broken thing, so different from the one I'm used to from her, the one that can light up a room and elicit a smile from me, even at my moodiest.

"I'm sure you can surmise that he climbed from there until he became the Theyn. I'm sure you can surmise what it means to climb to that position. My mother hated it. I heard her scream that she didn't want him to touch her, not with the blood of so many on his hands. She didn't realize, or maybe didn't care, that he did it all for her, to give her the life he thought she deserved."

She pauses and swallows. There are no tears in her eyes, but she looks like she's in physical pain. She's never spoken about this, I realize, not to any of her other friends or even to her father. This must have sat between them, heavy and unacknowledged, for the better part of her life.

"She didn't die when I was a baby. She didn't die at all, as far as I know, but it's easier to pretend, I suppose. She left us before we came here; she said she couldn't do it anymore. She wanted to take me with her, but my father wouldn't allow it, so she left me behind."

There, her voice cracks, and she hastily wipes away tears that have only just begun to form at the corners of her eyes. Normally, Cress's tears are weapons, employed against her father or a courtier who won't invite me to a party or a dressmaker who claims not to have time to make her something new that week. These tears are not weapons, though, they are a weakness and so she cannot show them. She is the Theyn's daughter, after all.

"Did you want to go with her?" I ask carefully.

She shrugs. "I was a child. My father was away most of the time, and he scared me a bit. My mother was the one I loved best, but I didn't have a choice. Don't misunderstand me, Thora," she says, shaking her head. "I'm glad my father kept me with him. I know you think he's awful, and I can't blame you for that, but he's my father. Still, sometimes I miss her."

Her voice breaks again and I reach out to take her hand. "You're a good friend, Cress," I tell her, because it's what she needs to hear. In a simpler world, her friendship would be enough. But in this one, it isn't.

She smiles and gives my hand a squeeze before releasing it.

"You should get some rest," she says, standing up. "I'll see you at the banquet tonight."

She pauses, eyes lingering on me warily for a moment.

"You didn't . . . you didn't have true feelings for him, did you? Søren, I mean." She says it like she doesn't really want to know the answer.

"No," I tell her, and the lie slides easily off my tongue. It isn't even a lie anymore, I realize.

She smiles, relieved. "I'll see you tonight," she repeats, turning to go.

"Cress?" I say when she's at the door.

She looks back to me, pale eyebrows raised, smile tentative. A confession bubbles to my lips. I don't know that I can let her walk to her death.

I see a scale in my mind, Cress on one side, the twenty thousand of my people still living on the other. It shouldn't be a difficult decision to make; it should be simple. It shouldn't feel like it's tearing my heart out.

I swallow. "I'll see you tonight," I say, knowing that my last words to her are just another lie.

BANQUET

ANOTHER BANQUET MEANS ANOTHER ASH crown, though I swear to myself this will be the last time I wear one. The guard who delivers it along with the gown I'm to wear looks perplexed to see me instead of Hoa, but I tell him she stepped out for a moment to deliver my dirty clothes to the laundresses and he accepts that easily enough, pressing the boxes into my arms and leaving without another word.

I set the smaller box on my vanity, then lay the larger one on my bed and open it. The gown always goes on first in Hoa's routine so that the crown is saved for the last possible second.

This one is a deep blood-red, and I can already tell it won't cover much more than what's necessary. *This is the last time I'll be his trophy,* I promise myself.

Heron and Artemisia haven't returned yet, so it's only Blaise here. I tell him to turn around before slipping out of the dress I'm wearing and stepping into the gown. Tiny buttons run down what little back there is, and it takes me a moment to manage them myself. Unlike other gowns the Kaiser has sent, this one doesn't just leave my back bare but exposes more cleavage than most courtesans show and has a slit cut up to my hip. I'm practically naked. The idea of anyone seeing me like this turns my stomach, but I reluctantly call for Blaise to turn back around.

For a long moment, he doesn't say anything.

"I'm sorry, Theo," he manages finally, his voice quiet.

"I know," I tell him before squaring my shoulders and walking toward the box on my vanity.

The lid lifts with ease, and inside, the crown is a perfect circlet of ash resting on a red silk pillow. It could almost be pretty under different circumstances, but seeing it fills me only with hatred.

"Blaise?" I say, glancing up to his wall. "I've never put it on myself. Hoa always does it and I don't want to give the Kaiser any reason to suspect anything is different tonight."

For a moment, Blaise doesn't say anything. "All right," he manages finally.

I hear him shifting behind the wall before his door opens out into the hallway. Seconds later, he's slipping through my door as quietly as he can. His eyes are heavy with worry and I almost regret asking for his help. I'm already worried enough myself; seeing it reflected on his face just reinforces how many ways this can go wrong.

I try to smile at him, but it's harder than it should be.

"Are you going to be all right tonight?" he asks as he looks into the box. "With the Kaiser?"

I've been struggling not to think of exactly that. I can still feel him touching my hip at the maskentanz, still feel his breath in my ear, his hand on my cheek when he promised me we would talk again soon. I try to suppress the shudder that runs through me, but I know Blaise sees it.

"I've survived ten years," I tell him, knowing better than to lie to him. "I can survive one more night."

Even as I say it, though, I wonder just how true that is. The Kaiserin is dead, so the Kaiser will grow bolder. If Blaise hadn't broken his chair on the pavilion and our conversation had continued, I don't know where it would have ended. I don't *want* to know what would have happened next.

"I'll be there the whole time," Blaise says. He means it as a comfort and I smile at him and pretend to be comforted, but we both know there will be nothing he can do.

"I can survive one more night," I tell him again. "But promise me something?"

He delicately lifts the crown from the box, eyes focused on it instead of me. "Anything," he says.

"When the Kaiser is dead, whenever that may be, I want to burn his body. I want to put the torch to him myself and I want to stay and watch until there is nothing left of him but ash. Will you promise me that?"

His eyes flicker to me and I realize that I'm shaking. I take a deep breath to calm myself.

"I swear it to Houzzah himself. And to you," he says quietly.

Neither of us so much as breathes while he gently sets the crown on top of my head, a few flakes falling on my nose and cheeks as he does. His eyes stay locked on mine as he reaches a hand up toward my cheek before hesitating and letting it fall away. Worry still creases his forehead.

"You will survive." He says it like he's trying to convince himself of the fact. He hesitates a second longer, as if he wants to say something else, before giving a brief nod and leaving the room just as quietly as he came in.

I take one last look at my reflection in the mirror. Ashes already flake down over my cheeks and nose, marking me. The red stain I used on my lips looks like fresh blood. Underneath, I see bits and pieces of my mother staring back at me, but twisted with hate and fury my mother never needed to know. I'm not sorry for it.

I am angry.

I am hungry.

And I promise myself that one day I will watch them all burn.

By the time I arrive at the banquet, it has already started; sitting at the long table are dozens of courtiers in rich, jewel-colored silks and velvets. The lot of them drip with Spiritgems of all shapes, sizes, and types, which glitter in the light of the chandelier overhead. Seeing them now, so *many*, sickens me. How many of my people have given their lives and sanity so that these people can have a little more beauty, an ounce more strength?

Crescentia isn't here, I realize as I scan the room, which means Elpis's trick with the treska seeds worked. At least that's one thing that's gone right so far, one less problem I have to worry about. But that relief is short-lived, because once my eyes find Søren's, everything in me tightens up again and I can hardly breathe.

He doesn't look like the boy who left three weeks ago. He is hollowed out, with stark dark circles under his eyes. His long blond hair is gone, shaved off so unevenly that I wonder if he did it himself. It's the traditional Kalovaxian expression of grief, and despite everything, I feel a pang of pity for him. I quickly drown it in more hatred, though. He might be mourning his mother, but he's still a murderer. How many of my people has he personally killed? I doubt even he could tell me the answer to that, let alone remember all their names.

I am rage and hurt and hatred, but I force that aside and give him a small, tentative smile, as if I'm glad to see him, before forcing my eyes away in case anyone else is watching.

"Ash Princess," the Kaiser bellows from his place at the head of the table, eyes suddenly heavy on me, oozing over the many inches of skin left exposed in the gaudy crimson dress.

He means to humiliate me, to put me on display like a stolen jewel, but for the first time I don't mind it. I can see the fury etched into the lines of Søren's face as he takes me in. The Kaiser is unwittingly doing my job for me—it won't be at all difficult to push Søren over the edge tonight. The real challenge will be keeping my anger toward both of them in check.

"Your Highness," I say, approaching the Kaiser and curtsying at his feet. His face is already a drunken shade of vermilion. As he always does, he tilts my chin up and places the palm of his hand against my cheek in order to leave his handprint in the ash that's already sprinkled down over my face. I keep my gaze lowered, but out of the corner of my eye I see Søren go rigid, eyes locked onto his father in cold rage.

"You'll sit at my side tonight," the Kaiser says when I rise, gesturing to the chair to his left. The one that used to belong to the Kaiserin. He takes a long swig from his jeweled goblet before setting it back on the table. There are drops of red wine in his beard; they look like specks of blood.

"I would be honored, Your Highness," I say.

Though it's nothing I wasn't expecting, dread still pools in the pit of my stomach as I take the seat, only inches away from the Kaiser and directly across from Søren. Though I know it's good that they're both staring at me, that it means the plan is working, it still takes every inch of effort not to shrink away.

"You look quite pretty tonight, Ash Princess," the Kaiser says, leering at me before turning his attention to his son and grinning. "Doesn't she look pretty, Søren?" he asks.

He's taunting him, I realize. The attention Søren's been paying me hasn't gone unnoticed by the Kaiser after all, but instead of angering him, it only seems to make him gleeful.

To his credit, Søren manages a nonchalant shrug, though he studiously avoids looking at me. He mutters something under his breath while staring down at the plate in front of him.

The Kaiser lifts his goblet for another long gulp before slamming it back down, making Søren and me jump, and startling all the courtiers at the table into silence. They try to pretend they aren't listening in, but of course they are.

"I don't think I heard that, Søren," the Kaiser says. "I asked you a question and I expect a proper answer."

Søren flinches from the Kaiser's voice and his eyes finally rise to meet mine, full of pain and apology.

"I said she looks beautiful, Father," he says, but each word is sharp as a knife.

The Kaiser frowns at his son's tone, like he's been presented with a puzzle he's never seen before. His mouth twists and he takes another gulp from his goblet. His eyes are unfocused as they turn back to me.

"I don't believe you thanked me, Ash Princess," he says. "Don't you like the dress I sent you?"

I want to stare the Kaiser down and spit at him. But I am not Queen Theodosia right now, I am Lady Thora, and so instead, I bite my bottom lip and fidget uncomfortably, tugging at the low neckline.

"Of course I do, Your Highness," I say, my voice shaking around each word. "I'm so grateful for it. It's lovely."

He smiles like a wolf closing in on its prey, and my heart hammers quicker in my chest, my palms sweat. People farther down the table resume their conversations, but across from me, Søren's gripping his dinner knife so tightly that his knuckles have turned white. The Kaiser's hand comes down to rest on my bare knee, exposed by the slit in the dress.

"Good girl," he says, low enough for only me to hear.

It takes everything I have not to recoil from him, but I manage, staring at the table in front of me instead.

I will burn your body to ash, I say in my mind. I imagine it, the torch in my hand, his body lying on top of a heap of hay. I will lower the torch and he will burn and I will smile and maybe then I will finally feel safe again.

"That's enough."

Søren's voice is so quiet I barely hear him above the music and the hum of conversation. The Kaiser hears him clearly, though, posture going stiff and his grip on my leg tightening painfully until I wince. For an impossibly long moment, he stares at Søren silently, eyes cold and hard. But Søren, to his credit, matches his stare until the other courtiers at the banquet table give up the pretense of not eavesdropping. The room is so quiet I can hear my heart thundering in my chest.

"What was that, Søren?" the Kaiser says, and though his tone is polite there is an undercurrent of broken glass and snake venom. I'm sure his words are heard in every corner of the room.

The lump in Søren's throat bobs, but he doesn't shrink away like I half expect him to. His eyes flicker to me for an instant before glancing out at the other courtiers watching. I can see the gears in his mind turning as he takes them in, sees the situation from their perspective. Søren doesn't understand how court works, but he knows battle and he knows that's what he's stepped into. He knows that his options now are to surrender or declare war. He knows to declare war over me would be to sign my execution warrant. He knows to surrender would do the same, more or less.

I can see him look at the situation from every point of view in the matter of a few seconds before he makes a decision, getting to his feet and bracing his hands on the table in front of him, looking beleaguered and exhausted.

"I said that's enough, Father," he says, loud enough now for the entire room to hear him. "This is not a night to celebrate a victory, not with so many of my men fallen in Vecturia."

If the Kaiser could execute someone with his gaze alone, Søren would be dead in seconds, but he says nothing.

"Instead," Søren says, tearing his eyes away from his father and staring out at the other courtiers, "tonight is a night of mourning and solemnity for those we lost in a battle we should never have entered. It was a vain mission; we had no reason to attack Vecturia, and hundreds of Kalovaxian men lost their lives for it."

Silence follows Søren's proclamation, stretching out for what feels like an eternity before a bald man seated at the other end of the banquet table gets to his feet. I recognize him from my last punishment; he's one of the courtiers who lost a son in Vecturia.

"Hear, hear," he calls, raising his wine goblet.

One by one, more men and women join him, raising their goblets toward Søren with shouts of agreement and solemn calls for remembering Vecturia. Before long, the vast majority of the hall has stood for him, and even those who remain seated look bewildered and uncertain.

The Kaiser's grip on my knee goes slack as he looks around the hall, glare nearly lethal. When he realizes he's outnumbered, he slowly rises from his chair, picking up his own goblet.

"Well said, my son," he says, and though he flashes a smile at Søren, the edges of it are razor sharp. "I propose a moment of silence for those who fell in Vecturia. Those men died for honor and they will receive an honored welcome from their ancestors."

Once the dam inside Søren has broken, though, there is no walling it up again.

"Those men didn't die for honor. They died for greed," he says through gritted teeth, and I know he's thinking not only of his men, but of his mother. He's not foolish enough to accuse the Kaiser of murder in front of his entire court, though.

The Kaiser's mouth thins into a line. "Well, perhaps next

time I will seek your opinion, Søren, before I make a decision for my people."

"Perhaps you should," Søren replies. "But as I said, this is not a night for celebration. We'll take your moment of silence and then I propose we end the night early to honor the dead."

The Kaiser is as tense as a bow stretched taut enough to break. "I believe that would be for the best," he allows.

Suddenly I wonder if I won't have to frame the Kaiser for murdering Søren, if he'll just do it himself. But the Kaiser is a man slow to action and I don't have the time to wait.

We bow our heads for the moment of silence. After a few seconds, I look up to find Søren watching me. Everyone around us has their eyes closed, so I mouth, *"Midnight tonight."* His gaze is heavy on mine as he nods once before bowing his head again.

CAGE

———— • ◆ • ————

I WALK BACK TO MY ROOMS alone after the banquet, though I'm sure everyone I pass assumes my Shadows are nearby. That's the good thing about having guards prized for their skill at going unnoticed—no one misses them when they aren't around.

The pounding of my heart thunders through my body, but I'm not sure if it's caused by excitement or panic or dread or some combination of the three. Despite the chill in the air, my skin feels clammy, and my sweat mixes with the ash flakes from my crown, causing it to streak down my face. With shaking hands, I wipe it off, my palms coming away black.

It's almost over, I tell myself. Almost. But no matter how far I get from this place and the Kaiser, I know I will never forget tonight, the leer in his eyes and his hand on my knee. I wonder if I'll ever sleep peacefully again.

I reach the door to my room and push it open, almost letting out a scream of surprise. Blaise and Heron sit on the edge of my bed, waiting in anxious silence.

Heron shoots to his feet at the sight of me, peppering me with questions that I only half hear, but Blaise just looks at me, his eyes boring into mine. He doesn't have to ask questions; I think he sees my every thought written plainly on my face.

I don't know what to say to them, so I say nothing, crossing to my vanity and looking at my reflection in the mirror—a wild-eyed girl in a garish dress with black streaks covering most of her face.

"Here," Heron says quietly, appearing behind me. "I can hold your hair back, if that helps."

"Please," I say, barely louder than a whisper.

His fingers are gentle as they rake through my hair, pulling it away from my face. Ash is there, too, coating the top of my head in a sheet of gray, but there is nothing to do about that. Søren won't be long, and now, more than ever, everything needs to happen perfectly. With Heron holding my hair, I splash water from the basin onto my face, washing away the sweat and ash and cosmetics.

I give myself one more moment as I pat my face dry with a towel, and Heron steps away from me, letting my hair fall down around my shoulders again. When I turn around to face them, I am strong and sure and ready to rise. I am Queen Theodosia.

"It worked," I tell Heron and Blaise, looking between them. "Better than I expected, even. The Prinz made a scene—called the Kaiser selfish and laid the lives of his fallen comrades at his feet. Honestly, given the way the Kaiser was looking at him, he might kill Søren himself, though that's not a risk I'm willing to take. Søren will be here soon and the plan is on track."

Blaise nods, eyes holding mine. "Elpis's family is on board

Dragonsbane's ship. Artemisia is waiting there to make sure her mother keeps her word."

Heron digs into the pocket of his pants and pulls out a leather hair tie, a scrap of crimson fabric embroidered with a gold dragon, and an Earth Gem.

"I nicked these," he says, passing them to me. "Scatter them on the ground, make it look like a fight."

I nod, taking them. I'll need a different dress, one with pockets to hold them, but I'm anxious to get out of this one anyway.

"Søren will be here soon," I tell them. "You should both already be gone when he gets here. I'll tell him I want to go for a sail and I'm sure he'll be happy to oblige—he's more comfortable on the water than here in the palace. Off the East Harbor, it's a small boat with a red sail."

"I'll be waiting in another boat nearby. We should have a signal for if you run into trouble," Blaise says.

"I'll scream. That'll be signal enough," I tell him before turning to Heron. "That leaves you to get Elpis. Do you remember where the Theyn lives?"

Heron nods. "I remember," he says. He takes a step toward the door before turning back toward me. "Is it all right if I hug you?"

"We're going to see each other in an hour or so," I say with a half smile. "But yes, I would like that."

Heron smiles back before closing the distance between us and wrapping his lanky arms around me. It's a good hug, the kind that feels like safety and home and love. I let myself get lost in it for a moment before pulling back.

"I'll see you soon," I tell him emphatically.

"Soon," he repeats before hugging me again, briefly, and letting me go. Quiet as a light breeze, he slips from the door, leaving Blaise and me alone.

"I don't like the idea of you taking on the Prinz on your own," he says quietly.

"I know," I tell him. "But you can't very well follow us through the tunnels without being noticed. And I can do it. You said it yourself: Søren won't hurt me."

"He will if he thinks you're trying to kill him."

"He won't," I say, certain of it.

Blaise is quiet for a long moment. "I believe you *can* kill him, but you shouldn't have to be the one to do it."

"It's war," I point out. "I won't lose sleep over it."

Blaise shakes his head, his eyes heavy. "Yes, you will."

A lump rises in my throat and I swallow it down. "You really need to go, Blaise," I tell him. "Søren will be here soon, and I need to change."

He nods, but he doesn't make a move to leave.

"Blaise—"

"I'll go, don't worry," he says, hands fidgeting in front of him. "It's just . . . we might never come back here, Theo. This is our *home*."

His words twist in my chest and I shake my head. "It's a cage, stained with the blood of too many people we've loved. It hasn't been home for a long time now."

"Still," he says, his voice hoarse as he takes a step toward me. "We took our first steps here. We said our first words. This was the last place we were truly happy."

I hold back tears that threaten to fall. "It's only walls,

Blaise, and roofs and floors. Yes, it's full of memories, but that's all they are."

He stays quiet for a moment, hands coming to rest on my shoulders. He leans in and presses a kiss to my forehead.

"Be safe," he says. "And don't do anything foolish. I'll see you soon, Your Highness."

It isn't until after he's gone that I realize he's never called me that before. I've always just been Theo with him, but maybe Theo—like Thora—won't exist for much longer. Soon, all that will be left of me is Queen Theodosia, and as much as I want that, I can't help but mourn the loss of those other parts of me.

DAGGER

—————•—•—————

I CAN'T SIT STILL WHILE I wait for Søren. Elpis said that Cress and her father would eat dinner late—usually not until ten—and I instructed Elpis to poison their dessert wine. Heron will get her from the Theyn's suite to Dragonsbane's ship. It's a tight schedule to keep, but unless something goes horribly wrong, there's no reason I won't be on the ship by the time the Theyn's body is discovered. They'll find Søren's soon after.

Every part of me buzzes like I'm covered head to toe in Spiritgems. I can't stop thinking about what I'm about to do. It's easy to focus on the Søren that Erik painted earlier, the Prinz so eager to earn his father's respect that he used my people as weapons, but I also remember the boy on the boat who resented his court, the boy desperate to turn his back on it all, the boy who stood up to his father in front of the entire court. The boy who needed me to assure him that he was nothing like his father. How can they both exist in one person?

The knock on the wardrobe comes just after the midnight bell tolls, followed by Søren stumbling out. Though he already seemed like a shadow of himself at the banquet, up close he's even rougher around the edges. With his shaved head, his face is all sharp, haggard angles. His bright eyes are darker than I remember, sunken deep in his skull. When he looks at me, it feels like he isn't seeing me at all.

He stands before me broken, and despite everything, I want to comfort him. Because I know what it is to be changed so irreparably and without consent.

"Søren?" I say, taking a tentative step closer.

He can't know anything's changed, but I can't look at him the way I used to, no matter how hard I try. Now when I look at him, I see blood and death. I see the Kaiser. Luckily, he's too lost in his own anguish to notice, and my voice seems to break whatever spell has come over him. His attention snaps to me, and in a few long strides, he has me in his arms. He buries his face against the side of my neck, the stubble on his jaw scratching my skin. I struggle between his warmth and the thought of the blood he's drenched in.

"I'm so glad you're safe," I tell him, bringing a hand up to run over his patchily shaved head.

He doesn't reply at first, keeping his face buried in my neck.

"Let me see it," he says, his voice muffled against my skin.

"See what?"

He tugs at the shoulder of my dress and I swallow, realizing what he means. My wounds. Erik must have told him. I turn my back to Søren and lower the shoulder of my chiton so he can see the tops of the fresh wounds. His breath hitches. He reaches out to touch my shoulder where the whip didn't.

"I'm so sorry, Thora," he says under his breath. "If I hadn't failed . . ." He trails off and shakes his head.

I turn back to face him fully and take his hand in mine. I don't have the patience to make him feel better about my pain, and I certainly don't have the time. I think of the Theyn and Crescentia sitting down for dessert and wine before bed and how they will not get up again.

"Take me away from here, please," I say. "Let's go for a sail, just for a few hours."

Søren nods, but the haunted look hasn't left his eyes. "I'll bring her back by sunrise," he says to my Shadows.

There's no response. They're long gone.

"Let's go," I tell him, pulling him toward the wardrobe. The time is now and the urgency of what I need to do is suddenly pushing me forward. My edges are fraying like a worn blanket, but I will hold it together for just a little while longer. And then I'll be free.

He doesn't protest, instead following me into the wardrobe and through the tunnel entrance as he did before. I don't stop, but continue down the tunnel path, this time pressing forward in tense silence.

When the tunnel becomes tall enough to walk upright, I get to my feet and brush my dirty hands over the skirt of my dress. I hear him behind me, but as soon as I turn to face him, his mouth falls on mine and I'm caught between him and the tunnel wall. He kisses me with a desperation I've never felt, like a man dying of thirst. I struggle between pulling him closer and shoving him away.

He must feel my hesitation, because he pulls back after a few seconds, resting his forehead against mine.

"I'm sorry," he says, his voice hoarse. "I just needed to do that one more time."

Panic shoots down my spine. "One more time?" I ask, resting my hand on the back of his neck and tugging him an inch closer. "But we have until sunrise, Søren."

I start to pull him into another kiss but he stops me with a gentle hand on my shoulder.

"I can't, Thora," he says quietly. "There are things you don't know, and once you do, you aren't going to want to see me again. I won't even blame you."

"The whipping wasn't your fault," I tell him. "There was nothing you could have done."

He drops his eyes. "It isn't that," he admits.

My hands fall away from him. "Then what is it?" I press.

He tries to rake a hand through his hair, forgetting it's all but gone. He paces a few steps away from me before turning back.

"I love you," he says after a deep breath. "I just want you to know that first. I love you and I would never want to do anything to hurt you."

"I love you, too," I say, careful to keep my voice even. My mother once told me it was a sin to lie to a dying man, but I don't know if that's true. Søren will be dead soon enough and my lies will die with him.

"At the mines," he starts, forcing the words out. "The slaves working in them, we had physicians observing them. Running tests. Experimenting."

No. I want to cover his mouth, stop him from talking, suffocate him with his own words. He doesn't get to do this; he doesn't get to confess to a crime I've already hanged him for. I have no use for his guilt and I am not here to make him feel better. But there are so many things I want to say to him, and it's almost a relief to get the chance, to stop acting for a moment and let my rage loose.

"What are you saying?" I force my voice into shock. "You've been experimenting on my people?"

"They aren't your people," he replies. "And you know better than to say that out loud."

"To anyone else, yes," I say, my anger finally able to rise to the surface. "But I didn't think I had to lie to you."

In the dark, I can barely make out his expression falling. "That's not what I meant," he says, shaking his head. "I'm sorry. It's . . . it's just . . . this is hard to talk about."

"Not nearly as hard as I would imagine it is to endure," I reply, struggling not to raise my voice.

He has the good sense to look chastened, and I can feel a fraction of my steeled heart soften ever so slightly. I ball my hands into fists at my sides, to keep from reaching out. He does not get to be the wronged hero.

"What were they looking for?" I press.

He hesitates another second before continuing. "Prolonged exposure in the mines . . . it does something to a person, it imbues them with qualities of the gems they mine, somehow. Some people can stand it, most can't. We knew this. *You* knew this. What we didn't know was why. But my father thought it was something that could be useful if it could be understood. And it turned out it was. The physicians have been running tests and comparisons for years. Months ago they finally concluded the cause. The magic in the mines is so thick that it's in the air itself. It gives the gems their power, but it also seeps into a person's body—into their blood, specifically. A rare few people can survive with it, but most aren't so lucky. The magic drives them mad.

"At first, we killed off anyone who showed signs of it, because we feared they were lethal. But my father decided that was wasteful. Maybe they were a danger to us, he said, but wouldn't that also make them a danger to others? He thought he could weaponize them, send them into battle on the front lines to do as much damage as possible and limit loss of life."

"But that doesn't limit loss of life at all," I say, struggling not to yell.

He flinches anyway. "I know. I *know*."

"And you used them in Vecturia," I continue. I'm no longer playing a part. My anger has bubbled to the surface, and it makes me dangerous. With so much at risk, I know I need to keep my temper, but it feels impossible. I realize that I don't know Søren any better than he knows me. "How many?"

He doesn't answer at first. "I don't know," he finally admits. "Hundreds, I think. My father gave the order."

"Your father was here, Søren. *You* gave the order."

His face blanches. "I didn't want to. It was always the plan, even before we set sail. He wanted to test them out in a battle he knew we could win so he could then begin selling them to other countries. My father always gets what he wants, you know that better than anyone," he says. His voice turns pleading as he reaches for my hand, but I pull away as if his touch burns.

He wants my forgiveness again, he wants me to cleanse him of his father's sins, but the blood is on his own hands this time.

"I do," I say, looking down at the ground between us. Anger is one thing, but disappointment will wound him worse. "I've withstood his wrath time and time again for things I didn't even do. But I know who I am because of it; I know what matters to me and what I'm willing to fight for. Can you say the same?"

He swallows. "I know that I'm willing to fight for you," he says quietly.

I don't doubt that he means it, especially after the banquet. Søren wants so badly to be different from his father. And I wanted this to be easy, one way or another, but I feel like I'm being torn in two.

My dagger presses against the skin of my forearm from where it's hidden in the sleeve of my cloak, but the weight isn't uncomfortable as it was earlier. It's almost welcome, an anchor in a stormy sea and the only thing keeping me from getting lost in the waves. I can't be taken over by anger, not when there is still so much to do and time is running out.

"Thora," Søren says, stepping closer to me. This time, I don't move away. I don't flinch when he reaches his hand up to touch my cheek. "I can't tell you how sorry I am, how I wish I could go back and undo it. I would, in a heartbeat."

"There's no going back," I say, though I'm not sure if I'm talking to him or myself. I force myself to look up and meet his eyes and let Thora take over, one last time, before I bury my dagger in his back. "It'll be all right, Søren. We'll get past it. I know you're nothing like your father," I say, because I know that's what he needs to hear.

Unbidden, the Kaiserin comes to mind, telling me about how she fell in love with the Kaiser, how she never imagined he was capable of everything he's done. What is Søren capable of? I wonder. What evil will fester in his soul and grow if I don't kill him now? In a dozen years, he could be worse than the Kaiser himself.

I twine my fingers through the short hair at the base of his skull, pulling him down into a slow and bruising kiss. After a second, he returns it, cradling my face in his hands like he's afraid he'll break me. There's wetness on my cheeks, but I'm not sure if the tears are mine or his. It doesn't matter, I suppose. For a breath, we're one person and I feel his sadness as acutely as I feel my own.

As I deepen the kiss, I slide the dagger down my free arm until its handle is clutched tightly in my hand. It takes some maneuvering to unsheathe it, but he's lost in my arms and his own pain so deeply he doesn't notice anything. Not until the sharp point of my blade is pressed to his back.

His lips break away from mine and his blue eyes fly open, searching for answers that he discovers quickly. Shock registers on his face, but it's all too soon replaced by resignation. The lump in his throat bobs as he swallows and gives an infinitesimal nod.

"An inch lower," he whispers against my lips. When I comply, a smile ghosts across his face, though it doesn't make it to his eyes. "There it is. Now strike hard and true, Thora."

I don't want to see his face when I kill him, but I can't look away. "My name is . . ." I break off, taking a steadying breath. "My name is Theodosia," I say quietly.

Confusion flickers across his expression before clearing. "Theodosia." It's the first time my real name has crossed his lips, and it sounds almost reverent. He rests his forehead against mine so that his eyes are all I see. "You know what to do."

He's right, I know *exactly* what to do. It's the same thing, more or less, that I did to Ampelio—my father. Killing the Prinz shouldn't be more difficult than that, surely, but in this moment he's just Søren, the sad-eyed lost boy who once let cats follow him everywhere, who befriended his bastard brother no matter the threat it posed, who kissed me like maybe we had the power to save one another.

And I can't watch him die any more than I could have watched Crescentia.

The dagger slips from my hand and clatters to the stone floor, echoing around us, and I shove him away. He looks as shocked as I am. He truly thought I would do it, and I'm not sure if I should be proud of that or not.

He crouches down to pick the dagger up and I expect him to press it to my own skin, but he only stares at it for a moment before tucking it into the waist of his breeches. A moment passes in silence before he speaks, his voice quiet but strong.

"You don't have to forgive me, I don't expect you to, but I know I need to get you away from here—away from him. We can run away tonight, just like we talked about. I made that promise to you, so please let me keep it."

My throat tightens so much that I can't speak, only nod. He thinks he's safe and I can't blame him for that. He doesn't know that Blaise is out there, waiting. I might not have been able to do it, but Blaise will.

* * *

A storm whips through the air as soon as we step out of the tunnel. I can't imagine how Søren is planning on sailing through it, but he seems strangely calm, his face carved white marble in the moonlight. If it weren't for how tightly he's clutching my hand in his, I wouldn't know he was nervous at all. I try not to look at him; I try not to even think about him walking next to me.

It's too dark to see Blaise's boat from the shore, but I know it's out there somewhere in the inky waves.

"My father will send men," Søren says, pulling me out of my thoughts. "But he doesn't have many friends among his warriors. I do. I'm hoping that will count for something if we're caught. But my ship is fast and light. Anything my father sends out for me will be weighed down with a heavier crew and artillery. We'll outpace them by miles."

I nod, trying to look placated, but my mind is still churning. I'll get him on the boat, *just far enough away* from shore that Blaise will be the only one around to hear me when I scream. He'll come quickly, and in the meantime I can tell Søren I saw a rat or some similar lie to keep him unaware until Blaise comes on board and slits his throat.

And then . . .

And then I'll be free. The thought sends a delicious shiver down my spine. *Free* is something I haven't been in ten years. And as soon as I can, I'll free my people as well.

When we're mere feet from the shore, Søren's grip on my hand tightens painfully and he pushes me behind him, trapping me between his body and the cresting waves. Sea spray mists my ankles. I hear them before I see them, boots marching in tandem on the beach, a shout turned to gibberish in the wind, the clatter of swords being drawn from their scabbards. A dozen of the Kaiser's men approach over the sand dunes from all sides, surrounding us and effectively trapping us between them and the water.

"Go," Søren whispers, nudging me into the water, toward the ship. I turn and take half a step before stopping short. The waters that were clear only a moment ago are already filling with ships. Even with Blaise lying in wait nearby, I don't stand half a chance of escaping. And even if I manage to get to Blaise before they catch me, even if we manage to escape them for a time, we'll lead them straight to where the others are waiting.

I won't do that. Artemisia was right: I am expendable.

So I stand with Søren and squeeze his hand as the soldiers close in around us, and I let him believe I'm doing it because I can't leave him behind. Maybe it will earn me a measure of mercy, though I doubt the Kaiser will be moved by the display.

In front of me, Søren forces himself to seem casual as they approach.

"Your Highness," the head guard says, his voice wary. He's the guard with the scar, the one Heron decided to frame.

"Johan," Søren replies, a smile in his voice. "What brings you lot out here tonight?"

But Johan isn't swayed. "I should ask you the same," he says. He tries to get a look at me, but Søren blocks him, hiding me from view.

"I had hoped for a midnight rendezvous, but I'm afraid you've quite ruined that plan." He sounds like the petulant prinz I once believed him to be.

"And that wouldn't happen to be the Ash Princess you're off to rendezvous with, would it?" Johan asks, sounding like he already knows the answer.

Søren's grip on my hand tightens, but he keeps his voice easy.

"I don't see what business it is of yours, Johan, considering that your job is to protect my father. Who is guarding his life right now while you're out here, interrupting my romantic plans?"

"Your father is protected enough," Johan says, bristling. "But Lady Thora orchestrated the murder of the Theyn tonight, and we believe she means the same fate for you."

My heart is pounding in my ears, but Søren doesn't lose his calm. He must be piecing together the puzzle, though. He must realize my attack on him was part of a larger plan. He must be wondering how far back that plan goes.

But when he speaks, his voice is untroubled. "I can't imagine that's true. How could she possibly murder the Theyn when she's here with me? And the man had no shortage of enemies, as I'm sure you're well aware. Lady Thora has been under my father's care for ten years without incident."

"There are witnesses," Johan says. "The Kaiser has ordered that she be brought in to answer for it. If she's truly innocent, let him decree it."

Witnesses. What kind of witnesses? The idea should terrify me, but I can't feel anything anymore. Every part of me is numb.

"Because we all know that my father is a reasonable man," Søren says, growling the words out.

Johan has the good sense to look a touch frightened.

Søren's skills in battle are legendary, and though he might not stand a chance against twenty men, he'll certainly take out a few on his way down if it comes to it.

I like to think even Blaise isn't fool enough to try to save me from this, but I can't say for sure. I hope he's far enough out that the other ships haven't spotted him, far enough that he can't see me like this. But then I realize that he must be. If he could see me, the ground would be trembling.

"Step aside, Your Highness," the guard says, straightening up. "Or we'll be forced to arrest you as well."

Søren doesn't so much as flinch. He stands firm, planted in front of me like an oak tree. He won't move because he knows that there isn't a chance the Kaiser will find me innocent, even if I didn't do it. He won't move because he knows that doing so will damn me.

He doesn't realize that I'm already damned, no matter what he does. He can't save me from this.

I pull my hand from his viselike grasp and step around him.

"It's all right, Søren," I say, and though my voice shakes, I try to sound as composed as he did. "I have nothing to answer for, and I'm sure the Kaiser will see that."

Søren reaches out to grab me, but one of the guards gets there first, aided by the Air Gems studding his shirt.

"Lady Thora, you are arrested for the murder of the Theyn, and the attempted murder of Lady Crescentia."

Even as he binds my hands behind my back with stone manacles, relief floods me. *Attempted murder.*

Crescentia is still alive.

TRIAL

———◆·◆———

THEY SEARCH ME BEFORE BRINGING me in to the Kaiser, and I'm grateful that Søren didn't trust me enough to give me my dagger back. They find nothing, but that won't help me. If Cress survived, I'd imagine she told the Kaiser everything— about my seducing Søren, my stealing her Spiritgems because I was working with others, the treasonous things I said about him in the garden. I've become more trouble than I'm worth to him now; he'll have no choice but to kill me.

But the Theyn is dead. The Theyn is dead. I repeat the words again and again in my mind, waiting for them to feel real. I no longer have to dread seeing him, no longer have to skitter deeper and deeper inside myself anytime we breathe the same air. This is what I've wanted—needed—for so long, yet strangely, all I feel is relief that Cress is alive.

How? I wonder. No one survives Encatrio.

As I'm shoved through the door to the throne room, I search the crowd for her face, but she isn't here. It's possible she didn't drink the wine. That's the only explanation; even a drop of Encatrio would have been enough to kill her. No matter what the guard said, I won't believe she's alive until I see her with my own eyes. Considering where today will lead, that doesn't seem likely.

Maybe I'll see her in the After one day. Maybe by then we will have forgiven each other.

When we reach the base of the Kaiser's dais, they push me roughly to my knees and I stare at the gilded carvings that wrap around it. Flames for Houzzah, but this close I can see they are more than that. The arcs of the flames form letters. The letters form words. Astrean words. It's so subtle I doubt any Kalovaxian would have noticed it. *I* hadn't even noticed before.

Long live the daughters of Houzzah, born of fire, protectors of Astrea.

They are words meant for my ancestors going back centuries. They are words meant for my mother. They are words meant for me. I will die today, but I will die with them in my heart. I will die fighting and my mother and Ampelio will be proud when I join them in the After. Maybe the Kaiserin will be there, too, finally at peace.

I could have done more, fought harder, wavered less, but I tried. And Artemisia was right: the rebellion won't end with me. She and Heron and Blaise will keep fighting. My people will keep fighting, and maybe one day, Astrea will know once again how freedom feels. I'll go to the After happy if I can believe that.

"Ash Princess." It has never been a title said with anything other than disdain, but now the words are full of venom as well.

I am not a Princess of Ashes anymore, though, and I am not Lady Thora. My name is Theodosia Eirene Houzzara, and like my mother and all my foremothers before her, I am a Fire Queen, with the blood of a god in my veins. Even if it is only for a few moments more. I square my shoulders and meet the Kaiser's cold gaze. I do not look away, even as my stomach churns.

His mouth twists. "You stand accused of orchestrating the murder of the Theyn. How do you answer these charges?"

There is no right answer. Even if I deny it, he will have me killed. But I will not die as Thora, begging for mercy on my knees.

"The Theyn slit my mother's throat ten years ago. I'm only sorry it took me so long to repay the debt," I say, projecting my voice loud enough that it echoes through the silent throne room.

The Kaiser's face sharpens and he grips the arms of my mother's throne. If we were alone, he would take pleasure in killing me himself, but he has to put on his show. He wants them to remember me a certain way, too: the little Ash Princess, small and cowering. But I won't let him win this time.

"What did you put in the wine?" he asks, his voice frighteningly calm, though I'd imagine he already knows the answer, given the state the Theyn's body must have been in. He wants me to say it, though. His eyes glint dangerously, matching the pendant around his neck. Ampelio's pendant. He means to frighten me, but he doesn't have that power over me anymore. He has already taken everything—my mother, Ampelio, my home. But now I have nothing left to lose and so I have nothing left to fear.

I lift my chin and keep my gaze level on him, unflinching. "Liquid fire that burns the drinker from the inside out," I tell him. "It's a merciless death. The throat burns first, you know, so that the drinker can't even scream as they die."

Horror flickers across his face for only a second before it's replaced by hunger.

"*Encatrio*," he murmurs. "Where did you obtain it?" he demands, leaning forward.

"There are many who know the rightful ruler of Astrea and were willing to help me. One day soon, you'll see just how many there are. I only wish I could be there when you do."

The Kaiser nods to the guard behind me, who steps forward and brings his sheathed sword down hard on my back so that I lurch forward, bracing myself with my hands against the tiled floor as I fall to my knees. I cry out as pain sings through my body and the wounds still fresh from the whipping come open again. One shout breaks through the silent crowd. Søren. I'm not sure whether his presence is a comfort or not, so I try my best to ignore it. I take a breath before getting to my feet.

I will not die on my knees.

The guard steps forward to hit me again, but the Kaiser holds up a hand to stop him.

"Do they know that you killed the Kaiserin?" I shout so that everyone in the room hears me. "You shoved her out that window. I saw it myself."

He leans forward, face turning red.

"It was probably you who killed my dear wife," he spits, motioning for the guard again.

This time, I'm ready for it, though. Just as the covered blade hits me, I drop to the ground, taking minimum impact from the blow while still making it look real. I get to my feet quicker this time, feeling only a dull throb in my shoulder.

"The Kaiserin was kind to me," I say. My voice wavers, but it's clear. "She knew what a monster you were. Her hate for you overwhelmed her to the point of madness. Is there anyone, *Your Highness,* who wouldn't happily see you dead? How many of them"—I gesture to the crowd behind me— "wouldn't gladly stab you in the back if they had a chance? They don't love you, they don't respect you, they *fear* you, and that is no way to rule a country."

"It is the *only* way to rule a country," he snarls. "Should I rule through *love* and *compassion* like your mother? That didn't end well for her."

I clench my teeth. He will not use my mother to bait me. "My mother was a better ruler than you will ever be," I say instead. "But then, a rat would make a better ruler than you. Even an ant."

He gestures to the guard again and this time the blows rain down one after another, even after I fall to the ground. The gashes are all open again and my dress is wet with blood. But the pain barely registers. All I feel is fury. It burns through me until my skin feels like fire. When the guard finally steps back again, I am gasping for breath. It takes me longer to get to my feet this time. My legs refuse to straighten, to hold up my weight, but I force them to. Only a little longer, and then there will be no pain. Only my mother. Only Ampelio.

"Bring them in," the Kaiser commands, waving a hand.

A guard steps forward to grab me roughly by the arm as the door behind the throne opens and two slave girls are dragged in, their hands cuffed together. It takes me a moment to recognize one of them as Elpis.

No. My heart plummets even as I tell myself I'm wrong.

It can't be Elpis. Elpis is on a boat, far away, with her family. Elpis is safe.

But she isn't. She looks even younger than usual, her round face wet with tears and her large eyes red and frightened. When they find mine, they widen and her tears start anew. I want to go to her, to tell her it's all right, to fight for her, but the guard's grip on me is strong.

Two more guards appear behind them, unlocking their shackles. One guides the other girl before the Kaiser. Crescentia's older slave, I realize. She limps as she walks and the skin around her left eye is dark and swollen. Unlike Elpis, though, she isn't frightened. She holds herself tall and confident.

"What is your name?" the Kaiser asks her.

"Gazzi, Your Highness," she says with a wobbly curtsy.

"Gazzi," he says with a kind smile. "Will you repeat what you told my guardsmen when the Theyn's body was found?"

She casts a glance back to me, but there is no softness in it. Astrean as she might be, I am not her queen. "I told them that earlier in the day Elpis had answered the door for a visitor. I was in another room, but they spoke for several minutes. I could tell it was Lady Thora—she visited Lady Crescentia so often I recognized her voice. When she finally left, I peeked out from the door and saw Elpis slip a glass vial into her apron. She was smiling bigger than I'd ever seen her."

"And you didn't mention this to Lady Crescentia or the Theyn?" the Kaiser asks.

"I didn't know what I'd seen," she admits. "I thought maybe it was a present for Lady Crescentia—they were such close friends, it wouldn't have been unusual. It wasn't until we were preparing dinner that I saw her take the vial from her apron and tip it into the dessert wine. I asked her what it was and she hit me, Your Highness." She motions to her bruised eye. "Locked me in a closet. She finished preparing dessert herself, and the next thing I knew, the guards had found me and I told them everything. But it was too late and the Theyn was dead. Luckily, poor Lady Crescentia only drank a sip of wine because she'd had a bit too much of the dinner wine already."

Only a sip. A sip alone should have killed her. It would have killed someone twice her size. But I can't imagine they have any reason to lie about that now. Even though I still don't really believe Cress is alive, my knees buckle with relief.

"Thank you, my dear," the Kaiser says, before motioning Elpis forward.

The guard shoves her along and her eyes meet mine. I give her an encouraging nod, but we both know what will come of this. To my surprise, the fear dissipates from her eyes. She nods once at me before turning her attention to the Kaiser.

"Do you dispute the charges leveled against you?" he asks.

"I don't," she says, her high voice strong and clear. "My queen offered me a chance to help her strike back at the people who have hurt everyone I love. I leapt at it." She smiles and it is wild and triumphant, despite everything.

But the Kaiser responds with a snap of his fingers and a grin that turns my skin to ice. The guard holding Gazzi unsheathes his sword.

Gazzi is too shocked to do anything before the guard holding her stabs his sword through her back, the bloody point of it coming through her chest. A quick death. My attention doesn't linger on her. I wait for Elpis's guard to do the same, but instead, he pulls a vial from the inside of his cloak and removes the cork. Keeping one arm firmly around Elpis's waist, he brings the vial to her lips.

Her eyes lock onto mine and I realize what the Kaiser has planned. I've confessed, yes, but I haven't told him everything. He's smart enough to know that.

"Just enough poisoned wine left for one," the Kaiser says. "You have a choice, Ash Princess. Tell me the truth and I'll send her to the mines instead. Otherwise . . ."

The guard pulls Elpis's hair back until she has no choice but to open her mouth and he tilts the potion closer. I struggle against the guard holding me, but his grip is like iron.

He won't spare her, no matter what I do—just like he didn't spare Ampelio. He's a liar and he doesn't show mercy. I know that and so does Elpis. So does everyone in the room. I cannot save her. I cannot save her. I cannot—

"Stop!" The word is wrenched from my throat like a sob, against my will. The guard freezes.

"I thought we could come to an understanding," the Kaiser says with a nauseating smile. "I'll ask again: Where did you get the Encatrio?"

I swallow. Suddenly I don't feel anything like a queen. A true queen could weigh the lives of many against the life of one, but I can't. All I see is Elpis. All I hear is Blaise's voice, telling me she's my responsibility. I asked this of her, I brought her here, I've as good as killed her. I owe her this. Even if the Kaiser doesn't spare her, he'll give her a clean death, like Gazzi. Not the Encatrio; he'll save that for some-one else.

"My Shadows," I say, trusting that they are long gone now.

"Rebels replaced them last month. Where they got it, I don't know."

The Kaiser frowns and motions to the guard, who tips the vial again.

"I don't know!" I shout, fighting against the guards who hold me, but it does no good. "I swear, I don't know anything more!"

They don't stop, though. Elpis's guard tips the vial just enough to give her a drop before pinching her nose until she swallows. The sound that erupts from her is like nothing I've heard before, the hoarse cry of a dying animal that vibrates through my whole body, scraping over my skin like claws. I fight against my guards, my elbow flying up. Something cracks and one of the guards lets out a string of curses, but their hold never loosens.

Elpis slumps against the guard, her eyes half shut. The skin of her neck is already charring, turning gray and dry. She can barely whimper.

"Still a few more sips to go," the Kaiser drawls. "What were you doing tonight?"

I swallow and tear my eyes away from Elpis. This, at least, will cost us nothing. "I was supposed to kill the Prinz before escaping."

With her throat burned, Elpis can't do more than shake her head an inch.

"Escaping where?" he presses. "With who?"

I open my mouth to answer, struggling for a lie—any lie. It won't matter; Elpis and I will both be dead by the time the lie is discovered, and Blaise and the others will be far gone. But it isn't so simple. The Kaiser will arrive at whatever country

I name with battalions and soldiers and berserkers. He will bring war to their doors. I can't form words.

The Kaiser seems to expect it. He seems to want it. Gleefully, he motions to the guard again, watching Elpis with a fascination that turns my stomach to lead.

Elpis is twitching against the guard now, and he struggles to hold her still as he lifts the vial to her lips again. She groans and her eyes find mine. The pain there clutches at my stomach, but there's something else as well. I put a name to it a second too late: resolution.

The guard goes to force another drop of the potion down her throat, but Elpis drinks it all instead, sucking each drop out before the surprised guard can pull it away.

I shout a string of Astrean words my mother never taught me and struggle against the guard holding me, fighting him with everything I have as my mind spins and blurs. But the guard doesn't loosen his grip, and all I can do is watch as Elpis falls to the ground, twitching and curling in on herself like the child she is. The charring spreads from her throat and the smell of broiling flesh fills the room. The courtiers behind me begin to gag, as if they were the ones suffering.

When she finally stills, her blackened mouth is frozen in a silent scream.

Dimly I hear the Kaiser order for the bodies to be removed. A guard drags Elpis away like she's no more than a rag doll, her head lolling on her neck limply, eyes mercifully closed. A trail of ash is left behind in her wake.

She was my responsibility and I killed her. If I have any regrets, it's this. Too many people have died for me, and now I'm almost grateful that no more will have to.

The Kaiser steps down from my mother's throne, his footsteps echoing loudly in the silent room as he comes toward me. I can't look at him, unable to take my eyes off the trail of ash Elpis's body has left in its wake, but he grabs my chin and forces me to look up so that all I see is his face, red and sharp and cold.

"It's a shame," he whispers so that only I and the guards holding me can hear him. "You would have made such a pretty kaiserin."

I swallow my tears. They're for Elpis; the Kaiser doesn't deserve to see them. If the guards weren't holding me as tightly as they are, I would throw myself at him and do whatever damage I could before I was stopped—claw his eyes out, smash his head against the stones, grab the guard's sword and stab him through the heart—there are so many ways to hurt someone in a matter of seconds, and I would invent a dozen more. But the guards must feel my desperation, because they hold me tight, like I'm a threat.

I do the only thing I can—I spit. It lands just below his eye, shiny and wet.

The back of his hand hits my face. The force of the blow should send me to the ground again, but the guards keep me standing.

"Take her away," the Kaiser says to my guards. "Set her execution for sunrise so that everyone will witness it. I want the world to know that the Ash Princess is dead."

CELL

———— • ————

THE KAISER DOESN'T MAKE MISTAKES often, but he made one when he didn't kill me. He thinks it's smart to wait until there's a larger audience, a more Astrean audience that will be further broken by seeing me killed. I see his logic but there is a flaw in his plan.

I was ready to die for my cause, before. I was ready to greet my mother and Ampelio in the After and watch my country rise again without me. But now I can't get the image of Elpis's ashen body out of my mind. I can't forget the way the Kaiser grinned as he watched her die. As much as I long to see my mother again, I am not ready yet.

I am not done with this world, and I am not done with him.

The guards led me down into the dungeons beneath the palace, a maze of cramped, dirty cells my mother never used during her reign. She thought them too cruel a fate even for criminals, sending them instead to work off their crimes in the Outlands.

These are the same cells Blaise and I explored as children. My feet recognized the path; I could see the layout in my mind as clear as any map. Blaise must remember them, too.

They locked me in a cold cell separate from other prisoners, with no blanket, or food, or even a set of clothes not covered in blood. It's so cramped that I can't lift both my arms, and it's the sort of dark that only exists in nightmares. The heavy lock creaked as it was slid into place, and their boots echoed down the hall.

As soon as I was alone, the laughter began. I couldn't control it and I didn't care to. There's no one to hear me this far below ground, and if there were, let them tell the Kaiser all about it.

Let him believe I'm mad. It won't be the biggest mistake he's made tonight. Somewhere out there, Blaise and Heron and Artemisia are getting word of my arrest and they're putting together a plan to get me out. I know that as certainly as I know my name.

The Kaiser should have killed me when he had the chance.

I don't know how long passes before my laughter dies down, or how much more time inches by before the footsteps break up the silence, these much softer than the guards'. Too soft to be Blaise's. Artemisia's, maybe? I scramble toward the bars and try to see down the hall, but it's too dark and I don't dare call out a name.

A candle's dim light turns a corner, coming toward me and growing brighter, illuminating the girl holding it. I have to stifle a cry of surprise when she stops in front of my cell door, face inches from mine.

Crescentia might have survived the Encatrio, but it didn't leave her unchanged. Her once soft, rosy skin has turned chalky, and even in the candlelight, it has a gray sheen, except for her neck, which is coal black from jawline to clavicle and rough as unpolished stone. Her hair, eyebrows, and eyelashes have all turned from pale gold to a blinding, brittle white. Before, her hair fell past her waist in waves, but now it ends bluntly at her shoulders, frayed and broken at the edges. Singed.

But it isn't only the poison. The girl standing on the other side of the cell bars isn't the one I've known for the past ten years, the one I pretended to be a siren with, the one I laughed and gossiped with. That Crescentia was pretty and sweet and always smiling, but this girl has red-rimmed eyes and an expression like ice. No one could call her pretty now—fierce, striking, beautiful maybe, but never pretty. When we met, I thought she looked like a goddess, and she still does. But it's no longer Evavia I see; it's her sister Nemia, the goddess of vengeance. Before, Crescentia looked at me with love, like we were sisters, but now hate rolls off her in palpable waves.

And I don't even blame her for it, though I can't regret murdering the Theyn.

"Do you want to know why I did it?" I ask her when several moments pass in silence.

Her flinch is nearly imperceptible, but it's there. "I know why you did it." Her throat is raw and burnt and every word seems to pain her, though I can see how badly she tries not to show it.

She doesn't know, not really, and I want her to understand. "For the last ten years I've lain awake at night with my mother's dying scream in my ear, with your father's cruel eyes haunting my nightmares. I thought he would kill me, too, sooner or later. The only way I could sleep was if I imagined killing him first. Poison wasn't ideal, I'll admit. A dagger would have been symmetrical; his own sword would have been poetic. But I worked with what I had."

I watch her face carefully for a reaction as I speak, trying to shock her, but she barely even blinks. She reads me like one of her more challenging poems, and I know she sees through my apathy. It's not surprising. We've always been able to read each other well. The difference is that for the first time, her mind is closed to me. I am looking at a stranger.

"Not killing you was the only time my father defied orders," she tells me after a moment of quiet, her voice cold. "The Kaiser wanted you dead. My father passed it off as strategy, and he wasn't wrong, but that's not the real reason he spared you. He told me once that he looked at you and saw me. That turned out to be the biggest mistake he made."

I remember the Theyn pulling me away from my mother's body, even as I clutched her dress as tightly as I could. I remember him taking me to another room, speaking with his soldiers in a halting, violent language I didn't understand at the time. I remember him asking me in terrible Astrean if I wanted something to eat or drink. I remember crying too hard to answer him.

I push the memories to the back of my mind and focus on Cress standing in front of me, expecting . . . what? Sympathy? An apology?

"After a life filled with senseless murders and brutalities, that's truly saying something," I tell her instead. "I won't lose any sleep over him, even if I had another night of sleep left."

Her jaw tenses. After a moment, she speaks again. "And why me?"

A laugh forces its way out of me. "Why you?" I repeat, surprised that she has to ask, after everything.

"I was your heart's sister."

The term that was once an endearment now sounds vile.

"You would have turned me over to the Kaiser if I didn't stay complacent and docile. I wasn't your heart's sister, Cress. I wasn't any different to you than a slave who forgot my place and stepped out of line. You cracked the whip and reminded me who was in charge."

There it is, a tremble so slight I would miss it if I hadn't known her as long as I have. She's wearing the mask of a stranger now, but it slipped for just a second. Just enough to remind me what we were once, how far we've fallen in such a short time. But as soon as it appears, it's gone. Sealed away behind cold gray eyes and stone skin.

I push forward, desperate to break through again, even if it only brings rage and hate. Anything is better than her cold, vacant eyes.

"Thora was your heart's sister, maybe," I say. "Sweet, obliging Thora, who never wanted anything. The broken little Ash Princess who depended on you because she had no one else. But that's not what I am."

A spark in her eyes, a clench of her jaw. "What you are is a monster," she tells me, biting out the words with more ferocity than I thought she possessed.

Despite myself, I flinch. "I'm a queen," I correct her softly, even as I wonder if I'm both. Maybe all rulers have to be at least part monster in order to survive.

But my mother wasn't, a small voice whispers in my head. I silence it. My mother wasn't a monster, it's true, but the

Kaiser was right: she ended up with a slit throat and a lost country. Blaise was right, too. My mother was a soft queen because she lived in a soft world. I don't have that luxury.

"Why did you come here, Cress?" I ask quietly. Her eyes narrow at the causal use of her old nickname, and I wish I could take it back. We are not friends; I need to remember that. It's not something she will forget so easily.

"I wanted to see your face one last time before you died, Ash Princess," she says, taking a step closer, until her face is pressed into the space between two iron bars, gray hands clenching the bar below her chin. "And I wanted you to know that I'll be there tomorrow, watching. When your blood spills and you hear the crowd cheer, I wanted you to know that my voice will be the one cheering the loudest. And one day, when I am the Kaiserin, I will have your country and all the people in it burned to the ground."

The viciousness in her voice scares me more than I'd like to admit. I don't doubt she means every word of it. So I say the only thing I can to fight back.

"Even if Søren does marry you, you'll always know," I tell her. She freezes.

"Know what?" she asks.

"That he's wishing you were me," I say, twisting my mouth into a cruel smile. "You'll end up like the Kaiserin, a lonely, mad old woman surrounded by ghosts."

Her mouth tightens and she mirrors my mockery of a smile. "I think I'll ask the Kaiser if I can keep your head," she says, before turning and leaving me alone again in the dark.

When she's gone, I bring a hand to the metal bar she'd been touching and jump back. The bar is scalding hot.

PLAN

———•———

I T TAKES BLAISE LONGER THAN I expect to find his way to me, though my sense of time is heavily skewed. I can't honestly say whether moments are passing or hours. For all I know, he isn't coming at all. I have to believe that Heron escaped after he couldn't get Elpis out of the palace; otherwise, the Kaiser would have killed him in front of me as well. It's a small comfort, but it's a comfort all the same.

He and Artemisia might be far away by now. I hope they are. But I know Blaise well enough to know that he would have come back, and it wouldn't have taken long for him to have gotten word of the Kaiser's announcement.

Still, it feels like half an eternity before I hear footsteps again, heavier this time. He doesn't risk carrying a candle with him, so I don't see his face until it's mere inches from mine, separated only by the bars of the cell.

He looks more haggard than usual. There are dark circles beneath his eyes, his jaw is covered in stubble, and his clothes are dirty and damp.

"You took your time," I say, getting to my feet.

"I had to wait for a change in the guard." He rakes a hand through his messy hair, eyes roving anxiously. "There are two of them posted at the entrance to the cells. We have twenty minutes before they'll do rounds."

"You used the entrance to the cells when there's a perfectly good tunnel hidden down here?"

He shakes his head. "That's the escape route—no need to risk exposing it before then. I was going to come earlier, but your friend messed up that plan."

I don't have to ask who he's talking about. "She's not my friend," I tell him. It isn't the first time I've said that to him, but it's the first time the words have been true.

"What happened?" he asks. His attention is on my dress, which is now more red than violet.

"I'm fine," I tell him, but he doesn't believe me. I can't meet his eyes when I tell him about Elpis.

I wait for the blame to come. He didn't want me to give her that responsibility and I insisted. Her blood is on my hands and he has every right to remind me of that. I deserve to hear it, though it might break me.

He's quiet for a moment, and though I still can't meet his gaze, I feel him looking at me. He reaches a hand between the bars to take mine. It's a comfort I don't deserve.

"You are not allowed to fall apart, Theo," he tells me. "Not now. Or else she died for nothing."

I press my lips together to keep my protest down. I know he's right, but I don't want him to be. I want to wrap my guilt around me like a cloak, but that doesn't help anyone but me. It certainly doesn't help Elpis.

"Her family?" I say after a moment. To my relief, I manage to sound like a queen again instead of the mess of a girl I know I really am.

"Safe. Already with Dragonsbane," he says.

"And Artemisia and Heron?"

"They're staying nearby, waiting for a plan."

"Do you have one?" I ask.

He lifts a shoulder in a shrug. "I can get you out of here easily enough," he says, placing his hands on the bars. With Glaidi's strength on his side, how easy will it be for him to pry them apart? The muscles of his arms flex and the steel begins to arc without him shedding a bead of sweat. "The tunnel out of the dungeons leads to the coves on the western shore."

I turn the idea over in my mind. It's simple—an escape, perfectly easy with no risk. And yet . . .

"Something's bothering you about that plan," he says, reading my expression. He takes his hands away from the bars. "What?"

I sigh and rest my head against the bars. "It isn't *enough*. We were always to strike and run, but we aren't striking," I say.

"We killed the Theyn," he points out.

I shake my head. "It doesn't matter. The Kaiser isn't weakened and there isn't enough for the Kalovaxians to turn against him. And after Elpis . . ."

"There will be time to avenge Elpis—all the time in the world once you're safe. But today isn't that day."

I don't want to admit that he's right. There is nothing to be gained by rushing things, but when will we have a chance to get close enough to strike the Kaiser again? I've seen the Kaiser's war strategy enough to know that it involves hiding behind others more than fighting himself. This very well might be our only chance to weaken him, and I don't want to waste it.

"Maybe it is," I say to him as a plan begins to form in my mind.

"Theo." Blaise says my name like a warning. "You tend to get that look on your face before you do something reckless."

I can't help but laugh.

"That might be true, but in your experience, Blaise, is there ever anything you can do to stop me?" His silence is all the answer I need. "Good. Because we're pressed for time, so let's skip the part where you tell me how reckless it is and list all the dozens of things that can go wrong, and instead just agree to do what I need you to do."

Blaise's mouth twitches, but whether it's with amusement or frustration, I can't tell. I suspect it's a bit of both.

"All right, Your Highness. What do you need me to do?"

"For starters, you can fix these bars," I say. "I'm not leaving just yet."

RESCUE

———— ✦ • ✦ ————

I MUST FALL ASLEEP AFTER BLAISE leaves, because the next
sound I hear is the jingling of a ring of keys. I bolt upright
and squint, half expecting to see a guard there, ready to lead
me to my execution, but instead, it's Søren. He's in the same
clothes he wore earlier, but now they're bloodied and torn.
A ring holding four large iron keys hangs from his hand. I
scramble to my feet, all tiredness leaving me immediately as
adrenaline courses through my body.

I should be surprised to see him standing there, but I'm
not. I knew he would come for me; I told Blaise as much. Now
here he is.

"There isn't much time." His breathing is ragged. "Someone will find the guards soon, and you'll be the first prisoner
they check on."

"You're rescuing me," I say slowly.

Even in the simplest plan I spun Blaise, it doesn't happen
like this. In my plan, he comes here angry, hurt, demanding
answers I'm not sure how to give.

"Trying to," he says, swinging the door open.

"I tried to kill you," I remind him.

"But you didn't."

"What I said to the Kaiser—"

"Yes, I would really like to hear more about that, but I'm not sure now is the best time," he says, glancing over his shoulder. "I promised to take you away from here, and I intend to follow through on that. First we have to live that long, though."

I can't begin to make sense of his open face and blind trust, but I know he's right. We don't have time for any of this right now. I thought that when he came, I would have to convince him to leave with me, but I'm not about to question this turn of luck.

"What's your plan?" I ask instead.

He slides one of the keys into the lock, and there's a heavy creaking as he turns it. "My father won't stop looking for us, no matter where we go," he says, pushing the door open. "Sooner or later, we'll have to take a stand."

The conviction in his voice takes me by surprise. "You're willing to do that?" I ask him as I step out of the cell.

"I've never wanted to be kaiser, Thora," he admits.

The name chafes, but I ignore it.

He begins to lead me down the hallway. "But I don't think I have a choice," he continues. "Not after Vecturia. What you said in your letter, what you accused him of . . . ," he starts, but he can't finish. For all the terrible things he thought his father capable of, he never imagined that.

"I saw it myself," I tell him.

He clears his throat, focusing on the present instead of the past as he takes a hard turn, pulling me with him. "As I said, we'll have to make a stand. You have allies, and there are

Kalovaxians who would follow me. We might have a chance if we do it together."

"Together," I echo.

He glances sideways at me. "I never thought I could go against my father until I saw you do it. You want a rebellion, I'll help you strike the match."

I hope my smile looks more real than it feels, but the idea of aligning with any Kalovaxians—even if they stand against the Kaiser—is a horrifying one.

We continue down the maze of hallways in silence, our pace hurried. The dungeon is cold and the air is wet, but I barely feel it with the energy coursing through me. I can't see a hair's breadth in front of my face, and Søren's hand clasping mine, warm and calloused, is more comforting than it has any right to be. It's the hand that gave the order to kill hundreds of my people, I remind myself.

A groan comes from one of the cells we pass, and I try to ignore it. The man is Astrean, more than likely, and if I were a more selfless person I would stop and save him. But that was the groan of a dying man, and I know there is nothing I can do for him. My hands are already so drenched in blood anyway—Ampelio's, the Theyn's, Elpis's.

My feet trip over something large and I nearly fall on top of it, but Søren holds me up.

"What . . . ," I start, but I trail off when I realize exactly what it is.

Someone will find the guards soon, Søren had said. I'd assumed he'd locked them in a cell, maybe knocked them unconscious. I didn't think he would have killed his own people, but I'm beginning to wonder if I know him at all.

I swallow down bile and step over one body, then the other. I've seen so much death it shouldn't affect me so deeply anymore, but it does. I push the thought of them out of my mind and quicken my pace to keep up with Søren's long, fast strides.

"What is your escape plan?" I ask quietly. "It doesn't involve walking through the palace, does it?"

"Well, it doesn't involve *walking*," he mutters under his breath. "I suppose you have a better one?"

"I have several."

Voices shout from the right, coming toward us, so the next chance I have I go left, pulling a reluctant Søren after me.

"This will bring us deeper into the dungeons," he says.

"Which means they won't look for us here, at least not at first," I say.

I let go of his hand so that I can feel the wall as we walk, trying to get an idea of where we are. It's been so long since I explored here with Blaise that I could be mistaken, but I don't think I am.

I miss the feel of Søren's hand in mine when it's gone, but I know he's still here. I can even hear him breathe in the silence, but as dark as it is, I feel utterly alone. As if he can hear my thoughts, he brings his hand to rest on the small of my back.

I want to shrug him off, but not as badly as I want to keep him near.

"What are you looking for?" he asks.

"A way out," I tell him, continuing to search. "There's a hole somewhere, about the size of my pinky, I think. If you press it with a stick, a door opens. It was meant as an escape path if there was ever a riot down here and a guard needed to go for help. This was centuries ago, when Astrean queens still kept prisoners here. I found it when I was exploring as a child, but I doubt the Kaiser knows about it."

"Where does it go?" he asks.

"It comes to a fork. One way goes to the throne room, the other goes all the way to a cove on the western shore—I would imagine it isn't far from your ship. It could also be used to get people out if the palace was under siege."

Ampelio begged my mother to use it when the Kalovaxians attacked, to take me and run until forces could be gathered, but she refused. Queens didn't run, she insisted. It didn't matter, in the end. Only moments later, when they were arguing over who would bring me through the tunnel, the Kalovaxians took the harbor.

"Who's there?" a voice rasps in Astrean from a nearby cell.

"It's a girl," another voice says from farther down.

Unlike the man before, they don't sound like they're dying. They sound thirsty and I'm sure they're starving, but they're still very much alive.

"That's not just any girl," a third chimes in, this one female. "That's the princess."

"The princess is locked in her golden cage," one of the men sneers before spitting.

The words bristle, though I can't blame them for it. It was true enough, once. "The *queen* is leaving this godsforsaken city, and you should be doing the same," I say in Astrean, taking the ring of keys from Søren's hand.

"They're criminals," Søren hisses behind me, though I'm sure they can still hear him.

"So are we," I remind him, holding up the ring of keys. "Which keys are they?"

He hesitates for a second before pointing to one. "It's the same for all the cell doors. The others go to the outer doors that separate the cells from the rest of the castle."

I nod, taking the key and sliding it into the first cell's lock.

"You're running?" the man in the first cell asks in Astrean as I push the door open and move on to the next one. All the cells smell like urine and feces and vomit, the odor strong enough to make me dizzy.

"Recuperating," I snap, ignoring my nausea as I push the second door open and move on. "You're welcome to stay here if you'd rather."

"Do your allies include the *prinkiti*?" he asks, spitting the word at Søren. I haven't heard the term before, but it's easy to piece together what it means. Roughly translated: *little yellow prince.* Søren might not know much Astrean, but he can guess it's an insult and he scowls beside me.

"Today they do," I reply, glad that Søren can't understand me. I open the last door and all three step out of their cells tentatively, as if they think I might be here to trap them. With Søren at my side, I can't blame them for their wariness.

The first man laughs, but it turns into a wheeze. "You really are Ampelio's daughter," he says.

The fact that I was the one who killed Ampelio must not have made it all the way down here. If he knew that, he wouldn't be laughing. Still, the comparison makes pride bloom in my chest.

The man gives a shallow bow. "Guardian Santino, at your service, Your Highness. Guardian Hylla and Guardian Olaric, as well."

The other two Guardians echo his sentiments, but I'm

too surprised to really hear them. Guardians, alive. I thought Ampelio had been the last, but the Kaiser was keeping three prisoner right below my feet. While their names don't sound familiar, I hardly knew all of them.

"Pleasure," I say, inclining my head. Despite everything, I can't help but smile. "I'm surprised the Kaiser didn't kill you. Foolish of him to leave Guardians alive."

Hylla gives a snort. "Ah, but why kill us when he can harvest us?" she says, showing me one of her arms, covered in deep cuts, old and new. There are gashes as well, where it looks like her flesh was carved out. "Blood drawn six, seven times a day for his experiments. Skin scraped away. Fingers cut off for the bones." She shows me a hand that has only her thumb, pointer, and ring finger remaining.

Just as quickly as it came, my smile slides away. Nausea rises in my stomach again, though this time it has nothing to do with the smell. Søren knew about this, I remind myself, and in his silence he approved of it. I want to step away from him, but I can't. I bury my fractured heart deep in my chest. "You'll join us?" I ask.

"We need to hurry," Søren says, and I can hear the irritation in his voice.

"We'll only slow you down," the other man—Olaric—says, leaning most of his weight against the cell door to keep upright. "But we can keep them busy."

"You can barely stand," I point out.

"If your rebel *prinkiti* could spare a few of his gems, we could certainly hold our own," Hylla says with a sniff. "Earth for me, Fire for the others."

Next to me, Søren tenses, knowing he's being mocked, and I put a hand on his arm to calm him.

"They were sworn to protect my mother," I tell him in Kalovaxian. "And therefore me. They want to give up their lives to buy us time, but they need gems to put up any kind of fight. One Earth, two Fire. Do you have any?" I ask, though I know he does. I can feel them even now, prickling the air between us. I've been around them so often, I barely notice them anymore, but I can always feel them.

He sighs before fiddling around for a moment. The Earth Gem he pries from the hilt of his sword, using the strength it provides him. The Fire Gems are torn from the lining of his cloak. Even in the dim light, they wink like distant stars. He passes them out, but I know he's not happy about it.

"You trust them?" he whispers to me.

I don't trust anybody. I certainly don't trust you.

"Yes," I say.

"We'll keep the men busy," Hylla tells me.

Next to her, Olaric grows a ball of fire in the palm of his hand, just large enough to illuminate the five of us. It's difficult to tell through the dirt and dried blood covering most of their faces, but they're younger than their voices led me to believe, a decade younger than Ampelio, at least. They might have been a little older than me before the siege, freshly trained and excited for the life laid out in front of them. I can't imagine they saw it leading here. When Olaric's eyes fall on me, the corners soften and he almost smiles. He must have been handsome once, and the kind of man who knew it.

"You look like your mother. Sound like her, too," he says

in Astrean. "When I see her in the After, I'll give her your regards."

I want to tell him not to be foolish, that we'll meet again, but I know better than that. The next time I see them will be in the After, and I hope I won't join them there for a long time yet. They go into this battle knowing they won't come out the other side alive.

More people dying for me. And why? What have I done to deserve it?

"Thank you," I say, and ignoring the stench, I step forward and kiss each of them on the cheek in turn. "May the gods guide you."

"Long live the Queen of Astrea," they recite back before Olaric snuffs out his fire again and their footsteps fall away.

I stay rooted to the spot until I can't hear them anymore. Finally, Søren puts a hand on my waist and guides me forward. For a long moment, he doesn't speak, but after we turn another corner, he clears his throat.

"I don't know any of my father's men who would willingly die for him," he says. "Your people love you."

"They don't even know me," I say. They wouldn't lift a finger for me if they knew the things I've done. "But they loved my mother more than enough to make up for it."

He doesn't know what to say to that, and I'm glad, because I'm not sure what I want to hear. The Guardians' words keep repeating in my mind, burning through me with enough hope to keep me putting one foot in front of the next into an uncertain future. *You really are Ampelio's daughter. You look like your mother. Sound like her, too. Long live the Queen of Astrea.*

ESCAPE

FOOTSTEPS GROW LOUDER BEHIND US as I wind through the maze of dank, dark hallways, running my hands over the walls, looking for the hidden passageway. The sound is heavy and synchronized. Soldiers. They're still far away, but they're approaching fast. Underneath that, I hear the sounds of a fight: shouts of surprise, cries of pain, the thud of bodies landing heavily on the stone floor. Søren listens intently while I search for the hole, more desperate than ever.

"They're a couple of minutes away," he says. I can hear the fear beneath his calm. "It's only a few men—three or four, maybe—but they have dogs tracking us. The rest stayed behind to fight your friends. They aren't going down easily."

"And how many can you manage if they catch us?" I ask him.

He hesitates. "Depends on who it is. If it were me commanding, I'd send the strongest ahead. We're the priority; your friends are just an obstacle. In that case, one or two. If I'm lucky."

"Those aren't inspiring odds," I say, desperately searching the walls.

"Which is why I suggest you hurry," he says. He fumbles around in his jacket, then nudges my arm with something blunt. I reach out to take it and realize it's the hilt of my dagger, the one I nearly stabbed him with. "Just in case," he whispers.

"Thank you," I say, keeping it clutched in my left hand and going back to feeling the wall with my right.

I don't remember it being this dark. When I was here as a child, I could see things better. For all I know, we passed the hole ages ago or made a wrong turn somewhere. Memory is such a fallible thing. Still, I drag my fingers over the rough, craggy stones, even as they begin to bleed.

A dog barks, and I don't need Søren to tell me they're closing in now. I press on faster, my mind a frantic blur. I must focus. All I can think of is this wall and my fingers. All I can think of is getting out.

The hole is so small I almost miss it. In the dark, I can't be sure it's what I remember—but it *has* to be, because the warriors are so close now that I can almost smell them. It has to be or we are dead.

"Thora," Søren warns, but I ignore him and draw my dagger.

Unsheathing it, I press the tip into the hole in the stone, pushing so hard I'm worried I'll break the dagger altogether. The footsteps are so loud I can't hear anything else, not even the sound of the tunnel door opening.

I fall through it.

* * *

I hear the splash before my skin registers the shock of the cold water, but when I hit, it turns my skin to ice. I push myself up on my hands. It's a stream. Though it's only a few inches deep, it ebbs and flows, and I suppose it must lead to the ocean.

"Thora?" Søren whispers, stepping in with more grace than I did and closing the door behind him. It's dark here as well, but there's some kind of dim light coming from the distance, just enough to see a few inches in front of me.

"I'm fine," I say, taking his hand and climbing to my feet.

I step back through the water to listen at the sealed door, Søren at my side. I can hear warriors thunder past. It's only seconds before the dogs double back, stop, and begin barking and snarling on the other side.

One of the warriors shoves against the wall and Søren grips my hand in his. I can nearly feel his pulse racing, and I squeeze back just as tightly.

The door holds, not giving so much as a breath, and the warrior curses at the dogs, trying to drag them away, but they don't budge.

"Leave them," another warrior says. "This deep in, the dogs lost the scent, but there's no way out. She can hide, but we'll find her before sunrise."

The footsteps hurry away and I feel Søren relax next to me, though he doesn't let go of my hand.

"Come on," I whisper, setting off down the tunnel.

The icy water gets deeper with each step, soaking my skirt and legs. Before long, we're in knee-deep and my legs are numb. I don't remember having to swim out of the tunnel when I was a child. Blaise and I walked right out to the shore, never going deeper in than our ankles. But that must have been low tide.

"You're shaking," he says, and I realize I am. The air is even colder than it was in the dungeon, and my dress is soaked. "Take my cloak."

Ever the gentleman, I think before putting a hand out to stop him. "I'd imagine you'll need it soon, too."

"I'll be fine," he insists, sliding it from his shoulders and passing it to me.

I hold it gingerly in my arms. The lining of the coat is studded with Fire Gems, I remember, a perfect way to stay warm in the winter. I've gotten used to ignoring the draw over years of being surrounded by them, but this close, the power calls to me. It buzzes through my blood and mind. If I wore the cloak, I could be unstoppable. All those Fire Gems, all that power.

We come to the fork in the tunnel: the water rushes to the left—the side that must lead to the ocean—but the other side inches uphill. That way goes to the throne room. The Kaiser is surely there, and he surely knows I've escaped by now. I can see his face—that furious, bloated red face—as he sits on my mother's throne and blusters threats at his guards.

How simple would it be to start a fire? I haven't tried it, but I've seen Kalovaxians light fireplaces with the aid of a few Fire Gems. It can't be that difficult, especially since I have the blood of Houzzah in my veins. I imagine watching the fire grow and grow and swallow the palace and everyone in it who ever hurt the people I love. For an instant, I think about ending this now. I could do it; it would even be easy, but it would cost me.

In one act of sacrilege, I would give up my chance to see my mother and Ampelio again. The gods would damn me, and they just might damn my country as well. I don't know if I believe that. I can't help but think about Artemisia and her lack of belief in the gods. After everything my country has suffered, I don't know if my mind believes in them anymore either. But I can still feel them in my heart, in the stories my mother told me. I *want* to believe in them.

"I can't take this," I tell Søren, though passing the cloak back is one of the hardest things I've done. He frowns. "Why not?"

"The gems. I . . ." I trail off. Now is not the time to explain, but I have no choice. "They are only meant to be handled by someone who has earned them, and never so many. Guardians spend years studying and worshipping in the mines for the privilege of carrying a single gem. Using one without proper training . . . it's sacrilege."

"But aren't you supposed to have the blood of a fire god in your veins? If anyone can use it—"

I shake my head. "My mother always said that we rulers were the last people who should have that kind of power. I never understood it before, but I'm starting to."

Søren hesitates, still holding the coat out to me. "You'll freeze without it," he says. "The water is only going to get deeper, and if my navigation skills are what I think they are, we should emerge close enough to the boat that swimming will be our best chance to avoid attention. You didn't come all this way to freeze to death."

"I'll survive," I tell him.

He holds the coat out for another second before realizing

that I'm serious. He starts to shrug it back on, but stops half-way and takes it off again. He holds it out to drop it, but I stop him, my hand on the cloth. Even through the thick wool, I can feel the pleasant hum of the gems rush through me again. It's dizzying, but I try to ignore it and focus.

"We might need that," I say. "If we manage to liberate the mines, there will be some Guardians there and they'll need gems. We need as many as we can get now."

He nods, taking the cloak back and hanging it over one of his shoulders.

"These allies of yours . . . ," he starts.

"You've seen some of them," I say. "My Shadows for the last few weeks."

Søren frowns. "Your Shadows?" he echoes. "What happened to the other ones?"

"Killed," I admit.

The water is up to my waist now. It's beginning to lick at my freshly opened wounds, stinging them so painfully that I have to bite my bottom lip to keep from crying out. I know it's cleaning them as well, but that doesn't make it hurt less. The light ahead is getting stronger.

"I'm tired of death," he says finally. "When I killed the guards . . . it didn't even faze me. I didn't think twice about it. I don't even feel guilty. What kind of person doesn't feel guilt over killing?"

"Someone who's done it too many times," I say. "But you don't need me to tell you that it was necessary."

"I know," he says. "It just feels like every time I do it, even in battle, I turn a little bit more into him."

I don't have to ask who he means.

"You aren't your father, Søren," I tell him.

I've said the same words to him a few times before, but each time I think he believes them less, even as I believe them more.

He doesn't answer me, and we lapse into silence as we wade deeper and deeper, each lost in our own thoughts. Blaise will have told the others my plan by now. How are they reacting? Not well, I imagine. Artemisia will scowl and roll her eyes and make some snarky comment. Heron will be subtler, but he'll wear his quiet disapproval in the crease of his brow, the twist at the corner of his mouth. I can make them understand, though. It's the right move.

"There." Søren's voice breaks into my thoughts.

The end of the tunnel appears in the distance, a small circle of indigo sky. We hurry toward it. The tunnel widens around us into a cove that opens directly into the ocean. There is just enough moonlight to confirm that we're facing west. There is nothing visible but a small ship bobbing in the distance. *Wås.*

"You're right," I say. "We're going to have to swim it."

He looks at me. "The current isn't strong, but it will be against us."

It's nothing for him, I'm sure, but he's worried about me. And he has good reason to be. The most swimming I've done has been in the heated pools below the palace. Still, bathwarm water. Nothing like this.

"Sounds like fun," I say lightly, hoping I sound more confident than I feel.

I don't. He sees right through me, but he also knows we don't have a choice. It's swim or die.

"Stay close to me," he says. "Let me know if you need a

break. We don't need to get to the ship itself, just those rocks."
He motions to the cluster of boulders the ship is tied to.

They're closer, but not enough to make much of a difference. There's also the added risk of being seen when we climb them. But as long as there's a chance, I have hope.

"Let's go," I tell Søren. We can't waste another moment.

It feels like every inch I gain, the waves knock me back two. If this is what Søren calls a weak current, I'd hate to see a strong one. I'm so cold that I don't feel it anymore. My fingers and toes have gone numb and I'm worried that they'll fall off before I reach the rocks.

Søren is ahead of me, but I can tell he's holding himself back to stay close.

"Break?" he asks, gasping out the words over the waves. Despite the Fire Gem cloak wrapped around him, the cold is getting to him as well.

My teeth rattle against each other, drowning out almost everything else. "We're almost there," I reply, pushing on.

"About halfway," he corrects.

I want to cry, but it would be a waste of energy I can't afford to spare. I can cry later, when I'm warm and safe. I can cry all I want then, but not now.

The only way I can survive this is if I let my mind leave my body, the way I do during the Kaiser's punishments—the way I *did*, I remind myself. He's never touching me again. Without my mind to get in the way, all I have to do is breathe and paddle and kick. My mind is far ahead of me, on the boat already, warm and safe and free.

Warm and safe and free.

Warm and safe and free.

I repeat the words to myself like a mantra, timing them to the beat of my heart and the rhythm of my strokes. Nothing else matters. I'm hardly even aware of Søren paddling ahead of me, though he keeps looking back to make sure I'm still afloat.

An eternity passes before we reach the rocks and he stops to help me up.

"Y-you ... said ... o-o-only thirty ... m-minutes," I manage to get out when I reach him, clutching the boulder so hard the jagged edges dig into my fingertips.

"I actually think we made good time," he tells me, sounding impressed. "You might have even done it in twenty-five."

My teeth are chattering so badly that I can't answer. He tries to give me the cloak again, but I push it away.

"Just for a minute," he says.

I shake my head. "I'm fine," I say, but I don't expect him to believe it.

"There are blankets on the ship," he says, tying the cloak around his shoulders. He grips my waist and helps boost me onto the boulder. "And a few changes of clothes."

"And c-c-coffee?" I ask him, scrambling for purchase on the rock. I lost my shoes long ago, so I have to do it barefoot. My poor fingers are bloodied and raw and stinging from the salt water. I'm surprised they can do anything, but they manage to hold on. I find my footing as well, and take the opportunity to get my bearings. The ship is a stone's throw away, maybe a few yards.

Søren pulls himself next to me.

"No coffee. But wine. Good wine," he tells me.

I take a deep breath and begin to move, inch by inch, toward the boat. The frigid wind freezes the joints in my hands, making it hard to grip, but I push through it. I know that I need to move faster, especially now that we're so visible from the shore, but I can't. Even this feels like it will kill me.

"You're doing fine," Søren tells me through clenched teeth. It makes me gladder than it should to see that he's struggling as well. He was born to be a warrior, made for worse things than this, and he's still having a hard time. "Just don't look down," he warns.

But of course, as soon as he says it, I do exactly that. And of course, I regret it immediately.

We've moved far enough and high enough along the boulders that the water is now a steep drop below us. At its edge, smaller, jagged rocks break the surface, threatening to tear me to pieces if I slip. I take a shuddering breath and draw my eyes away.

"I told you," he grunts. "Just keep looking ahead."

I grit my teeth but don't argue. It's close now, the bow almost close enough to touch, though it's tethered a few feet off to keep it from crashing into the rocks.

"We're going to have to climb higher," Søren says, as if reading my mind. "And then we're going to have to jump."

"I w-w-was a-f-f-fraid you were g-g-going to say s-s-something like th-that," I manage.

Though it sounds like it costs him, he laughs.

It's difficult to find traction under my feet farther up, and more often than not, my arms are doing most of the work holding me. They'll feel like seaweed after this, I'm sure, but there will be an *after this,* and that is what matters.

The Kaiserin was right. Sometimes just surviving is enough.

A shout from shore cuts through the air and next to me, Søren lets out a string of curses—only about half of which I'm familiar with.

"It's fine," he says, glancing over his shoulder. "We're almost there, and all their ships are on the other side of the peninsula. By the time that guard gets to anyone else, we'll be gone. It's *fine.*" I get the feeling that he's assuring himself more than me.

I want to turn around and look myself, but I don't need Søren to tell me that's a bad idea. All I can do is put one foot ahead of the other, one hand in front of the other, and climb. Everything else is out of my control. In a way, there is freedom in knowing that.

"All right," he says after a moment. "Now you're going to need to jump."

I look down at the ship a few feet below and swallow.

"I'm not going to lie to you, Thora, it's going to hurt," he says. His voice is so reassuring that I almost don't bristle at the name. "You're going to need to keep your knees soft and roll from the impact so you don't break anything. Can you do it?"

I nod, even though I'm not sure. It's the only answer I can give.

"On the count of three. I'll be right behind you. One. Two . . ."

I get ready, bending my knees.

"Three."

I push away from the rock with my last remaining burst of energy.

For a blissful moment, it feels like flying, with nothing but air around me. But when the impact comes, it's hard, and even though I do as Søren said and keep my body soft, I still hear a crack when I land, and pain floods my right side. My rib. I ignore it as best I can and roll away, making room for Søren to land as well.

His fall knocks the air out of him and he wheezes for a moment, struggling to catch his breath.

"Are you all right?" he asks, when he can speak.

"Broken rib, I think. But I'm fine, other than that."

He nods, but his eyes are troubled. He struggles to his feet and starts untying the boat from the rocks.

"I'll get us moving. Go down into the cabin and warm up. There are clothes in the chest at the end of the cot," he says. Even though he's limping and shaking, he still sounds like a commander. All business.

"Søren," I say softly. My voice almost gets carried away on the wind, but he hears it and turns to look at me. He's smiling, even after everything, ready to embark on a new adventure, ready to fight against the only family he has left. Ready to stand at my side no matter what.

If only it were that simple.

"It's going to be fine," he tells me, misreading my expression.

I shake my head before cupping my hands around my mouth.

"Attiz!" I call out, loud enough to hear over the wind. *Now.*

Before Søren has a chance to ask what's happening, three black-cloaked figures pour out from the cabin and rush toward us. Blaise, Artemisia, and Heron.

Søren draws his sword, but he's still weak from the swim and the climb, and shock slows his movements. Artemisia knocks it from his hand without any effort. Heron shoves him down onto his knees and drags his arms behind him, binding them with a length of rope.

I'm frozen in place, unable to do anything but watch. I put this into motion, I remind myself. It was the right thing to do. Still, seeing Søren hurt and unable to fight back breaks my heart.

"If you hurt her, I'll kill you all," Søren spits out, struggling against them.

I find my voice. "Søren," I say again, and he drags his eyes to me.

It's then that he realizes they aren't hurting me. Blaise comes forward to wrap a blanket around my shoulders. Confusion flashes across Søren's face but it's quickly replaced by a coldness I recognize only too easily. I saw it a few hours ago on Crescentia's face. He stops struggling, but his eyes stay hard.

"Take him below," I say, surprised that my voice comes out level. Even my shivering has stopped. "Let him change into something dry. He won't make a very good hostage if he's dead."

FREE

———— ◆·◆ ————

SØREN WAS RIGHT. WHEN *Wås* starts going at full speed, nothing can touch her. For a moment, the Kaiser's ships were dots trailing us, but we lose them quickly, and soon there is nothing behind us but water. Even Artemisia, who's taken charge of the ship, is impressed with how she moves. I want to tell her that Søren built it with his own hands, but I doubt she would find that as endearing as I did. She would give me that look she specializes in, the one that says she still isn't sure I'm trustworthy. I would hope I've more than proved it, but I don't think I ever will with her.

I understand, though. Girls like us have learned what trust gets you.

Heron hasn't learned that lesson yet. He sticks to my side, devoted, using his gift to mend my rib and the other scrapes and cuts. He fixes Søren as well, though no one asks him to and Artemisia even chides him for it.

Søren is drugged immediately, Heron deftly pouring a vial of something down his throat and holding his nose until he swallows. He said it will keep him unconscious until we reach Dragonsbane. Her ship will have a proper brig, he said, with bars and locks and chains, that will be more effective in keeping him captive.

Even though the cabin of *Wås* is small, and Søren is slumped in the corner only a few feet from me now, I force myself not to look at him. Like this, in sleep, he looks like a child, and guilt swells in my chest until I can't breathe.

It was necessary. It was the only way this could have ended. He had turned on his father, I truly believe that, but no one else will. And I can't be any kind of queen if I side with my enemies over my people. Søren *is* my enemy, even if we both wish he weren't. He has the blood of hundreds of innocents on his hands.

Though mine aren't quite clean anymore either.

I can't relax with him this close, even if I don't look at him from my place curled up on the cot. His cot. It even smells like him—salt water and fresh-cut wood. My body aches with exhaustion, but my mind spins and I can't find sleep—I'm not sure I want to. I don't know what will await me in my dreams.

The door to the cabin creaks open and Blaise slips in, holding two mugs of steam-plumed tea.

He looks worse than I feel, violet half-moons underlining his eyes, standing out starkly against his dull, ashen skin. I wonder when the last time he slept was. Unbidden, I hear Erik's voice in my mind, but I push it away. We are warm and safe and free and that is something to celebrate.

"I figured you would still be awake," he says, maneuvering nimbly around Heron's sleeping form and casting a suspicious glance at Søren's unconscious one. He sits at the edge of my cot and sets his mug down on the small folding table next to it before passing me the second one. Before I take a sip, he stops me.

"I drugged it," he says. "Not that badly," he adds, jerking a head toward Søren. "But you should get some sleep, and I thought that was the only way you would."

I nod my thanks and start to take a sip as he crouches down by Søren, checking his bonds. Before I can overthink it, I switch our mugs. When he turns back to me, his eyes dance over my features. He sees my guilt, but only part of it.

"You did what you had to do, Theo." It takes me a moment to realize he means Søren. "And it's over now."

I snort. "No, it's not," I tell him, taking a long gulp of my non-drugged tea.

"But you aren't alone anymore. You don't have to pretend to be anything you aren't," he says, coming to sit back down on the edge of the cot. "That's something."

I nod even though I'm not sure he's right. Queen Theodosia feels almost as much of a charade as Lady Thora was, and it's a much trickier role to fill. No one expected anything from Thora, but people will expect miracles from their queen. I force myself to finish the tea and watch warily as he does the same.

Already his eyelids begin to grow heavy, but he fights it. "Are you all right?" he asks.

I can't help but laugh. "Everyone keeps asking me that— you, Heron, even Art—and I keep saying I'm fine. *I'm fine, I'm fine, I'm fine.* But I'm not."

"I know," he says, frowning. His eyes are growing unfocused now, slipping over mine. He tries to blink away the sleep. "I don't think any of us are."

"I don't think we ever will be," I admit.

Blaise is quiet for a moment. He sags back against the pillows. "When Ampelio rescued me from the mines, I told him we should run. That you seemed to be perfectly fine being kept in the castle." He glances at me to see my reaction. "It's what everyone said; it's the impression the Kaiser was careful to give, unless he was having you punished. He wanted us to believe that you were happy to go along with his rule so that all of us would stay in line as well. But Ampelio never doubted you."

I swallow, trying not to think about the last time I saw Ampelio alive, the second before I plunged that sword through his back.

"Did he ever say anything to you about . . . Did he see me as his queen or . . ."

Blaise knows what I'm asking.

"He was careful to only ever speak of you as his queen," he tells me, but before my heart can sink too low, he continues. "After Ampelio rescued me from the mine a few years ago, we came to the capital. We were so close to infiltrating the castle and rescuing you, but it fell through, and Ampelio didn't want to risk your safety for anything less than a sure thing. But it was . . ." He swallows. "Dragonsbane had just sunk a cargo ship with thousands of gems, set for the North."

I stiffen, knowing the incident he's referring to. Dragonsbane sank a ship and I paid the price, as I always did. I was twelve or thirteen at the time, but I still have the scars from that punishment.

"We watched," he tells me. "Ampelio insisted. He said we had to see it, to know what we were fighting for. But I had to hold him back that day, and I almost couldn't do it. That fury, that desperation . . . it wasn't a subject wanting to protect his queen. It was a father trying to protect his daughter."

I swallow, feeling tears burn behind my eyes. I close them tight, trying to keep the tears at bay, and squeeze Blaise's hand.

"Thank you."

He squeezes my hand back, but neither of us pulls away. The question that's been weighing on my mind since I saw Cress bubbles up.

"What is Encatrio made of?" I ask. I think about the cell bars, scalding hot after Cress touched them. I think I might already know part of the answer, but I need to hear him say it.

He frowns. "Water, mostly," he says. "It isn't what it's made out of that makes it deadly, it's where the water comes from."

"The Fire Mine," I guess.

He nods. "There's a stream deep in the mine, almost impossible to find. As far as I know, the Kalovaxians have never found it, though they don't go in the mines for more than a few minutes a day to avoid the mine madness, so they've never explored much. Why do you ask?"

"You know Cress survived it," I say slowly. "But it . . . changed her."

"I saw," he says.

I shake my head. "Not just like that."

I tell him about the cell bars, how her touch had turned them hot.

"In theory, it's possible," he says after a moment. "The magic in the mines affects the water the same way it affects the gems, the same way it affects a person's blood. It kills most people, but . . ."

"But not everyone," I finish. "I never heard of Encatrio blessing anyone, though."

He yawns again, trying to shake the exhaustion from himself before slouching down further in the bed.

"No, but we were children and that was hardly the sort of thing anyone would have told us. And it wouldn't have happened often; the victim would have needed not just to be blessed by the gods, but by Houzzah in particular."

My stomach twists. "How could Houzzah have blessed a Kalovaxian?" I ask Blaise quietly. "How could he have blessed *her*?"

He doesn't answer. I turn to look at him to see that his eyes are closed and his face is slack. Asleep, he looks like a different person entirely. Giving him the drugged tea was wrong, I think, but I don't regret it. I keep hold of his hand in the dark. I hold it tight in my own until it doesn't feel so hot. Until it feels the same as mine.

Crescentia haunts my dreams. In them we are children again, playing in the underground pools and pretending to be sirens. Our laughter echoes through the cavern as we splash and dive while her nanny watches from far away. I arc down, keeping my legs together so they look like a tail. When I breach the surface again and open my eyes, the scene has changed.

Now I'm standing on the raised platform at the center of the capital square, and around me everyone jeers— Kalovaxians and Astreans alike. They are all shouting for my death, begging for it. Even Søren. Even Blaise. Behind me, I hear a sword being pulled from its sheath, and I turn, expecting the Kaiser or the Theyn. But it's Cress, holding her father's sword in her hands.

Like the last time I saw her, her neck is black and flaking, skin pale gray, hair charred white. My mother's crown gleams black on top of her head. She stares at me with such hate in her eyes, even as her mouth curves into a smile. Hands shove me to my knees and she comes closer, her steps dainty as ever.

She crouches down next to me and touches my shoulder gently, drawing my gaze to hers.

"You're my heart's sister, little lamb," she says, smiling wider. Her teeth have turned to sharp points.

She kisses my cheek like she has so many times before, but this time the print left behind is warm and sticky like blood. She stands back up, drawing the sword over her head and bringing it arcing down toward me, whistling through the air.

Time slows enough for me to realize that even now, I don't hate her. I pity her, I fear her, but I also love her.

I close my eyes and wait for the blade to find its mark.

I wake up in a cold sweat. The weight of the last day is heavy on my shoulders, but it's almost welcome. It's a reminder that I am alive, that I have survived to see another day—even if it is also a reminder of those who didn't. Elpis. Olaric. Hylla. Santino. I say a silent prayer to the gods that they are greeted warmly in the After, like the heroes they are.

Next to me, Blaise shifts in his sleep, brow furrowing

deeply. His head jerks to one side and he lets out a whimper that clenches around my heart. Even asleep, he is not at peace.

I roll onto my side to face him and place my hand on his chest, fingers spread. He's gained weight over the last few weeks in the palace, but I can still feel the hard line of his sternum through cloth and flesh. He continues to thrash for a moment, but I keep my hand steady until he calms and the tension smooths from his expression. Once more, he looks like the boy I knew in a different lifetime, before the world made ruins of us.

So many people I loved have been wrenched from my grasp. I have watched as the life left their eyes. I have mourned them and I have envied them and I have missed them every moment.

I will not lose Blaise, too.

Rustling comes from behind me and I pull away from Blaise, turning over to find Søren watching me with dazed, half-shut eyes.

Seeing him like this, bound and bewildered, causes guilt to rise in my chest until I can hardly breathe. Then Artemisia's voice echoes in my head: *We are not defined by the things we do in order to survive. We do not apologize for them.* I cannot apologize for doing what I had to.

"Was it ever real?" he asks, breaking the fragile silence.

I wish he would rage or yell or fight. It would be better than having him look at me like this, like I've destroyed him. Søren might be a prodigy warrior, but just now he's nothing more than a heartbroken boy.

It would be better to lie to him. It would make all of this easier, for both of us. Let him hate me and maybe one day I'll be able to hate him, too. But I've lied to him too many times already.

"Every time I look at you, I see your father," I say. The cruelest twist of the knife I can deliver, the words hurt me as much as him.

His body grows rigid and his fists clench. For a second, I'm worried he'll tear through the ropes like they're little more than straw, but he doesn't. He only watches me, cold blue eyes glowing in the dim light.

"That doesn't answer my question."

I dig my teeth hard into my bottom lip, as if that can keep the words in. "Yes," I admit finally. "There was something real."

He softens, the fight going out of him. He shakes his head. "We could have fixed things, Thora—"

"Don't call me that," I snap, before remembering Heron and Blaise are sleeping. This is not a conversation I want them to hear. I lower my voice but emphasize each word. "My name is Theodosia."

He shakes his head. It makes little difference to him—a name is a name—but to me it means the world. "Theodosia, then. I am on your side, you *know* that."

"I do," I say after a breath. I mean it. He went against his father for me; he was willing to leave behind his country and his people.

"Then why . . ." He trails off, finding the answer on his own. "Because you would lose their respect. They would say that you were letting your emotions cloud your judgment, that you were putting me before your country."

"And they wouldn't even be wrong," I say. "I can't do that, Søren."

If I didn't know about the berserkers, would I have betrayed him?

But that's the trouble with ifs. Once they start, there is no stopping them.

If he hadn't told me that ridiculous cat story, could *I* have killed him?

If he hadn't looked at me with such resignation, such self-loathing, could I have driven that knife home?

Paths stretch around me like cracks in a mirror, growing longer and fracturing off until I'm not sure where I stand anymore.

Søren shakes his head. "We want the same thing," he says. "We want *peace*."

A laugh bubbles up in my throat before I can stop it. It's such a simple solution, and such an impossible one.

"After a decade of oppression, Søren, after tens of thousands of my people have been killed and even more forced into insanity in the mines. After they have been *experimented on*. After *you* let them be used as weapons. How can you think peace is possible between our people?" It takes all my self-control not to shout, and I have to breathe deeply to calm myself. "Between us?"

"Isn't it?" he asks. "I know that I love you."

The words give me pause, and for a moment I don't know how to respond. He said that before, in the tunnel, but with everything happening there was no time to dwell on it. Søren isn't the type to throw the word *love* around lightly, and I don't doubt that he thinks he means it. But he doesn't. He can't.

"You love Thora, and Thora doesn't exist. You don't even know me."

He doesn't reply as I turn my back to him, curling my legs up to my chest. Tears sting at my eyes, but I hold them in. Nothing I said was untrue, but I wish it were. I wish there were some way for me to save my country and him. But there isn't, and I made my choice. I might care for him, but I can't forgive him for the berserkers, and I doubt he can forgive me for this betrayal, no matter what he says.

The earth between us has been scorched and frozen and salted for good measure. It's not a place where anything will grow again.

I'm not sure how long we stay silent, but I'm acutely aware of his presence, his eyes on me, his pain. I almost wish I'd taken the drugged tea. Oblivion would be better than this.

Blaise shudders in his sleep, arms flailing to fight whatever nightmares plague him. I hold his wrists, pinning them down before he hurts himself or me. When he's calm again, I release him, smoothing his short hair away from his face.

"It's not a cure," Søren says, his voice gentle. "You don't need me to tell you that."

I keep my back to him and curl in tighter, fitting my-self against Blaise's side. "I don't know what you're talking about," I say.

"Giving him a sleeping draft is like using a tea with special herbs to dull pain—it works for a time, but when it wears off, the pain is still there, just as bad. We tried similar things in the mines. It didn't change anything, in the end. There is no cure for mine madness."

Hearing the term sends a jolt through me. I roll over again to face him and the pity in his eyes sours my stomach.

"You're wrong," I say, the words barely a whisper.

He shakes his head. "I saw hundreds of men going through the same thing after the mines. First they can't sleep; then they lose control of their powers. It's only a matter of time before he turns volatile."

"He just has trouble sleeping," I say, forcing my voice to stay level. "After everything he went through in the mines, it's hardly surprising."

"He's one of the ones who tied me up," Søren replies. "I remember his skin was hot."

"Some people run warmer than others."

"There have been other things, though, haven't there?" he presses.

I think of the Kaiser's chair breaking. I think of the throne room, when the Theyn's whip bit into my back, the hairline cracks spreading out on the stones beneath my feet like spider legs. I think of the fear in Blaise's eyes as he told me later how there was something different about his gift. I think of how he told me he started the earthquake at the Air Mine because he lost control. How even Ampelio was frightened of him.

"You're wrong." But I don't even sound convincing to my own ears. "He's been out of the mines for five years. If he were mine-mad, he would be dead by now."

Søren doesn't argue, but he doesn't concede either. He licks his dry lips before bringing his eyes back to mine.

"If he is mine-mad, he's dangerous, even if he doesn't mean to be. I meant it when I said I trusted you. *Yana Crebesti,* remember?" he says. "Will you trust me on this?"

My feelings for Søren are messy and complicated and hopelessly entangled. But I do trust him, I realize.

"*Yana Crebesti,*" I tell him, even as it breaks my heart.

DRAGONSBANE

———◆·◆———

WHEN DAWN BREAKS, BLAISE IS still asleep next to me, and I'm sure he'll sleep for a while yet. It's good, I tell myself. When he was pretending to be one of my Shadows, he was too busy to sleep, and now he's catching up. That's all it is.

But I can't forget Søren's words last night, and I can't rid myself of the feeling that he's right.

The door creaks open and Artemisia lingers in the frame, hair blue and silver again. She doesn't have any reason to hide it anymore, after all.

"We're approaching the *Smoke*—my mother's ship," she tells me, without any preamble. "You should get up and try to make yourself look somewhat queenlike."

The barb doesn't sting, mostly because I'm sure she's right. My hair is stiff with seawater, and the bitter wind last night left my skin chapped and raw. I'm sure I don't look like anyone's queen right now.

"Get them up, too," she adds, nodding to Blaise and Heron. Her eyes glide over Søren's sleeping form like he isn't even there.

"Blaise needs sleep," I say. "You and Heron and I can do this on our own."

Art snorts, but she doesn't argue. "You'll tell him it was your idea when he wakes up, then. He's not going to be happy he missed it."

She slips away as silently as she came, and I lean over to where Heron is sleeping on the floor by the bed. I nudge his shoulder as gently as I can, but he still wakes with a jolt, hazel eyes wide and searching but seeing nothing. He gasps, but it sounds like he's choking.

"Heron," I say, keeping my voice soft even as his fingers grip my arm painfully tight. I know how nightmares like this work, and I know too well how to break the spell. "It's just me. Theo," I tell him, bringing my other hand on top of his. "You're all right, we're all right."

He comes back to himself slowly, blinking away whatever nightmares haunted him. I watch them fade away behind his eyes, his gaze finally meeting mine.

"I'm so sorry, Your Majesty," he says, sitting up and letting go of my hands. "I . . . I thought I was back in the mine for a moment."

"You don't have to apologize to me, Heron, though if we keep Art waiting much longer, she'll demand a few apologies of her own," I tell him. "And you can still call me Theo."

He climbs to his feet, though he's so tall he has to hunch over to keep from hitting his head on the low ceiling. He holds out a hand to help me stand, and I take it, more for the brief human contact than because I need help.

"All due respect, Your Majesty, but I'm not sure I can," he

says with a tired smile. "It'll be important to remind Dragons-bane of not just who you are but *what* you are."

My stomach clenches and I suddenly regret drugging Blaise's tea. It's selfish, but I can't imagine facing Dragons-bane without him, after everything I've heard. I try not to let my fear show.

We meet Art on the deck, where she's tethered us to a much larger ship with black sails that billow in the wind. Hundreds of expectant faces watch from its deck and the many porthole windows that dot its hull.

"You couldn't have done anything with your hair?" Art snaps.

"With *what*? Søren doesn't keep an assortment of groom-ing products aboard, surprisingly," I reply, matching her tone.

She rolls her eyes. "Then wave, at least, and smile. They'll tell their grandchildren about this one day. The first time they saw Queen Theodosia."

It's a surprisingly optimistic thought from Artemisia, and I let it buoy me. There will be future generations of Astreans. We will survive. We have to. But as soon as I think that, a sad-der thought shadows it.

"I'll want to see Elpis's mother and brother right away to relay my condolences," I tell Artemisia.

She glances sideways at me, but Heron is the first to reply.

"I'd like to go with you, if you don't mind," he says qui-etly, and I realize he must feel as guilty as I do. He was sup-posed to fetch her from the Theyn's after she administered the poison, but he wasn't able to.

Artemisia clears her throat. "She died a hero. We'll sing songs about her one day," he says."

"She was thirteen," I say. "She was too young to be a hero. I should have let her be a child a little longer."

"She never *was* a child," Art protests, eyes steely as she stares at the deck of the *Smoke,* where a rope ladder is being lowered to us. "*They* took that away from her, and don't you forget that. *They're* the enemy. You gave her a chance to be something other than a victim, and she took it happily. That is her legacy, and turning her into a helpless victim tarnishes it. I'll arrange for you to meet her family, but that is what you're going to tell them. You didn't kill Elpis. The Kaiser did."

I'm too shocked to reply, and Heron must be as well. It's a kinder sentiment than I ever expected from Artemisia, and though it doesn't alleviate my guilt wholly, it does help a bit.

"Come on," Art says when the ladder reaches us. "I'll go first, then Theo. Heron, you bring up the rear in case she falls."

"I won't fall," I scoff, though it suddenly occurs to me that I might. After the swimming and climbing yesterday, my arms feel limp and useless, but it's a short climb, at least.

"There will be a crowd gathered," Art continues, as if I hadn't spoken. "I'll push through it, so stay close to me. My mother will be waiting in her quarters, away from the madness."

She takes ahold of the rope ladder and begins to climb. I wait until she's a few feet up before following. The pain in my arms as I climb is almost a pleasant distraction from the worry rattling around my mind. I can feel hundreds of pairs of eyes on me, watching me like I'm someone worth watching—worth following—and I'm not sure I know how to be that person.

When I reach the top, Artemisia's waiting for me, leaning over the edge to take my hand. Her face is creased with panic.

"I'm sorry, Theo," she says, pulling me over the edge of the deck as she whispers in such a rush that I almost can't hear her. "My mother came out to meet you after all, and there's something you don't know—"

"Theodosia."

I know that voice. It sends shivers down my spine and sets my heart racing, fills me with hope that I haven't felt in a decade. I know it's impossible, but I would recognize that voice anywhere.

Art steps aside and the first thing I see is the thick ring of people gathered on the deck around me, all watching with joyous looks on their faces. A few have children on their hips or shoulders. Most of them look like they could use a few extra rations now and then, but none of them are starving, like the slaves in the capital.

The crowd parts and a woman approaches through the people.

The woman has my mother's face as well as her voice, the same dark eyes and round cheeks and full mouth. The same tall, reedy frame. The same untamable mess of black-cherry hair that she used to let me braid. The same freckles one famed Astrean poet referred to as *"the most divine of constellations."*

I want to cry out and run toward her, but Artemisia's

hand comes down on my shoulder and I understand the warning.

My mother is *not* alive. I know this. I saw the life leave her.

"Is this some kind of trick?" I hiss as the woman comes closer, mindful of the people watching. My people. I force myself not to cower, not to leap forward into her arms.

Her eyebrows arch the way my mother's used to, but her eyes are heavy with sadness.

"Not an intentional one," she says in my mother's voice. "You didn't think to warn her?" she asks Artemisia.

Next to me, Artemisia's posture has gone stiff as a soldier's. "We didn't want to risk . . . If Theo was tortured . . ." She trails off and clears her throat, turning to look at me. "Theo, this is Dragonsbane."

The woman smiles with my mother's mouth, but it doesn't have the warmth my mother's smile always held. There's a sharpness there, a bitterness my mother never had. "You, however, can call me Aunt Kallistrade, if you'd prefer."

"Our mothers were twins," Artemisia says, but I barely hear her. I barely hear Heron as he climbs over the deck railing and comes to stand on my other side.

The words make little sense to me. All I know is that I am staring into the face of my mother, a face I thought I would never see again. There are things I forgot about her, like how thick her eyebrows were and the bump at the bridge of her nose. I forgot how pieces of her hair would stand on end unless they were smoothed down with grease.

"Eirene was born five minutes before I was," the woman with my mother's face continues. "Small distance as it was, it made her the heir and me only the spare."

"If my mother had a twin, I would have known it," I say, still unwilling to believe what I can see.

She shrugs. "I was halfway around the world for most of your life," she says. "Court was never my place. I'm sure we would have met eventually, if the siege hadn't happened." She pauses and presses her lips together, her eyes softening as they take in my face. "I can't express how glad I am to have you here. It feels like getting a piece of her back."

She says the words, but I can tell she doesn't mean them. They're for the audience, not for me, and I know I should say something similar. I clear my throat.

"Looking at you, I can't help but feel the same," I tell her, even as I remind myself that she is not my mother. I don't know this woman, and I certainly don't know if I can believe anything she says.

I draw myself up to my full height. "I'm sure we have many things to discuss, Aunt," I tell her, pasting on the fake smile I always wore at court. The one I hoped I would never have to wear again.

"We do," she says, matching my smile. "I hear you've brought me a present."

I think of Søren, asleep with his limbs bound.

"Prinz Søren is not for you. He is a political prisoner," I say. "He'll be treated as civilly as possible while he's with us."

Her nostrils narrow. "You expect us to keep a Kalovaxian fed while the rest of us eat half rations?" she asks. "What justice is that?"

"The time for justice isn't here yet," I say levelly, raising my voice so the crowd can hear me as well. "We're still playing a game we have little chance of winning, and the Prinz is the only card we have. We need to keep him healthy and whole or else he'll be useless."

Dragonsbane's eyes flick over her shoulder to the crowd before she turns back to me, smile broader and more false than before.

"Of course, Your Highness. I'll see to it."

She shouts to two men on the fringe of the crowd. "Bring the prisoner to the brig."

"I'll be checking in on him to make sure he's being taken care of," I tell her.

When she turns back to me, her smile has gone feral. "I don't think that's necessary," she says. "Or wise, for that matter. There are already those who say you're too fond of him."

The words are a well-aimed jab, and I struggle to keep my face neutral. Next to me, Heron tenses like a bow ready to snap.

"You'll be wary of how you speak to your queen," he says, and though his voice is soft, there is a level of danger there.

Dragonsbane's eyebrows dart up in amusement. "I was merely sharing some advice with my niece. People say things, and we must be aware of them before they hurt us."

"Then let them say as much to my face," I tell her, keeping my voice cold. "In the meantime, you'll give him half of my rations."

"And mine," Heron says a second later.

For a second, I think Artemisia might repeat the sentiment, but in the presence of her mother, she's shrunken in on herself, quiet and unsure for the first time since I've met her. I understand. After all, I don't have many memories of my mother angry, but I'm sure she looked the same way

Dragonsbane looks at me now—jaw tight, eyes hard, mouth pursed. I can't help but feel like a child again, about to be sent to my room. But I am not a child. I am a queen, and I have faced far worse than her. So I stand straight and meet her gaze until she finally drops hers and speaks:

"As you wish, Your Majesty."

EPILOGUE

———◆•◆———

THE LAST PERSON WHO CALLED me Ash Princess was the heart's sister I orphaned.

We played together as children, learning to dance and pretending to be fantastical creatures, but when we meet again it will be as enemies. I saw the hatred in her eyes, felt her wrath like a hurricane ripping at my skin. She won't stop until she has my head, and I did that to her. This I do regret.

But she was right, in a way. I was a princess made of ashes; there is nothing left of me to burn.

Now it's time for a queen to rise.

Acknowledgments

"A book is a gift" was something Mrs. Lloyd, my first-grade teacher, was fond of saying. I remember that lens shifting into place and seeing books the way she did as something precious and priceless. I didn't realize at the time just how many people would go into dreaming up, creating, and wrapping it into the gift it is now.

Thank you to all of my stellar agents. Laura Biagi, who found *Ash Princess* in her slush pile and saw the potential in it, and in me. To Jennifer Weltz and Ariana Philips at JVNLA for extending the reach of my book to an audience I never could have imagined. And to John Cusick, for always being there to talk me through my anxiety attacks and writer's blocks.

Thank you to Krista Marino, the best editor I could ask for. Thank you for your guidance and your vision. Thank you for your patience. Thank you for seeing the story I was trying to tell and helping to shape it into the best book it could be. Thank you to Jillian Vandall, my incredible publicist, for her tireless energy and contagious enthusisam. Thank you to Monica Jean for all your insight and dedication. Thank you to Elizabeth Ward and the rest of the Underlined team for being so friendly and letting me hang out with them at conventions. And a huge thank you to Beverly Horowitz, Barbara Marcus, and everyone at Delacorte and Penguin Random House. This section alone could have taken up ten pages if I let it, but I am so excited to see Theo's journey through with all of you by my side.

Thank you to Billelis and Alison Impey for giving me the most beautiful cover I ever could have imagined. It's in large part thanks to you that many people will pick this book up in the first place.

Thank you to Macmillan UK and my editor there, Venetia Gosling, for connecting with Theo's story and bringing it across the pond. And to Greene & Heaton and my UK agents, Eleanor Teasdale and Nicola Barr, for finding *Ash Princess* the perfect home in Britain. I am eternally grateful.

Thank you to my parents for always being in my corner. You raised me to persevere, and I would not have lasted through the setbacks and rejections without that. And to my little brother, Jerry, whose fearlessness and dedication has always been an inspiration. I know that we will always have each other's backs, even when we're terrorizing one another.

Thank you to Deborah Brown and Jefrey Pollock for being my NYC family and trusting me to take care of your brilliant kids. Your support over the years has meant the world to me. And thank you to Jesse and Eden Pollock, for the constant inspiration and for reminding me who, exactly, my audience is. Eden often read scenes as I wrote them, and her feedback was incredibly astute. Jesse was too young, but I hope he'll enjoy it one day—sorry in advance for all the kissing scenes.

Thank you to my friends. Madison and Jake Levine, for almost twenty-five years of friendship. Cara Shaeffer, forever my inspiration in all things adulting and immature. Emily Hecht, for helping me embrace the weirdest parts of me. Lexi Wangler, for keeping me sane while in the publishing trenches. Patrice Caldwell, Lauryn Chamberlain, Cristina Arreola, Jeremy West, and Jeffrey West, for all the coffee and writing dates and snark.

Thank you to my fellow Electric Eighteens for all the support and commiseration and friendship. A special shout-out to my fellow NYCers, who have become incredible friends over the last year—Arvin Ahmadi, Sara Holland, Sarah Smetana, Kamilla Benko, Kit Frick, Emily X.R. Pan, Kheryn Callender, Melissa Albert, and Lauren Spieller.

Thank you to the many authors who provided so much guidance and support through the publishing process. Adam Silvera, Julie Dao, Gayle Forman, Melissa Walker, Libba Bray, Holly Black, Zoraida Cordova, Dhonielle Clayton, Karen McManus, S. K. Ali—I've been a fan of all of yours for some time, and I feel so lucky to now be able to call you friends as well.

Thank you to Maya Davis, whose insight was instrumental in fleshing out the cultures and characters.

Thank you to Molly Cusick for her support when I was going on submission and for answering questions I was afraid to ask my agent (and for helping me realize that was ridiculous).

Thank you to Birch Coffee on the Upper West Side and the incredible baristas there who kept me caffeinated and focused.

And last, but certainly not least, thank you to Mrs. Lloyd for planting the seeds for my lifelong love of reading and writing. They grew.

WHERE THERE'S SMOKE, THERE'S FIRE.

TURN THE PAGE FOR A PREVIEW OF THE SEQUEL TO *ASH PRINCESS*.

FREEDOM COMES AT A PRICE

LADY SMOKE

LAURA SEBASTIAN

The sequel to the *New York Times* bestseller *Ash Princess*

Excerpt copyright © 2019 by Laura Sebastian.
Published by Delacorte Press, an imprint of Random House Children's Books,
a division of Penguin Random House LLC, New York.

PROLOGUE

———— • ————

M Y MOTHER ONCE TOLD ME that peace was the only way
Astrea could survive. We had no need for vast armies,
she said, no need to force our children into becoming warriors. We didn't court war like other countries, in an effort to
take more than we needed. Astrea was enough, she said.

She never imagined that war would come to us, courted or
not. She would live just long enough to see how poorly peace
fared against the Kalovaxians' wrought-iron blades and savage greed.

My mother was the Queen of Peace, but I know too well
that peace isn't enough.

ALONE

—— • ——

THE SPICED COFFEE IS SWEET on my tongue, made with a generous dollop of honey. The way Crescentia always orders it.

We sit on the pavilion like we have a thousand times before, steaming porcelain mugs cradled in our hands to ward off the chill in the evening air. For a moment, it feels just like every time before, a comfortable silence hanging in the dark air around us. I've missed talking to her, but I've missed this, too—how we could sit together and not feel the need to fill the silence with meaningless small talk.

But that's silly. How can I miss Cress when she's sitting right in front of me?

She laughs like she can read my mind and sets her cup down on its saucer with a clatter that rattles my bones. She leans across the gilded table to take hold of my free hand in both of hers.

"Oh, Thora," she says, her voice lilting over my false name like a melody. "I missed you, too. But next time, I won't."

Before her words can make sense to me, the lighting overhead shifts, the sun growing brighter and brighter until she's fully illuminated, every awful inch of her. Her charred, flaking neck, burned black by the Encatrio I had her served, her hair white and brittle, her lips gray as the ersatz crown I used to wear.

Fear and guilt overwhelm me as the pieces fall into place in my mind. I remember what I did to her; I remember why I did it. I remember her face on the other side of the bars of my cell, full of rage as she told me she would cheer for my death. I remember the bars being scalding hot where she'd touched them.

I try to pull my hand away but she holds it fast, her storybook-princess smile sharpening into fangs tipped with ash and blood. Her skin burns hot against mine, hotter even than Blaise's. It is fire itself against my skin, and I try to scream, but no sound comes out. I stop feeling my hand altogether and I'm relieved for a second before I look down and see that it has turned to ash, crumbled to dust in Cress's grip. The fire works its way up my arm and down the other, spreading across my chest, my torso, my legs, and my feet. My head catches last, and the final thing I see is Cress with her monster's smile.

"There. Isn't that better? Now no one will mistake you for a queen."

My skin is drenched when I wake up, cotton sheets tangled around my legs and damp with sweat. My stomach churns, threatening to spill, though I'm not sure I've eaten anything to spill, apart from a few crusts of bread last night. I sit up in bed, placing a hand on my stomach to steady it and blinking to help my eyes adjust to the dark.

It takes a moment to realize that I am not in my own bed, not in my own room, not in the palace at all. The space is smaller, the bed little more than a narrow cot with a thin mattress and threadbare sheets and a quilt. My stomach pitches to the side, rolling in a way that makes me nauseous before I realize it isn't my stomach at all—the room itself is rocking from side to side. My stomach is only echoing the motion.

The events of the last two days filter back to me. The dungeon, the Kaiser's trial, Elpis dying at my feet. I remember Søren rescuing me only to be imprisoned himself. As quickly as that thought comes to me, I push it away. There are a good many things I have to feel guilty about—taking Søren hostage cannot be one of them.

I'm on the *Smoke,* I remember, heading toward the Anglamar ruins to begin to reclaim Astrea. I am in my cabin, safe and alone, while Søren is being kept in chains in the brig.

I close my eyes and drop my head into my hands, but as soon as I do, Cress's face swims through my mind, all rosy cheeks and dimples and wide gray eyes, just as she looked the first time I met her. My heart lurches in my chest at the thought of the girl she was, the girl *I* was, who latched on to her because she was my only salvation in the nightmare of my life. Too quickly, that image of Cress is replaced with her as I last saw her, with hate in her cold gray eyes and the skin of her throat charred and flaking.

She shouldn't have survived the poison. If I hadn't seen her with my own eyes, I wouldn't believe it. Part of me is relieved that she did, though the other part will never forget how she looked at me when she promised to raze Astrea to the ground, how she said she would ask the Kaiser if she could keep my head after he executed me.

I flop down on my back, hitting the thin pillow with a thud. My whole body aches with exhaustion, but my mind is a whirl of activity that shows no sign of quieting. Still, I close my eyes tight and try to banish all thoughts of Cress, though she lingers on the edges, a ghost of a presence.

The room is too quiet—so quiet it takes on a sound all its own. I hear it in the absence of my Shadows' breaths, their infinitesimal movements as they fidget, their whispers to one another. It is a deafening sort of silence. I turn onto one side, then the other. I shiver and pull the quilt tighter around me; I feel the fire of Cress's touch again and kick the quilt off entirely, so that it falls in a heap onto the floor.

Sleep isn't coming anytime soon. I roll out of bed and find the thick wool cloak Dragonsbane left in my cabin. I pull it over my nightgown. It swamps me, hanging down to my ankles, cozy and shapeless. The material is fraying, and it's been patched so many times that I doubt there is anything of the original cloak left, but I still prefer it to the fine silk gowns the Kaiser used to force me to wear.

As always, thinking of the Kaiser makes the flame of fury in my belly burn brighter until it scorches through me, turning my blood to lava. It's a feeling that frightens me, even as I relish it. Blaise promised me once that I would light the fire that would turn the Kaiser's body to ash, and I don't think this feeling will abate until I do.

SAFE

———— ⋅•⋅ ————

THE PASSAGEWAYS OF THE *SMOKE* are deserted and quiet, without a soul in sight. The only sound is the light patter of footsteps overhead and the muted din of waves crashing against the hull. I turn down one hallway, then another, looking for a way up to the deck before realizing how hopelessly lost I am. Though I thought I had a decent idea of the ship's layout during Dragonsbane's tour earlier in the evening, it looks like an entirely different place at this hour. I glance over my shoulder, expecting to see a flash of one of my Shadows before I realize they aren't there. No one is.

For ten years, the presence of others was a constant weight on my shoulders that suffocated me. I hungered for the day I could finally shrug it off and just be alone. Now, though, there is a part of me that misses the constant company. They would, at the very least, keep me from getting lost.

Finally, after another few turns, I find a steep set of stairs going up to the deck. The steps are rickety and loud and I climb slowly, terrified that someone will hear and come after me. I have to remind myself that I'm not sneaking anywhere— I'm free to wander as I please.

I push open the door and sea air whips at my face, blowing my hair in all directions. I smooth it back with one hand to keep it out of my eyes and pull my cloak tighter around me with the other. I didn't realize how stale the air belowdecks was until fresh air is in my lungs.

Up here, there are some crew members working, a skeleton crew to ensure that the *Smoke* doesn't go off course or sink in the middle of the night, but they're all too bleary-eyed and focused on their tasks to spare me more than a glance as I walk by.

The night is cold, especially with the wind as vicious as it is on the water. I cross my arms over my chest as I make my way up to the bow of the ship.

I might still be growing used to being alone, but I don't think I'll ever get enough of this: The sky open all around me. No walls, no restrictions. Just air and sea and stars. The sky above is overflowing with stars, so many that it's difficult to pick out any one in particular. Artemisia told me the navigators use the stars to steer the ship, but I can't imagine how such a thing is possible. There are too many to make any sense of.

The bow of the ship isn't as empty as I hoped it would be. There's a lone figure standing at the railing near the front, shoulders hunched as he stares at the ocean below. Even before I'm close enough to make out any of his features, I know it's Blaise. He's the only person I've met who can slouch with such a frantic energy about him.

Relief surges through me and I quicken my pace toward him.

"Blaise," I say, touching his arm. The heat of his skin and the fact that he's awake at this hour tugs at my mind, pulling it in still more directions, but I refuse to let them. Not now. Now, I just need my oldest friend.

He turns toward me, surprised, before smiling, though a little more tentatively than I'm used to.

We haven't spoken since we came aboard earlier in the afternoon, and truthfully, a part of me has been dreading it. He must know that I switched our cups on the trip here, giving him the tea that he'd laced with a sleeping draught for me. He must know why I did it. That isn't a conversation I want to have right now.

"Couldn't sleep?" he asks me, glancing around before looking back at me. He opens his mouth but closes it again. He clears his throat. "It can be difficult, getting used to sleeping on a ship. With the rocking and the sound of the waves—"

"It isn't that," I say. I want to tell him about my nightmare, but I can already imagine his response. *It was just a dream,* he will say. *It wasn't real. Cress isn't here, she can't hurt you.*

True as that might be, I can't make myself believe it. What's more, I don't want Blaise to know how Cress lingers in my thoughts, how guilty I feel about what I did to her. In Blaise's mind, it is clear: Cress is the enemy. He wouldn't understand my guilt, and he certainly wouldn't understand the longing that has taken root in the pit of my stomach. He wouldn't understand how much I miss her, even now.

"I didn't tell you about Dragonsbane," he says after a moment, unable to look at me. "I should have warned you. It couldn't have been a pleasant shock, meeting a stranger with your mother's face."

I lean on the railing next to him, both of us staring down to where the waves lap at the hull of the ship.

"You likely *would* have told me if I hadn't switched our cups of tea," I point out.

For a moment, he doesn't say anything, and the only sound comes from the sea. "Why did you?" he asks quietly, like he's not sure he wants to know the answer.

I'm not sure I want to give it to him, for that matter, but there is a part of me holding on to the hope that he will laugh it off and tell me I'm wrong.

I take a deep, steadying breath. "Before we left Astrea, when Erik was telling me what berserkers were, he mentioned the symptoms," I say slowly.

Next to me, Blaise stiffens, but he doesn't look at me and he doesn't interrupt, so I push on.

"He said that as their mine madness gets worse, their skin runs hot and they begin to lose control of their gifts. He said they don't sleep."

Blaise shudders out a breath. "It's not that simple," he says quietly.

I shake my head to clear it, then push off the railing, folding my arms over my chest. "You're blessed," I tell him. "It's how you survived the mine, how you've survived in the years since you left. You can't be . . ." I can't force myself to say the words. *Mine-mad*. It's only one word, two syllables, each one innocuous enough on its own. Together, though, they are so much bigger.

I want so badly for him to tell me I'm right, that of course it isn't mine madness, of course it isn't fatal. Instead, he says nothing. He stays frozen, hunched over the railing on his elbows, hands clutched tightly in front of him.

"I don't know, Theo," he says finally. "I don't think I am . . . sick," he says, unable to utter *mine-mad* either. "But I've never really felt like I was blessed either."

The confession comes out in a whisper lost in the night air, never to be spoken of again. I wonder if this is the first time he's said the words out loud.

I touch his shoulder, forcing him to face me before placing my hand on his chest, where I know he bears a mark, right over his heart. "I've seen what you can do, Blaise," I tell him. "Glaidi blessed you, I know it. Maybe your power is different from other Guardians', but it's not . . . it's not that. It's something more. It has to be."

For a second, he looks like he wants to argue, but then he places his hand over mine and holds it there. I try to ignore how hot his skin is.

"Why couldn't you sleep?" he asks me finally.

I can't tell him about my nightmare, but I can't lie to him either. I settle for something in the middle—a partial truth.

"I can't sleep alone," I tell him, as if it's as simple as that. We both know it isn't.

I wait for the judgment to come, for him to tell me how ridiculous that is, that I shouldn't *miss* having Shadows to watch my every move. But of course, he doesn't. He knows that's not what I'm saying at all.

"I'll sleep with you," he says before realizing what he said. It's too dark out to say for sure, but I think his ears turn red. "I mean . . . well, you know what I mean. I can be there, if that will help."

I smile slightly. "I think it will," I say, and because I can't resist, I don't stop there. "I would sleep even better if you tried to sleep, too."

"Theo," he says with a sigh.

"I know," I say. "It isn't that simple. I just wish it were."

As Blaise and I make our way to my cabin, I feel the eyes of the crew on us. I can imagine how this looks to them, the two of us walking together at this hour. By sunrise, they'll all be whispering that Blaise and I are lovers. I would rather people didn't whisper about me at all, but if that rumor eclipses the ones about Søren and me, I wouldn't mind.

A romance with Blaise is a much better rumor because it's one the crew will support wholeheartedly, if for no other reason than that he's Astrean. And the more support I have from the crew, the better. I can't help but remember how dismissive Dragonsbane was when I came on board, how she spoke to me like I was a lost child instead of a queen. *Her* queen. I worry it's going to get worse.

I force myself to stop that line of thought. How did I become so conniving? I do have feelings for Blaise and I know he has them for me as well, but I didn't even consider that. I went straight to plotting, straight to seeing how he could be used to my political advantage. How did I become that sort of person?

I'm thinking like the Kaiser. The realization sends a shudder through me.

Blaise feels it. "Are you all right?" he asks as I open the door to my cabin and lead him inside.

I turn to look at him, and push the Kaiser's voice out of my mind. I don't think about who saw us come in or what they'll say or how I can work that to my advantage. I don't think about what we talked about a few moments ago. I just think about us, alone in a room together.

"Thank you for staying with me," I say instead of answering.

He smiles briefly before glancing away. "It's you who's doing me a favor. I'm bunking with Heron, and he snores loud enough to shake the whole ship."

I laugh.

"I'll lie on the floor while you sleep," he says.

"Don't," I say, surprising myself.

His eyes widen slightly as he looks at me. It feels like we're going to stand here in frozen, awkward silence for eons, so I break the spell. I step toward him and take him by the hand.

"Theo," he says, but I press a finger to his lips before he can ruin this with warnings I don't want to hear.

"Just . . . hold me?" I say.

He sighs and I know he's going to say no, that he should keep his distance because I am not his childhood friend anymore. I am his queen, and that makes everything so much more complicated. So I play a cheap card, one I know he won't say no to.

"I'll feel safer, Blaise. Please."

His eyes soften and I know I have him. Without a word, I let my hand fall away from his lips and I pull him with me to the bed. We fit together perfectly, his body curling around mine, his arms around me. Even here at sea, he smells like hearth fire and spice—like home. His skin is scorching hot, but I try not to think about that. Instead, I feel his heartbeat thrumming through me, falling into a rhythm with my own, and I let it lull me to sleep.

GET **BOOKS** GET **PERKS** GET **INSPIRED**

GET
Underlined

Your destination for all things books, writing, YA news, pop culture, and more!

Check Out What We Underlined for You...

READ
Book recommendations, reading lists, and the latest YA news

LIFE
Quizzes, trend alerts, and pop culture news

PERKS
Exclusive content, Book Nerd merch, sneak peeks, and chances to win prizes

VIDEO
Book trailers, author videos, and more

CREATE
Create an account on Underlined to build a personal bookshelf, write original stories, and connect with fellow book nerds and authors!

Visit us at **GetUnderlined.com** and follow **@GetUnderlined** on

Did you love this book? Use **#UnderlinedReviews** to tell us what you thought!